THE DIFFICULT SUBJECT

By Molly Macallen

Book Two of
the MADDY SHANKS *Mystery Series*

First edition published April 2023.

Designed by Cait Palmiter.

ISBN 979-8-9881130-0-3 (Hardcover)

ISBN 979-8-9881130-2-7 (Paperback)

Author's note: The author thanks PGM, EKF, KLL, MDT, +1 for assistance editing this work. This is an original work of fiction and any resemblance to real-life events or real-life persons (dead or living) is entirely coincidental, with the exception of references to actual historical works as identified in the text and below:

ABBA, "Take a Chance On Me," from *ABBA: The Album* (Polar Music, 1977).

Percivall Pott, *Chirurgical Observations relative to the cataract, the polypus of the nose, the cancer of the scrotum, the different kinds of ruptures, and the mortification of the toes and feet* (London: Hawes, W. Clarke, and R. Collins, 1775).

Walt Whitman, *Leaves of Grass* (originally published in 1856, now public domain in the USA).

THE DIFFICULT SUBJECT

By Molly Macallen

Chapter 1

Madelaine Shanks arrived in Minneapolis with the singular goal of becoming a complete nobody again. The nondescript commercial district abutting the University of Minnesota Medical Center's East Bank campus where her office would be felt like the perfect setting for her plan. A drug store here; a Vietnamese lunch place there; an all-purpose commuter shop selling umbrellas, messenger bags, notebooks, and the kinds of birthday cards one grabs at the last minute. Perfect. Aside from the fact that the sidewalks all around Washington Avenue were Midwestern-tidy and seemingly devoid of homeless people, in the late summer warmth of 2004, this scene felt like it could easily be almost anywhere in North America. Which meant Maddy could just be some academic nobody again, and not who she had lately become.

Looking up to take stock of her new university home, she felt that the brick-and-cement architecture of the medical school's complex would only help. With an utter lack of aesthetic imagination, it combined the soulless, institutional styles of the last century, each new building section having been pasted to the last like chunky warts and benign tumors grown upon a hard face. The tallest bit, Moos Tower, looked to Maddy as if it had been designed by an unimaginative undergraduate taking a mechanical drawing class; she pictured an angsty fellow who had understood his grade to depend on how many right angles he could work in. The ill-shaped structure loomed above the complex, covered in a drab pebble facing that seemed to grab ahold of the soot of passing delivery vehicles. At the big, lumpy feet of Moos, a steady stream of people entered and exited the various doorways carrying backpacks, briefcases, and lunch sacks, looking like they had been handpicked by a stock-image photographer to represent Any Man and Any Woman going and coming to work, earnestly, wearily, thoughtlessly.

She tightened the cinch of her straw sun hat under her chin a little, to keep it from blowing off in the updrafts caught between the buildings.

Yes. She could do this. She could be just another young, underpaid instructor with a PhD—just another short-term humanities hire with little job security and no fashion sense, working in a grinding state university machine.

Of course, this plan would require avoiding reporters. And upon arrival, Maddy had been disappointed to discover her office would not be in a secured section of the complex. This left the possibility that a journalist could show up at her office and catch her off guard.

But the solution to that was simple: Avoid her assigned office and work instead in the nearby history of medicine library. Since her unit's administrator had stuck her in the only empty office he could secure quickly—an eight-by-ten-foot closet of a room in a wing mostly occupied by neurology researchers—odds were good no one would notice if she did not frequent her official location. Productivity was what mattered, not sticking to one's assigned office. The neurologists weren't going to think twice if a visiting assistant professor in the history of medicine didn't show up very much. In fact, it would just match their stereotype of the lazy humanities prof.

The chief librarian of the history of medicine collection—a maternal, gregarious, corn-fed Minnesotan who sported a strawberry blonde coif and a dip of meaty cleavage—told Maddy she'd be perfectly happy to give Maddy regular space to work in the small library's main reading room. The space wasn't big, but it was at least five times the size of Maddy's office, and the windows looked out across a series of flat commercial roofs right down to the thick, sliding serpent that was the Mississippi River. The furnishings felt humane: antique wooden tables; simple leather chairs; low, incandescent lighting. Not fancy, but not spartan.

"But *of course* you can work here, Professor Shanks! It's always a joy to have a real historian of anatomy in the house!" the librarian had cried out in answer to Maddy's request.

Unasked, the librarian also offered to provide space in the break room for Maddy to meet with her students if they came for her help and another patron wanted quiet in the library's central space. There was a linoleum-topped lunch table in the break room with a few chairs alongside a kitchenette.

Maddy had instinctively lied when she sought this kind of accommodation from the librarian, never mentioning the problem of reporters. She just said she found her tiny, assigned office more than a little depressing, with a window facing a brick wall and tossed-off furnishings that looked army-surplus, all of it too far from old books.

Well, that wasn't a complete lie.

"You prefer the company of the dead," the librarian had said to her with a wink.

"I like old books," Maddy had answered. "I guess I'm a typical historian that way."

"The dead are so much easier to deal with than the living," the librarian replied with a singsong voice and a broad smile, as if Maddy had never answered.

"Eighteenth-century books smell so good, don't you think?" Maddy observed in return, picking up a circa-1750 midwifery manual from one of the display shelves and giving it a sniff as if it were a wildflower plucked in a field on an afternoon walk. That unique aromatic blend of dried-book mold and aged leather binding always made her feel calmer, more in her natural place. She breathed it in again and thought to herself that some chemist in some sparkling clean New Jersey corporate laboratory should concoct a perfume that matched this scent. "Thesis," it could be called, marketed in tiny bottles that looked like those of late-nineteenth-century opioid tinctures, with a tea-stained paper label. She would sprinkle it in her evening bath.

"Old books smell better than pickled bodies, I'm sure!" the librarian exclaimed. "But you would know better than I?"

Maddy forced a lip-closed smile, paused, and asked if the collection here included an original Vesalius *De Humani Corporis Fabrica*? (The best way to distract a history of medicine librarian, Maddy had long since learned, was to ask to see her first-edition Vesalius.)

The librarian suddenly fluffed like a chicken disturbed by a farmer come to collect her eggs.

"I'll get the key to the vault!" she cried out. "You'll want to see our Harvey, too."

. . .

All this work of holding off people's curiosity—it was already exhausting, and it had only been a couple of days here so far. Maddy had imagined before arriving that she might manage to start with a clean slate here. When she had called to tell her best friend, Liz, that the Minnesota job offer had come through, Maddy had even burst into tears at the idea of a fresh start.

She had met Liz, a behavioral rat researcher, through a cross-departmental grad course on gender and science at Indiana University, where they had both been earning PhDs. On the call, Liz just waited until Maddy composed herself. Maddy knew well that Liz didn't much care for crying women, unless they were specifically crying on her shoulder—in which case, she found them irresistible.

"Freedom?" Liz had asked, when Maddy had stopped sniffling.

"Freedom," Maddy answered, blowing her nose. "I can move on, get out of Indiana, get back to work. Get on with the rest of my life."

"The trial will be going on in Philly."

"But that won't matter. That won't matter," Maddy said firmly again as if trying to discipline the unruly dog that was the anxiety in her gut. "I'll get a couple of articles out, get an academic book contract in the works. The teaching load is light—two and two—and it'll position me well. It's just a two-year—so being on the market again no later than next year will be hard. But it's *something*."

"It is something," Liz agreed.

Liz thought about what it was going to be like without Maddy to share a six-mile run or a pitcher of cheap beer in the dull of Bloomington weekday evenings. Then she realized she should be sounding happier for Maddy.

"Seriously, congratulations! It's something! *Something* is what we all hope for. *Something* is what we aspire to when we go for a PhD. *Something* is what everyone wants to put on her CV!"

Liz paused, wondering if Maddy was annoyed with her joking.

"Would you like a couple of little young fellas to take with you to Minneapolis? They're not as good company as me, but they also eat a lot less than me."

"I can't, really," Maddy said, although she liked the idea of a pair of rats from Liz's line for the lonely moments. Without the lab's principal investigator noticing, Liz had managed to breed one subgroup to be particularly smart and welcoming of human companionship. Liz had taught Maddy the visceral pleasure of a small, furry, sleeping creature on her belly, tucked under her shirt, when everything else felt like a shit show. Liz wasn't supposed to take rats out of the lab, but she told Maddy that it wasn't as if anyone noticed or cared. The lab's research was behavioral, not the biohazard sort.

"Why can't you, *really*?" Liz asked in a tone that suggested Maddy might be acting a bit snobbish regarding Liz's species preferences. "You know they'll keep each other company if you're busy. And you'll have some mammals to come home to. Warm, short-term mammals who like how you smell and who'll be happy when you drop crumbs all over. That's the best kind of mammal to come home to, and you know it."

"The associate dean who offered me the job also offered to put me up in a small house he owns, and I can't bring rats to someone else's house."

"Oh?" asked Liz, her voice rising.

"Oh, come on, Liz," Maddy answered. "It's not like that. It's an *empty house*. Well, I mean it has furniture. Probably grown-up furniture, not grad-school furniture. More something! I just have to pay utilities. It'll save me a fortune, especially compared to what a whole nice house would cost to rent. And *I'll be living alone*. You can come visit. You can drive and bring my palm tree since I won't be able to ship it or fly it there with me."

"It's not a setup?" Liz asked.

Maddy didn't answer.

"He installs you in a tenuous position and in his *house* at the same time, Maddy?"

Liz's voice had that low timbre it took on when she felt that combination of annoyance and vigilance about her friends.

"He knew I'm coming on short notice to take over for Alex Shugar. So, he offered me what had been her house since it's sitting unused anyway. He says it's a nice small house in a quiet spot in the Lake Minnetonka area, twenty-five or thirty minutes west from school. If there's no traffic. If there's traffic, more."

"That's kind of far. You're gonna waste a lot of work time getting there and back. And is that how you say her name? SHUG-er?"

"Yeah, apparently they used to say, 'Shugar, rhymes with slugger,'" Maddy answered. "I guess that made it easy to remember. Alex Shugar was a bit of a slugger by all accounts. Anyway, he has her house because he inherited it. She was his wife. Well, his ex-wife."

"Oh. *Oh*. And he hired her replacement. . . . Hang on. How are you going to get from there to the university? Is he giving you a ride every day?"

"He's lending me *her* car," Maddy replied, sounding annoyed with Liz. She was in fact annoyed with herself. She hadn't thought about this all as a possible arranged entanglement. Why hadn't she? Desperation in terms of jobs? No other offer had come through. Of course, she had barely applied for positions, being afraid of being offered interviews by search committees only interested in meeting a fifteen-minute celebrity. Plus, her dissertation director had assured her she could stay in Indiana one more year—that the college would find a way to make it work if she needed one more year given everything that had happened. The dean didn't seem to mind the good publicity of the celebrity grad student.

"Well," Liz said, "with all the money you're saving, what with being lent a house and a car of the ex-wife you're replacing, you can afford to install a couple of fresh deadbolts to ward off any drunken late-night visits that might occur when this associate dean forgets where he lives *now*."

"Stop, Liz," Maddy pleaded. "Stop. Honestly, he a dorky academic, not a player. He's remarried. For fuck's sake, Liz, he's a *sociologist*. And it'll be great. Because you can come visit."

"There *is* a bar there in Minneapolis that I like," Liz answered. "Had a good time there during a genetics conference a couple of years ago."

"I was actually thinking you'd be visiting with *me*," Maddy replied, a little exasperated.

"Don't worry, Chicken Little. You can always bring another friend if we go out. You make friends easily enough."

Chapter 2

Maddy wasn't sure how Jordan Fitzpatrick had managed to slip away from the paparazzi this time, but he had—and now he had followed her into a back stairwell of her hotel. She could feel his hot breath on the back of her head as he held her close from behind, his arms around her waist. He was pushing her hair off her neck with the tip of his nose, landing his lips just below her left ear, kissing her on the sternocleidomastoid, that strong, long muscle running up her neck from the shoulder, though he made it feel as if that muscle ran straight down to her inner thigh.

She turned her head toward him suddenly, as if he had hit a reflex point with his lips.

"Not here, not here," she whispered. "We should go up to my room."

"Someone might see us in the hallway." He turned her around to face him, pushing her back gently up against the yellow cinder-block wall. "Plus, I can't wait."

His whisper seemed to echo in the quiet stairway. Light streamed in from a window on the landing. (Wait, why did this hotel stairwell have a window, she wondered?)

He kissed her on the neck again and laid his right hand on her left shoulder, slowly dragging it down, running ever so lightly over her left breast while he looked into her eyes. She could feel all her blood rushing from her head to her groin, and her eyes felt as if they might cross. Her knees went from locked to buckled. She tried to lock them again. His hand settled momentarily on her hip and then drifted down, finding the hem of her dress. Slowly up then went his hand, under her dress, up the front of her right thigh, to the top of her panties. She could feel his warm fingers reach down inside. His three middle digits drifted around a bit, like a trio of mice settling into a familiar nest of straw. He lay one fingertip on her clitoris and held it there motionless, still looking into her eyes, knowingly. He smiled and moved his head slowly left to right, right to left, left to right . . . She was sure she was going to fall.

"*You* can't wait either," he said with a soft laugh. And then he stroked her gently, and soon she came with a guttural moan and a rush of disorientation.

After just a moment, the pleasant shudder turned into a nasty chill. Feeling the cold, Maddy pulled the bedclothes closer to her body. She wondered anew why this sometimes happened. Shouldn't the sudden rush of blood here and there make one feel *warmer* all over? She tried to remember the sympathetic nervous response—heart rate increase, pupillary dilation, goose bumps, perspiration. Winslow, 1732, *Exposition Anatomique de la Structure du Corps Humain*, was it?

Maybe she should try an A-level Hollywood star next time. But ever since she had seen him in that dumb costume drama in the university's indie film festival, the B-level Jordan Fitzpatrick had been so damned reliable.

She threw off the covers, got up, and bent over, hands to the floor. She pulled her legs up carefully into the air to take a free-of-the-convent morning handstand. Her nightgown fell asymmetrically down around her arms and head. She noted as usual—and yet also with a fresh bit of delight—being blinded to the room by the fabric while the cold air tickled the naked majority of her body. She split her legs slowly front to back, brought them back together, and split them to her sides.

She held the pose for a minute before standing up. Then she tried to make a bit of clatter as she moved about the room to dress, trying to fill the house with some noise. *Too quiet for my taste,* she thought as she pulled on underwear, jeans, and a sweatshirt. As if the universe had read her mind, the landline in the kitchen let out a piercing squeal.

It was the first time she'd heard it ring. At first she wasn't even sure what the sharp electronic sound was. She rushed over to the phone on the wall, her bare feet cold on the kitchen floor tile.

"Hello?"

"Finally!" answered a man's voice. "Finally, I get you! Listen, it's Leonard, and I only got a minute. You home on Friday?"

The accent sounded like New York to her. Lower Manhattan, maybe Brooklyn.

"Yes, I'll be here," Maddy said, trying to add a question of who Leonard was. But all she got out was "Who . . . ?"

"Great. It's coming then. You'll love it. It sings! It sings, my dear! Call me after."

And with that, he hung up.

Maddy stood there for a minute, trying to figure out what to do. It had to have been a call meant for Alex Shugar—why the landline hadn't been turned off, she could not figure, other than simple neglect of the task, as others. Scott Willingham, Shugar's ex and the associate dean who hired her, had not been dealing much with Shugar's effects. Rather than getting rid of Alex's clothes before Maddy's arrival, Scott was still boxing them up and moving the boxes to the garage when Maddy arrived by airport cab with her suitcases. He'd even left all of Alex's food here, except for the most perishable. When Maddy asked him what she should do with all the food in the cupboards and tins, Scott apologized for not having thought that part through. He suggested Maddy go ahead and use it if Maddy didn't think that was morbid. She had brightened inside, happy to have access to a significant store of decent free food. (She'd already spotted some good vinegar and curry pastes.) She said that would be fine, that it didn't trouble her in the least.

Now she thought that maybe adding "in the least" hadn't been the best choice. Well, in any case, what to do about this delivery coming in six days, the delivery of a something that wasn't meant for her? A something that would sing? Maddy thought about emailing or texting Scott but didn't want to talk to him more than necessary, given Liz's instincts about why Scott had hired her.

She made herself some oatmeal with raisins and a cup of tea, all from

Shugar's pantry. She added a bit of honey to the bowl and the cup, subconsciously accounting with satisfaction having saved at least a dollar and a half on this perfectly satisfying little meal. After putting her empty dish in the sink, she took the mug and wandered into the small house's second bedroom, the one in the back of the house that Shugar had used as her study. The room looked out to the expanse of woods behind the house, a few acres of land Scott explained were too wet for building. It had been set aside as a small nature preserve. He warned her that in the spring the mosquitoes would be unpleasant and that she might hear the sump pumps come on.

The other houses in this subdivision's enclave were invisible from here, hidden like this house in the stands of the woods. The feeling of remoteness reminded her enough of the convent to set off a clenched-belly muscle memory of being in a place that was all wrong yet magnificently safe.

Wolf wouldn't like this place for her. With no picket fence of nuns surrounding her, he would say it was too far off the beaten path. Still, it felt such a luxury. A whole little atheistic convent to herself! No one to object if she had a late-night party or sang loudly in the shower first thing in the morning. No one to wake her up if she felt like sleeping in. And the picture window in this back room made it seem almost as if Maddy were in a treehouse. Shugar's choice of dark wood furniture for the room only accentuated the sensation.

Maddy switched on the room's overhead light and then the desk lamp. She figured she would use this room when working from home on teaching duties or research. It had a desk with a decent chair plus a comfortable modern couch positioned against the picture window wall, good for reading. She pulled up the seat cushions and confirmed that the couch had a pull-out bed, one that Liz could use when she visited. She poked around the room, figuring Alex must have kept sheets for this couch somewhere, and soon found them with spare blankets and a pillow, all hidden inside the matching ottoman. Lovely—Liz would like this quiet bedroom, the view of the woods, the air coming off the trees. It might make her visit more than once.

But in this room, too, Maddy noticed, Scott Willingham had not really put Alex Shugar away. While the desk was basically cleared, holding only a glazed ceramic plant pot full of standard-issue pens and pencils, Alex's presence could still be felt all over the room. Maddy looked at the series of photographs in silver frames. Here was one of Shugar with Willingham from years earlier. They were smiling; a friendly divorce, presumably. Well, of course—she had apparently left him her house? And her car.

And here was another photo from at least a decade before showing Shugar with two other women, all in academic robes, all looking smart and self-assured. And another with a different woman—taken on a sunny day against the railing of a boat—both of them in sunglasses and hats.

And a fourth, this one seemingly recent given the crows' feet around Shugar's joyful eyes, with a man about her age looking as happy as she did. Maddy wondered if he was the man whose small toilet kit she'd found in a drawer in the bathroom. She had opened the zippered case to find it held a toothbrush, dental floss, nail clippers, a stick of deodorant, and a small bottle of cologne. But no toothpaste, which meant that whoever he was, he must have been accustomed to using Alex's. Most people, Maddy had come to observe, were picky about their toothpaste. (Liz went for a "natural" brand that Maddy thought tasted too much like food.) Whoever had left this toilet kit had almost certainly been a regular here.

Maddy looked next at the books lining the walls of the study. Most were what she would have expected given Shugar's career history: a PhD in English literature earned about twenty-five years before she shifted her career to focus on literature and medicine, eventually drifting into working with people born intersex. These were people who had been born with anatomies between the male and the female—some born with confusing genitals, some born with bodies where doctors later discovered that the internal reproductive organs didn't match the external sex.

Maddy knew from the obituary posted on the program's webpage that Alex had gotten into this work because she had written a well-regarded paper about an eighteenth-century autobiography of a person born with what was then called hermaphroditism, and this had led living intersex people to ask her to help advocate for their rights. Maddy knew from Alex's scholarship that from the mid-twentieth century on, intersex people had been subjected as babies to surgeries meant to make them sexually acceptable to their parents and others, surgeries to which many of them later objected. Moved by the activists' autobiographies, Alex had gone from being a traditional academic to an activist herself, tracking the real histories, fighting with surgeons, trying to get them to change.

Wilhelm's type—the academic medical elite—would surely have snickered at Alex's work, writing it all off as PC feminism and gay politics. But Shugar had focused years of her scholarship on contemporary clinical criticism anyway, ultimately working for a decade with this population, arguing with the surgeons that everyone deserved the right of sexual self-determination.

In the absence of anyone else around to do the work, Shugar had acted as a proper historian, tracing out the centuries of experiences before pediatric surgery became the norm. She had shown how most intersex people had lived normal lives before surgery became ubiquitous, challenging the conventional wisdom that "no one could live like this." Lots of people had, she showed.

It reminded Maddy now so much of the arguments the psychologist Nick DesJardins had made to Maddy—arguments she knew to be true from her own research: that the negative social experience of dwarfism, like intersex, arose from the *cultural* context, not the biological conditions themselves. She wished she could call and talk with Nick about this connection between his ideas about his own condition—dwarfism—and Alex's ideas about intersex. But like Alex, Nick was dead.

Would there be a trial for him someday? A trial in Washington?

Maddy stared out the window a moment, watching a crow jump its way down a tree, branch by branch. How it did seem to her as if the crow was meant to have arms, the way it moved as if it had a sudden case of phocomelia. Had this dusky Minnesotan forest robbed the crow of its arms, slapping on wings as a consolation prize?

She shook her head like a child shaking an Etch A Sketch to clear the irrational image from her brain and took Alex Shugar's last-authored book off the shelf to slowly page through the ending. It recalled to her Shugar's series of angry polemics against the way medical subspecialties favored traditional assumptions over actual evidence of what helped or hurt people with atypical bodies. But Shugar made clear she had had just as little patience for most of the scholarship in the humanities. Alex had called many humanities scholars' treatment of people's stories, including patients' memories, "secondary abuse," the way they took real people's histories of trauma as if they were just stories to be deconstructed and analyzed, used as mere academic objects of fascination. How was this different from how the doctors treated them, she asked? How did it reduce the problem of attributed shame? What had they done to help other than "represent" the issues?

("What have you done to help?" Maddy pictured herself for a moment as a teenager, asking the question impatiently of Sister Severe, standing there having one of their periodic ontological arguments in the convent's front sitting room as they waited to accept a scheduled delivery of food from a grocer who gave the sisters past-date products.)

But if Shugar's argument was correct, what was one supposed to do as a humanities scholar, Maddy wondered now? How could one do reasonably objective history—tell it like it was, represent it like it had really been—while worrying first and foremost about the *effects* of that history, worrying about whether one's work was helping today with the problems of shame and injustice? If you worried too much about the effects of your work, worried too much about helping or hurting, you could not free your vision to go where the evidence would lead. Right?

If Shugar wanted real justice, Maddy thought to herself as if she were arguing with Shugar in a proper seminar room, Shugar had to recognize that sometimes the digging would find what *hurt* subjects. Sometimes the very act of digging would necessarily harm people.

Maddy had spent the past many months considering what her investigation into Wilhelm had wrought. At the very least, her digging had brought about Jimmy Heathcote's death in New York. And Nick DesJardin's in Washington, too? She knew, rationally, these deaths were Wilhelm's fault, not hers. Yet she could not think of them without feeling remorse and contrition, wanting someone to wash her soul in icy water with a great deal of dish soap. If only she had not made Wilhelm and them her subjects. But then, what choice had she had?

She remembered then a conversation with Wolf, one had over a pot roast with new potatoes, a roast he had cooked at her Bloomington flat in a combination of a good Burgundy and fresh orange juice and herbes de Provence. He had been there for her dissertation defense and it had become a conversation in her little kitchen about what you are supposed to do when you've become interested in someone who doesn't want to be the subject of your curiosity. Wolf wasn't talking about Wilhelm; he was talking about an abused woman who would not cooperate with him or any other officer, and how there was consequently almost nothing they could do to stop the man who finally killed her.

"But *why?*" Maddy had asked. "*Why* would she not testify against him? Why would she not help you help her?"

"Love?" he had replied. "Fear? Shame?"

"Shame?" Maddy had asked, using her fingernail to pick a piece of dried rosemary off her incisor where it had adhered. "What do you mean?"

"That you have to admit you have a humiliating problem before you can exit the problem," Wolf had responded. "You know, that thing you are so bad at."

He had let out a short laugh while spooning more gravy onto her plate.

18

"But my problems in Philadelphia were never problems of humiliation, never problems of *shame*," she had answered, pushing her plate a little closer to help him with his ladling. "Were they, Wolf?"

"Then why did you have such a hard time telling me about The Jerk? Why could you not just *tell me* what had happened to you? Why did I have to find out by accident?"

He wasn't saying any of this in an accusatory fashion. It was more as if he were just curious. Perhaps he would have even shrugged his shoulders if his arms hadn't been involved in the task of serving food.

"I think there is a way, Wolf, that *speaking* of The Jerk means he's *fucking* me again. Fucking me *over* again."

"And you're ashamed of that?"

"Why wouldn't I be?"

Now Maddy cleared her throat, as if to stop herself saying something aloud to continue the conversation that had ended months before. What was it about this study of Alex's that seemed to disorient her so? Was it the intense silence, so reminiscent of an archive?

She used her finger to trace out Shugar's concluding words in this book. Here was the argument Shugar had lately come to be known for: Culturally relativistic, jargon-laden, academic conversations about "representation" were all well and good if you weren't someone who had suffered real-life injustice. In that case, reality mattered. Action mattered. Clarity mattered.

Maddy recalled now that one especially uncertain stretch just after Philadelphia, when Wolf had gone back home from visiting her in Indiana and she could barely sleep, when she had come across an ongoing dueling-essay debate in the *Chronicle of Higher Education* between Shugar and a famed literary theorist, with Shugar arguing that scholarship required attention to flesh and bones and scalpels—to lived reality, to justice, beyond the coldly medical, and beyond the merely academic. It was as if Shugar knew this wasn't just a mind game. It had felt for that moment like Shugar had been speaking directly to her, had been urging Maddy to accept that justice mattered more than just the pleasure of ideas. It had been as if Shugar was telling Maddy to buck up and carry on.

She wished for a moment that she had reached out to Shugar then—that she had gotten to talk to this woman before she had died. Maybe she could have talked to Alex confidentially about the trial. The prosecutors had said Maddy shouldn't talk to anyone about it, not until it was over. But given her own work with intersex people, Shugar had probably known how to keep secret a conversation like the one Maddy needed with her, how to hold a hand while listening to a story that everyone would say was unbelievable until everyone said it was obviously true.

Alex would surely have laughed if Maddy had been able to tell her about the conversation with that woman from the University of Chicago, only slightly senior to Maddy, just after Maddy's talk at the midwestern medical humanities meeting—tenure-track with expensive heels and a Florentine scarf wrapped around her shoulders, just so. She had told Maddy derisively that her "little murder investigation" wasn't scholarship and that she shouldn't mistake it.

"Nobody does a dissertation that is simply an unpacking of a series of murders, with good reason, Dr. Shanks! It doesn't take a PhD to do that kind of thing, now, does it? How many police officers do you know with PhDs? All practice, no theory, what you figured out. *Not. Scholarship.*"

Oh, how good it would be to tell Professor Shugar of this stupid point of view. How good it would be to tell Alex Shugar of *how* she had figured it all out in Philadelphia.

But, then, Maddy wouldn't have this job if Alex were alive. She wouldn't have all the food in the pantry. She wouldn't have free use of this beautiful little house, with what might just be the best bathtub in the world....

Maddy noticed now, in the study, there was one low shelf near the desk that was uniquely empty—empty but for a lonely bookend. She wondered what this was about. Had Scott emptied this shelf for Maddy to use? But if so, where were the books that had been there, and why clear a shelf so hard to reach?

She then opened the drawers of the wooden filing cabinet near the desk. The tags on the hanging folders indicated these had been places where Shugar had kept correspondence and research notes on major projects. There were tabs for "hermaphroditism" in various periods—early-modern, Victorian, contemporary—and tabs for various modern intersex patient rights groups, children's hospitals, and medical specialty groups. But nothing in these hanging folders.

Hanging folders marked with subject headings, but nothing in them—it felt to Maddy like an abandoned building with the windows knocked out, frayed curtains blowing through the jagged holes in the glass. Had Scott just cleared this out to make space for Maddy, storing the material in the garage or the basement or somewhere else? Had he given the material to someone else—an archive, a student of Alex's who might follow up?

Maddy kept looking, soon finding that, by contrast, the file drawer in the desk itself had plenty of research material in it. This made no sense. If Scott had wanted to empty space for Maddy's use, why hadn't he made space in the desk drawer where it would be most logically convenient? Perhaps he had just started cleaning out the space and not finished?

Here in the desk file drawer Maddy found a series of folders on various sexual behaviors—exhibitionism, pedophilia, polyamory, foot fetishism— some marked with scientific terms Maddy didn't know but that she could tell from the Greek root *philia* referred to sexual orientations. She couldn't recall Shugar having published on any of this. Inside the folders were jumbles of printouts of articles on these subjects, photocopies of case studies from various literatures, and notes in what must have been Alex's hand. Was this what she was working on when she died?

Is it snooping, Maddy suddenly wondered, *if the snoopee is dead and the snooper has been invited to occupy the space?*

She couldn't seem to stop looking and skimming. It felt like being in an underappreciated archive with no uptight staff to scold one for taking inadequate care with the papers. Still, she tried to keep them organized exactly as they had been, to keep her mug of tea well away from the material. A major scholar's work had to be kept just so, for history.

Chapter 3

It was too late by the time Maddy realized she had done something wrong while lighting a fire in the living room fireplace. Now the room was filling up with smoke and she started to panic. The fire was catching the kindling she had laid below the logs, and the smoke was getting worse. Waving her hands around, she soon realized, amounted to nothing but sheer idiocy.

She ran to the nearest windows and opened them and then hastily pulled her cell phone out of her pocket, flipping it open and dialing Scott Willingham's cell phone. When he answered, she tried her best to tell him what she had done. The peaceful drifting of the smoke around the room in the early evening light felt like a mockery of her panic.

"Did you open the flue?" Scott asked her tensely.

"The what?"

"The flue!" he yelled. "Did you open the flue?!"

"I'm sorry—"

"I'm thirty miles away right now!" he said, adding rapidly that he'd call someone. He hung up.

Unsure what to do, she ran around opening more windows and looking for a fan. Fifteen minutes into this mess, she was wondering whether to call the local fire department—do you call the fire department when you're filling a house with just smoke?—when she heard a car pull up fast and a key inserted into the front door lock. A man rushed in, slammed the door, and ran to the living room. He grabbed a tool next to the fireplace and used it to pull open what Maddy realized must be the flue. The smoke started to redirect up the chimney like sheep herded through a gate.

He sat down on the rug facing the fireplace and gave out a loud sigh.

Maddy sat down on the couch behind him unsure what to say or do. She felt about as stupid as ever. She wished she had paid more attention at the convent to how the fireplaces worked, but Sister Thomas Aquinas had always been the one to handle starting the fires.

She probably should not have said yes to living in this house. Who even was this guy whose back of the head she was now looking at, someone who could let himself into her house at will? Were there other men who could?

The light from the window picked off the here-and-there strands of gray in his otherwise black hair. He watched the fireplace until the smoke was steadily going in the right direction. Then he looked up to the mantle, and then to his left and his right, as if slowly reorienting himself to this space.

Finally, he turned to face Maddy and stood up. She looked at his face as he rose and judged him right about fifty years—twice her age. Now she recognized this face from the happy-couple photo in Alex's study. Only he did not look happy now.

"Lucky I was not too far. And the good news is you build a shitty fire," he said. His voice was low and reedy, as if he'd spent the last night out in a loud place. "It has mostly died out. If you're going to build another one, *open the flue first*," he told her, picking up and shaking the hooked tool, looking as if Maddy had run over his beloved dog.

She felt awful realizing she had almost certainly pulled him back to where he did not want to be—the house of his dead lover. Though he was tall and muscular, he looked weakened by being in this room. His shoulders sloped down in defeat.

"Dean Willingham called you?" she asked, standing up as if to attention. He was a good bit taller than her own five-foot-three, and she felt her puniness add to her sense of incompetence.

"Yes," he answered. He extended a hand, looking embarrassed at his rude introductory tone. "Hank Merriman."

"Madeleine Shanks," she said, taking his hand and shaking it wanly. "Maddy."

She usually tried to shake more firmly. She nearly told him so.

Hank looked again around the room. He was standing a few feet away from her, but even so, he stood close enough for her to smell his cologne. She hastened to the master bathroom and brought him back the toilet kit.

"This is you...?" she said, dragging the "you" out from a statement to a question.

Not that she had a question. Maddy's sense of smell, Liz had once observed, suggested that her DNA overlapped more with the canine genome than was true for the typical human. She handed him the small black nylon case.

"Yes," Hank said, turning it over in his right hand and then gripping it in both. "How did you know that it is mine?"

"How you smell. Well, and your photo. And, also, you having a key and you knowing how to open the door fast. Plus, Scott calling you," she answered.

Maddy caught herself embarrassed at having rattled off the reasons as if taking an easy quiz. He nodded silently. After putting down the toilet kit on the couch and rubbing his eyes with the palms of his hands, Hank looked at her straight on again.

"So, you will have by now also discovered my good Scotch. Want some? I could use it."

He walked toward the kitchen.

"Yes, please," she answered. "With an ice cube."

"I think you can close the windows now?"

Instead of closing the windows, she followed him to the kitchen. She wanted to see how he moved in this space that was once his. He pulled two tumblers and poured them each a glass, hers iced, his neat, his actions clearly second nature. He then went back to the living room, closed the windows, fixed the fire so that it took on a reliable burn, and settled himself into the armchair that she figured he must have occupied many times before. Maddy sat on the couch, unsure whether to sit on the end nearest Hank or the end farthest, finally settling awkwardly in the middle.

"Hey, who else can get in that front door as easily as you?" she asked.

"Just me and Scott," he said. "You don't need to worry."

24

Maybe Liz was right about adding a new lock?

Maddy noticed that Hank kept looking to the daybed set in the bay window that faced the long driveway to the house. The way he looked to that daybed, it must have been where Alex liked to be, at least when he was in that armchair.

"Is this what Alex drank—Scotch?" she asked in a quiet voice. He responded absentmindedly that Alex generally preferred a gin and tonic, double the usual lime.

As Maddy sipped, trying not to watch Hank too closely, she felt the heat of the Scotch radiate from her throat to her belly to her arms and felt, too, a calm finally settling over her. What a good old drug alcohol was. No wonder they used it as an anesthetic for bone-setting and dental work and such before the days of the modern stuff. Such a reliable slide into the pool of ego abandonment where pleasure could wash over you.

She looked down at her knees just to stop looking at him and wondered if at such a juncture it was better to try to make small talk or to be quiet. He finally broke what had become a long silence.

"So, you're living here, then, in Alex's house?"

She explained that Scott had hired her to be Alex's replacement—to teach Alex's courses as scheduled—and had offered her the house since she had had to move on relatively short notice.

"Your PhD is in what?" he asked.

"History—history of medicine and science," she answered. "I know it's not what Professor Shugar's PhD was in—that hers was in literature, that she did literature and medicine," she added. "But our scholarly interests did sort of overlap. And she was in a medical humanities program, not a literature program, so they could take me on as an historian in such a program. My degree didn't have to be in literature. So."

"You don't need to apologize for your degree."

"And you?" she asked.

"Me, what?"

"Your PhD field?"

She could not put her finger on why she knew him to be an academic. Maybe it was that Alex seemed too smart and too busy to be with anyone but another PhD? And Hank seemed too knowing in his responses to Maddy not to be one of the tribe.

"Psychology," he said. "I'm a sex researcher in the psych department."

"Full professor?" she asked.

He nodded.

"Promotion to University Distinguished Professor soon?"

He huffed.

"Not a chance," he answered. "I've earned it, easily, but I'm too much trouble to the administration."

There was another silence. Maddy wondered—were the files in the desk Hank's, the ones on various sexual interests? But if so, he would have taken them back by now. Alex Shugar had been dead about three months. She looked at his face, lit now by the fire, as darkness was falling steadily. He was ruggedly handsome, not like your typical professor. She didn't think it just the Scotch telling her that. He had what looked like that kind of intentional two-days-without shave. Well-cut hair. Good nails. No rings. A watch, nothing too fancy; just functional with an aged leather band.

She looked at his face again and suddenly thought he might be near tears. This was her own stupid fault. Alex would say she'd been treating Hank as a mere subject. Should Maddy do something? Might doing something for him get her somewhere better, too?

As if he could see her noisy thoughts, Hank closed his eyes.

"So, you were Alex Shugar's lover?" Maddy asked, surprising herself perhaps more than him.

"Not exactly."

He opened his eyes, looked at her, and wrinkled his brow a little.

"Not exactly?" she asked.

The Scotch had peeled away what little hesitation she had in her. She wanted a little more of it for just that reason. Oh, to feel the body of a strong man who wasn't a jerk. And he probably wasn't a jerk. Not if Alex had had him.

"We did not have sex. We were not sexual partners. I'm guessing that's what you're asking."

"How odd," Maddy answered, suddenly wondering if there was something wrong with him. "You were both so interested in sex. She was straight? You are straight?"

"Yes," he said, and he let out a short laugh at her impetuousness. "Very straight. In both cases."

"And you were both single?"

"Yes," he answered. He stood up, took the Scotch bottle from the mantle, and poured himself some more. He was about to pour her more as well when he stopped to ask, "Hey, how come I feel like I know your name,

Madeline Shanks?"

"Possibly the news," she said with no little dread, lifting her glass up in front of her forehead signaling for him to pour more, as if making a superstitious gesture. She sighed as he refilled the glass an inch. She looked at it and thought she shouldn't drink this much. But she drank most of it back anyway, coughing a little from the burn.

"You know the trial about to happen, of the doctor who killed a bunch of little people—a bunch of patients with dwarfism—to obtain them for research specimen purposes? In Philadelphia?"

His eyes got wide as he sat back down.

"That was *you*? The grad student who put it together while doing her dissertation?"

She pursed her lips and nodded.

"Oh, wow. Ally would have liked to have met you. I remember she said you had really done it, gone after the truth, gotten some justice. I wonder if that's why Scott hired you—as a kind of tribute to her. No bullshit postmodern take. Just reality. Your work was the ultimate in patients' rights, Alex said, though a little too late for the victims, I guess!"

"Alex said *that*?" Maddy asked, genuinely surprised. "She knew about what I found?"

"Everybody knew about it," he answered, looking at her face now more closely. His gaze made her feel caught in the roadway. She wanted to pull back behind a bush.

She moved to offense.

"So, why didn't you sleep together? Why were you here so often?"

He paused and looked to the daybed. Maddy wondered if he had fantasized about taking Alex there?

"I don't know how to answer that question," he finally answered. "We did *sleep* together. At least a couple days a week. For years. You know that because you figured that out." Before she could say more, he added, "We just didn't have sex."

"Why not? Is there something wrong with you—or was there something wrong with her?"

"Not that!" Hank said, laughing. He was settling in now, it seemed—settling well into the chair and into a comfortable honesty. This gave her a little hope. "You're a pushy one. You sound like me. No, Alex and I didn't have sex because *I* was used to younger women, and *she* was used to better men."

He chuckled. Then he said it again, as if he was quite proud of the construction: "I was used to younger women, and she was used to better men. My relationship with Ally was the most intense of my life. It didn't fit your categories. Frankly, it took a lot more effort than a sexual relationship takes."

She wondered what he meant by that.

"You and Scott—her ex-husband, the deanlette—the two of you are friends?" she asked.

He snorted.

"Oh, no. I wouldn't say that."

"So, Scott didn't like you because he *thought* you were having sex with Alex?"

"No," Hank answered, running the tip of his right index finger around the rim of his glass. "No. I expect Scott didn't like me because he knew I *wasn't* having sex with Ally." He brought the glass to his lips and sipped. "Look," he said, "by our age—the age that Alex and I and Scott were, or *are*—things present themselves unexpectedly. Things get sorted out in ways you don't expect. You'll discover that someday. Life is complicated."

Death more so, Maddy thought, but she said nothing aloud. Death was supposed to make subjects stable. They stopped doing, thinking, writing, dreaming. As problems, this ending of action should make them more contained, more manageable, easier to describe, to understand, to solve. Yet, in truth, so rarely did death make a complex subject like Alex easier. Just quieter, like a sullen child. Less likely to be forthcoming. Less likely to argue in convincing ways with her historian. But somehow more demanding of her.

"She died how?" Maddy asked aloud, knowing from the obituaries she had looked up that Alex had died at age forty-nine from drowning. She wanted to hear how Hank would put it.

"She drowned by accident. She went for a swim alone in one of the smaller lakes, tucked back in some woods near here," he said.

He tilted his head to the right, stared at the fire, and blinked two or three times.

"She liked to swim in open water, and she liked it best when there was nobody else around. She didn't worry about doing it alone. She liked the feeling. Like riding her bicycle with no helmet to feel the air. But water was everything for her."

He paused then, opening his mouth and closing it a few times as if struggling to think how to translate a sentence. He looked at the daybed again, as if he could see Alex there for a moment.

"She said to me—she said to me sometimes—that we both had intense

28

survival instincts, and we had no choice but to test them constantly if we were going to stay out of real trouble. That we had to run down our survival instincts every now and then, wear them out, to keep them from doing something crazy. Like mad dogs who have to run."

Then he looked as if the ghost had disappeared.

"So, she used to swim alone," he said. "In open water. To tire the survival instinct?" He breathed in deeply, audibly, and sighed, as if there was no answer to his own question. "Neither of us was very good at staying out of real trouble."

As if this statement had jogged his memory, he looked at his watch. Seeing the time, he stood up, turned to Maddy, and handed her his glass.

"I have to go," he said. "I have a date. I mean, an appointment."

He grabbed his toilet kit from the couch and tucked it between his upper arm and side. She stood up to see him to the door. He seemed unaffected by the drink, but she felt dizzy and liquid. He opened the door, flipped on the ceiling light in the foyer, and turned to her.

"Listen," he said, looking her in the eyes, a hawk fixed on a target. Maddy was struck by his height and by the breadth of his shoulders and nearly giggled at the obviousness of all this. "There are probably still some good steaks in the freezer. I know because I bought them. If you treat steak like you do fires, call me if you want one, and *I'll* make it. They weren't cheap."

With a glass in each hand, Maddy had to close the door after him with her back. She waited to listen to his car leave. It sounded like a sports car. Predictable, that. Predictable, too, her response to his anatomy and his age and his status. Leaning against the door, she could feel the evening cold seep from the surface of the door through her clothes to her skin. She could hear the fire in the living room crackling, popping, sighing, as the wood dried in the heat of the flames.

She thought about her own survival instinct. She could see it now in her mind as if it were a big black bear—muscular haunches and a heavy breath. Dark and large and staring at her. She wondered what would ever tire that beast out.

Chapter 4

It was the kind of weeknight after a twelve-hour lab day that Liz would have usually spent with Maddy watching bad TV or going to one of the university gyms together. But Maddy was gone to Minnesota and Liz felt disinclined to call her when they had talked just a few days ago. So, Liz called on her simpler companions.

"Hey, Newton. Hey, Einstein."

She settled on the couch with a light blanket over herself and four chocolate chips in her left hand, held loosely so they wouldn't melt. She stretched forward using her right hand to open the door of the cage next to the couch, turning the wire door into a small drawbridge to the seat of the couch. She leaned back again.

"Come on, Newton. Come on, Einstein," she called softly to the black-and-white brothers. "I have your chocolate."

The two small hooded rats climbed up the inside of the cage, lumbered out, ducked under the blanket, and crawled to Liz's upper thigh, where they reappeared. Each then stood on his haunches to greet Liz and wait for the chocolate treats. She scratched Newton on the neck, tickled Einstein's belly, and gave each one a chocolate chip. Liz watched with delight as the rodents finished off the chips and washed vigorously behind their ears with their front paws. There was nothing as satisfying as watching a rat give himself a good cleaning after something tasty.

This was the castrated duo she had hoped to give Maddy. She'd chosen males because they had the advantage of being less industrious than the females—better at settling down for mutual comfort. Castrated, they would get along fine and not be marking everything with pee. Males were good for some things, at least when you castrated them.

Liz had outfitted Newton and Einstein's favorite bedding spot with a pair of Maddy's dirty gym socks—swiped from Maddy's hamper while Liz had been helping her friend pack—so that the brothers would be used to Maddy's scent and immediately treat her as a colony-mate were she to appear and take them as her own. But, Liz thought to herself sadly, having them recognize Maddy's smell as kin would only matter if Maddy came to visit. And what were the odds of that with her schedule? At least Liz had these warm little guys to play with.

As if reading her thoughts, Newton crawled up the front of Liz's sweat-shirt, perched on her shoulder, and sniffed the side of her face with his pointy snout. Then he put his front paws up on her scalp and started examining her hair with his nose and fingers. Newton was perpetually fascinated by Liz's buzz-cut hair. His fingers tickled her, and she reached up and gave him several strokes with her fingers. Einstein, meanwhile, was busy cleaning up the cuticles on Liz's other hand, gently trimming off dead skin with his teeth, using his tongue to clean her short nail tips. She reached under him to tickle his belly. He wrestled her finger, making clear his intent to finish grooming her if only she would behave.

While Newton wandered around the couch under and over the blanket, Liz let Einstein do his work on her fingertips. She wondered what Maddy was up to at that moment. Maybe her evening bath? When she had called after taking possession of the house, Maddy had exclaimed to Liz that it had a beautiful big bathtub, set off by itself in a dedicated solarium, just off the master bedroom, with big skylights and windows all around, on a slate floor. She said she wasn't sure how she'd ever go to work with that tub calling.

But it seemed more likely Maddy would now be frantically prepping for

Shugar's two courses, one a history of medicine survey for a mix of upper-division undergraduate plus graduate students, the other a small grad seminar on the history and politics of anatomy. Maddy did seem to Liz exceptionally well qualified to replace Shugar. While plenty of PhDs could teach that survey class, there could not be a lot of scholars around—well, not junior ones in need of jobs, anyway—who would be so well prepared to conduct a seminar on the history and politics of anatomy. Still, taking over someone else's courses without much notice, especially someone with as complicated and as big a reputation as Shugar, could not be easy. Liz hoped her friend would not fall into the usual problem faced by junior academics, where teaching duties take up so much energy, there'd be no time for what the system values: grants, research, publication. And even with Wilhelm's trial going on, Maddy would have to be looking for another job essentially at the same time. Where, Liz wondered, would Maddy end up next? Where would Liz?

Academia was like the military, where you're almost never in control of where you go. You make friends and leave them in one unpredictable round after another. Liz had reminded Maddy of this as she warned her off developing any real romantic relationship during a temporary job, especially a relationship with another hard-to-employ junior academic or with a settled academic who would not be willing to move for Maddy's career. Liz remembered now how Maddy had responded to this. Not with words, but with fifty quick push-ups and several sighs.

. . .

Maddy was kicking herself for not looking closely at the class roster before the seminar. If she had, she would have known what names she was going to have to match with faces, and then she wouldn't be in this position of trying to remember the eight seminar students' names while also trying to learn which name went with which body.

Now she had gotten through the first seminar meeting, and it had gone pretty well, she thought, but she still couldn't remember with any confidence who was called what. Why did grad students have the habit of never calling each other by their names in these seminars? Was it just to torture the new prof? And now they were headed out to the Loring Pasta Bar for a shared meal and drinks—she had been informed this was the traditional thing to do in her program after the first seminar meeting—and they would be joined by other students affiliated with the program, with more names and bodies she didn't know and couldn't keep matched.

As the seminar group walked through campus toward the restaurant in Dinkytown from their assigned classroom in Rapson Hall, Maddy pulled back the one student whose name she *could* remember to walk with her: Josiah. He was older than her, perhaps by as much as ten years, and was earning his PhD in the History of Science program. He was clean-cut and upbeat and had held a job in the real world as an engineer before deciding to get a PhD. Josiah was taking Maddy's class as an elective as he had with a couple of other classes in the Medical Humanities master's degree program into which she'd been hired.

"Help me out, Josiah. I'm forgetting everyone's names already."

"It won't matter, Dr. Shanks," he assured her. "You'll learn them soon. They know you're new. No one's going to hold it against you."

His vowels had hints of the South and she wondered if she could ask where he was from, or if that would come across as sounding too date-like.

"The orange-haired guy?" she asked him.

"Peter. Just think *Peter, Peter, Pumpkin-eater*," Josiah suggested. "You know, orange hair, like a pumpkin. That's what I did to remember his name."

"You're good," Maddy said. "And the blond woman?"

"Lateesha."

"Yeah," Maddy answered, as they continued to follow the others in the group. "About that?"

"You want to know why a woman who looks all white has a Black woman's name?"

She admitted that was her question.

"Somebody told me her parents did it as some kind of cultural support for African-Americans," Josiah said. "I met her mother when she was visiting— she's *all about* indigenous beads and oppression, so I could see that being the explanation. But to be honest, none of us have had the guts to ask."

"And the Asian guy?"

"He's from Hong Kong and his real name is Cheung," Josiah told her, "but he goes by Kevin. We tried calling him Cheung and he just got mad at us and asked us why we wouldn't call him Kevin."

"Ironically," Maddy said, "I could have remembered 'Cheung.' Any of you guys could be named Kevin."

The group turned a corner and continued down the path past Jones Hall.

Josiah pulled Maddy back a touch more.

"Listen, I have to tell you something before we get to the restaurant. There's likely to be a post-doc joining us. Thin and tall. Brunette. Very pretty, I guess I'm not supposed to notice that. Her name is Sarah. And she hates you."

"What?" Maddy let out a little laugh, to let him know she understood him to be joking.

"Yeah," Josiah answered in a serious tone, "she hates you. She wanted your job. She was sure when Dr. Shugar died that she'd be given the temporary replacement position. Instead, she had to scramble to put together another year of funding while she looks for a job, because *you* got the job. As far as Sarah is concerned, you stole her starter job. Her mentor is dead, and you stole her job. And she needs a starter job. Well, we all do. You know that."

"She got her degree in your PhD program?"

"Yes," said Josiah, "and Alex Shugar was her dissertation director. So, naturally, she thought she had a lock on Shugar's job when . . ."

He stopped speaking then because they had reached the Loring Pasta Bar. With Josiah holding the door open for her, Maddy walked in and stopped dead, taken aback by the look of the place. It was not what she had expected from Minnesota—a fantastical space with a soaring ceiling, an atrium surrounded by a mezzanine dining space lined with intricate ironwork, the whole layer cake of this feasting hall held up by modern steel trusses. The nineteenth-century iron and twentieth-century steel contrasted so confusingly with the mounds and mounds of heavy interior brick—brick that appeared almost medieval, laid as if by some drunken man with huge hands, with one-foot-thick swooping brick arches opening here and there, the curved openings allowing newcomers visual hints of all the different tile used to cover the floors in this place. Maddy turned to look around more. The front wall through which they had entered held such big windows— clear glass, block glass, etched transoms—and along that front wall stood a row of banquette booths lined in maroon leather, looking as if they had been stolen from some Little Italy Mafia club.

Maddy became aware Josiah and Kevin were watching her take it all in with her mouth stuck open. They laughed aloud at her and told her to follow them to the table. A couple of students not in the seminar had arrived twenty minutes ahead to order up plates of appetizers, entrees to share, and several bottles of wine so that they would not have to wait too long, knowing many had schoolwork to complete yet tonight. They introduced themselves quickly as Marissa and Seo-Yeon.

Maddy settled roughly into the center of the long table set for fourteen as the students grabbed chairs and started passing the dishes—fried calamari, potstickers, beef skewers, fettuccini and linguini in various sauces, and a gooey artichoke-laden dish served in ramekins. Kevin filled Maddy's wineglass as Josiah dished her various appetizers and several pieces of garlic toast.

"We may have over-ordered," said Peter Peter Pumpkin Eater to Maddy above the din, "because tradition holds the new professor pays, and we get to take all the leftovers home!"

"Um, okay," Maddy answered, and the group all laughed at her.

"He's kidding you," Kevin told her loudly, over the noise. "They tried to tell me the same thing when I first came, that the new *student* pays for everything."

Three more people arrived, one smiling woman pushing in to take the seat Josiah had been saving next to himself.

"Jenna," she said, extending her hand to Maddy over Josiah. "Nice to meet you, Professor."

"Jenna is a med student," Josiah explained to Maddy, "and she is simultaneously working on a master's degree in the Medical Humanities program. If you're lucky, you will have her next year. If I'm lucky, she will fall in love with me and marry me so I can have a steady income from a *real* doctor when I graduate as a doctor-ette and can't get a job."

Jenna told him to remember she liked sapphires more than diamonds.

"You'll have to give me a loan to get you a ring," Josiah answered.

She elbowed Josiah in a friendly manner.

"This is Farhan," Jenna said, pointing at a man who had arrived at the same time as her. "He's also a med student, same master's cohort as me. Oh, and here is Sarah."

Maddy didn't need to be told here was Sarah. She could tell by the brunette prettiness combined with the glare. Maddy reminded herself it was just a form of sexism for one woman to dislike a woman just because she was so pretty. Then she quickly decided she could legitimately dislike Sarah, because Sarah already disliked her.

"So, hey, Professor Shanks," Lateesha called to Maddy from down the table, interrupting Maddy's petty rationalization. Maddy realized she had somehow already downed her wine, as Jenna was now refilling Maddy's glass after filling her own. "Now that we're out of class," Lateesha continued, "can we ask you about extracurricular stuff?"

"You want to know my astrological sign?" Maddy replied.

"You know what they want to know," Sarah answered with a chilly smile. "The coming trial."

"I'm just reading about it in the papers, same as all of you!" Maddy said, shrugging her shoulders and trying to sound collegial. She wasn't being honest; she was *avoiding* reading about it in the papers. She was avoiding news altogether.

"Five first-degree murder charges!" Josiah exclaimed. "For a researcher they say was short-listed for a Nobel in physiology!"

"His research on growth was really important—he was working out some key mechanisms," Maddy answered. "Can you pass those potstickers again?"

"If it *was* real research," Peter noted, handing Maddy the plate. "If he did what you think he did—killed all those special dwarf patients to have their bodies available for his work—then how do you know *anything* he published was real?"

"Repeatability," Maddy answered. "Others replicated his findings on growth."

She thought she must appear bizarre, defending the work of a man who was now on trial for five murders because of her. Scooping two potstickers onto her plate, she tried to broaden the point, as if to lecture a little, legitimize her place as the teacher at the table: "Replication makes a finding more likely to be real, of course."

She popped an entire potsticker in her mouth, realizing too late it was going to be very difficult to chew with that much food on her tongue.

"How did you even figure it out?" Lateesha asked, just as two more plates of food arrived.

Maddy hoped the fact that she obviously had her mouth full meant the subject would change, but there seemed no sign it would let up. She chewed as best she could, swallowing down more wine as she tried to figure out how to manage the rest of this potsticker and move onto a new topic of conversation. Should she mention how much she liked that artichoke dish? Surely everyone would agree, and they could move on to guessing how it was made. The prosecutors had asked her to lie low on all this, not engage with people on it, especially not random people. They didn't see the case as simple to prosecute and had told her so several times, each time making her feel as if what they were saying is that she hadn't done it quite right, she hadn't quite made the argument well enough before handing it off to the police and the prosecutors. A bad debate partner. No—an unreliable research assistant. That's what she had turned out to be?

"Figuring it out was just like all good historical research," Josiah answered for her, since Maddy was still chewing and hesitating. "You put the pieces together, and when something doesn't add up, you figure out where the missing parts are until it *does* add up. You triangulate sources. You look for patterns. Wilhelm claimed many of his patients died of heart failure—and Wilhelm claimed that was a side-effect of several particular forms of dwarfism. But, if it was a consistent side-effect, then why wasn't it well documented in the rest of the literature?"

"It *could* have just been that no one found the heart problem pattern before him," Maddy explained, rejoining the conversation, again wondering to herself why she sounded like she was defending Wilhelm. "In fact, there was a text from the nineteenth century, where a physician had noted heart failure as an apparent cause of death seen in one form of dwarfism. The text recounted the deaths from heart failure of two brothers with the same condition. So, there was *that* historical trail to support all those alleged cardiac deaths—that heart failure was a long-known, documented cause of death with some of these growth conditions."

"So?" Sarah asked, wrinkling her lips as if Maddy had defeated herself. Except for Sarah, the students were all eating hungrily while their eyes remained glued to Maddy's face, as if she were putting on some riveting show.

"*So,*" Maddy answered, meeting Sarah's eyes and her challenge, "the older text was a *fake*. I looked into it and realized it was a rather elaborate fake. And that seemed significant. Why would someone have bothered to fake this text? Why would anyone go through all that trouble to fake a text that wouldn't be worth much at all as a fake? It wasn't like someone had faked a Leonardo drawing. And why hadn't anyone else cited that text until Wilhelm? Why did that text seem to be completely unknown, never cited—until Wilhelm?"

The group let out a delighted murmur. This bit had not been reported in the press. She probably should not have mentioned it. But the wine had accidentally had the opposite of the usual effect of alcohol on her; it had amplified her defensive ego rather than letting it fall away. At least she had not mentioned the discrepancies between the death certificates and Wilhelm's grant reports.

"Professor, can I ask you a question?"

This came from down the table, from a squat, gruff MD student whose name Maddy couldn't now recall, except to remember it was too silly a name for the woman's serious demeanor. Brittany? Tiffany? She was taking Maddy's course to fulfill a requirement for the master's.

"If the jury finds Dr. Wilhelm *not* guilty, does that mean you lose your PhD?"

Maddy couldn't tell if she was joking, but the group laughed.

"I'm kind of serious," the medical student chimed back. "I'm assuming your dissertation lays all this out. If the jury finds him not guilty, does that mean you were wrong? Does it negate your dissertation? Do you have to do a new one?"

"Come on," answered Josiah twirling some pasta on his fork with the help of a spoon, his elbows out to the sides. "You can't seriously think that a jury of ordinary people is qualified to judge Professor Shanks' dissertation in History of Science and Medicine and strip her of her PhD?"

"Plus," Peter added, "Since when was getting a PhD based on being *right*? Especially in the humanities! Can you imagine if that's what people's degrees depended on?"

There was some awkward laughing at this, but the conversation seemed to be quickly becoming uncomfortable. Maddy thought maybe it was due to her own pinched body language. Or maybe it reminded them all too much of the kinds of criticisms of the humanities Alex Shugar used to press upon the students, according to what her departmental chair had told Maddy over a coffee the day before—arguments about truth, accuracy, justice—as Alex had scolded the students to be more, to do more, more than her colleagues ever asked of them.

"My dissertation," Maddy explained now, dredging her garlic toast point through the sauces pooled on her plate, "my dissertation is not just about Wilhelm. In fact, it's mostly about where anatomy museum specimens have come from historically—in the *past*. My committee suggested I mostly leave the Wilhelm story out." She took a bite out of the moistened bread.

"Any subject in the last fifty years is for *journalists*, not historians," another student offered, appearing to be quoting a mentor.

"There's that," Maddy said after a swallow. "And it's a bit of a distraction, the Wilhelm story."

That was what her own dissertation director had said in that meeting where she had told him she thought she had ruined her career before it had ever started by catching a murderer and heading off an academic cliff.

"Murder is a *distraction*?" Sarah responded, quoting Maddy in an aghast tone, twirling a piece of stringy cheese around her fingertip. "Only in academia does what the whole world is *titillated* by count as a distraction while all the *boring* material counts as meaningful. The duller it is, the more important to academia, right? Murdering people is not important! Justice is not important!"

"You do sound like Professor Shugar, Sarah!" Lateesha exclaimed.

"Well," Sarah answered, wiping the cheese off her finger onto the side of her plate, "I *was* her student."

"Obviously, justice is important," Maddy said, looking around the table. "Obviously I believe justice is important. I mean . . . obviously."

She drank down more wine, emptying her glass again. She was drinking way too much since arriving to take this job. Now she was going to have to go back to her assigned office and sober up before she could drive back home to Alex's house, especially since Josiah was already refilling her glass and she was already drinking more. The history of medicine library would be long since locked up for the night when they finished this fast but heavy dinner, but she wished she could go there, pull an all-nighter with musty books, soak up that smell in silence under some underpowered lightbulb while her python belly digested this bolus of weirdly varied foods. Just read, just try to understand a passage where the words sounded familiar but were used in unfamiliar ways. Just do deep history, about something only three or four people would ever care about.

"Listen," Maddy told the group, rousing herself. "I need some help re-membering your names. Why don't you each tell me your name again—as if I can't remember them, which, you know, I *totally* can, but humor me anyway—and tell me something unusual about yourself that the rest of the group probably doesn't know about you. That will help me with names."

Kevin went first, announcing sarcastically that he was from Hong Kong, not St. Paul. The group laughed politely. Lateesha went next, revealing she had been born on an airplane over the Atlantic Ocean. (Maddy and Josiah exchanged a look: did *that* somehow explain her name?) Josiah offered that, contrary to malicious rumors, he didn't own a pocket protector.

Around the table the revelations went, until Maddy was the only one who had not said something. She had not meant to include herself in the exercise.

"Come on, Dr. Shanks," said Sarah, "you have to tell us *something*. Something *unexpected*."

Maddy thought to herself about what to offer. Two years in a convent? No, not that. That she didn't much care for mice but had grown quite fond of rats? No, not that. That she was an heiress to a stupid billboard? No, not that.

She finally answered that she could do a backflip from a standing position.

"Show us," dared Sarah, without missing a beat.

At this, Maddy had two tipsy thoughts simultaneously: what a stupid thing to have mentioned; and Sarah probably thought she was lying.

Maddy stood up, cleared a couple of chairs, and without further ado, did a near-perfect backflip. As the students (save Sarah) let up a surprised cheer, momentarily drawing attention to their part of the busy dining hall, she made a mental note not to offer this trick while wearing dress boots with wooden heels. At least she had on pants.

The commotion was interrupted by someone yelling "Darlings!" behind Maddy and slapping her on the shoulder. Maddy turned to see it was Professor Lew Meadows, the chair of her program. She was glad to see him; he was invariably kind to her—kind to everyone.

"A flipping professor! Look what we landed for you, kids. A flipping assistant professor."

He wore his usual uniform of a starched white dress shirt with French cuffs, a well-fitted vest, and a brightly colored bowtie.

"Did they tell you you have to pay the whole bill, Professor Shanks? They tell everyone new that. Well, have no fear. I am here to be your knight with shining credit card, thanks to a generous alum who has paid for the Loring Pasta Bar for the seminar kids in perpetuity. Where 'in perpetuity' means until this here silver card expires."

As Lew Meadows paid the bill, the group began to disperse, talking of their next day's classes and who could give a ride home to whom. Lew used a nod of his head to Josiah and Jenna to signal that they should move to a booth with him and Maddy.

As the four of them settled into the deep banquette, Lew said to Maddy, "I know I'm not supposed to have favorites among our darlings, but the twins here are my chief remaining reason to live since Alex's passing."

Jenna and Josiah nodded at him, and Josiah asked if he should go fetch Lew a Manhattan from the bar.

"See?" Lew said to Maddy, handing Josiah a ten-dollar bill. "I've raised these two right."

As Josiah went to get the drink, Lew asked Maddy how the seminar had gone. Maddy answered she thought it had gone okay—that all the students had done the assigned reading and that the discussion had been reasonably lively. He told her he was pleased she had assigned reading for the first meeting. Some faculty just showed up and handed out the syllabus and left on the first day, he noted aloud, but Maddy obviously thought there wasn't a teachable minute to be wasted.

"I like your work ethic."

Lew looked over the menu and started giggling just as Josiah returned with the drink.

"Did ya see the footnote to the pastas?" Lew asked. "It says, 'Vegetarians available upon request.' *Someone* didn't proof the menu. Well then!"

Lew looked around the room and spotted the best-looking waiter. He signaled for him to come over, and asked him, "Are you by any chance a vegetarian?"

The four of them smiled with amusement as the waiter, looking confused, shrugged and said no.

"Too bad," Lew answered. "Too bad."

The waiter asked them what he could bring. Lew ordered a brownie ice cream sundae for Jenna and Josiah to share and two apple pie slices á la mode for Maddy and himself.

"You'll need to keep up your strength," Lew told Maddy. "Our students can be quite demanding. And that's *without* them making you do backflips."

"Plus," Jenna added, "you have to not wither away in the face of Sarah's laser-gaze."

"Oh, Lord," Lew said, rolling his eyes. "Was she shooting you daggers? As if Scott was gonna give her the job after Sarah filed a complaint against Alex. Please!"

Maddy asked what the complaint was about.

"I think I'm supposed to be sworn to secrecy by university rules about sexual harassment complaints," Lew told her. "But . . . seeing as how Ally is gone, can't see as how it can do any harm to tell you."

He sipped his Manhattan and put it back down, twirling the cherry around in the drink with his fingertip.

"See, Sarah had been making googly-eyes at a certain male faculty member who shall remain nameless. Mind you, she was a post-doc by then, fully graduated. And he's single, and she's single, so far as we all know. And they weren't even in the same department! She was following him around, practically offering to pack his lunch and do his laundry. So, he asked her out. And she promptly filed a sexual harassment charge against him, just for asking her out!"

Jenna and Josiah tsked and shook their heads, looking as if they had been trained to agree with Lew.

"I'm confused," Maddy said. "What did this have to do with Professor Shugar?"

"Wait for it," Lew answered, taking another slow sip of his drink. He patted his lips with his napkin. "*Sarah* went to *Alex* to tell her she was filing this charge—that she had been sexually harassed by being a post-doc asked by a faculty member to go out. *Please.* Alex basically told her off. Probably told her to *fuck off*, knowing Ally, and not just because the guy was a friend of Ally's. She explained to Sarah that if you didn't want to go out with a guy, what you do is say 'no, thank you,' not file charges against him." He paused. "So, Sarah filed a charge against *Alex*, too. For contributing to the harassment environment or some such."

Josiah and Jenna gasped in unison, bringing their hands to their faces in a gesture of horror while also laughing sharply.

"Smart!" Josiah exclaimed, with obvious sarcasm. "File a charge against your major professor when you need her help to get a job?!"

"Oh, but see, that was the genius of it," Lew replied. "I think it's quite possible Alex would not have given Sarah a glowing recommendation out on the market. Sarah probably knew that. Alex often told me she had problems with Sarah's work and with her overall attitude. And Alex never lied—she was *incapable* of lying, even to save someone's feelings. She wasn't going to lie on a reference letter. Sarah probably knew that. But *now*, with this complaint against Alex filed, if Alex didn't give her the strongest recommendation, Sarah could claim it was *retaliation* by Alex. She kind of had Alex in her grip with this business. Sarah was going to force a good letter out of Alex."

He took another sip of his drink, patted his lips again, and went on.

"In fact, Scott Willingham let drop last week that now Sarah has filed a charge of retaliation against *him*—because he didn't give Sarah Alex's job, after Alex died. Sarah's logic is that Scott was mad about the charge against Alex, so he's punishing Sarah unfairly. So now supposedly it's *Scott* committing retaliation, by giving Maddy and not Sarah the job. Isn't that precious? What a clever method to bottom your way to the top!"

He picked up his fork and polished it with a clean paper napkin, looking around the room to see if the desserts were coming. Jenna and Josiah were shaking their heads in wonder at Sarah's maneuvers while Maddy sat still wondering how she was going to avoid having Sarah accuse her of something.

"Junior high!" Lew cried out. "Just like junior high. But, again, bit of a genius move on Sarah's part, charging Scott. The administration doesn't want to deal with the public scandal of a sexual harassment suit, especially not one tangled up with a professor whose sudden death made the news and whose ex-husband, a deanlette, is somehow also involved in the harassment charge.

So, they basically gave Sarah an extra year of funding just to keep her quiet. And, of course, as disgusted as we may be, none of us can *talk* about it."

He rolled his eyes and then his whole head.

"We can't talk about it, my dears, *unless* we're in this secret, magical Loring Pasta Bar booth together where you all will forget what I told you as soon as we leave it! God, I love this booth." He ran his hand across the wine-colored upholstery. "I need to hold the next program faculty meeting in this booth," he said, as if talking to himself out loud. "And my next date."

The waiter brought the desserts on a round tray, resting the end of the tray on the edge of the table. As the waiter put the plates in front of them, Jenna asked him if he was sure he was not a vegetarian. He told her yes, he was sure—he was raised on a cattle farm in western Minnesota, and he still ate meat.

"Too bad," she told him. "Was thinking of asking for carryout."

Maddy could feel Josiah kick Jenna under the table.

Chapter 5

The next morning, Maddy found herself perched uncomfortably on a shallow wooden armchair just outside Associate Dean Scott Willingham's door in the anteroom that served as his secretary's office. Trying to stay quiet and not trouble the secretary who had been kind enough to find fifteen minutes to fit her in, Maddy was trying to figure out what she was going to say.

I'm not who you think I am.

I came here for a job, not a side-job.

I wish you had told me why you were really hiring me.

She paused on that last one and thought about it more. Even if Lew Meadows was right about Scott's hidden motive for hiring Maddy—even if what Lew had told Maddy after Jenna and Josiah had left the pasta bar *was* true—it wasn't as if Maddy was unqualified to fill in for Alex Shugar in her scheduled courses. Lew had made that clear, that Maddy was *fully qualified* for this position. And maybe Lew was wrong about Scott's motives. Maybe he was seeking drama where there was none.

Yet Lew had shown repeatedly that he had her best interests in mind, and this seemed another case. He had been genuinely kind to her since she had arrived, apologizing repeatedly for her horrid closet of an office, making sure she had the photocopier codes and knew exactly where her classrooms were, giving her coupons for good lunch places. This little bombshell he had dropped on her last night—telling her he thought Scott had an ulterior motive for hiring her—was just part of Lew's way of taking care of her. Right?

Wouldn't it have been so much simpler, Maddy thought, if Liz had been right and Scott had brought Maddy here just to set her up for sex with him? And wouldn't it have been good if Scott were sexy and she *could* use him for a lay now and then, getting off on the power trip? That would have all been so much simpler.

Maddy looked up at the big, round, institutional clock on the wall and wondered how much longer Scott would be. Maybe she should just go. Leave it all alone. Through his closed door, she could just barely hear him talking on the phone, doing his work as associate dean for graduate education in the college. It sounded as if he was negotiating with some departmental chair over a position. Listening to his flat tone, she wondered if he had any sense of humor. He never seemed to smile, to joke, to laugh, at least not around her. Was that just because Maddy kept representing Alex's death to him?

A moment later, he opened his door and called her in, closing the door behind her. He sat back down behind his desk, posture straight, his salty-blond hair matched by flecks of gold in his necktie. She wondered if a woman had picked out the tie for him. It seemed a smoother, more coordinated look than he would have found on his own.

"What can I help you with?" Scott asked perfunctorily, gesturing to Maddy to sit down. "Everything at the house okay?"

"Yes," Maddy said, taking a seat across the desk. She told him that the garage door wouldn't open reliably from the remote device in the car but that she had changed the battery and now it was working. She added, as if the conversation required it, that she was closing the skylights when she went out, as he had asked.

"Good," he replied. "Because you never know when it will rain. So, what do you need? I only have a few minutes. Wasn't expecting you this morning."

"Yes," Maddy said, trying to think of what to say. "Thanks for seeing me." She paused. He looked at her over his glasses and raised his eyebrows.

"Well," she started, "well, I had a conversation last night with Lew Meadows."

He huffed. "I wish Professor Meadows would tell my administrative assistant when he's having conversations with new faculty so she could mark space in my calendar for the next day."

Maddy couldn't tell if he was joking.

"So, what did Lew tell you?"

"He suggested—he wondered—he intimated—that you brought me here not just to *fill in* for Professor Shugar?"

"I'm not sure what you mean," Scott answered, leaning back in his tall desk chair, looking uncomfortable. "Explain."

Maddy wasn't sure how to put it without leaving him pissed off at Lew or her or both of them. She noticed the framed photo of Scott and a younger woman on his desk, between them a young child of about three years.

"Your family?" Maddy asked.

"Yes," Scott answered. "My wife, Maya, and our son Matthew."

"But she is not faculty."

"Maya works in central administration, in accounting," Scott replied.

"She doesn't *look* like an accountant," Maddy said, immediately regretting making the observation. But Maya was much too sexy looking to be crunching budget numbers all day long. She had a glamour about her. A perfect hourglass figure and serious jewelry. The kind of hair that looked as if it were naturally gorgeous but must have taken a lot of work.

"Alex introduced Maya and me," Scott said. "After our divorce. She thought Maya and I would do well together. She was right. Alex was almost always right about people."

This little bit of history struck Maddy as odd. Why would Alex have picked out a spouse for Scott? A little controlling, no? Well, Alex was by all accounts *a lot*.

Still, how odd to see Scott was now with a woman of such a different type from Alex. Usually men had a physical type. It wasn't just that Maya was at least fifteen years younger than Alex and Scott, maybe twenty. Her whole style was rather Hollywood whereas Alex had been a classic academic based on the photos Maddy had seen—largely uninterested in her appearance, dressing for ease, and straight-framed, not curvy.

"Listen," Scott said, interrupting her thoughts. "I only have a few minutes. What did Lew intimate?"

"That you brought me here because you want me to figure out how Professor Shugar died."

Scott didn't respond. He took off his glasses, cleaned them on a cloth he pulled from his top desk drawer, and put his glasses back on. He returned the cloth to the drawer and closed it slowly, watching his own hand push the drawer in, as if he was in a furniture showroom trying out the desk's quality. Maddy's mind involuntarily started to name the muscles Scott could now not seem to relax: procerus, risorius, trapezius.

"Well, Dr. Shanks, I hired you to teach Professor Shugar's classes and to do the other duties required of faculty of your rank."

Maddy scrunched her closed lips to one side of her face.

"Sure," she said. "That's why you *hired* me. But is that why you *brought* me here?"

"A distinction without a difference," he replied.

This was one of those stupid, in-fashion phrases Maddy hated. And it didn't answer her question.

"What do you think she died of?" Maddy asked.

At that, Scott stood up unexpectedly. He turned to the wall behind him and looked at the photos and diplomas hanging there, reviewing them one by one almost as if they weren't his own. He spoke without turning back around.

"What do I think she died of? Drowning, obviously. Beyond that, how would I know?"

"What did the medical examiner rule?" Maddy asked.

Scott turned and looked her in the eye. "Drowning. Probable suicide."

"I assumed it had been ruled an accident!" Maddy answered, failing to hide her surprise. "Swimming alone, drowned *by accident*, I thought. Probable suicide?"

"The medical examiner has done me the favor of not broadcasting his theory," Scott answered. "I mean, I had to know, since I am her executor."

"And heir," Maddy said. "Sole heir?"

"Her will dated back to just after we divorced. Our lawyer—we shared a lawyer for the divorce—it was a friendly divorce—said we needed to update our wills. And so we just had him at that point make our individual wills so we each left each other what we had, made each other executors. It was partly to prove—I mean, we had nothing to *prove*—but it showed we still cared about each other, just the same, that there was no shame in this divorce. No one had anything to be *ashamed* of. Alex had wanted to emphasize that."

His back was up against the wall and Maddy wondered if he might knock off one of the framed items. He went on:

"We each said we'd update them later. I updated my own for Maya when I remarried. Alex simply never updated hers. I doubt she would have left me as the heir on purpose, although we still cared very much about each other."

"Who would she have chosen, do you think?"

Scott didn't answer. Did he not know or not want to say? She could not tell from the expression on his face, some combination of startled and self-defensive.

"When I told the police that I thought the medical examiner was wrong—Alex wasn't depressed; it made no sense—they thought I just didn't want the suicide ruling because her life insurance had the usual clause. That it wouldn't pay on a suicide. They didn't really care what I thought. They thought I just wanted a different ruling for the *insurance* money."

"How much?" Maddy asked.

"How much what?"

"How much is that policy worth?"

"Three hundred thousand," Scott said, as Maddy's left eyebrow went up involuntarily.

"I see," she said, consciously pulling her eyebrow down. But the motion just furrowed her brow. This—she thought to herself, as she tried to fix her facial expression—was exactly why she'd quit playing poker at Liz's weekly game. "So, you'd like to show it was an accident. You think that *I* can prove that it was an accident. That's worth a lot to you."

"I think you could see that it was *not suicide*. I mean, not for the money!" he said, flopping down in his chair as if he were a misunderstood child. "I don't need the money. Surely you can see *that*."

"I don't know a lot of academics who couldn't use an extra three hundred thousand dollars, even the ass-deans," she said, accidentally using the derisive term for associate deans. "If it's not the money, why do you care? I know there's stigma around a suicide ruling, but if no one but you knows, why does it matter?"

"It *does* matter," Scott said emphatically. "Someone might well turn it up—they might turn up that ruling—some student journalist, some biographer, poking around. And then it'll all be such a mess. And, well, the much bigger deal for me is that Alexandra was all about knowing *reality*. And I can't get it out of my head that this isn't the right answer. She'd want us to know. Her friends would be furious with me if they thought I'd put up with the wrong ruling. *And it doesn't make sense*. If she'd been depressed, she would've told me. She would've had me help her."

"Depressed people don't always tell others. They often can't ask for help."

"It doesn't make sense," he repeated, as if she had not answered. "So much was going on. Sure, some of it was rough. But she was in full fight mode, totally herself. She wasn't depressed. She seemed, if anything, even *more* engaged in the world than usual right then. Not *depressed*. Not defeated. Makes no sense."

"And an accidental drowning does?"

"It certainly makes more sense for Alex than suicide," he answered, licking his lower lip and then biting it. "We all *figured* she might accidentally drown someday, the way she went off swimming alone. We all kept telling her that it's dangerous, her habit of just jumping in water and swimming alone in places no one else even thought to swim."

"Then tell yourself it was that—an accident—and be done with it."

"No! NO!"

Maddy visibly startled at his anger. Catching himself, in an earnest and quiet voice Scott apologized for yelling. He looked to the door clearly wondering what his secretary was thinking. Then, in a strained voice, he went on:

"One doesn't just *decide* these things according to what one *wants* to be true. Surely you of all people understand *that*. You're like Alex that way. Or so I thought. This isn't about *representation*, Dr. Shanks. It isn't about what's written on a piece of paper. This is about *reality*. You're the kind of historian who is truly a social scientist, not a humanities scholar, aren't you? Driven by evidence, not feelings? I thought that when I hired you."

"Look," Maddy said, rubbing her eyes with two of her fingertips. She could feel her pulse tapping against her chest wall like a hotel housekeeper knocking fast on a guest room door, looking to get in to clean up for the next guest.

She started pulling from the lines she had prepared:

"Look, I came here for a job, not a *side-job*," she said.

That didn't quite work.

"I'm not who you think I am," she added.

It still fell flat.

"I wish you had told me why you were *really* hiring me. *I'm not a fucking amateur cop.*"

She flashed to Philadelphia for a moment, that moment when she had realized she was totally in over her head. It felt as if Wolf were in the room now, looking straight at her.

"Listen!" she exclaimed. "What happened in Philadelphia wasn't intentional. It happened because I was doing a history of specimen collection. I was working on my dissertation, just working on my research—"

"I know, I know," he said, cutting her off as if she were being tiresome. "I'm not asking you to go out of your way. You're in her job. You're in her house. You're talking to her colleagues and her students. I'm just asking you to be open to . . . to . . . a *possibility*."

"Of what?" Maddy asked.

"You wouldn't find this *intellectually interesting*?" Scott asked, faking a coy smile.

"Lots of work is *intellectually interesting*, Dr. Willingham," she answered, with a tone of exasperation, the wisdom of which she then doubted.

"You could get a publication out of it, maybe! Some publicity, too."

"I have *other work*," she said, now using as polite a tone as she could muster. "I'm not lacking for work I need to get done." (There was her heart banging again: "Housekeeping!")

"I'm not asking you to go out of your way," he insisted. "I just thought, maybe—"

At that, Scott's door opened suddenly and his secretary entered. She apologized for the interruption and told him the provost was on the line. The secretary left but not before pausing to look at Maddy as if to try to ascertain what was going on with this new hire.

Maddy asked Scott if she should step out and he said no, he would only be a minute. She sat quietly while he took the call.

What would Liz say? If Scott was serious that he was just asking Maddy to be casual about this so-called intellectual problem, then surely she could just be casual about this. And just *do nothing*. Stay too busy with other work. She couldn't very well refuse him outright, could she? He had given her the job and she supposed he could take it away if he wanted to, at least after this first year. A replacement position, short-term—no security there. Her health insurance was dependent on him. And her housing.

Damn it.

Sure. She could just be casual about it. As in *ignore it*. She could just stop noticing things that didn't matter to her real work—things like, well, that on Scott's wall, two of his diplomas had a middle name (Robert) and one did not. She could stop taking note of the detritus left in the wake of Alex's death—Hank's toilet kit, the files left in Alex's desk—stop noticing things like that the child between Scott and Maya in the photo didn't look like it could be his child. (Maya was white like Scott, and the child looked mixed-race somehow?)

She could stop noticing these kinds of things, no matter if she lived in Alex's house and drove Alex's car and was coming to know Alex's students and colleagues and a quasi-lover who had slept with Alex but didn't have sex with her . . .

Maddy pulled her phone out of her pocket, flipped it open, and went down through her contacts to find Hank Merriman's number. She had emailed him the morning after he came to help her with the fireplace to ask him for his phone number in case she needed it. He had immediately obliged.

Scott was still deep in conversation with the provost on the phone, something about a training grant on a tight deadline. She opened a text window on her phone and started pecking out the message.

Steak Friday?

Ok, came the reply shortly thereafter. *Move 2 to fridge today.*

Need me to get anything? she asked.

I got it. 7 p.m.?

Yes TY

There was a pause.

Should she not have added "thank you"? What the hell did it sound like she was thanking him for? *Jesus, Maddy*, she thought to herself. *Someday just be normal.*

Hey, Hank added to the text conversation just then, *you eat like bird or horse?*

She thought for a moment and then answered: *Omnivorous pony.*

He didn't reply.

Scott hung up his phone and showed Maddy the door.

"I'm not asking you to go out of your way," he said again. "I want to be very clear about that."

Chapter 6

Smell is perhaps the most elusive sense. Touch, taste, sight, sound—the stimuli of these other senses are readily translated into human words. One can say that a sound is sharp, long, dull, or low or that a taste is salty, bitter, or sweet, and the idea is sufficiently contained. But how can one adequately contain a *smell* in words such that the brain can create an adequate facsimile? Smell refuses to cohere to mirrored language even when it fills the mouth.

Smell—Maddy realized, thinking about her first and last encounter with Hank, over the smoke in the fireplace—smell is quite like pain. While reference can be made back to it, while it can be indexed in the brain with a date and a place, while a person can remember the experience of it *just well enough* to know that she wants to avoid ever reencountering it or to know that she wants to experience it again, there seemed to be no truly recalled memory of a smell or a pain in its immediate absence. You couldn't effectively experience it again on recall, the way it seemed you could a sound or a sight.

And yet, as with pain, when a scent reappeared, it felt paradoxically indelible. As if it had never left you. As if you could never leave it, hard as you tried.

Hank knocked awkwardly on the door. Maddy came out of this thought and answered, opening the air between them. He handed her one of the two bags of groceries and closed the door behind him, telling her he was sorry that last time he had burst in with his copy of the house key, that he hadn't been thinking, and she stopped him from apologizing and said of course, nothing to be sorry for. He offered to return the key, but she said no. She took the groceries to the kitchen and he followed. No, she said again, no, because she had a habit of locking herself out of places. Would he be so kind as to keep the spare key in case? And he said yes, of course.

He put his bag of groceries on the counter and went immediately to the drawer where Alex and he had kept the wine opener. He pulled out one of the bottles he had brought and moved to open it. He and Maddy had now passed by each other's orbits just closely enough that the texture of his cologne—a little like antique wood, a little like an electric transformer—had come fully to kiss her philtrum, that vestigial vertical groove of flesh between the upper lip and the nose into which one's index fingertip fits so perfectly, as if when we were born each of our mothers pressed her index fingertip there to say, "Shhh, don't cry," and the dimple had stayed.

She pressed her own finger there, on her philtrum, for just a second.

He looked approvingly at the steaks she had earlier taken out of the refrigerator, poking them with a finger. He rinsed the finger, ground salt and pepper over each of the steaks, and poured and handed her a glass of wine. He took a sip from his own glass and said it needed some time. She took a sip and let the liquid sit on her tongue for a few seconds. He watched her and, when he could see she swallowed, suggested they go into the living room to sit while the meat came more fully to room temperature.

Maddy stopped him by putting her hand on his forearm.

"Listen," she said, holding him back a moment. "Something happened."

He looked at her confused.

"Something came. I'm hoping you can explain," she added.

Then she walked before him into the living room and stood looking at what was now in the bay window, where Alex's daybed had been: a shiny black grand piano.

Hank came and stood next to her. He became preternaturally still.

Finally, he asked, "Why is that here?"

"I take it that means you didn't know Professor Shugar had ordered a Steinway."

"Why is that here?" he asked again, sitting down now in his usual armchair while keeping his eye on the piano as if it were a stranger whom he knew he couldn't trust.

Maddy wanted to tell him that what had happened, *obviously*, was that she had decided to disregard Scott's request from a couple of days before— that she had firmly resolved to ignore the details of Alex's life and death— and that, *therefore*, the universe had decided to send a grand piano so black and so shiny it made Maddy think of the darkest and most perfect eggplant. (It made her think of Wolf.)

And why would the universe send a piano? Because, in her experience, the universe loved a good *Fuck your little resolutions, Madeleine Shanks*, and it was hard to disregard an instrument of this size, especially when it's being carried in your front door to be set up and comes to a rest such that it takes up what felt like a good third of your living room.

Because, clearly, the universe had decided it was going to send either a Steinway or a giant taxidermied rhinoceros with a great big horn. Or a biplane!

But she didn't say that to Hank. She didn't want to tell him—at least not yet—what Scott had told her about Alex's death, about the ruling of probable suicide. It wasn't just that she didn't want to bias Hank's answers to her forthcoming questions. She had also realized that if she did fully take up Scott's request, and Hank knew she had tried and ultimately couldn't figure out why Alex died, then Hank would know Maddy had failed. And she didn't want Hank knowing she had failed. She wanted him to think her quite brilliant, quite wonderful, quite—quite *necessary*.

"Apparently," Maddy said to Hank, settling herself on the couch, "well, apparently, Alex ordered a piano a couple of days before she died. And now that piano has been delivered."

"When it arrived you didn't tell them that . . . ?"

"I honestly wasn't sure what to do."

Honestly wasn't sure? Posh. The truth was that she had been somewhat fascinated by this great black beast's arrival. Even as the delivery crew was only just beginning to wedge the door to prepare to bring it in, Maddy had gotten to doing the math: If Alex had ordered a grand piano and someone had known about it, that someone would have told Maddy to expect it— someone other than that fellow Leonard, the man on the telephone who six days earlier had obviously been calling *Alex* about this long-awaited delivery.

Why would a woman go to New York, to Steinway, to order a new piano if she'd been thinking of ending her life? Just to be a pain in the ass to her ex-husband, to leave him a piano to deal with? Or to leave it for her ex-husband as some special kind of gift? But what if Scott had sold the house by the time it had been meant to arrive?

And depressed people don't go and arrange things like that. Although Alex wasn't your typical person.

Maddy took another sip of wine and, staring at the piano, involuntarily narrowed her eyes. She rather liked Alex's style, sending this thing to her old house from the Great Beyond. What a way to suggest maybe Scott was onto something. *Shugar, rhymes with slugger.*

I mean, Maddy thought to herself, as if talking to Alex, *it's not like you really sent it from the other side. There is no other side. But, oh, it feels like you did. They all tell me you had such strength, the kind of strength that could reach from the dead . . .*

Just like Margaret Lovisa staring at Maddy from that preservation jar, egging her on to understand how Wilhelm had come to own quite so many interesting bodies.

"Do you play?" Maddy asked aloud, turning to Hank and feeling a little electrified. She already knew the answer because of how he had reacted to this instrument.

"No," he said, looking disoriented and wary. "Neither did Alex. Can't imagine why she would have ordered this."

"Does Scott play?"

"No," he said, with some impatience evident in his voice. "And anyway, Alex would not have ordered him a gift like this. It must be a mistake."

"No mistake," Maddy told him. "Alex's name was on it, and her address. Came this morning. It even came with a tuner, a very skinny, rather tall man with wire-rim glasses. He spent about three hours tuning it. I tried to give him something to eat, he was here so long, but he wanted nothing to do with me, with food, with anything but this piano. Guess he really liked it. I finally had to shoo him out so I could shower and get dressed for— "

She realized she sounded stupid talking about showering and dressing for the man she was talking to. She thought about the underwear she had picked out, matched to her bra, ivory with a little bit of lace trim, the set she had bought *not* on sale in Washington one day, on a hope.

"Do *you* play?" he asked her.

"Only a little," she said. "Mostly churchy tunes. Nothing you'd want to hear on such a beautiful instrument. I haven't tried it yet."

She realized as she said it *why* she hadn't touched it yet: She had been unconsciously hesitant to get her fingerprints on it.

"Where did the daybed go?" Hank asked, gesturing towards the piano with his fingers splayed, looking somewhat desperate, as if Alex herself had gone suddenly missing again. "Where did—"

"It's *okay*," Maddy urged. A strong man looking unstable always unsettled her. It reminded her too much of her father.

"It's okay," she said again. "I had them put it in the basement, and I draped it carefully with clean sheets. It'll stay clean. We can put it back once we figure out what to do with the piano. I guess Scott has to figure that out?"

Hank wandered back to the kitchen looking disturbed, and she followed. He said nothing as he pulled what must have been his apron from a drawer, a big red apron with almost invisible grey pinstripes. He put it on, tied it behind him, and started to cook, first pulling out a large roasting pan that had been stored in the oven to get to the cookie sheets also kept there and then turning the oven on to preheat. She watched as he cross-sliced three big russet potatoes on a mandolin and laid them on paper towels to dry before tossing them in salt and oil and laying them out flat in a single layer on a cookie sheet.

Seeing her glass nearly empty, he poured her more wine and did the same for himself. He looked rapidly up from the glass to her eyes and back down again. His brow remained furrowed, his lips silent.

Now he washed lettuce and spun it the spinner. He felt it with his fingertips and dried it a little more with a towel before assembling a salad with chopped cherry tomatoes and red onion and cucumber in a bowl he reached for without apparent thought. He put the potatoes in the oven.

She lifted herself onto the counter out of his way and sat there watching him. She wanted to ask him the things you are supposed to ask in a situation like this: How long have you been cooking? What do you like to cook? But she wanted much more to ask him things that went well beyond.

Why does this piano bother you this much? Did it have something to do with another man who was going to be moving in with her?

Did you wake up with an erection next to her, and was it for her?

Did you lie on the bed and read a book while she took a bath in that beautiful tub, the one (Scott had explained during the house tour with embarrassment) that Alex had insisted on installing in a new sunroom just off her bedroom, windows all around, right under two huge skylights? Those skylights under which one could lie back and look at the moon sliced up by the trees while warmed by the wood stove off to the side?

When you weren't here, did Alex take other men to that tub, those "better men" she was used to? Did she take them to the bed you shared for sleep, or did she always save that spot in the bed for you, for when you were done with those younger women?

He was heating a large cast-iron pan on the stove and held his hand just above the surface to feel the heat as it intensified. He pulled his hand back a moment, turned to Maddy, and looked her in the eye.

"Why so quiet?" he demanded. He took off his apron rapidly and rumpled it up on the counter, taking a swig of wine.

"Why so quiet?" she asked back quite softly.

"How are the classes?" he went on without pause, and she told him they were going well but that she had accidentally done a backflip at the Loring Pasta Bar in front of her seminar students and now they wanted her to do acrobatic tricks for them and she was afraid it was just going to give her a reputation for being weird and stupid.

"All academics are weird," he said, moving the steaks to the pan. "And if you were stupid, you wouldn't have a PhD, would you?"

"I have met some pretty stupid PhDs," she replied, and he laughed briefly in agreement as the meat gave off the sound of flesh searing.

His laugh was soft and pleasant, a relief from his tension, and she found herself staring at his arms as he stood at the stove. He was wearing a short-sleeved fitted black T-shirt, and his arms were strong and tan. And his chest and his legs looked just so.

A Renaissance artist would find him quite perfect. A stonecutter, perhaps, or a farmer, perfect as a model, or better a fresh body for a theatre dissection after a public hanging for some crime of passion. They would have started the dissection with the gut to prevent the rot problem as they worked over the next three days, swatting flies away. Eventually they would have gotten down to his bones, put them in the bone box with its drilled holes and laid the box in the river to let the water wash through, to wash the last of the flesh away. The bone box, that clever closed colander for letting a callous river do the work of cleaning bones. Then, after a few weeks, they would have dried out his bones in the sun and assembled his skeleton.

But for now, here he was, still alive. So alive, so fleshy with warm blood and warm breath.

"Hey," she said, "turn to me, then stand with your legs apart and your arms out to the side?"

He gave her a quizzical look but did as she asked.

Yes, there it was. There he was: DaVinci's Vitruvian Man, filling the circle of the universe with his proportionate arms and legs and head and trunk. She suddenly realized that was what Wolf's body had also recalled to her. *That* was why she had once dreamed Wolf was DaVinci—of course. She felt her face momentarily flush.

"Thanks," she said, letting herself down off the counter to get a glass of water. He went back to the stove.

"All academics are weird," he repeated. "But you, Professor Shanks, are exceptionally weird."

He turned with his wine glass in hand, and she met him with her glass of water. They clinked the glasses together gently. Each took a drink.

She was now having a telegraphic conversation in her head with Liz.

You and your daddy complex, said Liz to her, adding, *he's easily old enough to be your father, as you well know—just like Wolf*, and Maddy answered that she had never wanted to fuck her father so Liz should just fuck *off* with her notion of a daddy complex, thanks very much.

"So, what do you want to know?" Hank asked.

"Hmm?"

"You invited me over because you wanted to know . . . ?"

"*Know*, in the biblical sense?" she said laughing, and he laughed back at her and said it obviously wasn't what he meant.

He looked as if her remark had turned him a little pink. He could see that it delighted her.

"I think I give you too much to drink," he said, taking her water glass from her hand and refilling it for her. "You may eat like a pony, and you may have a reputation as big as an elephant, but you're really a little thing. More water, less wine, and tell me what it is you wanted to know."

She wasn't sure where to start. If she asked him this and that, would she remember what he answered? Because she hadn't decided yet if she'd try to figure it all out—how Alex had died. She had no mental filing cabinet in which to put his answers. If she was going to try to figure it out, she knew, she'd have to do the usual thing she did in historical research: She'd have to make a timeline and organize the knowns, make a list of the unknowns, note the sources to keep track of certainty levels, be open especially to shoring up or changing out the things that were rather uncertain and therefore very possibly wrong. Figure out the gaps and try to fill them. Try to understand which were related as cause and effect. Triangulate. Understand personalities.

And if she was going to do all that, she'd have to remember his answers about what happened when, and why, and . . . well, she was a little tipsy and wanting to get more so, wanting to know what he felt like on the couch, wanting to know what his thighs and his ass felt like in her hands. And remembering whatever he might tell her about Alex with the precision that research required seemed quite unlikely. No one went purposefully tipsy to an archive.

Anyway, she didn't want to know about all the possible *whens* right now. She wanted to know about the *hows*.

When was a question of the cerebral cortex, all proper and mature.

How was a question of the adductors, those big muscles in the upper inner thigh. *How* got you so much closer to *why*, that question that would fool you into thinking your very subjective response was a perfectly ontological fact.

. . .

Hank made it about a mile away from Alex's house before he pulled over realizing he had to properly dry off his eyes before he could continue driving home. The thought of feeling humiliated at having broken down crying in front of Maddy helped to cool him. He found a small stack of napkins in the glove compartment left over from some take-out run and dried his eyes one at a time. The napkins all smelled of fry oil.

Why had Maddy insisted on asking all these questions? Was she just a gossip like Lew Meadows? And where did she get off, pushing him until she could pull the string hard enough to make him cry like a child's doll? Hank had assumed she'd invited him over as much for sexual possibilities as anything else, a feeling only confirmed by the way she had seemed at first. Playful. Appealing.

What was with her? When he had managed during dinner to casually ask her at what age she'd started having sex—he prided himself in always making it sound like it was just a professional question he asked everyone, and not a probative icebreaker on a date—had she been *serious* when she had said she'd stopped being a virgin half her life ago? She'd told him before that she was now twenty-six. She'd started at thirteen?

That was awfully young, yet she seemed not at all like the women he knew who had been brought to their sexual lives through abuse. But then, he thought to himself, cooling down more, he knew from the research the outcomes on women who had been introduced to sex like that were scatter-shot. And yet she seemed so sexually naive in certain ways; she didn't know how to flirt in a normal way. Or didn't care to? Was this just the problem of her being an academic, hanging around theorizing feminists?

God, *what an ass*, to have broken down like that in front of her. Why did he lose it?

He banged his right hand on the steering wheel.

Well, in fact, he knew why he had lost it. Right as they finished off the dessert, she had been asking so many questions about Alex. Asking about who Ally was as a person, telling him to answer in one sentence. ("That's easy," he had answered. "She was a force of nature.")

About why Alex and Scott had divorced. (Hank told Maddy plainly he wasn't going to tell her that. He was only willing to confirm that Alex had introduced Scott to Maya, Scott's second wife.)

About what Hank had felt in the days Ally was missing, before they found her body. ("Lonely, mostly. I wasn't used to dealing with uncertainty and stress without her by that point. I felt angry at her, leaving me to deal with the stress alone. And then stupid at the irrationality of that.")

About how he had heard she was dead. (Scott had come to his office where Hank had not really been working—just sitting since he had realized she was truly missing. All he could do was sit and stare at the wall waiting to find out where she was. Her cell phone had been turned off or had run out of battery, but he kept dialing it every hour or so. One of his senior graduate students ended up sitting quietly with him, keeping people out of the office, and was there when Scott came with the news.)

About what he knew about how she had died. (Swimming alone, Memorial Day weekend, Cottontail Lake. She liked to swim alone.)

Was it because he had not cried even that deep into the conversation that Madeleine Shanks had asked the series of questions that would set him off? Was she *trying* to push him to lose it when had she asked when had it really hit him that Ally was gone forever? That he would never feel her hand alive again?

That last question had caused him to remember and reveal something still raw: It was two days after Alex's body had been found and taken by the coroner. Scott had come back to Hank's office. Scott hadn't said anything. He just took Hank's hand, opened it palm-side up, and put Alex's silver necklace in it. Scott knew it was the necklace Hank had given her, the one she wore almost every day to mark their strange relationship. The coroner had returned it to Scott by then, and Scott had come to give it back to Hank. It

60

was a rare moment: Scott acknowledging the significance of Hank's relationship with Ally.

He started now crying again silently with his mouth open. A tear made it into his mouth. The problem was this: Every time Hank pictured Scott giving the necklace back by dropping it into his open palm, Hank pictured not Scott doing it, but Ally. As if Ally had come to purposefully say goodbye once and for all by handing him back the necklace. He wanted to go back. To talk her out of it.

. . .

Maddy laid back in Alex's bath, looking up at Alex's trees, wondering if Alex's moon would show its face tonight. The room was dark save for the sparkling bits of light coming from inside the seven old Johnny Walker Blue bottles someone had drilled and filled with short strands of white Christmas lights. The bottles were standing directly on the slate floor spaced around the bathtub, all lit, reflecting tiny dots of light in the glass of the windows and the skylights, everything else dark, all of it leaving Maddy with the feeling she was floating so pleasantly in the twinkling night sky.

"Alex," Maddy said aloud, "you knew how to do a bath."

Ever since the piano had arrived that morning, Maddy had fallen into a long on-and-off conversation with Alex Shugar. It was something Maddy sometimes involuntarily did with major historical subjects in her work as she found herself getting to know them. Now, Maddy found herself asking Alex what Hank had meant over dinner a few hours earlier, about someone he said Maddy should talk to—a good friend of Alex's named Everett Inskeep, who was also named Sophie Inskeep. What did Hank mean, that Inskeep had two names and lived sometimes as a man and sometimes as a woman?

"You want me to do your work for you, Professor Shanks?" Alex asked in a slightly annoyed tone, like a dissertation director talking to her slacking student.

"No," Maddy answered. "I just don't want to embarrass myself when I meet this good friend of yours."

"What did Hank tell you about my thoughts on shame?"

"That you called it 'the difficult subject,'" Maddy answered. "That you said we didn't discuss the problem of shame enough. That you thought shame was the thing that too often kept us from living. That you believed shame was the manifestation of the sin of pride. How interesting an idea— that when pride metastasizes, it grows to shame! He said that you believed that we should not bother too much with shame. Especially in terms of sex." (Maddy remembered, too, what Scott had said—that Alex and he had made each other heirs and executors to show there was nothing in their divorce of which to be ashamed.)

"Right," Alex answered. "People think sex is the problem, but sex isn't the problem—shame about sex is always the problem."

"Yes, Hank said you said that," Maddy said. "I like how you think. We think alike."

"So, go talk to my good friend Everett Sophie Inskeep," Alex answered, "and do so without bringing your silly shame about who is what sex."

Maddy assured Alex she was generally very good at lacking shame. Then she told Alex she felt a little stupid for having blown the chance tonight of getting laid with Hank, asking him so many questions that she had driven him out in tears. And driving him out right after that nice dessert he had made—sugared, sliced-up strawberries with mascarpone, dotted with chopped fresh leaves of mint, drizzled with a bourbon-casked maple syrup, served with a perfectly paired Riesling that had finally rendered her good and drunk. What Maddy had wanted was not to drive him out with her inquiries. What she'd wanted, at the very least, was a good round of necking. He had nice arms, a lovely chest. And American men her own age, she explained to Alex, were shitty kissers. It was like they never learned anything from the movies. She figured Hank was a good kisser.

"How would I know?" Alex asked. "Anyway, I think good kissing is less about generational differences than experiential differences. Hank comes with a lot of *experience*, that is true."

Maddy chuckled aloud at that and raised her hands to the top of the bath water to let them now just float atop the surface. That's what she wanted—a guy with a lot of experience who would give her what she needed, not be a jerk, and then go home. He would go home, right? Not think this was still his bed?

She looked at her hands, fingers splayed, floating. She wondered how long it took for a drowned body to surface. She'd have to look it up sometime. And why did it sink and then surface? Did it always surface? The physiology and physics of all that were probably pretty interesting.

For now, she lay back deeper in the tub, letting her hair get wet, feeling the warm water touch her scalp. She moved her hands to lie on her thighs and used the tips of her thumbs to feel her adductor muscles. Her right index fingertip met her right thumb tip and they rolled one on the other. The waves caused by her movements left the water lapping at her belly.

Chapter 7

"Was I right?" Lew Meadows asked before sitting down in the chair across from Maddy.

"You're not going to order a coffee?" Maddy asked back, as she cleared her laptop computer and stack of papers off the coffee shop's small round café table to make room for Lew.

"They know me here. The barista will bring mine in a minute."

He plunked down in the wooden chair, lifted the strap of his bright yellow messenger bag over his head, and shoved the bag under his chair. "So, come on, was I right?"

"You know, Professor Meadows," Maddy said with an unwitting smile and a bit of a yawn, "telling someone like you 'you're right' is pretty much inviting more trouble."

She paused.

"But yes, you were right."

"I knew it!" he yelled, thrusting one finger into the air like a rocket.

Several other people in the coffee shop turned to look at him as Maddy shushed him.

"It's okay," he said, "now the barista definitely knows I'm here. I'll get my cappuccino sooner. Tell me *everything*."

He slapped his hands down on the table in front of her as if to indicate that he would control the table until he got the gossip he craved. Maddy proceeded to tell him some about her meeting with Scott, specifically leaving out the part about "probable suicide." When she asked Lew what he knew about Alex arranging Scott's second marriage, Lew shrugged.

"How would I know? They never tell me the good stuff."

"Gee, I wonder why," laughed Maddy.

"But Maya cheats on him *constantly*. And he doesn't seem to mind."

"Seriously?!"

"She's a looker. He's probably just as happy to have first dibs if not a total lock," Lew said.

He wrapped his palms around Maddy's cup, to see if it was hot or cold.

"You want a warm-up? I can get you one." She shook her head no. He leaned over and whispered. "Have you seen their child?"

"I saw a photo in Scott's office."

"Darling kid," Lew observed, now leaning back. "And they love him to pieces. But he's obviously not the fruit of Scott's loins."

"You don't know that."

Lew lifted his eyebrows.

"Okay," Maddy went on, "maybe they adopted the kid."

"Pssh. She was preggers all over campus. A glowing mother-goddess."

"Well, okay, maybe it was *his* sperm and *she* used a donor egg from a woman of color," Maddy offered.

"Or, *or* it was a spontaneous genetic mutation that caused the child to look like he doesn't have two white parents! Or, *or*," Lew went on, sarcastically, "or she *could* have faked the pregnancy and stolen the child from the hospital nursery! Or they could have brought the wrong baby home and never noticed! But do consider, Professor Shanks, that Occam's razor would suggest the explanation to be *another gentleman putting his baguette in her oven*."

Maddy took a drink of coffee.

"I see your point, Professor Meadows. I see your point."

A young man with a goatee soon came over to deliver Lew his cappuccino, a vanilla cookie perched on the saucer. Lew handed him a five-dollar bill

64

and made a puckered kissing motion.

"Anyway," Maddy told him, "the question of other gentlemen and their baked goods aside, I resolved just after I spoke with him to *ignore* Scott's request to think about Alex's death."

"Damn it, woman," he said, kicking her foot with his and taking a sip of his drink. "Why would you do *that*?"

She didn't answer. She looked out the window. She was wondering whether Lew, too, wanted Maddy to look into Alex's death or was just hoping for any kind of excitement. She was also wondering whether to tell Lew about what Scott had told her about the ruling of probable suicide.

Seeing her hesitation, Lew suddenly announced that he wasn't playing a very good departmental chair. He sat up straight and asked how her classes were going. It was a rather mechanical ask, but he genuinely listened to her answers and reassured her as needed.

Then he asked how her research was going. More mechanics, more gentle cheerleading.

Then he asked her how the house was going as a place to live.

He stopped her as she began to answer, admitting to her he didn't really care how the house was. He kicked her again.

"It's not like I am *happy* Ally died, you know—God, I miss her every day—but I think it's pretty *interesting* that Scott would think there's something more to know. That he'd make a point of hiring *you*. Don't you?"

"Yes," Maddy said. "It's *interesting*. How did you know that's why he wanted me to take this job?"

Lew answered that he hadn't known for sure. It just seemed strange, he said, that Scott had made clear to Lew he wanted Madeleine Shanks hired and no one else. Scott had decided to go external for a temporary replacement for Alex after she died but not to run a normal, open job search to see who would apply. Why would *that* be? It all seemed odd, Lew said, and it pushed the bounds of the affirmative action hiring policy, not doing an open search but just calling Maddy, doing a perfunctory interview, and hiring her after Lew had reviewed and okayed her CV.

"And no offense, Professor Shanks," he added, "but it's not like people know you nationally for your *scholarship*. They will someday, I'm sure, but not yet. Plus, he changed the seminar topic to fit your work exactly."

"What? I thought Professor Shugar had been teaching a seminar on the history of anatomy!"

"Hell, no," Lew answered. "She hadn't taught a seminar in that vein in years and even when she did, it was a course on the *politics* of anatomy. Not the *history* of anatomy. It was a completely different course from yours. He changed the seminar topic specifically to fit your work. I mean, he checked with me first to make sure it'd be okay for our students. But still. Lately Alex had been teaching the seminar on sexuality—kind of a philosophy of sex course. If he'd really been hiring to replace her, that wouldn't have been a course for *you* to be hired to teach. I already love you, you brainy little lady, and I'm glad you're here. And you're doing great. But I wouldn't have hired you if Scott hadn't basically insisted."

Maddy thought for a second how strange the idea that she had landed an academic job because of what had happened in Philadelphia. This was not the kind of approach people said would get you a real leg up in the tough market. She roused herself from the tangent and asked Lew if that was what Alex had been working on when she had died—a philosophy of sex. He explained that he'd been away on sabbatical in Europe the previous semester so they hadn't been in touch as much as usual, but he said that yes, she had started a book project about sexual desire and it had been inspired, he thought, by work her good friend Hank Merriman had done. Lew said Maddy should ask Hank more about it.

"It's not like Hank knew everything she was up to," Maddy replied. And then she went on to tell him about the piano and Hank's shock at its delivery.

"What on earth?" Lew exclaimed. "A grand piano! Ordered in New York! What was that woman up to?"

He paused, clearly going through possibilities in his mind.

"So, wait, Hank doesn't play, does he?" asked Lew.

"He told me last night he doesn't. He said he had no idea why Alex would have purchased a Steinway a few days before she died."

"Oooh, you talked to him last night?"

"He came over," Maddy replied, putting her chin down and rolling her eyes up like a naughty child caught.

"Huh! He came *over* to you! You *do know* his reputation, young lady?" asked Lew, wagging a finger at her.

"I was *counting* on his reputation, my good man," she answered, and they both cracked up. "You know what my best friend, Liz, says? She studies mammals—rats, mostly—and this is what she says about us mammals: *Gotta sleep, gotta eat, gotta fuck.*"

"This Liz person and I would get along just fine," Lew answered, taking a bite of his cookie. "So, did ya get a little? My, he's a handsome specimen, that one."

"Alas, no," said Maddy. "I made him cry and he left."

"Shut up," said Lew.

Maddy told him that it was true.

"Oh, you pushed on him about Ally and her dying, didn't you. You meanie."

"What *was* their relationship like, Lew?"

"Volatile and tender," said Lew, getting wistful. Now he waved his right hand, side to side, just in front of her face. "I know, I know—that sounds like a contradiction. But that's what I'd say: volatile and tender. They were like an old married couple, sometimes arguing at public lectures or in university committee meetings, and then you'd see them walking on campus together, laughing and touching each other gently like two college kids in love. Then, that night, you'd see him out on a date with some young thing, her out to dinner with some guy or a woman friend her own age. The next day they'd be together again, maybe laughing, maybe dressing each other down about some paper on which they disagreed."

He paused like he was remembering some scene in particular.

"All of us who loved her took it hard when she left us. But Hank, he was like a lost soul. He still looks lost. Like a faithful dog without his owner."

Maddy was now picturing Hank and Alex curled up together in her bed, waking up slowly together on a lazy weekend. She suddenly missed her own dog in Philadelphia.

"Lew," she said, pushing herself forward from that thought, "tell me— Hank said I should talk to a friend of Alex's. Last name 'Inskeep'?"

"Sophie!" said Lew. "I haven't seen her in way too long. Give her my very best when you do."

"But," Maddy said, "Hank said he—I mean she—I mean—"

"Yes," answered Lew, anticipating her question. "Sophie-slash-Everett spends part of the time as a woman and part as a man. Depends on the day. The good news for you is it makes Everett Sophie Inskeep a lot less tense than it makes *you*, so you just have to deal with your own anxieties over this. Pull it together! You can do it, girl."

"Fair enough," Maddy answered, realizing she ought to be able to manage it. She had managed an entire conference of people with various forms of dwarfism and had even felt in the company of her peers there. Perhaps Everett-Sophie Inskeep, too, would make her feel a little more normal through the sympathetic kinship of those who don't fit in.

"Sophie was a great friend to Ally," Lew added quite seriously, ending their momentary silence. "Ally told Sophie so much that I think she didn't tell the rest of us."

"Why would anyone tell you *anything*?"

Lew laughed and finished off his cappuccino. He pulled out and waved another five-dollar bill in the air above his head as if flying a flag. Then he slapped it down on the table.

"So, when I contact Inskeep," Maddy asked him, "I should ask for Sophie and not for Everett? Because Ally told Sophie more than she told Everett?"

"Don't be daft!" Lew snorted. "They're not *two different people*, you silly woman. *One person.* You're dealing with *one person.* Don't you have different sides to you? One an up-and-coming professor of the history of medicine, the other a horny acrobat?"

"Gotta research, gotta fuck," she answered, laughing at his observation.

Lew told her he saw her doing a handstand on a bike rack near the medical school earlier in the week.

"Sometimes a girl just has to be upside down, Lew."

"With that attitude, you'd think you could get laid. Let me get you Sophie's contact info," he went on, pulling his tiny red address book out of his vest pocket. "She and I should take you shopping, get you something cute to wear. Improve your odds. She'd enjoy dressing you. She has good taste. And I can brilliantly accessorize that good taste."

This time another member of the coffee shop staff, a young woman dressed in a tan shop apron, brought over the cappuccino for Lew. As she took the five-dollar bill and his used cup and saucer, he made the same kissing motion as he had to the barista. She smiled, hesitated, and then asked nervously whether Professor Meadows would look over a draft paper she had written for a class that wasn't his. She said she thought he might be at the café today so she had brought it with her, hoping for his help on the thesis statement and on some of the transitions.

"Of course, sugar," he said to her. He tilted his eyeglasses down to read the name badge pinned to her apron. "Jenny. I remember you well from my class. Jenny. Of course."

While Lew jotted down Inskeep's contact info on the napkin for Maddy, Maddy sat amazed at how Lew could sound simultaneously like he was completely bullshitting and completely genuine, as with this former student. He handed the napkin to Maddy. Then he waved his hand in Maddy's face again.

"Run along, little darling, and file your sexual harassment complaint against me for this *deeply inappropriate* conversation while I help out Jenny

68

at this nice table you procured for us. The Title IX investigators probably haven't gotten a grievance about me *in a week,* and they'll be fearing I'm dead. Go reassure the suits I'm still around to keep them in business."

Chapter 8

Maddy pulled the car into the garage, turned off the engine, and pushed the remote to close the door. She sat silently in the dim glow of the ceiling fixture, the one that allowed her about three minutes to exit the garage in some light before it automatically turned off.

If she had been actually looking in the direction she was staring, she would have noticed Alex's garden tools hung on nails and hooks in a slightly haphazard fashion along the wall. She might have seen Alex's thick canvas gardening gloves laid atop one of the crossbeams in the garage wall's structure, or the spider's web stretching from the rake to the shovel.

But she wasn't really looking. She was instead sitting the way she had so many times in the pews, her hands gripping her knees like the talons of a bird on a branch in a sharp wind, her brain vaguely trying to plan an escape. It was that old feeling of needing to save herself from unjust condemnation.

But was it *unjust* condemnation? That was always the knotty question, wasn't it? If one traced out in any history the whole web of action, inaction, knowledge, and ignorance, one could always find at least a little guilt, at least a little innocence.

She figured it would only be an hour or two at most before the Philadelphia prosecutors' office would call to tell her what was now obvious from the news spreading across media outlets: that Maddy had screwed up. That she was an idiot.

She tried to look on the bright side: She hadn't talked to Wolf in several weeks. Their calls had been tapering off as the trial approached, as if they were afraid of jinxing it with too much talk. So, the odds that he would be the one to call now to speak the new humiliation seemed very low. It would be one of the prosecutors. It would probably be Jill.

It would be better if it were Wolf. She could change the subject quickly by asking him what she was supposed to do about the public lecture she had to give the day after tomorrow. The lecture had been planned as a low-key departmental affair: She would present her work the way one does when one is new to the faculty; there would be maybe twenty or thirty people, a mix of students and professors, with dry cookies, dark-pink punch, and institutional coffee. Perhaps the technology would be a little uncooperative and someone would have to jiggle various plugs. That happened often enough to be part of the ritual. Various people would suggest during the Q&A that she look at various texts and she would duly take notes, mostly in order to be polite as someone in her low position—especially as a woman—must be.

If Wolf called, she would tell him that she had been ready for all that. The prospect of these normal troubles had made her only mildly nervous. What she hadn't been ready for was what had happened today as a result of the spreading news—four hundred people would RSVP to say they would attend her lecture and that Lew would then, without asking her, move the event to a large lecture hall to accommodate the huge interest. She would tell Wolf that she wasn't sure how to deal with the prospect of suffering humiliation in so public a forum. No one would be there to hear about her scholarship. They would be there because of the murders. Which meant she was sure to disappoint. Because she wasn't allowed to talk about them.

But she had.

The ceiling light timed out and shut off with a click, leaving her mostly in the dark save one strand of light coming in the garage's single dusty window. She pulled out her phone and sent Liz a text:

Call?

She shoved the phone back in her pants' pocket.

She got out of the car, throwing her book bag over one shoulder, and exited the detached garage. She paused then on the crushed gravel path to the house, first to look at the stone house, then to look at the expanse of woods behind the garage and house. She let out a long sigh. The sun was setting, turning the sky to a cake-batter yellow—such a pretty color. The trees' branches swayed slowly in the wind, the leaves of the poplars shushing like a bristly push broom on a cement floor. The firs whispered to each other.

The worst thing, really, was how the dream she had woken up from that morning kept ducking its head back through the window of her consciousness. She was back in the convent, in the front hall in the middle of the night. Maddy was standing there in her white nightgown, no socks on her feet. Sister Ruth was there, dressed in her full habit as if for daytime, saying to her, "There's a wolf at the door." And Maddy was trying to get past her to open the front door, trying to explain her the wolf was not a problem.

"I *have* to go," she told the nun. She could feel in her gut the safety that lay *outside* the door if she could only get there.

But Sister Ruth kept blocking the door, answering, "No, Madeleine. You're in your nightgown. And the wolf is not here for you. You know that."

Maddy finally dropped her book bag on the gravel path and took off. She ran straight into the woods, jumping over downed limbs, tripping and slipping on wet spots, occasionally startling a squirrel. She felt her hair fall out of her ponytail band but kept going. She started to feel sweat forming on her chest and under her arms. She kept running. Every time she became conscious that her step had grown more tired, she pushed herself to run a little faster.

. . .

The printout of the article from the University of Minnesota's student newspaper was passed around the Philadelphia DA's office to quiet sighs. Each having seen it, Jill Strauss and Andre Grey sat down together at the small round table to which they naturally gravitated when they had a problem. They sat in silence for a minute or two, Jill chewing on her lip, Andre twirling a pen in his right hand around the tip of his middle finger.

Another staff member soon came by to interrupt the silence, telling them the story had been picked up by the *Star Tribune* and that a national-desk *USA Today* reporter had called to ask for confirmation. The story would be national soon. It wasn't a big story, but any tidbit on the Wilhelm case caused widespread fascination, which meant copycat front-page stories with sensational headlines.

"Toss a coin to decide who calls her?" Jill suggested.

"Nah," Andre answered. "You have to call her. You can do the worried big sister thing. You know—express concern about her and at the same time kick her ass a little."

Jill sighed. "I thought she understood not to talk to reporters."

Andre said nothing and looked over the printout again.

"You know what? I'm not sure she did," he said, handing her the paper. "If you read it closely, it's clear she told somebody about Wilhelm's faked article and how that tipped her off that he was up to something. She told *somebody* that recently by the look of it. But it isn't clear whether she told that—the bit about the forgery—to the student reporter, or just to someone else who told the reporter. Look at the article."

He poked his finger at the text.

"There's no fresh interview with Shanks. You *know* they would have quoted her if there had been an actual interview. Everyone wants an interview with her. Most of this story is just pieced together from priors."

Jill read it again a little more slowly and then agreed with Andre.

"You're right—and this bit about her doing a backflip for her class at a pasta place? What the hell is that even in there for? Looks like the reporter was just fishing for anything sexy."

She shoved the paper back at Andre.

"So, do I bother calling her? She'll know we know."

"Yeah," Andre answered, pushing his chair back, "you have to call her. You know Shanks. She's not gonna relax until one of us gives her the dressing-down she's expecting. Call her and yell at her so she can feel okay."

Jill stood up.

"You don't suppose she did this on purpose to get attention, to get our attention or something? We haven't checked in with her in a long time. Maybe she's feeling neglected? Maybe she wants to be in the papers? For someone's attention?"

"Nah. Not her style. I think she would have just called us if she wanted to know what was going on."

Jill made herself plainer.

"She hasn't called Wolf?"

"He knows to let us know if she needs anything," Andre answered. "I'm confident Wolf would tell us if there was something up. They both under-stood the need to keep . . . all complications to a minimum until we clear the trial."

...

Liz called to find Maddy up a tree.

She didn't realize this until, a few minutes into the call, she asked Maddy why there were bird sounds and Maddy said, oh, it was because she had had a true train crash of a day and so she'd gone running in the woods behind Alex's house and had ended up climbing a very tall tree.

"I think it's a fir," Maddy told Liz. "But, you know, I suck at tree identifi-cation. I think this is what firs smell like, though."

"Do I need to send the fire department to get you out of the tree, you crazy cat?" Liz asked, masking her worry with sarcasm.

"They'd never be able to get a truck back here. Too wooded," Maddy explained. "Too wet."

She went on to tell Liz about the day, that it had started with a student stopping by the library where Maddy was working on revising a manuscript to ask her if she'd seen that she was featured as the front-page story in the student newspaper. About the Wilhelm case—the one she wasn't supposed to be talking about. Giving away new information in the press right before the trial.

From there it was a series of phone calls. First it was Dean Scott Willingham reminding her that when she'd first come to campus, the campus police (following a call from Wolf?) had specifically asked her to keep a low profile, and this wasn't very low-profile. Then the university's media people called to let her know various reporters were trying to get ahold of her, asking her if she wanted to do interviews. Then calls from unknown numbers, presumably press, none of which she answered but the sum of which meant she'd probably have to change her phone number again.

And then the history of medicine librarian had come over to tell Maddy excitedly that Lew had moved the location for the talk because of so many people reading in the article about her upcoming lecture and indicating they wanted to attend. The librarian had asked if Maddy wanted her to pick up extra copies of the school paper so Maddy could have them to keep. As if Maddy would be excited at this point to be in a student newspaper when her story and photo had been spread by every major reporting outlet nation-ally and even internationally when Wilhelm had been charged.

"I'm a freak show," Maddy told Liz. "A fucking freak show."

Liz didn't know what to say. After a pause, Maddy told Liz that she had finally called Lew to ask where she could possibly hide out until her class, and he had suggested the map library—nobody ever went to the map library—and he had said he'd meet her there because he wanted to make sure she was okay and because she'd had some mail delivered he thought she might want. And then what was in the mail but the annual early-fall letter from Sister Ruth reminding her she could always come to the convent for the holidays. She was always welcome.

The letter was signed, as always, "with love and prayers."

"And I know she means it," Maddy said to Liz. "I mean, I know she loves me, which just makes me feel like *a shit*. And it was weird—I had a dream about the convent and Sister Ruth just this morning."

"Maddy," Liz interrupted her, "you know you can always come home with me for Thanksgiving or whatever."

"Right. Because being with your family while your grandmother keeps asking you if you've outgrown the lesbian phase is so relaxing. That sounds just awesome. I'm sure I would sit there quietly and not say anything to make it worse this year. Right?"

She went on to tell Liz that she had spent most of the day with dread waiting for the DA's office to call and scold her. Her phone beeped as she said it.

"Oh great," Maddy said, "looks like they're calling now. I think I'll ignore it and let them call again later."

"No! Go take the call! Get it over with."

Maddy switched the call over.

"I know!" Maddy answered the call, rather than saying hello. She said it again: "I know. I know I know I know. *I know!*"

"Hey, Maddy, it's Jill Strauss from the prosecutors' office. How are you, Maddy?"

Maddy didn't answer.

"Yeah, listen," Jill said, "I know you know."

Again, Maddy didn't answer.

"Is that birds I'm hearing?"

"Yes," Maddy said. "I'm up a tree."

"You're up a tree?"

Maddy answered in the affirmative.

"Is it a big tree?" Jill asked.

Maddy answered again in the affirmative.

"Is there a tree house that you're in? Or are you just holding onto the tree?"

Maddy explained she was straddling a branch with her legs and leaning on the main trunk with her back, sitting in the tree, and that this wasn't the most comfortable thing in the world, sitting in a tree. There were sharp bits and some sap. A tree house, she observed, would definitely be nicer.

"I've always admired your coping mechanisms, Maddy," Jill said, honestly. "So, I get climbing a tree right now. But if you fall out of that tree, someone who cares about you is gonna be upset."

Maddy got the reference to Wolf.

"Will you come down out of the tree?"

"History would suggest I will at some point come down out of this tree, yes," Maddy answered. "I do tend to get hungry every few hours."

She sighed, remembering the need to come out of the trees at the convent because of hunger.

"I know I fucked up, Jill. But I didn't talk to that reporter. I have ignored them all equally."

"We figured that," Jill replied. "Well, Andre figured that. The backflip story kind of gave away that they were stretching to report anything about you. At least the students of yours, the ones they interviewed, had nice things to say about you as a teacher."

When Maddy didn't reply, Jill added that she was trying to determine what bird she was hearing through the phone.

"Meadowlark?"

"I don't know," Maddy answered. "I don't really know Minnesota birds. I only know the common West Virginia birds, from when I was in a convent."

There was another pause. Maddy figured Jill probably thought she was joking about being in a convent.

"Is there anything I can do to reassure you it's okay?" Jill asked.

"Oh, for God's sake!" Maddy answered, her voice starting to crack. "Please don't be *nice* about this. It's been a little stressful, you know—all of it—first, reading about the trial preparations long-distance, wondering whether you're going to be able to convince the jury, or if he's going to go free and I'm going to be the one who's a liar or an idiot. A defamer of a major researcher, a hero! I don't get to even make the argument myself. At least if I got to make the argument myself, and they found him not guilty, I would know the best argument that could be made had been made. I would know it was me that fucked it all up."

She paused, realizing she had just insulted Jill.

"I'm sorry," Maddy said.

"No, don't be sorry. I know exactly what you mean. When I was lower in the chain and someone else got to argue my case, I had exactly the same frustration. I still run into it. I totally get it."

"And then," Maddy went on, as if Jill had said nothing, "having people ask me things I can't answer. Unless I've had too much to drink, and then I stupidly answer, I guess. And having to wonder if...."

"If what?" Jill asked.

There was another pause, now with the sound of a woodpecker not very far away.

"Is Hunter okay?" Maddy asked.

"So far as I know. Do you want me to call Detective Wolf and find out?"

"No. No, I don't want him to know you had to call me because I fucked up. Although he probably already knows."

"It really is okay," Jill told her. "Everyone messes up. Neither Detective Wolf nor I nor any one of us expects you to be some paragon of perfection, you know, especially when you have no experience with this kind of thing. It's unfamiliar. It's stressful. You shouldn't be so hard on yourself."

"Christ, Jill, I didn't make it this far by being *easy* on myself," Maddy said with a tone of disgust. "Where are we, anyway, on the schedule?"

"No one told you?" Jill asked. "You didn't read the article, or see any of the news this week? Jury selection finished. Judge'll start the trial Monday."

Maddy gulped. She leaned up a little harder against the tree and gripped the branch between her legs a little more firmly.

"Did you hear me, Maddy?"

"Yeah. I didn't realize we were there now."

"It's hard to say how long it will take to play out, Maddy. And you should know that even if we get convictions on some of the counts, there are likely to be appeals. But it's a safe bet you're going to get calls from reporters, and it's best if you just don't take them. Our case will go best if you don't talk to people. It will give his lawyers less ammunition with the judge."

Maddy nodded and then realized Jill couldn't hear her.

"Okay," she mumbled. "I know." She added more quietly, "I know I know I know. Don't fuck it up, Jill. Don't let anyone fuck it up."

"I'll do my best."

With that, they hung up. Maddy sat quietly for a few minutes listening to the woodpecker. She looked west and noticed anew the lush color of the yellowed sky. Then she looked east to see the periwinkle of evening coming on. Venus was just now visible. The shushing sound of the branches in the wind swelled and faded and a small flock of geese flew by a few hundred feet away, honking lazily as if there wasn't much to say but someone had to say something, to pass the time.

She thought she'd have to climb down before it was too dark to see well. These were very much like the trees at the convent—the sort that accelerated the darkness in unpredictable ways. Just like the memory of The Jerk.

She called Liz back and told her in a quiet voice that Jill Strauss had been as understanding as ever.

"Did you know the trial starts Monday, Liz? That jury selection is complete?"

"Mad girl, I thought you knew. I'm sorry. I didn't want to mention it unless you brought it up first."

"It's okay. In a way I'm glad. I mean, of course I'm glad. It's the point of the whole thing—well, I mean conviction is the whole point."

Liz suggested Maddy carefully climb down the tree and drown her sorrows in a combination of chocolate ice cream and rum, a recipe the two of them one late night had named "milk of malaise." Maddy answered that she couldn't, she had so much class work to prep, plus the talk to finish prepping. She asked Liz how on earth she was going to do this talk now, with all these people coming wanting to hear about the Wilhelm history, when she couldn't give them what they wanted. Liz said Maddy should just open with a joke, explain briefly why she couldn't talk about the case, promise the audience that she would talk about it when the trial was over, do a flip, then give a great talk on her work, so that people got to know her for her scholarship.

Maddy mentally filed away what Liz said but changed the subject.

"I need to get laid," Maddy told Liz in a firm voice. "I need to feel somebody against me, around me, in that way. Forget my troubles. That's what I need more than milk of malaise."

Liz asked Maddy what she wanted Liz to do about it.

"Find me somebody through your network," Maddy told her. "You know a million people who are chill about sex, and one of them is bound to know somebody here who is safe and not a jerk and won't ask much of me. There was one guy here, a psych professor—but I think I drove him off. Anyway, you'd say he was too old for me."

Liz said she was willing to try.

"But just so we are perfectly clear, I'm not feeding your stupid Daddy complex, Mad. It *will* be a guy about our age."

Liz asked her how much was in the billboard account. Maddy guessed around six thousand.

"You're not going to buy me a gigolo, are you?" Maddy asked. "I'm not really into that idea. It's probably illegal. Wait, I'm sure it's illegal."

"Don't be an ass, Mad. You don't have to pay for sex with men if you're a *woman*. That's the single upside of being a straight woman. Well, that and having an easy route to pregnancy if you want a kid. I'm asking about the billboard account because I just wanna be able to offer whomever I find some money to take you out so you don't feel like you have to put out if you don't want to. You'll know it's your money."

"So why don't I just pull out my own wallet if we go out?" Maddy asked. "Simpler than giving him my money to spend on me."

"Stupid woman," Liz answered. "You don't want to wrestle over the check—that is so not sexy. And I know you like good food and females respond to resource-display. You want resource display beforehand, trust me. This way, knowing I can give him some of your money, if all I can find is a poor grad student or post-doc—which is what everyone is at our age—he can still take you out somewhere nice. So that you're sexually primed."

"You're a true friend, being so considerate about my need for re-source-display and sexual priming," Maddy answered.

"Shut up," Liz responded with a snort-laugh. "*You* know that *I* know a thing or two about how to properly bed a femme woman."

"Yes, yes you do. I just never thought that knowledge would benefit me."

"Get out of the fucking tree, Maddy. You're not a monkey, even if you can swing from branches like one."

"I'm planning an impressive dismount, though. The Russian judges will be forced to score me higher than they want."

Chapter 9

Everett Inskeep opened the door to his craftsman-style 1920s-era home in the Uptown neighborhood of Minneapolis and motioned to Maddy to come in quickly from the dense rain. As Everett took her fold-up travel umbrella, Maddy realized what a good thing it was she had not borrowed Alex's elegant wooden-handled umbrella, as she had the week before. How awkward it would have been to show up with an item borrowed from the grave of Everett's good friend.

Stepping out to the covered porch, Everett shook off the umbrella and collapsed it. He came back in, closed the heavy wooden door, secured the umbrella with its snap-sash, and hung it from its loop on a handsome cast-iron coat stand. Then he showed Maddy into his living room and invited her to sit on the sofa.

"Your home is so beautiful," Maddy exclaimed, looking around at the perfectly appointed house and wondering if she should have taken off her wet shoes. It looked like something out of one of those design magazines Maddy occasionally spoiled herself with on a trip—the kind of magazine that they'd all pass around for weeks at the convent until Nancy, another orphan boarder, cut it up for the scrapbook she kept to imagine the house she would keep after she found a Catholic doctor or senator to marry.

Everything in Everett's home appeared freshly painted. The ceilings had elegant crown moldings and the doorways and windows were lined in wood that looked to Maddy to be red oak. The furnishings were a stylish mix of period and contemporary, the colors muted so as to work together within a palette of yellows, greens, and dark pinks. Maddy could not help but notice that Inskeep had a baby grand piano in the living room.

He thanked her for her compliment on his home, explaining that he was by profession an architect. He said he did interior design work, too.

"Yes, I know that you were the person who designed the sunroom addition to Alex's bedroom—with the bathtub! And the separate master bath, with that lovely shower, with the cherry blossom tiles," Maddy answered. "Hank Merriman told me all about your design. It's all so beautiful. *Especially* the solarium with the bathtub. It is the most beautiful bathtub I've ever seen—the way it is set up in the space full of glass, among the trees."

Maddy could see that Everett was very happy that she appreciated it. He looked to her to be in his early sixties—tall and thin and more graceful in his movements than the average man. He seemed to move almost as if he had taken acting lessons to play a part, as if for participation in a local theater, though he did not come across as trying too hard. He wore, she noted mentally, the classic uniform of architects—well-cut slacks and a mock turtleneck sweater with stylish leather shoes. His wristwatch gave off a flash of silver as he moved.

"Were the Johnny Walker Blue bottles with the lights around Alex's bathtub your idea?" she asked.

"Yes," Everett smiled. "Alex had been saving up the empties in the basement, not sure what to do with them. She'd given Hank a bottle of it twice a year, once on his birthday and once on the anniversary of the fight that had started their unlikely friendship. She'd saved up the empties because she liked the heavy blue glass too much to just throw them out. It occurred to me we could use them in the final design of the space, to give it a warmer and more personal touch. She especially liked to take baths at night. She was out in the woods where no one could see her, so."

"It's all positively ethereal at night. Is that how you met Alex, by her hiring you?"

"No," Everett replied. "No, that's not it."

He stood up to his full height and asked Maddy if he could offer her a cup of coffee or tea. Maddy told him she was happy to drink whatever was easiest. She was trying to figure out what visage to maintain given that she was there to talk about the loss of his close friend.

"I have some tea in the kitchen just freshly made. I'll bring it out," he responded. He left and returned with a tray that he set down on the wide ottoman that doubled as a coffee table. He poured Maddy a cup and handed it to her. Then he poured himself another and sat down in an armchair. She noticed he held the cup with his pinky extended and that he had a simple silver ring on that pinky. It matched the flash of his wristwatch's face.

"I would offer you sugar or milk," he said, "but it's a green. Genmaicha. Now I've forgotten your question."

"How you met Alex Shugar," Maddy replied, shifting her face through various expressions trying to find a neutral one. "Hank said you were one of her closest friends."

"Yes, yes." He stared across the room for a moment and then turned his face to Maddy. "Hank told you about me?"

Maddy nodded and sipped her tea, holding the cup in imitation of his grasp, pinky up.

"So, you'll surely be thinking about what he told you—that I am bigendered—that I sometimes live out as my male side and sometimes as my female side?"

Relieved he had brought it up, Maddy nodded.

"Well, to answer your question, Ally and I met because she was giving a public lecture on intersex at another nearby university and I was interested to hear that. We got to talking afterwards, and then we met for a lunch to talk some more. I told her about my life, she told me about her work, and then she told me about her life, too. She wanted someone to help her with some changes to her house, so I became her architect and interior designer. We became good friends. She was my best friend, and I think I was hers."

"Hank told me she talked to you as much as anyone," Maddy responded earnestly.

"I think that is true. We were similar in some fundamental ways, Ally and I. We both loved design that was sensual without being garish or pretentious. And neither of us had a lot of patience for people being thick or self-deceptive."

He got up and went to his mantle and brought back a framed photograph to show Maddy, sitting down next to her on the couch. The photo was of Alex and another woman standing on a bridge, arms around each other's waists looking like they were having a lovely time out. It took Maddy a minute to realize the woman was Everett—or, rather, Sophie. Maddy looked from the photo to Everett's face and back. Everett laughed.

"Yes, that's me when I am Sophie—*en femme*. I surely do miss Ally."

He took the photograph and put it back on the mantle. Sitting back down, he asked Maddy why she wanted to talk.

"Well . . ."

Yes, why *was* she here if she wasn't trying to learn more about how Alex had died?

"Well," Maddy said, "something a bit odd happened and I just hate not knowing why something happened."

Everett cocked his head and looked at her quizzically.

"You sound like Alex. She hated not understanding something she saw as different from the expected."

"I'm curious," Maddy said with some hesitancy in her voice. "If you don't mind my asking, what was she like before she died? I mean just before? I know she was under a lot of stress."

Everett looked into the distance again and then bit his lower lip. How funny, Maddy thought, that the metaphor of biting one's lip described the actual act.

"Yes," Everett said, releasing the bite. "Yes. There was a lot of stress in her life. There was some difficulty with a postdoc of hers"—Maddy figured this must have been a reference to Sarah and the sexual harassment complaint—"and she was working on some complicated research, and the activists were acting up, and then there was the Gnat—"

Maddy stopped him. What activists acting up?

Everett explained that Alex's work on sex and identity had led to various activists angry that she didn't subscribe to this or that viewpoint. He said they were lately trying to get people to boycott talks she had been asked to give at various universities and conferences and that some of the talks had ended up involving some degree of security.

"And the Gnat?"

"A graduate student in philosophy here, doing his dissertation on her work. According to him, she had undertheorized her work. I take it his complaint amounted essentially to that Alex was just too clear in her prose. He was saying she had overstated—well, he was saying that she overstated the importance of *reality*, as I understood it from what Alex told me. He was basically acting as if she were naïve in her work. At least that's what she told me. He had made her very angry."

"Why did she call him 'the Gnat,' though? That was her name for him?"

"Yes," Everett answered. "He had become obnoxious, constantly following in her wake to reanalyze her latest work, feeding the grouchy activists here and there. He would follow her around to talks and always manage to get in a hostile question during the Q and A. Making her look defensive. Making her look *wrong*. She was angry at him because his pursuit was starting to impact her ability to publish. Not because the editors wouldn't take her work but because her attempt to anticipate his foolish criticisms were weighing on her mind as she tried to write, and she hated that, being mentally controlled in that way by an impertinent young man who hadn't even finished his PhD. She was afraid he was about to start using the Freedom of Information Act to get her correspondence. You know, she was at a public university, so people could use the public records rules against her. Or so she thought. Perhaps he had intimated it."

Maddy sat up at the mention of the Freedom of Information Act as if she had been pinched by a ghost. Everett took a long sip of tea and went on.

"She decided to start destroying records, he irritated her so much. I remember, I told her I wasn't sure she was legally allowed to destroy records of her published research or that he was legally allowed to get them. I told her to talk to a friend of hers who is a lawyer, or else her own lawyer. And she shushed me and told me she'd prefer to be ignorant of the law. But she didn't like the idea of anyone working on her papers after her death. She said there were better topics than her and she couldn't respect anyone who would bother with her as a subject. She told me she had started purging. Destroying her records."

Maddy wasn't sure what to say to this. Perhaps this explained the strange absence in Alex's home office of some of her files. And that empty bookshelf?

And then suddenly she realized perhaps Alex wouldn't like Maddy thinking about her so much after her death.

But then, Maddy thought rather matter-of-factly, Alex is dead.

"So, she was pretty agitated? Just before she died?"

"Well, it was strange," Everett answered, rising a bit from his seated position to peak into Maddy's teacup. Seeing she still had half a cup, he sat back down.

"All of that was going on but she also had, the last time I saw her, a new vibrancy about her. Almost a peacefulness, too. I asked her what was going on. She was quiet. She would only say that she thought she had found—how did she put it?—a new source of sexual insight? She said she wasn't ready to tell me. No, wait—she said there were *no words* for it. She said very specifically there were no words."

"No words for it?"

"That's what she said. *No words for it.* She smiled when she said that. And it seemed odd that she would say such a thing happily when she was so interested in words. Much as she complained about the fashionable obsession with representation in academe, her life was *words*."

"Do you think she told anyone what was going on? Maybe Hank? Maybe Scott?"

Everett shook his head and pinched his eyes closed in an awkward manner.

"Perhaps this sounds a little conceited," he said, opening his eyes, "but I seriously doubt she would have told Hank or Scott before telling me what was going on. Hank is one-hundred-percent *man*. And a sexist at that. He doesn't mean to be, but he drove her crazy sometimes in his sexist assumptions. There was so much he couldn't understand about her experiences, her feelings, the way she approached the world and felt in it as a woman. And Scott and Alex were not very close, except in a kind of family-protective way. They watched out for each other but they weren't intimate emotionally. They hadn't been in years. Alex didn't trust him emotionally."

Maddy asked Everett bluntly why Alex and Scott had gotten divorced.

"That's not for me to say, really," Everett answered. "I mean, I know. But it's not for me to say."

The doorbell rang and Everett stood up quickly, saying, "Forgive me."

Maddy wasn't sure if the "forgive me" was a reference to getting up to answer the door or to not being willing to say why Alex and Scott had divorced. As Everett opened the door, Maddy could see it was a delivery driver coming to drop what looked like a book. Everett put the package on the table near the door and came back and sat back down.

"Do you play the piano?" Maddy asked, nodding her head towards the piano.

"Yes," he responded, looking at his instrument. "Why would I own a piano if I didn't play?"

"Well, that's a good question. Did you know that Alex had ordered a grand from Steinway in New York just before she died? It arrived the other day. And I don't know why she would have ordered it."

"I cannot understand that either!" Everett exclaimed. "She told me nothing of it."

Looking agitated, he stood back up, went over to the piano, pulled out the bench, sat down, and opened the cover to the keys. He played one note.

"Very strange. Alex said nothing to me about this. It is the sort of thing she would have told me."

Maddy asked, maybe Alex had just ordered it for the way it looked in the room? But Everett responded that you don't buy a Steinway grand like it's a new vase for the table.

"And besides, she would have asked me first. She didn't make major design changes without asking what I thought. She enjoyed thinking about design with me. And a Steinway isn't exactly an impulse buy," he added. "It's not like she was a rich woman. Why buy a hundred-thousand-dollar instrument she could not play?"

He played another note three times, as if it were a bell ringing the hour.

"She didn't order it for *you* to play it?" Maddy asked him, just as he hit the third note and stopped.

He shook his head no.

"Are you sure she didn't buy it so that you could play when you were visiting her?"

"Buying a new Steinway for your piano-playing friend for when she *happens* to come over is a bit like buying a sugar plantation in case your friend *happens* to take two lumps in her tea, Dr. Shanks," Everett replied.

Now he put both his hands on the keys and played a short phrase from what Maddy recognized as Mozart. She watched his long fingers crawl over the keys like a crab along the beach. He stopped suddenly and said simply, "Strange."

He turned to Maddy while shifting himself to sit on the end of the bench.

"I'm afraid I honestly don't know the answer to your puzzle. But I do at least know why she went to New York sometimes."

Maddy's eyebrows went up.

"She had a wealthy gentleman friend there whom she visited every few months. I recall she was there seeing him just a couple days before she died. Perhaps he knows the answer. Perhaps it was a gift from him. But why would he have given her a piano?"

"Do you know who he is?" Maddy asked.

"Yes," Everett answered, "but I'm not sure if it is okay with him to tell you. I can call him to ask, to ask if you can contact him. He may not want you to know of him."

Maddy asked him why the relationship between Alex and this man would need to be a secret.

"He's prominent," Everett replied. After a pause, he added, "And prominently married."

"Ah. He and Alex were having an affair."

Everett stood up now somewhat stiffly and asked Maddy if she wanted to see the rest of the house. Maddy put her cup on the tray, stood up, and said she would very much enjoy that.

Everett showed her the downstairs first, the kitchen, the butler's pantry, the formal dining room, the parlor, the powder room, and an added home office off the back—then the upstairs with three bedrooms and two baths, the master bathroom obviously added to the house above the home office, but in such a way as to feel as if it fit in perfectly with the bones of the structure. One guest bedroom had a queen size bed, the other, two twin beds.

"My niece and her husband come and visit at the holidays with their two children."

Oh, this was a house Maddy's convent bunkmate Nancy would have happily taken for her marital nest. Every room was meticulous in both design and cleanliness. It reminded Maddy of the convent in how everything was in its proper place, everything perfectly dusted, only it felt much warmer, more welcoming. They came back down to the living room and sat down again.

"Can I ask you something?" Maddy asked, picking back up her cup. "Are you intersex? Were you born between male and female?"

"Oh, no, my dear."

He opened the teapot to see how much was left and closed it again.

"I should put more hot water in. No, my dear, I was born male. My body still is male. I just feel the female gender in me in a strong way sometimes—I feel bigendered—and I'm fortunate enough in my life to be able to live as both a man and a woman. I have the money, the safety, and a lack of angst—a healthy or unhealthy lack of angst depending on who you ask."

"Alex was comfortable with it, I guess?"

"Alex was comfortable with just about everyone except people who spent too much time being ashamed of themselves. I wasn't one of those people. I learned a long time ago that shame was a waste of energy you could be using on something productive."

"Like what?" Maddy asked.

Everett laughed lightly like a society woman and said in a full voice, "Oh, like getting dressed up." And then more quietly, with a wink, "Or getting off."

Maddy laughed with him at that. She sipped a little more tea.

"Sorry," he said, blushing a little. "You remind me of Alex somehow and I'm talking rudely, as if I'm talking with her. I sound a little like her now."

"I don't mind at all," Maddy answered. "So, it's a sexual thing? Your life with two genders?"

Everett leaned in and warned Maddy in a conspiratorial voice that what he was about to explain was sometimes hard for people to wrap their heads around because they'd been led to believe there were only three sexual orientations—gay, straight, and bi. But there were many subsets and variations of human sexuality, he said, involving orientations towards particular types of bodies, orientations towards people of particular races or ages, orientations towards particular situations.

He explained to Maddy in a way that was much more animated that he himself had an orientation that meant he was bisexual but not in the usual way. He explained that, as a man, he was attracted to women. But, he said, he also felt attracted to the idea of *being* a woman himself. And he felt aroused as a woman. So, he enjoyed sometimes immersing himself in life as a woman, and in that life taking men as partners.

"But the two genders, they are both *sexual* for you," Maddy answered, finding herself surprised that she sounded critical.

"*Your* gender is *not* sexual?" he asked back, his tone making it clear he didn't expect her to answer. "I'm guessing you're straight. When you have sex with a man, aren't you doing it *as a woman*?"

Maddy narrowed her eyes and stared at the ceiling fixture. She was thinking about the fantasies she drew to mind when she took care of herself. Then she thought about what she was hoping Liz would arrange for her.

"Yes," she finally said. "Yes. You're right. When I want sex with a man, I want it as a woman. As a woman with a man. Does that sound horridly heterosexist?"

He ignored her question and went on as if teaching a lesson about how to pronounce a word or do a dance step.

"So, for me, it's just that sometimes I feel like a man—a man who, when he wants sex, wants sex with a woman—and sometimes I feel as a woman—a woman who, when she wants sex, wants to feel like a woman with a man. The term for it in French is quite lovely," he added. "*Amour de soi en femme.* Love for oneself as a woman."

"I see."

"No, you don't," said Everett, sighing and taking note of her earnestness with a look of paternalistic sympathy. He leaned over and tapped his finger lightly on her wrist. "It's very kind of you to *act* like you do understand. The truth is that it takes a while to wrap one's head around. It's one reason you won't hear it talked about in public. Simple straight people like you presumably are, they hear about it and ask the kinds of questions they used to ask about gay sex. 'But how do the parts fit together?!'"

He chuckled a little now at his analogy.

"Do you think about transitioning your body to be more female—with surgery and hormones?" Maddy asked.

Everett told her he'd thought about it a few times, but he liked having his body working the way it did—that he had realized he liked being bigendered.

"Unlike some of my *amoir de soi* sisters who used to be male," he said, "I don't mind being a man part of the time. I like it. It doesn't make me feel wrong. I understand that for some of us, switching the body over is necessary to feeling good, to feeling whole, to surviving. There are lots of different ways people get to a gender-cross—I mean lots of different feelings that put one there or get one there—and lots of different ways they go when they get there. Mine is just one of so many different experiences. This body, this way, well, it works for me. I've had electrolysis on my skin to stop facial hair from growing. But so far, I haven't felt the need to change my body a lot in terms of permanent work, just some electrolysis here and there. I was blessed with not too big an apple."

He stroked his neck briefly as if lost in thought.

"Some of my sisters need more physical transition to feel good, to be well. Some get breasts, some also do bottom surgery. Some go as far as they can. If it helps them feel good, I say more power to them. I helped one friend pay for her surgeries. But some of us are okay this way. Someday the world will be okay with it all, I like to think, the way Alex was fine with it all, and then people won't feel they have to live as one or the other. Some will still switch over medically and socially and legally, but more people may live like I do, out in the open and bigendered without feeling a need to be closeted or to choose one gender. No shame."

"Alex had a folder on this," Maddy said aloud but as if to herself. She turned to Everett. "She was working on a book about sexual arousal—about human sexuality—I think maybe she was going to write about this, about your bigendered experiences of sexuality?"

"Yes, that's right. It was partly because of our friendship that she became interested in this. She wanted to develop a moral philosophy of sexuality and she was using different arousal patterns to think about the meaning and the ethics of sex. She had asked me if she could use me as a case study, and I said of course. I mean, she was changing the names and identifying details of those of us she was using as illustrations. So, in the book I would have been under some other name and profession even though I'm hardly in the closet. She was using Hank's work some, reading into the sexology literature. Asking people a lot of questions, trying out some new ideas."

He bent his neck to the left until it let out a little crack.

"It was getting her in *more* trouble." He sighed.

Maddy asked what he meant.

"It's not okay to talk openly about this particular way of living among some transgender activists," Everett explained. "They say it's suggesting they are just sexual fetishists. I don't begrudge them the desire for transition. I truly get why some choose it. And how do I know what they feel and what they need? Earlier in my life, I thought about transition. If I had a different life, if surgery were magic and really gave me a body like you were born with, a full female body, I might go there? I'm not sure. I do like how my parts work, and I would always worry I would not like the 'after' in terms of the physical feeling, post-surgery. But what bothers me is that, for the ones who are like me, when they deny it, they're doing so out of shame. And we have nothing to be ashamed of. I'm not ashamed of who I am and how I feel. We don't choose what turns us on. So shame is useless. And exhausting."

"The difficult subject," Maddy said. "Shame, I mean."

"Yes!" Everett cried out. "What Alex said! That shame was the difficult subject, not sex. And of course she was right. The difficult subject isn't sex, it's the *shame around sex*. Sex is easy to talk about if you're not steeped in shame. Sex becomes a joy when you let yourself go. But we are so ashamed of sex, we act as if sex is the problem."

Maddy looked at her watch. Then she realized it must have come across as a rude gesture.

"I'm sorry," Maddy said. "I just have to keep an eye on the time because of my office hours."

"I'm embarrassing you," Everett said, standing up and picking up the tray. "I'm talking too much about my own world."

"No," Maddy answered, also standing up. She put her teacup on the tray.

"Honestly, you're not. I find what you're saying really interesting. The truth is it is very hard to embarrass me. I'm weird. And it's true, I don't understand what you're telling me about how you feel, but I also know from what you asked me that I realize I haven't even thought enough about how *I* feel to judge you about how *you* feel."

Everett paused and looked at her. He relaxed his shoulders. He put the tray back down.

"I appreciate that," he said.

"I forgot to tell you that Lew Meadows asked me to say hello to you—well, to Sophie."

Everett smiled broadly.

"Ah, Llewellyn. We haven't seen each other in forever. Give him my best when you see him."

Maddy told Everett that Lew had said they should all go shopping together and Everett lit up like he had just spotted a shooting star.

"That would be delightful!" he cried out. "I'll go ahead and call him then, and we'll find a time."

Maddy apologized that she had to go, thanked him for his hospitality, and reminded him to please call the gentleman friend of Alex's in New York. Everett asked what exactly he should tell him.

"That I'm an historian of medicine," Maddy said, "interested in Alex's life. That I'm discreet and won't reveal anything he doesn't wish. I suppose I can give him references if he wants that, to attest to my being trustworthy?"

She paused a moment to think.

"Tell him—well, tell him that I think Alex would want someone to figure out one puzzle she left."

He saw her to the door, opening her umbrella for her on the vestibule and handing it to her. She turned back to him just before he closed the door.

"Please don't tell him the puzzle came in the form of a piano. I want to see if he knows."

Chapter 10

"Is that okay, miss?" the driver asked.

He received no answer but kept inching his black Town Car forward through the traffic over the Brooklyn-side tower. While two cars nearby exchanged an angry volley of horn blasts, Maddy noticed how the light from the falling sun grabbed at the cables of the great bridge, dancing along the dull bronze of its exoskeleton like a spider scrambling up a wall.

Yawning, Maddy pulled from her brain the recollection of some history of medicine she related to this structure. The Brooklyn Bridge had been built in the 1870s through the innovative creation of a chamber into which workers had descended to dig down into the sediment to find a sure stone footing on which the great beast's legs could stand. The change in air pressure experienced by laborers going in and out of the chamber had brought on decompression sickness for many of them—bubbles in the blood, excruciating joint pain, dizziness, an urge to gasp for breath, occasionally death.

In 1879, Dr. Andrew Smith had named the occupational illness "caisson disease" after the engineering term for the underwater excavation chambers used during construction. Laypeople called it "the bends."

Maddy herself felt a bit dizzy riding in the backseat as the car slowly approached Manhattan. She bent over for a moment, the seatbelt straining against her, clasping her hands around her ankles, her head draped over her knees. Her nylon pantyhose felt slick and cheap against the skin of her fingers. She yawned again. She had not slept nearly enough the night before, getting home at about two o'clock in the morning and then having trouble getting to sleep in her cold bed (dumb to have skipped a bath; it would have settled her). She got up at six thirty to throw together what she'd need for this overnight trip, rushing to get to work in time to finish grading students' draft papers from the history of medicine class and to drop them off in the mailroom before hurrying to Everett Sophie's house to get Alex's letter, then on to the airport to catch the flight to New York to meet Alex's former lover, worried she would not quickly find the discount long-term parking . . .

Why had she said yes to this trip yesterday afternoon? Now she felt unsettled at the thought that no one but Everett Sophie Inskeep knew where she was going. Liz would not be happy. Wolf would not approve.

The car pushed forward suddenly, moving up two full car lengths through the rush hour traffic, and stopped again. Maddy sat up and turned to look over her shoulder out the back window. To get to Philadelphia from the southern end of Manhattan, which way was it? Did you go back through Brooklyn? No. It would make more sense to go on a bit through Manhattan, then cut west to New Jersey, then south to Philadelphia.

And if someone were looking to come the other way, from Philly to New York? No matter, she told herself. If Wilhelm didn't know she was here, he certainly wouldn't find her here. Not that he would ever approach her anyway. Jill Strauss and Wolf had both told Maddy that so long as Wilhelm thought he was going to get away with it—which Wilhelm seemed to think was true and Jill and Wolf seemed to worry was possible—it didn't matter that Wilhelm's lawyers had gotten him out on two million dollars' bail. He'd leave her alone. If he did otherwise, it would be like admitting guilt.

And at this point it seemed clear they weren't going to call her as a witness, so whatever damage she had done to Wilhelm, he would figure there was no *more* she could do. The evidence had been largely identified by her, sure, but now it could and would be presented without her. Much as she wished she could present her argument to the jury, she didn't mind not getting the citation credit to her dissertation research in the court record.

Still, now that she thought about the geography consciously, being only about two hours away from Wolf felt wrong. She ought to be farther. Or nearer?

She picked up a police siren in the distance beyond the bridge, and she could feel for a split second his solid body against her solid body in his kitchen when he held her for that long stretch, as he had leaned back against the counter and she leaned on him, her head turned to the side to rest on his warm, breathing chest. Her arms had been limp at her side, his hands clasped together on the small of her back. She could vaguely sense the presence of his service revolver nearby, as if it were a second obedient dog on watch.

Now, in the car on the bridge, dopey from stress and exhaustion, she just wanted Wolf there to ask her once again as he had then, *Are you okay?* She wanted him to ask again because, when he asked it, he hadn't been asking how she *felt*. No. He had clearly been asking what the hell was wrong with her. She had looked at his face when he asked, and she had seen his disturbance. His implied diagnosis of her profound pathology had been such a relief. Like someone had finally told her the prognosis. *You're all wrong, Madeleine Shanks. You'll suffer some more. You'll fuck up more. Then you'll die.* And knowing that was how it was going to go made it all feel perfectly doable to her then.

But today, worn out and sitting in the back of this Town Car inching across the Brooklyn Bridge, she could imagine him refusing her the pleasure of suggesting she'd fuck up again and die and instead simply scolding her for what she'd done the night before with Maarten. Telling her with derision that she lacked basic self-respect. That she still didn't know how to take care of herself.

Now she brought the back of her left hand to her face. If she could evoke the smell of last night, the smell of Maarten or his apartment or that boozy drink, the reminder of that pleasant sexual novelty might exorcise this dreaded frustration, this sense she'd never feel fully safe with Wolf again.

It wasn't like she was craving Wolf. No, she thought. She was just craving that extraordinary feeling, the feeling he had given her, that she could close her eyes and *sleep*, knowing that he'd keep watch. Did anyone ever really crave another person, or just what the person might give?

"I woulda normally taken you through the Midtown Tunnel from JFK to the Upper East, miss, but there's an accident totally backing it up. Basically closed. Plus, this way you get to see the city skyline from this side, coming in from Brooklyn. Not for nothing, right? You from New York?"

"Yes. I mean, not the city. Long Island." She hastened to look out the back window again.

"Long Island! I'm from Bayshore. Which part you from?" the driver asked.

"I'm sorry, I need to think about something for a moment," she responded more curtly than she meant.

The driver apologized as Maddy opened her backpack to check again that the letter Everett Sophie had given her was there. *Was* it even a letter in this envelope? She ran her finger over the seal across which Alex Shugar had signed her name. She tried momentarily holding it up to the light of the setting sun to see if she could make anything out. But the envelope was too thick. She turned it over and looked again at Alex's signature and then at the name Alex had written on the front, the name of her gentleman friend in New York: Liberty Whitaker, IV.

Sophie said Alex had called him "Whit."

Maddy put the envelope back in her bag, zipped the bag shut, and sighed. What an insane twenty-four hours it had been. Good thing she had slept most of the time in the air. It was only about this time yesterday when her phone had rung while she was parking the car at the university lot to go teach. It was Liz calling to tell her she'd found Maddy a man. Or as Liz put it, "a live one."

"Are you kidding me?" Maddy had asked nervously, juggling her phone, her sweater, and her book bag. "I only asked you a couple of days ago."

"Listen," Liz answered, "after you made your surprisingly reasonable request, my choices were: *a*, rerun some complicated new study data I've run three times from which I've still found no statistical significance, *b*, mark up a stack of papers for Professor Bundi's grade-obsessed, premed twits, or *c*, work on finding someone to lay you. Which do you think I was going to spend time on?"

"But it's so quick—I don't have anything to wear!"

"Good news, Mad! Last I checked, straight people were still having sex without clothes."

"But who is he?"

"Dutch post-doc at your place," Liz answered like a bus driver announcing a stop. "Political science. Dutch is good, by the way. They teach real sex ed in the Netherlands. Hell, he may know more about your lady parts than you do. Nah. But he'll at least know the difference between a vagina and a vulva. Anyway, I'll pull and send you his publications so you can sniff each other's theses and whatnot."

"But—"

"But, but, but!" Liz scolded her. "Give it a try. If you don't like him, you don't have to do it. I made sure he understood consent."

"What did he want to know about me?"

"You know, the usual—what you research. Academics! We *are* a fucked-up bunch. Oh, and he asked me if you were ugly. I think he thought that's why you are looking for a guy to have sex with."

"Oh, Christ," Maddy answered. "What did you tell him?"

"I told him not to worry, that your face is *completely forgettable.* Which he understood you can't say about a really ugly person."

Maddy agreed with Liz that all that was true.

"I also said you clean up okay. So clean up okay, okay? He's going to be in touch. His name is Maarten. Two a's, the way they do it on the canals of Amsterdam."

There was a pause.

"This is where you say, 'Liz, you are the *best friend* a girl could ever have, and I am so grateful! And, Liz, I'll make him use a condom and I still have my IUD, so you don't need to worry at all!'"

"Liz! You are the most *bat-shit crazy friend ever*, and I *think* I am grateful but I will tell you after I meet this guy. And I still have my IUD, so you don't need to worry *at all* about pregnancy."

"That'll do," Liz replied. "Aren't you late for class?"

"What else did he say?"

"Oh, right," Liz said. "He said 'nothing kinky.' He said it twice. So don't ask for anything kinky."

"What counts?" Maddy asked.

"Mad Girl," Liz laughed, "here's a good rule. If Madeleine Shanks is familiar with something sexual, it probably counts as 'plain vanilla.' That means 'not kinky,' by the way."

Dashing off to teach had let Maddy shift into mental autopilot. Right from the classroom she had to run off to give the public lecture at the big hall they'd arranged, the talk she'd been dreading. But the event had gone okay. She had taken Liz's advice and told the audience outright that she couldn't speak about the trial, joking that she could confirm only *one* thing that had been in the papers. She then came out in front of the podium and executed a fine backflip. While the audience gasped and applauded, she realized she really had to stop wearing her wood-heeled dress boots if she was going to be doing gymnastics at work. . . .

Yes, the talk had worked out okay, all in all. It didn't hurt her feelings about it that Maarten had shown up fifteen minutes before the start time to introduce himself and that he had flirted so pleasantly. Saying it was for good luck, he had offered her a bar of single-varietal chocolate from Tanzania and a bottle of water. The chocolate had come in such evocative wrapping, waxy brown butcher paper tied with twine. And he amused her so when she admitted to him that she felt nauseous with nerves, and he said that she could *not* vomit up the chocolate she had just tasted because Liz had told him to buy it with Maddy's money. It would be so hard to sort out the economic theory of who would ultimately pay for it if *he* had bought it with *her* money but Maddy *consumed* it but then *threw it up*.

"Economics isn't my major field," he had said. "If you keep the chocolate down, my life will be so much simpler."

Then he had pulled out his laptop, telling her he always found that a little dancing before a lecture could shoo away the jitters. He put on ABBA's "Take a Chance on Me," shrugging his shoulders with a smile. Though he was a terrible dancer and had to keep pushing his glasses back up his nose, he did make Maddy feel less overwhelmed. If only Lew had not walked in on them dancing and become immediately determined to find out who this Dutchman was to Maddy.

When Sophie Inskeep had also shown up in the green room five minutes later, it had given Maddy the hope Lew would be distracted in that direction and leave the mystery of Maarten alone. But after greeting Lew warmly, Sophie had told Lew she had to talk to Maddy right away about something confidential and Lew had turned back to Maarten.

While Maddy was overcome by the thought of how much Sophie looked like she could be Everett's younger sister—a similar face to Everett's but with higher cheekbones, roughly the same body shape but flesh that now gave off a feminine whiff of rosemary and baby powder—Sophie told Maddy excitedly that she had called Alex's friend in New York. Liberty Whitaker wanted Maddy to go to New York the very next day, before he had to leave for a long trip. Sophie said they needed Maddy to deliver an envelope Alex had left behind for Mr. Whitaker. And, if she went, Maddy could ask him in person about the piano.

Mr. Whitaker would pay for the trip, Sophie assured Maddy, urging her to go. When Maddy acquiesced, Sophie assured Maddy she would call Whit back right after the lecture and have all the arrangements made.

"You just go give your talk," Sophie had said. "We'll get you to New York in time for dinner tomorrow."

. . .

Once they reached Mr. Whitaker's private club, the driver from Bayshore in the off-the-rack black suit and cap handed Maddy off to a doorman in a uniform that looked like something from the Queen's brigade.

A few steps later, that man handed her off to another fellow standing just inside the door, dressed in a significantly less absurd outfit, something like a black tux.

That man walked her up a few steps to another man, this time a handsomely kept forty-something in a cappuccino-colored wool suit with the kind of shoes Maddy had only ever seen in Europe. He introduced himself as Joseph, the club manager. Maddy noticed that he smelled lightly of clove cigarettes as Joseph asked Maddy if she wished him to store her bag for her. When she answered that she needed to keep her bag with her, he quickly answered, "Of course," as if she had expressed real insight.

They proceeded into a small elevator up one level, down a hall of closed doors, a hall lined with traditional landscape paintings in gold frames, to a private dining room. Upon entry, Maddy quickly made an account of the room: a coffered ceiling; built-in mahogany cabinets and bookcases at either end, the books bound in fabric and leather; a seating area at one end, with two upholstered armchairs facing the windows and a Chesterfield sofa facing back at them, all centered around a heavy coffee table. At the other end of the room, a dining table that could seat six, set for only two, candles not yet lit, fresh flowers including an expensive-looking orchid blossom. Lamps around the room, three of them already switched on to meet the approaching dusk.

She glanced over to the table and mentally noted the number of spoons, forks, and knives at the place settings. She felt grateful that, one rainy Saturday, Sister Mary Grace had schooled her in formal table rituals, reading slowly to Maddy from *Tiffany's Table Manners for Teenagers* as if it were a second catechism, drilling her with a starched cloth napkin and freshly polished silverware.

A small flash of light from outside drew Maddy's eyes to the large window and then to the window seat tucked between two segments of the room's heavy curtains. She realized, with something of a start, that this building overlooked Central Park. How had she not noticed that significant landmark on the way in?

"May I get you a drink, Dr. Shanks? Are you hungry right away?" Joseph asked. "Mr. Whitaker should be here for your dinner in not more than about twenty minutes."

Maddy said she wouldn't mind some water and a snack. She asked which way the bathroom was.

"I'll send someone to show you," Joseph answered. He had, she thought, a remarkable ability to sound warm and distant at the same time. The tone must have been well practiced.

Joseph closed the door behind him, and as Maddy waited for her bathroom escort, she adjusted her bag on her shoulder and straightened the front of her dress with the palms of her hands. She was glad she had guessed correctly what to wear—a simple small-print dress with a cardigan sweater, nude hose, and flats; nothing showy, nothing sloppy. But she felt sure everyone in the building including the staff was wearing something that cost at least ten times her outfit.

Soon a woman in a well-cut black dress and simple pearls came to show her to the bathroom. She told Maddy she was welcome to leave her bag in the dining room, but Maddy again didn't want to leave the bag (not with the envelope signed by Alex inside). They walked down a hallway, and the woman showed her into a lounge that had an anteroom before a suite of several small washrooms. When Maddy came back out to the anteroom, the woman mumbled into a small microphone that Maddy realized was attached to the woman's collar.

"Oh, now I see!" Maddy exclaimed, as this staff member was opening the door of the dining room for Maddy again. "You have to be sure there are no awkward encounters in the hallway or the ladies' room. *Certain people* shouldn't be meeting *certain people*."

Wives who shouldn't be running into mistresses, Maddy thought. The woman smiled conspiratorially at Maddy.

"Dr. Shanks," she said, gesturing toward the coffee table, "here are refreshments for you."

Someone had left a glass of water, a glass of champagne, and a plate of three baguette slices toasted and topped with cream cheese, smoked salmon, capers, and a tiny bit of purple onion. Just enough onion to taste, not enough to make one's breath troubling.

The woman left, closing the door again. Maddy sat down on the sofa and tasted the drink and then the food. The slight sour note of the champagne so perfectly matched the appetizer that the full flavor of the salmon came forward without tasting at all fishy. Last night, Maddy now remembered, the dinner after her public talk had been at a not-bad Thai place with white tablecloths and little votive candles, but by comparison it now seemed a veritable hole-in-the-wall. Lew had arranged the standard post-talk gathering, with him playing host to Maddy and a handful of tenured faculty in allied disciplines. Still trying to figure out who Maarten was to Maddy, Lew had invited Maarten to dinner, and Maarten had turned out to be perfectly un-embarrassing: not showy, deflecting inquiries about his own work to keep the focus on Maddy, asking questions that advanced the conversation, mostly just listening.

They had all walked to dinner from Maddy's lecture and afterwards, to separate from Lew, Maarten asked Maddy if she had a car at the university and might give him a ride to his place. On the short drive, he asked her how she thought her talk had gone, telling her he thought she had given an exceptionally good lecture. She said he was just buttering her up but she liked it just fine. In the parking lot at his place, he had leaned over and kissed her just under her ear, letting out a small moist breath at the end. Her heart had quickened at that airy echo of the kiss. Then he leaned over and kissed her on the lips for about two seconds, just long enough that when he pulled away slowly the skin of her lip tugged at his.

In his apartment, he had put on calming piano jazz, lit some candles, and pulled out a cocktail shaker, mixing various fluids with some fresh-squeezed lime juice and ice.

"Hey," she had asked, "you're not going to be disappointed in me if we don't—"

"I am *already* not disappointed," he said, pouring the drink through the ice strainer into two martini glasses. "Your company and the company of your colleagues at dinner has already been most welcome in a week when all I've done is toil alone. Whatever you'd like to do or not do is fine with me. I only gave you a bar of chocolate, remember."

"And a bottle of water," she corrected him.

"True. Although I'll get reimbursed through Liz for the chocolate and maybe even the water. The little dancing before your talk was free—no charge. But wait! Professor Meadows bought you *dinner*! So, if you think someone buying you dinner means you owe them sex, that would be *him*. Now that I think of it, he also bought *me* dinner! Maybe I had better call him now and settle up? A threesome."

"He'd much rather have you than me, as I'm sure you picked up," she giggled.

Maarten handed her one of the martini glasses, the sides already slippery from condensation. He said he couldn't remember what it was officially called, so he was calling it "Divestiture."

"Because," he said, "I find I divest from work as soon as I drink it. What else can I give you?"

. . .

The ringing of Maddy's cell phone brought her back to consciousness, to the realization that she had a glass of champagne in her hand and was in New York, sitting on a window seat on the Upper East Side. Mr. Whittaker had still not shown up. She pulled the phone out of her bag and saw that it was Hank. She had not seen or thought of him since spotting him at her big lecture yesterday. There, five rows away from her, he had looked so off.

"Hi," she answered awkwardly, feeling a bit as if Maarten's kisses were still on her lips. "What's up?"

"Can I come talk to you?" he asked.

She told him that she wasn't in town. When he asked where she was, she didn't answer.

"Well, listen," he said. "Something is bothering me. I don't know why I didn't think of it before. Apparently, well, apparently when Alex died, she was wearing the necklace I had given her. Scott gave it back to me a couple of days later, as I told you. He gave it back to me when the coroner gave it to him. The coroner gave it to him along with the other jewelry she was wearing—two rings and a bracelet. I called Scott today and he told me that I had remembered that all right."

"So?"

"Well—and I don't know why I didn't think of this before—it doesn't make sense."

Maddy thought he was now sounding just like Scott had in his office: *It doesn't make sense.* Were they purposefully both using this line in coordination, a line they maybe knew was attractive bait to her mental fish? She squirmed a little.

101

"Alex always took off all of her jewelry before she went swimming," Hank continued. "Did it consistently after she lost a necklace she loved, a necklace a former student had given her, when she went swimming spontaneously in a river when we were out on a day trip. She was so upset about having not thought to take it off and having lost it forever. I bought her that special necklace later, after that, when I figured out that was the kind of thing she liked. And after that, she always made a point of taking off *all* her jewelry before she went swimming. To not lose anything ever again. Even if she'd been drinking or whatever—even if she was swimming without much warning, like she sometimes did, even in her clothes—she'd take off all her jewelry. Like a ritual."

"Perhaps she was distracted and just forgot before . . . before she died?" Maddy asked, sitting up straighter at what Hank was saying. The ghost of Maarten had been suddenly shooed away with this information, down the hall and past the gold-framed pastoral scenes.

"Look. It doesn't make sense," Hank said again. "What would have been so distracting? She always took her jewelry off before swimming—even if she kept on her clothes. And at that time of year, she would have been wearing her warmest wet suit. It was still cold. So why . . . ?"

"I don't know, Hank. How would I know?"

She wondered if she sounded too unsympathetic.

There was a soft knock, and the door of the dining room started to open.

"I'm sorry," Maddy said, "I have to go now. I'll call you soon?"

She hung up and stood.

It turned out to be a waiter come to check on whether she needed anything more. She politely declined.

After closing the door, Maddy sat back down in the window seat and looked out. People were walking in and out of the park, some rapidly, others lazily, one older woman pushing a double stroller of two children, and next to her a dog walker with five or six charges getting tangled up with each other. . . .

What had Alex been wearing? Maddy wondered, trying to come up with a logical answer for Hank, the way she had always tried since she was a girl to come up with a logical answer to "it doesn't make sense," to stave off those annoying familial appeals to divine intervention.

Surely, if one put on a wetsuit, one noticed one's jewelry in the process, at least bracelets and necklaces. They would get caught on the tight collar and arms of the suit otherwise. You'd notice a necklace and bracelets. Did Alex not wear a full bodysuit that day? When she wore a full suit to swim, did she drive to the lake already wearing it?

Maddy tried to slow down and picture the process. But it just raised more questions. Did Alex wear a bathing cap, or a suit with a hood, particularly when it was cold? Had Alex been in the habit of changing to her suit at home, changing to street clothes before getting back into her car?

Suddenly Maddy pictured Alex's car.

The car Maddy had left at the Minneapolis airport in long-term parking earlier that day.

The car where Maddy had been kissed last night by Maarten.

That was the car Maddy had been driving around for weeks without thinking about the fact that Alex must have been driving it just before she died.

How was it she had stepped into all these places Alex had been—her classrooms, her car, her study, her kitchen, her garage, her bath—without thinking about those moments that must have existed in the hours before her unexpected ending? Had Alex, too, had dinner with Liberty Whitaker IV in this particular dining room just a few days before she died? Had she sat on this very window seat waiting for Whit to arrive, the way Maddy now was?

What was Maddy doing here?

She had resolved to *ignore* Scott's request to ascertain how Alex had died. Yet because of what Alex's ex-husband had said to her, somehow now she was sitting here, waiting for Whitaker. Whitaker—Alex's secret lover who was in turn waiting for Maddy to deliver a letter to him that had been kept quiet for months for no apparent reason by Alex's odd friend Everett Sophie. (Why hadn't Everett Sophie gotten Whitaker this letter sooner?) And now with Hank, Alex's other lover-of-sorts, calling her to say what Alex was wearing at death didn't make sense.

What the hell was she doing, triangulating spaces between all these irregular relationships in Alex's life? Driving her car and teaching her classes and . . . how had she let this happen? Why was she trying to answer all these people's questions about Alex?

Suddenly her mind flooded with what she knew was a completely irrational thought—but there it was, taking over her mind like a tsunami meeting a flood plain—that Wilhelm, not Whitaker, was going to come in next and close the door behind him. That she had misunderstood the names from Sophie—Wilhelm, Whitaker. Or that Everett Sophie had set her up. That Maddy had been sent by Everett Sophie to *Wilhelm.*

And who would know that she was there?

Her heart was pounding so, it felt almost audible. Her mind was summoning Wolf, but it was the useless Wolf of the dream where she was yelling to him for help from the street, but he could not hear her through his painted-shut, third-floor bedroom window and his comatose sleep.

She stood up and put the champagne glass and the plate of crumbs on the dining table. She threw her bag strap over her shoulder and headed to the door. She flung it open. And she found herself facing not the blanched face of Dr. Wilhelm but the somewhat reddened face of an unfamiliar man who was wiping one eye and then the other with a handkerchief.

"Ms. Shanks?" he asked. "Forgive me—*Dr.* Shanks? I am Liberty Whitaker."

Chapter 11

"Forgive me," Whitaker said again as he stepped into the dining room and closed the door. He put his handkerchief in the pocket of his pants and gave a hard sniff, his nose wrinkling up momentarily. "I've kept you waiting so long you were going to leave?"

He took Maddy's bag from her and put it down in a corner.

"No, no. That isn't it," she said, her heart still racing. "I was just spooked by something."

"This place can feel a bit like a well-appointed insane asylum," Whitaker replied, sighing and gesturing for her to sit down on the settee. He waited for Maddy to be seated and then settled himself into an armchair facing her. Joseph appeared with a tumbler of what looked like Scotch or bourbon for Whitaker and a fresh glass of champagne for Maddy. This time the champagne had two crushed raspberries in it and a moistened mint leaf folded over the edge of the glass. Intrigued by this unfamiliar concoction, Maddy looked up at Joseph, but he did not meet her eye.

"Give us ten minutes or so?" Whitaker asked.

Joseph nodded and was gone as silently as he had come, taking Maddy's empty plate and glass.

Maddy breathed deeply for a moment to bring her heart back to normal. Then she tried the cocktail, figuring she was supposed to drink the champagne over the mint. The leaf was lemon-flavored and it shocked the taste of the champagne. The drifting flavor of the raspberry soon followed. It was weird and delightful and Maddy gave off a shaky smile at the novelty of these flavors and textures. She had to struggle a little not to get the mint stuck to her lips, and she wasn't sure what to do about the raspberries. She finally fished her pinky into the drink to pull one raspberry out and ate it.

"Is this the drink Alex liked?" she asked Whitaker, putting it down and looking at it curiously.

"No," he said, furrowing his brow. "I don't know why Joseph brought you that if you didn't ask for it. Why would anyone do that to perfectly good champagne? Alex usually took gin and tonic, with extra lime."

Maddy remembered Hank had said the same thing about her preference. So, Alex hadn't changed her drink as she shifted situations. It seemed by all accounts that she was always who she was.

Maddy lifted the glass and took another sip, wondering if this drink had been delivered to her in error. But this didn't seem like the kind of place where staff made any errors. She ended up with the second raspberry in her mouth, which meant she suddenly had to chew while drinking, and then the mint got stuck to her lip and she had to pull it in with her tongue rather like a cat eating up the last bits of a mouse. She must look pretty stupid, she thought.

Whitaker just watched her and waited for her to finish the clumsy maneuver. Then he asked, "What spooked you?"

Maddy wasn't sure how to answer and said nothing.

"No matter," he soon said. "How was your trip?"

She said it had been fine. She added, feeling that she was supposed to supply some details, that she'd slept most of the way on the plane and that the driver had had to come via Brooklyn from JFK because the Midtown Tunnel was blocked with an accident.

The small talk quickly felt ridiculous. So she just said it:

"This small talk feels ridiculous."

"Yes," he answered. "It *is* ridiculous."

106

He leaned back and took a sip of his drink.

"One of the things I loved about Alex was that she had absolutely no use for small talk. Of course, it was also one of the frightening things about her. No small talk. All big talk."

He looked past her for a moment, towards the window.

"How did you meet her?"

"In the Hamptons," Whitaker answered, "ten summers ago. My wife and I were at a formal late-afternoon garden party, some fundraiser—*one of the cancers*, as Alex would have said. She used to say that without the cancers there would be no summer season for my set. One of the other guests brought her."

"As a date?" Maddy asked, knowing that would have been when Scott and Alex were married.

"Oh, no, no," Whitaker said. He took another sip of his drink. "She was married at the time. She was out on the island visiting an ancient mentor of hers, a woman whose extended family had an old, small house next door to the party. One of the men got drunk and wandered over to the property where Alex was staying. Alex was outside doing some gardening for her friend. Trimming the roses. The drunk fellow got into a conversation with Alex. She told me later that he asked her if she could foxtrot and, when she said she could, he brought her back to the party."

He took another sip and sighed.

"I remember it well. She was wearing frumpy olive-green gardening pants and the kind of loose long-sleeve shirt that keeps mosquitoes off, and an electric-blue straw hat that was obviously borrowed from her friend because it was too big for her head. Her dirty gardening gloves were hanging out of her back pants' pocket. Everyone else was in formal wear. So, this man fox-trotted a bit with Alex until he fell and banged his head. When others were attending to him, I asked her if she'd like me to walk her back, and she said yes, that she felt horribly overdressed."

He chewed the inside of his cheek a little at the memory.

"I was myself quite relieved to get out of that scene. We ended up going for a walk. Talking. And one thing led to another."

"But never to more than this?" As soon as Maddy said it, she realized what that sounded like—that Whitaker had simply used Alex for casual sex. Which she'd meant, but perhaps not meant to say. "I mean . . ."

"You mean we became lovers. And nobody knew. Right. Honestly, we were both fine with that."

"*Was* Alex really fine with that? For ten years? Even after her divorce?"

Whitaker leaned forward and put his drink down. He clasped his hands together, his elbows resting on his knees, and looked at Maddy intensely.

"I suppose there's no reason for you to take my word for it, Madeleine." It sounded, as intended, like a dressing down of a child. "But Ally was fine with it. She never asked for more. Rather, I would say that she never asked for something *else*, nor did I. It wasn't more or less than what else each of us had in the rest of our lives. It was just a separate relationship in our lives, one that existed on a different pace, in a different place. We saw each other every few months. We talked more frequently than that."

"So, when she left Scott, it wasn't for you?" He shook his head. "Why did she, then? Why did she divorce Scott?"

"I would not feel right telling you that," he said.

Maddy wondered why no one wanted to tell her the cause of Alex and Scott's divorce. Not Hank, not Everett, not Whitaker. She could presume that if she asked Scott, he wouldn't tell her either.

"I can just tell you she didn't leave him for me."

A soft knock came on the door and Whitaker indicated the person could enter. The waiter from earlier came in and set down a tray. He lit the candles on the table and set down two bowls of soup and a silver basket of bread. He poured water from a pitcher and wine from a decanter into the glasses set at the table, and then he left. Whitaker motioned to Maddy to sit at the table in the place that faced the window. He sat at the end of the table, just to her right.

"You have an odd background, Dr. Shanks, if I may say so."

She tasted the soup. It was creamed and made from a base vegetable she could not place, something like a potato that had crossed with a sweet sort of radish. She tasted it again.

"What is it?" she asked him. "What's the main vegetable?"

He tasted it.

"Sunchoke, I should think."

"What is sunchoke?"

"It's a kind of root, I think. It's also called a Jerusalem artichoke."

She made a mental note, trying not to eat it too quickly. Then she thought about what he'd said before she asked about the soup.

"Hang on. What do you know about my background?" she asked, tilting her head in a gesture of curiosity.

"You mean besides the matter of the alleged murders in Philadelphia?"

She nodded.

"You're an orphan, no surviving family. You had one sibling, a sister, but she is not surviving. You are single—never married—and twenty-six years old. You started attending Georgetown University at age seventeen. Finished up in three years, then on to graduate school at Indiana University. You earned your PhD in history of medicine, rather quickly. Particularly considering the discovery of the murders."

"History of medicine and science," she corrected him, sitting up a little taller. "Not history of medicine. History of medicine and science. How did you know all of that?"

"I'm a senior partner at a sizable law firm," he said. "It isn't very difficult for me to have staff look these things up."

"I see." She tucked back into the soup. She was trying to place the flavor of the tiny bits of chopped green on the top. Marjoram? Greek oregano?

"You seem to have no history before Georgetown, Madeleine. I find that curious."

"On the contrary," she said to him, licking her lips. "I had *too much* history before Georgetown. Got rid of it, best I could."

She ate another spoonful of soup.

"And you grew up on Long Island, but you have no accent, hmm?"

"I have always felt as if I didn't really come from there," she said. "I think that's why I never picked up the accent. It wasn't my place."

"How did your parents and your sister perish, if I may ask? I know they all died on the same day. When you were fifteen."

"Car crash," Maddy answered, putting down her spoon and taking a sip of wine. Another perfect pairing, like the salmon and champagne. She closed her eyes for a minute to taste it all better. "And yes, that's right, they all died together, all on the same day."

"I'm sorry," Whitaker said.

She realized with some embarrassment that he must have thought she had closed her eyes out of grief over her family, not out of the pleasure of the food and drink. She cleared her throat and opened her eyes.

"It was a long time ago now. My sister was seventeen. To be honest, it settled some things in my life that would have taken longer to resolve."

He looked surprised at her blunt response.

"And where did you go from there?"

"Is that part missing in the records?" she asked, genuinely curious. "My people didn't look all that deeply."

"I was shipped off to a convent. In West Virginia. I didn't have other family to go to. But there was another issue that made them want to send me away—you know, the way the convent used to happen to young women who were social problems? A very medieval maneuver."

"You were pregnant?"

"Fortunately, no," she answered, drinking the last of the wine in her glass, realizing she had probably imbibed it faster than was polite. "Just deflowered. I thought I might be pregnant at the end there, but then my period came on, *oh blessed blood*."

She laughed darkly and low for a moment.

"I was so underweight, I wasn't properly developed, my cycle was completely irregular back then. So I wasn't too horribly worried about pregnancy, but at the end there . . . well, there was a delay that had me nervous. But it was probably just a reaction to the deaths. Threw my cycle off more than usual."

"Who was it?"

She took another sip of the soup. She thought she could taste a hint of curry. Perhaps just cumin.

"Hmm?"

"Who would have gotten you pregnant?"

"Oh. My gymnastics coach. He'd started in on me when I was twelve. Fucking me outright when I was thirteen. My father had just found out, and he was on his way to kill him or something, with my mother and my sister in tow, when he crashed the car. I had refused to go. He never made it there. I don't think he did it on purpose—the crash? Because I'm pretty sure he was planning to come back and kill *me* after that."

She sighed.

"I don't mean *kill* in the literal sense. But you know. He blamed me as much as The Jerk. I knew that's what he was going to think when he found out. That I was responsible. I just didn't think he'd ever find out before I'd grown and left the house."

"And what happened to The Jerk?"

Maddy looked Whitaker in the eyes. They were a muddy brown, his hair a sandy blond mixed with some grey, his skin darkened by the end of a summer tan, his eyebrows perfectly neatened up by someone. He was the kind of middle-aged man who would have looked quite ordinary but was instead handsome from so many years of being among the rich and the attended. His teeth were perfect, his skin was healthy, his hair was trimmed just so. He looked like someone had shaved him not thirty minutes before.

"Nothing," she finally answered.

"*Nothing* happened to that man?"

"Well, maybe not *nothing*. I became friends with a police detective—you know, the deal with the mess in Philadelphia. He learned of it through me, and he told some of his colleagues. They said they'd let me know if they needed help with a prosecution. I wasn't clear on the statute of limitations and all that. I didn't want to deal with it. So, I didn't really ask."

She played for a moment with the soft wax that had formed on one of the candles.

"I—I had trouble dealing with it. My policeman friend knew that. Sometimes you just have to carry on with your life, you know? Let other people handle some things? A serial murderer seemed more worthy of my attention at that point in my life—far more interesting, not so dull as a jerk fucking a young girl. It was something new I could research—the possibility of these murders—not something I already knew plenty about."

She pulled her finger away and peeled off the tab of wax that had adhered to her fingertip. She tucked the bit under the edge of her soup bowl.

"Anyway, yes, he had been a teacher and the gymnastics coach at the school, the Catholic school where my parents had sent me and my sister. And, well, you know the Church, well, the Church doesn't appreciate girls—or boys, for that matter—causing sexual scandal. It's considered *bad behavior* by the children. So, I was sent off, just after the funerals, presumably to not complicate matters further with the revelation of what he had been up to with me. That would have gotten out, I think. It would have caused the school and the Church *difficulties*. It would have added to anti-Catholic sentiments in the general populace. The things they worried about."

She cleared her throat briefly.

"So, I was packed off. Sister Ann Marie, it was, who came. I remember, she brought an egg salad sandwich for me, and it wasn't smelling so good by the time I ate it. But I was hungry, so I ate it. I don't know what happened to my parents' house, but my impression was it was mortgaged to the hilt, so presumably it went to the bank. Maybe you know?"

He shook his head. She took a drink of water and stuck her finger back into the soft wax.

"Like I said, it resolved some things earlier than otherwise."

She pulled her finger back and again peeled off the wax, adding the new bit to the last bit under the bowl's rim.

"The nuns' convent was in West Virginia?"

"Yes," Maddy answered, "in the middle of nowhere. I found it basically agreeable as a situation. Green hills, big storms. Nice change of scenery. And it felt like a fortress, which was what I needed right about then. They were Dominicans. The order that brought us the Inquisition, you know."

She twirled the empty wine glass in her hand, hoping he'd notice it was empty and give her some of his. He didn't.

"Anyway, I essentially home-schooled myself there, alongside a couple of equally pathetic girls for whom I didn't much care. I had a reputation of being 'cold.' That was useful because it meant I didn't have to try to be warm."

She gave up on the glass and dabbed the napkin at the corner of her mouth, where she thought she felt a little soup.

"When I was turning seventeen, I wrote to the Jesuits at Georgetown and asked them to save me from Dominican life. I told them I was a social liberal and an orphan, which I was. They admitted me with a full scholarship that fall. I also told them, quite frankly, that I was a hopeless atheist in desperate need of liberation from a convent. Jesuits, they respond to these things as a kind of metaphysical challenge. I suggested in my letter that if I ever grew rich from the billboard I was about to fully inherit at age eighteen—my entire inheritance, a stupid billboard that produces a few thousand a year—I would leave them my billboard upon my death, in exchange for taking care of me now. And I said I might be good enough for the gymnastics team. The sisters had managed to get me a little equipment to keep my gymnastic skills up. They seemed to think it would keep me out of more trouble or something. Sister Mary Grace learned the basics of the sport to give me help. She *read* about it. I had no idea until then that there were *books* on gymnastics! What a waste of paper and ink."

She took a sip of water and adjusted the napkin on her lap.

"Anyhow, apparently that letter I sent to Georgetown was good enough to get me in the door. I didn't have too much trouble proving myself after that. I work hard, and I'm smart. I finished fast—in three years—because I didn't dare not finish before the funding ran out. From there, it was on to a funded fellowship at Indiana. I made sure I'd have funding for graduate school before I graduated from Georgetown. Now I have this two-year deal at Minnesota. So far, so good. And this meal and this trip is costing me nothing. Except airport parking in Minneapolis. So far, quite good, I guess."

Whitaker blinked several times.

Maddy looked to the small silver basket of bread on the table. She took a piece, smeared some butter on it, and ate it. The crumb was of sourdough and the butter sweet. She noted how it caused her salivary glands to wince a little.

He kept looking at her and blinking.

Soon the waiter knocked and took away the soup bowls, spoons, and wine glasses—Maddy hastily threw the bit of wax into her bowl—and brought in the next course. Maddy looked down at the artistic plate: in the center, half of some small bird, the skin perfectly browned and glistening, and on the side what looked like some kind of exotic rice, plus a bouquet of colorful vegetables, drizzled in an aromatic sauce. The waiter poured a different wine in fresh glasses.

"Do you want that envelope now? From Alex?" Maddy asked Whitaker.

He shook his head.

"Okay then, my turn," Maddy said, as the waiter was leaving. She waited until the door was shut. "What was Alex like in bed?"

Whitaker looked surprised but did not immediately answer. He watched Maddy as she dug into the dinner. She let out a gentle moan at the flavor, took a sip of the new wine, and moaned quietly again. This could well be the best meal she had ever eaten out. It might even be as good as anything Wolf had ever made for her at home in Philly, though it was hard to tell because she so much preferred his company to Whitaker. Wolf didn't just blink at her. He advised her in his heavy way; he listened to her in a way that almost scared her; he laughed at her unintentional jokes. He didn't just blink.

"Come on. What was Alex like in bed?"

"She was a lover like you are an eater," he answered, after another moment's thought. "Enthusiastic. Inquisitive." He paused. "Sometimes joyful, sometimes deadly serious, fast, slow. As everything else with her, she was unpredictable. Frighteningly, wonderfully unpredictable."

Maddy chewed and swallowed and pointed her fork slightly at him.

"Were you worried your wife would find out?"

"No," Whitaker answered. "It wouldn't have made any difference. We have a French marriage."

Maddy asked him what he meant.

"Our marriage isn't about some girlish romantic fantasy. We merged two old families when we married—two wealthy, established families. We are raising three fine children together. She supports my career, and I support her very significant charity work. A great number of people rely on us, and we take that responsibility very seriously. It doesn't matter if there are other . . . relationships. We would each always be careful not to embarrass each other with an affair—neither of us would take such a risk. Which is one reason I love her. We have a mutual respect that is very deep."

Maddy wasn't sure what to say to all that. He made it sound very noble. But she couldn't help but hear it as an arrangement of the kind wealthy people primarily make to keep their money secure. Just the sort of thing she had heard about at Georgetown from the pre-weds, sent to school to marry Catholics of the right class. Their families set up foundations that looked charitable but gave their children jobs and gave the parents big tax deductions. Her boyfriend at Georgetown had explained it all to her.

She tried to think of a question that would get at what she was wondering about Whitaker's relationship with Alex. She wanted to know if Alex was comfortable being a mistress. It finally came to her.

"Did you show Alex recent pictures of your children when you saw her?"

"Yes," he said, raising his eyebrows. "She always asked after each of them, by name. She used to recommend to me books she thought they would each enjoy. She was often right. Sometimes she brought the books with her, so I could deliver them as if they were gifts from me."

Whitaker's phone rang and he apologized that he had to step out for just a minute. She wasn't sure whether she should continue eating while he was gone, so she just dabbled her finger in the sauce and licked it. Tarragon? She wanted to tell Wolf about the dish in the hopes he could recreate it for her sometime.

Seeing no sign of Whitaker coming back, to stop herself from gobbling up her dinner before his return, she took her glass of wine and went back to the window seat, looking out at the park and the paths that wound their way in. She wondered to herself if she could be satisfied in a marriage like the Whitakers'. But then she wondered how she could ever be satisfied in a marriage, period.

The night before with Maarten had been . . . Well, no wonder Alex had sought a more expensive version of the same. Maddy remembered how Maarten had kissed his way down her neck, right to her manubrium, the top of the sternum. When she had asked him with a false pout as to why he had stopped there, he had said that that was as far as he could go before reaching the fabric of her shirt. So she had undone one button, and then another, and another, as he kept kissing his way down. (How good she had chosen a front-closure bra for the day, purely by chance.) At some point, he asked her if she wanted to die with her boots on—*la petite mort*, he clarified—and she could only just mumble a "yes, *shut up*, yes," before he had used his lips and his fingers to—

Whitaker came back in and she stood up. Her face flushed red and, seeing it, he looked confused. He apologized and said he didn't expect an interruption to happen again. They sat back down at the table, and she took a belly breath to bring the blood back to her head. She tucked back into the bird and laughed silently a little at herself.

"I don't quite understand something, Madeleine," he said to her, as he watched her eat. "How is it you've come to live in Alex's house? My staff told me your current home address. It is Ally's house."

"Yes," Maddy said, licking a bit of sauce off her lips. Wolf had told her once that French tarragon was different from American tarragon; maybe that's why she couldn't quite figure out if this *was* the flavor of tarragon. Or it was enhanced with something else. Fresh coriander? "Scott offered me Alex's house as a place to stay. I took it."

"Scott offered you her job *and* her house?"

"Well, a temporary replacement for her job. And a temporary place to live, yes."

"Why did you take the house?"

Maddy thought for a second.

"Um, *free housing*?" she replied, as though she thought the answer was obvious. "Although I have to pay the utilities. I hope it isn't too cold a winter. I don't want to be too cold."

"So, if someone offers you a free place to stay, you just take it?"

"You mean like tonight, when you're buying me a hotel room?" She paused. "Yes."

He cleared his throat at the awkward observation.

"You *are* buying me a hotel room tonight, yes? I haven't got any place else to stay."

"It's all arranged," he assured her. "The staff here will get you there."

"Well, listen, when you've had a life like mine, and someone offers you shelter you don't have to pay for, your instinct is to just say 'yes.' I realize you've not had a life like mine. I tend to take free housing, free transportation, and free food. Definitely free books, if they're any good. I sometimes take free shoes, too."

"I'm sorry," he said, embarrassed.

She asked him what he was sorry about.

"It's not," she added, "as if I have been poor and you have been rich because you've personally set it up that way."

"I meant I am sorry I hadn't thought about your position."

"If only I had *cancer*," she said, laughing at him, "then you would have thought of my *position*."

He let out a sarcastic laugh at her impetuousness.

"Hey, where are you putting me up?"

"My secretary made the reservation," he answered. "She will have conveyed it to Joseph. I presume it is the Ritz Carlton. That's the usual place."

Maddy let out a sort of soft whistle. She nearly asked if breakfast would be included. But then she realized she wanted to know something else more.

"Can I ask you something?"

"Can you stop yourself?" he replied.

"Did you go swimming with Alex? Like in the Hamptons?"

"Yes," he said, squinting his eyes to bring the memory back to focus. "The evening I met her, she told me she was planning to swim around midnight, because there was going to be a full moon. She asked me if I felt like meeting up with her. So, I did."

"What happened?"

"It was incredible," he said. "In fact, it was so incredible, I had trouble even paying attention to Alex. You don't realize how dark the ocean is until the sun is gone and you are in it. The whitecaps were so white in the trace of moonlight. I was lost in the night ocean, not even talking to her. She was nearby, but I was just lost in the night ocean wonder. But she didn't mind that. She appreciated that I found myself wanting this ocean more than her at that moment. I think she felt like someone else understood. Someone else understood the water."

Maddy noticed he was holding his gold wedding ring on his outstretched finger just over the candle, staring at the flame. He pulled it up when the ring grew too hot.

"Understood the water?" Maddy asked.

Whitaker took a drink of his wine and set it back down.

"How much do you know of Alex Shugar's scholarship, Dr. Shanks?"

"Pretend I know nothing. Tell me what you were going to say."

"People in her field—your field?—they had been writing at that point for years about the social construction of the body. About how the body was understood differently in different social circumstances. The eyes, the mind, the womb, the—"

"The clitoris," Maddy said, being a little tipsy and thinking of Alex's work and of Maarten simultaneously. "Lots of people have written that, about the clitoris."

"Yes, that, too."

He tapped his water glass.

"Well, Ally knew it was true that how we think about our bodies is partly determined by cultural beliefs. *Of course* that's true. Rather obvious. Like beliefs about skin color. Cultural beliefs persist, and they matter. But she felt they had all gone so far overboard, the people in her field, claiming that everything we believed about the body, *everything we experienced about flesh*, was culturally determined. And in her life—in her own life, as in her scholarship—she wanted to get back to physical reality. *To flesh.* She wanted to *get back to flesh.* So she sought the sensual. She wanted to remember—to make other people remember—the unmitigated sensations of the flesh. That there's more than words. That there's skin, and nerves, and sweat. Life. That there's pleasurable life before death."

He drank more wine, leaned his head back, and looked at the ceiling.

"Swimming in the ocean at midnight under the moon. . . . She asked me afterwards what I had felt. I told her. The seaweed brushes up against your skin, the salt splashes up into your nostrils, the roar of the waves comes and goes like—well, like a threat. Like a thrilling threat. There's the pull of the undercurrent, the sand scraping against your skin, your eyes picking off the whitecaps—"

"Sensual. Yes."

"It was kind of like I had just discovered sex all over again," he said, as if Maddy had not spoken. "Like I was seventeen again. Only it was the ocean, not a woman. I had never truly *felt* the ocean. And all that time I had been near it, and on it, and in it. I had seen it. Smelled it. Tasted it. But I had never *felt* it. Alex brought me the ocean."

They both sat very still. After a few minutes, the waiter knocked and came in, removing the dinner course. Maddy asked Whitaker what was coming next.

"A salad, I expect."

Whitaker refilled her water glass from the pitcher as the waiter worked around them, indeed bringing a plate of salad for each of them. Maddy tried to figure out visually what the components were before she tasted them. The waiter departed.

"Did *you* discover sex again?" Whitaker asked. "I mean, you don't—if you don't mind my saying it—you don't come across as a frigid, damaged girl. The way you eat and talk suggests that, like Alex, you live rather sensually."

Maddy chuckled at his observation.

"There was nothing good to eat at the convent. There was nothing good to eat before that, either. Except the fried dough at the church fairs. Dusted with powdered sugar, that sort of melted into a sugary cream if they put it on when the dough was just out of the oil. And there were sometimes wild raspberries in the sump behind our house."

She took a piece of the ribbon of cheese sitting atop of the salad and smelled it to try to figure out what it was. Made from goat's milk, she thought.

"Manchego?" she asked him, and he said he wasn't sure.

She nibbled and swallowed. The taste of the cheese stayed in her mouth like a spirit, then disappeared after a moment.

"At Georgetown, the Jesuits gave us pretty good wine and pretty good cheese. And I found myself a good therapist there, with a little help from the admissions officer who had shepherded me in. The therapist, she was very pragmatic. Her attitude was that I didn't need to feel that my whole life was determined by my parents and my first sexual experience, particularly when I hadn't chosen any of that. She encouraged me to do what I had done to get there—make choices about what to do, take risks, not feel weighted or stuck in the past."

"So what did she tell you to do *sexually?*"

Maddy tried a forkful of the salad. The bitter greens were offset by what seemed to be pomegranate seeds. And the dressing—an orange essence there? Blood orange, with some rind? She swallowed and followed it with a little water.

"She suggested I masturbate."

She was now smiling at Whitaker, because what could you do but smile when telling a man whom you didn't know such a thing? Maddy saw him turn a little red.

"I hadn't really *thought* about it. But once she made the suggestion, and I *thought* about it, I thought it a *very good idea.*" She tapped the back of his hand with her index finger in rhythm with her words: "And then I found myself *thinking* on it a lot. I became quite an intellectual!"

She laughed with a silly smile, and Whitaker laughed, too.

"Somehow, I still managed to graduate. That poor therapist at Georgetown, mind you, because of where she was, she was dealing with almost nothing but repressed Catholics. So, she was very good at helping with sex. I wasn't a repressed Catholic. I wasn't either of those things by that point—repressed or Catholic. I was just a confused mass of unfettered teenage thinking. So, it was pretty easy for her to help me out of the sex hole. She helped me see I had nothing to be ashamed of; I had not exactly chosen to have sex with The Jerk. I mean, when it was going on, I had sometimes been pleased by the thought of doing something that would make my father crazy with anger. And I was sometimes satisfied in the thought that it proved there was no god, because what kind of god lets that kind of thing happen to a girl? So, The Jerk was helpful in being proof of my personal theology. But I had nothing to be feel guilty about, of that the therapist was clear. And of that, I became clear."

Maddy picked up a piece of the salad greens with her fingers, ate it, and licked the bit of dressing from the tips of her fingers.

"That therapist, she made sure I knew that everyone makes a bunch of sexual mistakes on the way to the main part of life. That meant I didn't worry so much when things didn't go like I planned. I stumbled. I just reminded myself she said that's what everyone does. Stumbling is part of normal sexual development, she said. So I could be normal." She paused. "I mean, not that I'm *normal*. But you know. Normal-*ish*."

She noticed Whitaker was looking at her in a way that suggested he was feeling sorry for her. She couldn't quite put her finger on it, but he looked suddenly paternalistic. She found herself impatient. He was obviously approaching her in the typical way—a man feeling protective of a damaged girl, as if these were the proper roles.

"Listen," she said, in a firm and slightly angry voice. "I realized something, along the way—that anyone I were to tell my story to about The Jerk, they wanted me to be a permanently damaged little thing. Well, everyone except the therapist. My being a permanently damaged piece of discarded sexual trash would somehow serve *their* sense of justice—their *need* for justice."

He looked at her confused. She went on.

"They could believe that even if The Jerk were never brought to justice, by leaving me horribly damaged, *their* world would still make sense. Evil must beget permanent harm! An evil man like him must lead to a permanently damaged girl! I must be a permanent wreck. Only good experiences beget *well* people. So I had to be a mess because that made them feel good. It fit their stories."

She wanted to stand up and do a handstand, but she resisted.

"Well," Maddy continued, "you know what? I didn't need to be sacrificed to other people's senses of justice that way. I didn't need to be permanently harmed just so they could feel like they could trust the world's moral mechanisms of evil begetting harm. Fuck that. So, I mostly just didn't tell people what had happened. And I moved on with my life, including my sexual life, as if I still had myself. I don't tell most people. And not because I am ashamed. I am not ashamed. I am not ashamed."

She drank a little more wine.

"Because I did still have myself, after it all. The first guy—I mean the *next* guy I slept with, when I was eighteen, I just told him I'd had a little experience previously, not the best. He was in the same class as me, we were both second-years then, and he was nice. He was not a jerk. He was a clunky lover, but I was also a clunky lover, and he really tried, and he was *nice*. And now I hear he's becoming a priest. Which I don't take at all personally."

She ate more of the salad and asked him why he wasn't eating his.

"I don't know," he said. "It's just a lot to hear from a young woman—a young person. And I think—I think the way you talk, you are making me miss Ally. You are like her in the way you talk. You just say what you want to say. Like her, you have your own ideas about justice. But you are here, not her, because she is really gone."

His eyes welled, and a tear fell from his left eye. Maddy put her fork down.

"Do you want that letter now? I mean the envelope?"

"No," he said, "not yet."

She wondered why. What was in it? Did he know and not want to deal with it? Did he not want to know? She had to know.

"You saw her a few days before?" Maddy asked, putting her right hand on his left. "How did she seem? Did she ask you for anything?"

She listened to herself and wondered if she was being kind to him, or if she was simply prying to get information, or if she was just covering up for embarrassing herself momentarily for having said all that she had said about her own sexual history. He pulled out his handkerchief with his right hand and wiped his eyes one at a time. He put the cloth back in his pocket.

"Yes, she was here for a visit a few days before she died. She noted we had been together ten years," he said. "Of all things, out of the blue, she asked me for a baby."

He chuckled and looked like he was going to cry again.

"What?! A baby?"

"A baby grand." He smiled. "A piano. A funny request, but I figured why not. She went to Steinway on that trip and picked one out. Only she selected a grand, not a baby grand. I paid for it anyway. I loved her. I was so grateful to her."

"It arrived a few days ago."

"Did it?" he said, his eyes widening. "I suppose you weren't expecting it."

"That's putting it mildly." She took a drink of water.

Whitaker asked what Scott had said about it.

"I haven't told him. I suppose I have to, but I'm not sure what to tell him. Do you know why Alex wanted a piano?"

"No," Whitaker said. "She didn't volunteer an explanation, and I was afraid to ask. I knew she didn't play, and I knew Hank doesn't play—I know Hank stays at her place sometimes, just to crash there. She told me that. So when she asked about the piano, I asked her if he played. She said no. So, who was going to play it? I was a little worried she was about to move on from our relationship with someone new. And—well, honestly, in bed she seemed different on that trip. Like maybe there was someone else? Almost as if she was thinking about someone else? But after all those years of meeting up, it was the least I could do. So, I gave her the baby. A big, beautiful baby."

He sighed.

"What else did you buy her over the years?"

He thought for a moment before answering. He leaned on his hand, his elbow on the arm of his dining chair.

"A lot of plane tickets. A lot of dinners. A lot of hotel rooms. Some trips to Europe and the Caribbean with me. One trip to the Outer Banks for her and two of her women friends. And a solarium. A solarium with a bathtub."

Maddy nearly threw her arms around him to thank him for the tub but decided she had better not. She wondered if he knew it was surrounded with blue scotch bottles filled with little white lights, because of Hank.

"How is that piano?"

"It is indeed *so* beautiful," Maddy told him. "I had to throw the piano tuner out or he never would have stopped playing it. But me, I only play churchy tunes—what I picked up in the convent. Do you play?"

"No," Whitaker said. "I play the guitar."

He asked Maddy if she would like tea or coffee. He slid his hand under the table to the edge. Maddy bent over and looked under the table.

"Oh!" she said. "There are buttons you can push to call the attendants! Now I understand how this works."

He looked at her, obviously wondering how she could be so childish in her manners while so wizened in her attitude.

"Tea sounds good," she said.

The waiter came in and Whitaker asked for tea for Maddy and decaf coffee for himself. She turned and watched the waiter go. Then she turned back.

"Mr. Whitaker . . . there's something I don't understand," Maddy said slowly, trying to figure out how to word her question so she got the real answer. "When Alex died—when you found out—why didn't you cancel the order for the piano? Why did you want the piano to come to her home, even after she was gone?"

He folded his napkin and laid it on the table.

"Pride," he finally answered.

"Pride?"

"I thought, when I heard—I mean, after I managed to pull myself back together—I thought I should cancel the order. Get the money back and not have a piano delivered pointlessly, not risk having someone trace such a large gift back to me. But then I realized, as people were memorializing her, as I read long distance about what people were saying, talking about who she had been to them, that no one had any idea of what we had been to each other. No one knew what she had been to me, or I to her. And, so, I figured if a piano showed up eventually on the doorstep of Scott or Hank or whomever would end up with it, well, then they would know Ally had had something with someone. And that something had been as big and as loud and as delicate and as lyrical as a fine piano. So, I decided not to abort the baby she had asked me for, after ten years together. I decided it should be born. I wasn't sure in what house it would live, but I wanted our baby born."

"Oh," said Maddy very quietly. "I see. But she was dead by the time it was born. I see."

She got up and walked over to her bag to retrieve the envelope. She sat back down and put the envelope on the table between the two of them. It was face up, with his name written in Alex's hand facing him. He looked down at it but didn't touch it. The waiter came in and served the tea and the coffee and left.

"You already know what's in it?" she finally asked, tapping on the envelope.

He nodded.

"So, can I open it?"

He nodded again.

She ran her finger under the seal and tore open the envelope. Doing so ripped through a bit of Alex's signature, which made Maddy wish she had used a knife. She pulled out the folded page therein and read it. Then she read it again.

Without looking at it, he leaned back in his chair, sipped his cup of coffee, and told her, "It's a codicil to her will. It leaves some smallish amount to Scott, asking him to spend it on his son's education, and then it leaves the rest evenly divided between Hank and Sophie—I mean, Everett, as Everett would be Sophie's legal name. It's notarized by someone at a bank."

"How did you know all that? You're right. It reduces Scott's portion to ten percent, asking him to use it for the child's education, and splits the rest between Everett and Hank."

"Because," Whitaker explained, sounding somewhat weary, "I'm a lawyer and my area of specialty is estates and trusts. Alex asked me how to change her will in a just-in-case fashion while her personal lawyer was laid up from cancer surgery. I think his situation made her realize she should update her own will. I told her she should go to a different lawyer and get her will properly fixed. She told me she generally didn't like lawyers and didn't want to find a new one, especially given that hers had some horrible cancer and she didn't want him thinking she figured he would die, so she just wanted to do a temporary fix in the meantime. I explained to her she could do this as a temporary approach but she should fix her will properly."

"And she did this something like a month before she died?"

Whitaker nodded without apparent interest. "I suppose. Good thing she did, I guess. Or Scott would have gotten it all, which wasn't what she wanted by that point."

"But wait," Maddy said. "If you knew what was in the envelope, why did you have me bring it to New York?"

Whitaker got up to move to the seating-area armchair again. He put his feet up on the coffee table and waited for her to join him. Maddy followed him over, settling herself into the settee with her cup of tea. She asked again:

"If you knew what was in the envelope, why did you have me come?"

"Sophie—I mean, Everett—he knew what was in it, too, Madeleine. We both knew what Alex had left in that envelope."

She wrinkled her brow. Why would Everett have waited on producing this documentation if Everett knew it shifted Alex's inheritance from Scott to Everett? Why would Everett risk giving this envelope to Maddy? What if she had lost it? Why would Whitaker have had her bring it to him rather than just giving it to whomever was supposed to deal with her will—Scott, presumably? Why had Scott not moved to sell the house, get rid of Alex's car, clean up all this by now?

"What's going on?" Maddy asked.

She put her teacup on the coffee table, got up, and walked over to the window seat. But she did not sit down.

She suddenly felt that strange combination she had felt with Wilhelm, when she was starting to realize there was something not right—that combination of a desire to stay and figure it out fighting with an urge to escape very quickly to a less fraught place. She was keeping an eye on Whitaker, but he was just sitting there, now slumped.

"I think you're looking for rationality," he finally said. "You're looking for rationality where you're meeting only emotion. Look, I don't know why Everett would hold onto it. As for why I wanted you to come here, I don't even know that."

He paused while she watched him.

"I think, irrationally," he went on, "well, I guess I thought maybe it would be Alex coming? That maybe she wasn't really dead? You were coming from Ally's house, from Ally's job, with Ally's signature on that envelope, sent by her good friend, and I think part of me thought it was going to be Ally. That's why I was standing outside that door when I arrived. I couldn't come in. Because I had finally realized of course it *wasn't* going to be Ally. But it was only when I was standing there that I realized I had been thinking maybe it would be her. It was going to be someone effectively just confirming her death. You."

This made no sense to Maddy. How could he have expected it to be Alex? Even irrationally? Was he interested in meeting Maddy because of something about Maddy? Was it because he knew she was wondering about the death? Did he know that Scott had asked her to think about why and how Alex had died? Had Whitaker brought her here to try to stop her?

Suddenly the perfectly appointed room of this club felt too familiar—the books, the just-so furniture, the large window looking out on the city park. Just like the study at Wilhelm's house in Philadelphia. Just like when she had realized what might be going on then.

"Did *you* kill her?"

She'd blurted it out without it first going fully through her brain. It was a brain-stem question. Now she felt foolish for having said it, especially with the emphasis she seemed to have placed on *you*. His head was turned to her fully, his eyes grabbing hers.

"Did someone *kill* her?"

"I don't know," Maddy answered, as if he had insulted her somehow. "I don't know how she died."

"She drowned, right?"

Whitaker stood up and came over to Maddy. He stood less than a foot from her, still holding her eyes with his.

"She *drowned*," he said now, as if he was telling her something she didn't know. Then again, as a question: "She *drowned*, right?"

Was he asking Maddy, or was he trying to persuade her?

Was the problem that, with her heart racing, she was reading Wilhelm onto him?

She did not answer him. He grabbed her firmly by the elbows. He gave her a good shake.

"How did she die? How did Alex die? Tell me."

His fingers' grip grew stronger on her arms.

"I don't know how she died," Maddy said, pulling back an inch though he held on. "How would I know how she died? I don't even have the autopsy report. I haven't looked up what drowning looks like. I haven't figured out what she was wearing. I haven't researched it. *I haven't done a timeline.*"

She tried pulling away again. He let go her elbows but kept staring at her. He looked as if he was doing math calculations in his head. Now he stared past her, his focus shifting to far in the distance. His mouth was hanging partway open. She tried to search his face for emotion. All she could see was a kind of exquisite intensity, followed by a hard swallow.

He brought his eyes and focus back to her.

"What did Scott tell you?" he asked.

"That they ruled it probable suicide."

"That's not right. That can't be right. She wasn't depressed. I saw her just days before. She wanted the piano. She wasn't depressed. That's not right." He paused. "What made them think it was that?"

"I don't know," Maddy answered. She felt dizzy. Caisson disease; the bends. What time was it? What time was it in Philadelphia?

"It never occurred to me—"

He paused. He drew his breath sharply in. She asked him what had not occurred to him.

"It never occurred to me maybe it wasn't an accident." He gulped hard again. "But no way was it suicide."

"Sometimes," Maddy said, trying to call up a calming voice, "sometimes people who love a person who kills herself have to believe it was not suicide. They tell themselves that to spare themselves the guilt they feel over the suicide."

He drew back for a second, as if she had spit on him. His face was red and angry. Then he slapped her hard with his open palm, right across her face.

Chapter 12

"I am so sorry," Whitaker said to her earnestly, kneeling and holding his hands to his mouth in a gesture of horror.

All Maddy could do with her heart racing so was to wonder why she could never seem to pick out the right shoes. Ballet flats for meeting a strange man alone, really? These were nothing to kick with. For once, her hard-heeled dress boots would have been the right choice.

"I am so sorry," Whitaker said again. "I don't know why I hit you. I don't know what made me do that."

Her face was stinging as her heart struggled to slow to a walk. She inched her way forward a bit, around him, keeping as wide a path as she could while hastening to the dining table. She looked quickly underneath and found and pressed the button she figured was used to call the staff. She pressed it again five times fast and backed herself to the bookcase. Joseph appeared in a relative instant. He looked at Whitaker kneeling on the floor and Maddy standing with her back to the books, visibly shaking. He closed the door quickly behind him and went over to Maddy.

Why hadn't she just run for the door, she wondered to herself? After all that had happened with Wilhelm, how could she still be this incompetent?

"Are you okay, miss?" Joseph asked her, putting his hand very lightly on her shoulder, as if she might break.

"He hit me," she said, meeting Joseph's eye as if she needed to convince him. "Hard."

"I am sorry," Whitaker said, rising and backing himself to the other side of the room. "It is true. I don't know why."

"I've never known Mr. Whitaker to be violent, miss," Joseph told her, pulling a handkerchief out of his pocket and offering it to her. He looked for a moment over his shoulder, at Whitaker. It seemed to Maddy as if Joseph's forehead was starting to sweat. She took the cloth from Joseph and dried her face of the tears she hadn't fully realized were there.

"I'm not excusing what he did, miss, and I'm not blaming you. I am just trying to let you know he is not usually violent."

Joseph took a cloth napkin from the table and dunked it in one of the water glasses. He took the cold, wet cloth and held it to Maddy's red cheek.

"You're trying to protect your master," Maddy said, pulling away from Joseph and the wet cloth, flopping herself down in one of the dining chairs. She was sitting only because her knees were too wobbly to stand. She wanted to leave but kept thinking she wasn't even sure where she would be staying that night. Was it too late to take a train to Philadelphia? Would Wolf even be home?

"It is true, miss," Joseph said, "that part of my job is to reduce problems for our members. You're right to be suspicious. But it is also true that I have known Mr. Whitaker for many years, and I am genuinely confused about why he would have hit you. Again, I am not blaming you. But I can assure you, it is not like him. Would you like me to ask him to leave?"

Maddy shook her head "no." Much as she wanted to get away from Whitaker, she also wanted to understand what his reaction to the idea of Alex committing suicide had meant.

Joseph handed Maddy the wet napkin and walked over to the bookcase. As she pressed the cloth to her face, she saw Joseph draw a small key from his pocket and unlock a cabinet. From the cabinet, he pulled a bottle of Scotch and, from a shelf above, three tumblers. He put the three glasses on the table and poured some liquor into each. His hand seemed to Maddy to be shaking a little. He walked over to hand Whitaker one and then came back and sat next to Maddy at the dining table. He handed her one of the glasses. Smelling the heavy peat of the liquor, she took a sip and coughed a little. Joseph also took a drink and set then his glass down. His imitation of her movements seemed designed to signal that he was on her side.

"Why did you hit me?" Maddy asked Whitaker without looking at him. He came nearer to the table and asked if he could sit. She nodded once, still without looking at him.

"I don't know why I did that," he said, taking a seat with obvious discomfort. "You said something about how I didn't understand Alex, that I didn't understand her enough—and—and I was suddenly picturing her drowning and—"

"And you felt like I had accused you of letting her drown."

"Yes."

"You felt I said you *let her drown*," Maddy said, still not looking at him. "You must feel like you *did* let her drown. No one slaps back like that at a statement unless he thinks it is true. That it *is* true, and he doesn't *want* it to be."

He did not respond.

She sighed, closing her eyes, wishing she had not come here. She tried to think about the exquisite food, the excellent drink, the interesting conversation and characters, to tell herself it had been worth it, this short adventure to New York. But it was just like the time she had let a guy who should have remained an ex fuck her in Paris just because he'd bought her a good dinner at an expensive place.

Well, she had at least figured out this much from this trip: If someone had let Alex drown—or set her up to drown—it obviously wasn't Whitaker. His reaction had been too emotionally disorganized. Emotional self-defense, not criminal self-defense. All hot, no cold. Not like Wilhelm.

So, that led nowhere. Maybe this trip had just been a waste of time.

She moved her chair back a few inches to lay her head down on the table, on her arms, her still-stinging cheek facing the ceiling, her face pointed away from Whitaker. Joseph picked up the wet napkin again and laid it on her red cheek. She didn't fight him.

Whitaker cleared his throat and stood up.

"I have no business continuing to trouble you," he said to her. He cleared his throat again. "I will go, as Joseph will take care of you. I will apologize to you in writing. If you wish to use my written apology to charge me with assault, you'll have that. And Joseph knows what I did. He'll back you up, not that I would argue. I'm a man of honor. Normally."

She pulled her head up, holding the napkin to her face, to get one more look at him. She wondered the point of his saying all this. He looked to her quite ashen.

"Joseph," Whitaker said, before he left, "please tell Dr. Shanks anything she wants to know. Answer all of her questions."

Joseph stood up to get the door for him.

"Anything? Mr. Whitaker?"

"Anything!" Whitaker barked at him and left.

Joseph closed the door and sat back down next to Maddy. He took another swig of his drink and pulled a gold cigarette case out of his pocket. Opening the case, he retrieved a cigarette and a match. He struck the match on the case and lit the cigarette with a short drag. He offered it to Maddy, but she declined. So he put it between his lips and took a serious drag.

"Well," he said to Maddy, blowing out the smoke to the side away from her, "maybe I should tell you *what* you should ask me?"

He took another drag from the cigarette, held it a moment, and blew out slowly.

"You'll get more interesting answers if you have the right questions, Dr. Shanks. I'm not usually in a position like this. And you'll presumably never be here again."

He knocked his ashes into Whitaker's empty glass.

"Do you want me to order you some dessert, first? I hear you like our food."

She nodded glumly. Joseph pushed a button under the table and then suggested to Maddy that she looked tired enough that she ought to put her feet up. He said it as if nothing unusual had just happened between her and Whitaker—as if it was simply that time of evening when one puts one's feet up and waits for dessert to be delivered.

He rearranged the pillows on the settee and tapped the pillow, gesturing to her. She came over and assumed the suggested pose, lying across the settee with her feet draped over one side. She watched Joseph sit down in one of the armchairs across the coffee table. He finished his cigarette, tapping the ashes into the saucer of what had been her teacup.

"Traditionally, in this relative position," she said to him, "me prone on this couch and you seated in that chair, *you* are supposed to ask *me* deep and penetrating questions, and *I* am supposed to answer. But we'll have to reverse since I am supposed to ask you questions."

She closed her eyes and wondered which topic to pick first. Maybe she *should* have him tell her what to ask; she was so tired and just wanted to sleep. The surge of adrenaline brought on by Whitaker's hit was subsiding. She could feel her blood chemistry returning to baseline. But that baseline was flat-out exhaustion, tinged with too much drink.

"You'll want to know," Joseph said after a moment of quiet, "whether it's true I would testify against Mr. Whitaker if you opted to file charges."

Maddy momentarily mulled what he'd just said and realized that wasn't a question she had—she didn't care at this point that Whitaker had hit her—but it seemed to her interesting that it mattered to Joseph. She could hear him lighting up another cigarette. His tobacco didn't smell like commercial cigarettes. It had a pleasant, sweet overtone, almost like butternut squash that had burned just a bit on the bottom of a pan.

"The fact is," he went on, "the club had to decide a year or so ago whether it was my job to protect one member who had violated a young woman on the premises or protect the club itself in the long run by letting me testify against him. I would have quit had they not decided I should testify and tell the whole truth. The pay here is quite good, and the food and drink, as you have learned, is excellent. But none of it would have been worth doing any-thing other than telling the truth about what had happened to that young lady. At the end of the day, no matter who you are sleeping with, you have to sleep with yourself. That's a bit of wisdom imparted to me by a very aged and distinguished member of the club."

He had a calming, low voice as if he were a very big man, though he was not. Maddy wondered to herself if that low voice was obtained via practice, or via the cigarettes and Scotch, or if he came by it naturally. Some dogs didn't look like their barks. She thought for a moment she could smell the lanolin of the wool of his jacket. But maybe it was also the cigarette.

"Did he have other women, besides his wife and Alex?" Maddy asked without emotion, her eyes still closed.

She was picturing Alex in this room with Whitaker, drinking her gin and tonic, pulling a clip from her hair to let it down, speaking something other than small talk, knowing what was coming. Did it leave her bored after all those years, Maddy wondered, this particular sexual routine? Or excited? Or perhaps that strange feeling, of mentally bored physical arousal that Liz said came with a regular sexual relation? Did Alex ever feel as Maddy did now, that she had come all this way to see Whitaker but that all she wanted was to sleep?

"He had a small number of other women over the years during their relationship," Joseph answered. "That said, he had a particular fondness for

Professor Shugar. And she was his own age, which suggests, I think, more than just sexual conquest. I think he really loved her."

Maddy opened her eyes to sit up to look at Joseph. She wanted to ask what that looked like—how he could tell Whit may have loved Alex. She was curious what love looked like.

He went on as if he knew her question.

"Whitaker lit up when Alex was coming. He bothered to check the menu to see if she would like what was on it, and if he thought she wouldn't care for what was planned, he'd ask us to make her something different for her, something more to her taste. He once even brought a whole fish here on ice, a species he knew she particularly liked—bluefish from Long Island—and asked the duty chef to fix it some way Professor Shugar had once described. He felt the need to remind me she liked her gin and tonics with extra lime and not too much ice, as if I would ever forget such things when he knew I wouldn't."

He paused and added, as if in summary, "He made her presence here larger, the way one does when one is a powerful man in love. We didn't mind it. We all liked her. She treated everybody well here. I would never just kick back and talk with a guest the way I did with Alex Shugar. She invited comfortable connection—intimate conversation."

Maddy noticed Joseph's feet were up on the coffee table, so she put hers up as well.

"You're kicking back and talking with me," she said. "You must do it often enough."

"Not at all," he said somewhat defensively, as if she had uttered a minor insult. He pulled his feet off the coffee table. "It's just we're talking about Alex—it feels a bit like she is here, almost like she brought you along. It feels like it used to when I'd be able to relax with her after he'd left, before I walked her to the hotel. Plus, to be frank, opening the door to find you and Whitaker the way you both were, well, that did throw me off. We only just finished dealing with that other member and the girl."

She stretched her back and her neck and yawned, and asked him why he had brought her that odd concoction—the champagne with the wet-draped mint leaf and the crushed raspberries? He smiled a wry smile.

"I figured it would turn Whitaker off of you, if he had any interest," Joseph answered. "Call me old-fashioned, but I am inclined to believe that, at your age, with your dime-store stockings, you didn't need to get too involved with a guy like him. Not good for you. And it would be nothing to a man like him."

She gave him a faux-insulted look.

"Dime-store stockings!"

She stood up, reached up under her dress with both hands, and pulled her pantyhose down to her knees.

"God, they hurt after a few hours. They all come with control-top, whether you want it or not. And for the record, I got them at the *drug store*. Not the dime store. On sale: two for one. I always wait for the sale."

She stepped out of her shoes and pulled the hose off all the way. She went over to her bag and shoved the stockings inside. Then she settled back down on the settee, now with her bare feet on the table. She wriggled her toes, looking at the pink polish she had painted on a few days before, and asked Joseph how the drink was meant to stop her getting involved with Whitaker. He explained that if Whitaker had not been adequately appalled by what Maddy was drinking—good champagne mangled with mint and raspberries—he'd surely be utterly appalled by the messy way in which she had to drink it. Joseph knew there was not going to be any elegant way to manage that drink. She smiled a real smile at that.

"Clever. Do you call that cocktail The Chastity Belt?"

He chuckled but did not reply. She looked at the door for a moment, wondering if dessert would ever come. She just wanted to get to the hotel and collapse. But she didn't want to go before dessert.

"So, why did Alex stay with him?"

Joseph mulled aloud her question's formulation.

"*Stay* with him? Well, she didn't *stay*. She came and went. At her own pace. He paid for her trips, but he was never in control of her. I suspect that was part of the attraction for him—that he couldn't control her in the least. And it was okay for her. It was all okay."

A knock came on the door and Joseph stood quickly as Maddy yanked her feet off the table and sat up straight. He answered the door and took the tray offered, closing the door behind him. He set the tray down on the coffee table.

"A raspberry soufflé," he explained, "with a crème Anglaise and a late-harvest Riesling that will go very nicely with it."

Maddy let out an involuntary squeak of excitement and plunged the spoon into the dish. After two bites and a sip of the wine she paused, thinking she needed to make this delight last.

She asked Joseph how well he had known Alex.

"I sometimes kept her company when Whitaker was running late, and

I almost always walked her to her hotel," he answered. "Whitaker couldn't be seen walking with her to a hotel, and he didn't want her to have to walk alone in the dark. Sometimes we sent her bag ahead while she and I took a long route, through the park or up and down the avenues. I assume in such cases he was left waiting at the hotel, or something. He must have wondered sometimes where we were. Over the years, she and I ended up in quite a few conversations. She liked to ask me why she was doing this. It turned into something of a ritual between us, that question."

"What did you answer, when she asked you why she was doing this?" Maddy asked, quite curious, dipping her spoon into the soufflé.

"I reminded her the food and drink were very good, the company pretty intelligent and genuinely interested in her and her work, the arrangement easily and harmlessly discontinued at any time, if that's what she wished. That seemed to be the answer she was looking for."

He moved to light another cigarette and then, looking at her enjoying the dessert, stopped as if he didn't want to spoil it with the smoke.

"Not that that's why I gave Alex those answers—not because that was what she wanted to hear. I told her those things because all of that was the truth. This position of mine would be utterly intolerable if I were required to pretend black is white. I wasn't going to tell her she was doing it because of pure love and devotion, or anything like that."

"Did she love him?"

"She may have. Occasionally. There was one time when one of his children was unexpectedly hospitalized, and she was quite distressed for him. Almost beside herself."

He put back in his case the cigarette he hadn't lit and told her to keep eating, that the soufflé would start to sag soon. "It has no control top to help it out."

She smiled at his joke and took another spoonful and drank some more of the wine. He went on:

"Alex Shugar was generally not the sort of person who bothered with convention, like questions of love. She would not have been troubled by the idea of feeling one thing for someone one day and another emotion entirely on another day. To put it plainly, she had no patience for bullshit—for pretense. It made her extremely attractive, and extremely repulsive, I suppose, depending on the situation. Depending on one's taste. Depending on what one would get from it."

"Why did she divorce her husband?"

At that question, Joseph licked his bottom lip, then pulled his tongue back in, but said nothing.

Maddy reminded him that Whitaker said to answer all her questions.

"I suppose he did say to do that."

He sat up a little, as if he had found himself at a bet he suddenly wanted in on.

"Do you know what a cuckold fetish is, young lady?"

Maddy shook her head no.

"Alex didn't know that was her husband's thing when she married Scott. Maybe even *he* didn't even know that about himself early on. But it turns out that Scott found, through Alex's affair with Whitaker, that he was excited by Alex cheating on him. He was turned on by the idea of another man 'stealing' his wife—having her. Scott confessed to Alex that he liked it. That it turned him on."

Maddy's eyebrows went up.

"So, why did she divorce Scott?"

"For a while," Joseph explained, "Alex thought this worked out rather well. She could have what she wanted with Whitaker or whomever without upsetting her husband—delighting Scott, in fact. But after a while, she realized that it meant that her sexual pleasure was being pushed and shaped by her husband's. He was egging her on for his own sexual satisfaction. And as a feminist, she was troubled by that."

He paused as if to think how to explain it better.

"She realized eventually that she didn't want her sexual life to be that much about her husband's pleasure. Scott was encouraging her to go cheat on him, so she became confused. Was she going to see Whitaker and the other men she might see for her *own* enjoyment? And at a baser level, she also felt Scott's particular desire emasculated him. Scott, at some level, was into being humiliated by having another man take his wife. That became clear over time. And she found that a turnoff. She told me she had come to realize she liked strong men, not men who were into being humiliated sexually. She particularly wanted men who wanted her, for real, not men who wanted other men to have her."

Maddy thought back to what Lew had told her about Scott's second wife, Maya—how Alex had found Maya for Scott, how Maya had been cheating steadily on Scott. Alex must have suggested or even arranged that Scott pursue Maya as a partner to help Scott have what he wanted—what he needed? Perhaps so Alex could get out of her own marriage without guilt?

Maddy also realized suddenly what Hank had meant when he had said that Scott didn't like Hank because Hank was *not* having sex with Alex. Scott would have preferred Alex have sex with other men, not have a loving relationship with Hank that wasn't even sexual.

And Maddy realized now, too, why Scott had emphasized the divorce was done to make clear no one had anything to be ashamed of. Because he had, in fact, been ashamed of his desires. But Alex saw no point in his being ashamed.

"Alex told you all that—about how she had realized she was turned off by Scott's desires, how she had come to realize she liked strong men?"

Joseph nodded.

"Like I said, she had no patience for bullshit, and we ended up in a fair number of conversations over the years. And, although I think she liked to think that her visits with Whitaker didn't leave her troubled, she often felt the need to talk about all of that when we would walk together to her hotel," Joseph said. "I suppose part of the reason she talked to me about it was that I knew about her and Whitaker, and not a lot of people did, or could know. He had to be careful for the sake of his wife and children. She understood that. She also knew I don't bother to judge people over these things, so I was easy to talk to, I suppose. If I did judge people over these consensual things, it would be all I would have time for in my job."

"But you didn't want Whitaker hitting on *me*."

"That's not about judging him, or you," Joseph said, somewhat earnestly. "That's just about being a little bit protective of women. Which any decent man is."

Maddy thought it was funny that he felt the need to defend his desire to protect her from a guy who was perhaps a bit of a cad. Joseph was right; it was something any relatively normal man sought to do. But did they do it to protect women, or to try to keep the playing field level for themselves?

"What did Alex say in your most recent conversation?"

"She was mostly quiet on the last visit," he answered, "more quiet than usual. You know, it turned out to be just a few days before she died."

He paused now, for a good long minute. Maddy tried to read his face but could not.

"You know what? She asked me something different that time—whether I thought it mattered who we have sex with. I wasn't sure what she meant. She said she was wondering about whether what really mattered with sex was *who* you were having it with, or *what happened*—what you *felt*. She wanted to know if in the end sex was just about one's own experience. The other person's pleasure might matter to you, but it might not, she said, if you weren't violating them. She wondered to me if perhaps the identity of the other person simply did not matter."

"What did you say in answer?"

"Well, frankly, it made me wonder if she'd recently had sex with a woman. Anyway, I thought about her question, and I told her I wasn't sure, and that maybe the answer was different for different people. Or maybe even different in different circumstances. That maybe you couldn't feel the same thing with just anyone—well, *of course* that is true, you won't feel the same regardless of who it is—but that maybe what mattered wasn't just what you felt at the time, but what you believed—what you knew—afterwards?"

Maddy nodded.

"Alex told me on one of her last visits that she thought she was strange as a woman, because she rarely experienced sexual regret the way many women did. No matter how bad a sexual encounter turned out to be, she rarely felt upset about it afterwards—she rarely felt regret or anger. And she thought maybe that was because she had no shame about sex, or maybe because she had focused so much on feeling her body during sex. That she was more focused on the feeling of her body than the relationship during sex. More like a man than a woman, she thought."

Maddy stopped him. "Sexual regret?"

"You know," he answered, "regretting having had sex, the next day. Feeling like you shouldn't have done what you did. She called it 'sexual regret,' so I assume it was some scientific term. You know she was working on a book about sex?"

"Yes. Sexual regret—so, for her it was the shame thing?"

He nodded.

"But maybe more than shame. Even if you don't feel *ashamed* the next day, you can *regret* having had sex with someone. You could, for example, regret not having expressed what you yourself needed, and having had bad sex because of that. You could regret creating complications in a friendship by having sex. There's plenty you can regret after sex. Especially if you're a woman, I guess, the way women are liable to get pregnant, liable to be judged more harshly than a man. Concern about sexual regret was the reason, she told me, that she didn't have sex with the friend of hers—the Lothario who stayed with her sometimes at her home. What is his name?"

"Hank," Maddy answered.

"Yes, Hank," Joseph said, taking out his gold case and reorganizing his remaining cigarettes into neater rows. "She didn't want to spoil their special friendship. Anyway, she wasn't asking me about this like she was regretting her relationship with Whitaker. She was asking me, I think, like she was onto something new—a new lover about whom she felt confused?"

"Did you have sex with her?"

Joseph smiled and didn't answer, though Maddy thought he shook his head "no" ever so slightly. She decided not to push it.

"Do you know why she would have wanted a piano—why she would have ordered a grand piano here in New York, right before she died?"

Joseph shook his head.

"Alex Shugar was nothing if not unpredictable," he replied. "Even unexplainable."

"I don't know why I assume the piano she got right before she died had something to do with sex—why I assume with her that everything was about sex."

Joseph wrinkled up his lips, yet he looked like he might be smiling again.

"Well, I'm not sure you're wrong. She certainly thought about it more than any woman I've ever known, particularly in the last year. I don't mean that she was—well, hornier than other women, if you'll pardon that crass language. Just that she really thought about it. Somehow she managed to study it like a lab experiment while also enjoying it. That's quite a trick, if you ask me. She just thought about pleasure—feelings of the flesh—more than most ever do."

They sat quietly for a while as Maddy finished off the dessert and the wine. She suddenly assumed for a moment that while she was here asking all these questions, Alex must right now be back home in her bath, steaming up the bottle lights and the windows. Then she remembered Alex was dead.

She lay back down lengthwise on the settee, draping her feet over the edge again with her hands crossed on her full belly to try to remember what Joseph had just said. Sleep began to wash over her, like a fog rolling in. She opened her eyes wider in an attempt to stay awake. Staring at the ceiling, she could just picture Liz hearing from her about this conversation and enjoying it, not least because it would mean Maddy had learned something about sex that never would have occurred to her—that there were men who liked having other men take their women. Liz liked nothing better than seeing Maddy shocked or surprised at something sexual. It gave her that feeling of moral superiority.

Maddy closed her eyes now involuntarily and then opened them suddenly again. She went over to the table, put the codicil from Alex back into its envelope, and put the envelope into her bag. Then she laid back down. As she did, she felt a little dizzy. She was starting to think she had had far too much to drink.

"Can I ask you something?" Joseph queried as Maddy closed her eyes again. She nodded.

"How did she die? I mean, I know she drowned. *Why* did she die?"

Maddy's right hand moved sleepily to her thigh, creating a crease in her dress between her legs.

"Why," she said. "Why is such a *thing*."

She sighed as if she had come upon an unexpected mess she would have to clean up before taking to bed. Spilled milk.

"I haven't timelined it."

He waited for her to say more, but she did not.

"I don't understand," he finally said. "I mean, I don't understand what you mean when you say you 'haven't timelined it.'"

Maddy sighed again.

"To know *why* Alex died—to know any *why*—one must know *who*, *what*, *when*, *where*, and generally *how*. Even then, *why* is a bit of a guess. *Why* is cause and effect—direct, global, motivational. *Why* is the god's-eye view. It's very hard to access historically. And, without a solid timeline, a historian can't know to any degree of certainty who, what, when, where, or how. So, at least at the moment, there is no chance of my knowing *why*."

"Do you need paper?" Joseph asked. "If that's the issue, I could get you some paper."

Chapter 13

The letter from Whitaker came around one o'clock in the morning, slipped under the door. The soft sounds of the delivery—the envelope brushing against the bottom of the door, the steady rhythm of feet walking away—pulled Maddy out of a restless sleep.

She turned on the desk lamp and sat down to read it. Her yawn tasted of wine. She wondered if she had forgotten to brush her teeth.

...

Dear Dr. Shanks,

After delivering you to the hotel, Joseph conveyed to me your questions, which I will herein answer. Forgive my handwriting: the only option for getting this to you by morning, i.e., before you depart New York.

First, allow me again to apologize for striking you. I expect you are right that something you said about my failing to help Ally must have rung true enough to sting. But that is no excuse for my action; I hope you will forgive it.

I now take your questions sent through Joseph, not in the order they were written but in the order in which they seem to make some sense to me:

My calendar indicates that I saw Ally last the night of Thursday, May 26. I believe she would have gone to Steinway the day after. I will call over there first thing in the morning and ask them to answer your questions when you come by. (As I paid for it, I shouldn't think there would be a problem.) I honestly have no idea why she asked for the piano, as I told you, or why she went and bought it. But she wasn't the kind of person to do something like obtain a piano without a good reason. She wouldn't have spent my money for no reason. She wasn't that kind of person, to trifle with one.

As you know, she died a few days later, in Minnesota.

That night in New York, Thursday, May 26, was the last time we spoke. Everett Sophie Inskeep was the person who called to tell me Ally had been found drowned.

We had never spoken before, and I was not even aware Sophie knew about our relationship until then. Sophie said she thought it best if I heard it early from her, not some random news source. She reached me through my firm and told me simply that Ally had been swimming alone and had drowned.

I was grateful to her for telling me. I knew well of Sophie's good friend-ship with Ally; Ally often spoke of her with affection.

I don't know why Sophie did not tell you what was in the envelope that you brought. Sophie knew what was in it. I know that because she told me on the phone what was in the envelope when she called to ask if you could come to see me. (I expect she didn't want me getting my hopes up that it was some meaningful final letter from Ally when it was just the codicil to her will that she and I had discussed.)

I also don't know why Sophie hasn't pursued the estate (i.e., portion of estate) she knew she had coming to her according to that codicil. Alex only ever spoke of Everett Sophie with great affection. About Hank, who would be her other main heir (as you now know), she spoke with a combination of warmth and exasperation.

But there isn't any question why she would have left the two of them her estate; she loved them, daily. They loved her, daily. They were fortunate that way.

You asked if she loved me. I don't know the answer to that. Alexandra Shugar didn't tend to follow the normal rules of emotion, or of expression of emotion, or of love and sex, or of anything else for that matter, so we rarely said, "I love you." I'm not sure that it is because she felt different things than most of us feel; I suspect it is more that she felt what we all do but that she was more willing to allow for her own recognition and airing of "inappropriate" feelings. She was without filter.

She was less willing than most of us to pretend steady or unconditional love, for example. She had no myths about parental love, romantic love, erotic love, and so forth. She believed they existed, but she did not pretend they were pure or purely beautiful. She didn't ever want us (her and me) to become conventional partners, i.e., man and wife. After her experience with Scott, she did not want to be married again. She said life was simpler without the fiction that got in the way of the facts.

When she told me that, early in our relationship—that she didn't want the fiction of marriage—I thought at first she was criticizing my marriage, calling it fiction. But then I came to realize she was at some level acknowledging what my marriage was (one thing in public, another in private) and accepting it, not blaming me for anything, not criticizing my choices. Or my wife's, for that matter.

You asked if I loved Ally. Yes, I did. I was simpler than she was. (I was easier, I suppose.)

Who would be happy that she's gone? I am not sure I am qualified to answer. There were some scholars who strongly disliked her, and some activists. She'd had an unsettling dispute with a creepy fellow, a plumber she felt had ripped her off because she was a woman, although I think that ugliness had petered out and he was leaving her alone by then. She hadn't mentioned it in a long time.

There were colleagues and students, including the "gnat." That was a graduate student who was—well, kind of intellectually harassing her for his professional gain. Attaching himself to her reputation through opposition.

Ally wasn't someone inclined to hold her tongue. So, who would be happy she was gone? Probably plenty of people. Anyway, that is a better question for Sophie, Hank, and Scott, I think?

The car service is set to collect you at the hotel at noon. If you would prefer to be picked up somewhere else, please call my secretary at the number listed below and ask her to change the arrangement with the service. I would appreciate if you would keep me apprised, as you are obviously trying to find out some more about her death, or at least her life. My mobile is also provided below.

Yours truly,

L. Whitaker/IV

. . .

Maddy put the letter back in the envelope and tucked it into her bag right next to the envelope Alex had signed. She turned off the light and lay back in bed, suddenly overwhelmed with a desire to call Wolf.

If she called him, would he hop into his car and arrive within two hours as she fantasized? Knock to be let in, give her a firm kiss on the top of her head, put his keys and his wallet on the nightstand, take off his shoes and his gun, climb into bed, curl up with his arms around her, and tell her that she could go to sleep, that they'd talk about whatever it was over breakfast?

Or would he see her number and not answer? Or answer only to tell her they shouldn't talk just now if she had nothing urgent? Or ask her why she had been so stupid, talking publicly about how Wilhelm had forged Schlesinger 1888, getting that into the press just now at exactly the wrong time.

What would she even say to him if she called? That she was in New York City because she had managed to get herself entangled in some strange web of a dead woman's relationships without thinking about it? She had done exactly what he had told her not to do—go wherever a scent took her. ("You have too thin an economic safety margin in your life to go off the main path again, Rabbit. You picked a difficult profession. Stay absolutely focused on your work.")

She could call Wolf and play, "I'm too scared to sleep. I've stumbled on something strange, and I'm only two hours away from you," hint, hint. But when she did the calculation of her emotions, she had to admit to herself that, much as she didn't trust Whitaker not to be sly and self-serving, particularly given what Joseph had told her, she wasn't really frightened by this scene around Alex. Joseph had made patently clear there was nothing to fear here; that one slap had been out of character and wouldn't happen again. The letter confirmed her impression of Whitaker—and that it had already arrived suggested he was not planning to come in person to try to see her again.

No, she wasn't acutely scared, and she had no interest in playing stupid games with Wolf. One of the best things about being with Wolf was the lack of the requirement to play a limp girl, to dumb down her strengths. As conventional as he was about men and women and relationships, he never asked her to be anything she wasn't. He never asked her to be soft. She knew that made her tougher. Which just made him respect her more. Which just left her stronger still.

Liz had told Maddy impatiently over drinks one night that Maddy was just attracted to men who would rescue her. But Maddy had realized a few days later, while mulling this out on a run, that the truth was she was attracted to men like her—smart and strong—like Wolf and Hank and Whitaker. In older masculine packages, sure, but simply to meet her more agile, feminine one. Men who would amplify, not diminish, her.

But Wolf didn't need the complication of Maddy in his life. As it was, she had so complicated his life. She wondered if it really was the prosecutors' idea that they hold off on talking much or whether Wolf had just asked Jill to tell Maddy that.

She let out an audible sigh and tried to shake off that unpleasant snippet of memory—of the last time she and Wolf had been together, when they were drinking too much—the memory of giving him a prolonged erection when it wasn't what he wanted. How many Hail Marys had that cost the poor guy? And did he ever want to be alone with her again?

In any case, she wasn't scared now and did not need to call Wolf to tell him she was. Because this was nothing like it had been with Wilhelm. It was almost certainly the case that Alex Shugar had either accidentally drowned or purposefully set herself up to drown in a low moment. Maddy had seen nothing to suggest otherwise. Well—except why did Alex go swimming without taking her jewelry off? Hank seemed to think this was very abnormal.

Still, this wasn't like with Wilhelm, where *all* kinds of things had not made sense in terms of Wilhelm's representations and the historical record, where Maddy had *had* to acknowledge the strangeness of the situation. No, this scene with Alex Shugar had none of that undeniable obviousness to it, the obviousness about Wilhelm that she had at first almost set aside, hoping to ignore, before she had then given fully into and pursued like the straightest route to a train she had to catch.

And there was no one trying to scare her off in this case as Wilhelm had done. Even if Whit had slapped her and slapped her hard, he hadn't done it to push Maddy off looking at Alex's death. He had struck Maddy impetuously, probably because he had been feeling guilty for ten aimless years with Alex, not because he had felt guilty for something terrible he had done to her at the end. Why else would he have authorized Joseph to tell her anything she wanted to know? Why else would he not have attempted to cancel the piano's delivery before it arrived?

Maddy tried to pull herself off these thoughts. What else should she think about?

Maarten and last night? It had been awfully nice. Perhaps she could just go back to that feeling of being tipsy and pleasantly touched by someone who was as into the light eroticism of the encounter as she was. She could get off and go to sleep finally.

But, first, maybe the pleasure of just a little mental math?

The two people who stood to gain financially from Alex's death, as it turned out, were Hank and Everett Sophie. And yet neither of them seemed anything but genuinely distressed by Alex's death and seemingly uninterested in any financial gain. Scott might have thought he would gain financially by proving it wasn't suicide, but if he were looking primarily for the money to be had from Alex's death, why had he still not moved to sell her house? And would he want Maddy poking around about Alex's death if he had something to hide?

Perhaps even Scott had known about this codicil to her will. It seemed like Alex would have told Scott before changing her estate, cutting him away from the bulk of it but leaving him the executor. She seemed to be frank with everyone. Alex had probably just changed the beneficiaries because she had known who had plenty of money (Scott and Maya) and who probably had had less (Hank, if not also Everett Sophie)—or because of who was in her daily life more. Whatever the reason for the change, Scott seemed unlikely to have wanted her dead.

So, Scott was probably right that her death had been an accident.

But *had* he told Maddy he thought Alex's death was an *accident*? Or had he just said that Alex wasn't depressed and thus it couldn't have been suicide? Maddy couldn't quite remember now.

In any case, everyone who had known Alex seemed to think she had *not* been depressed just before she died. Sure, there were all those people she had been struggling with—the activists, the "gnat" grad student pursuing her work, her own grad student Sarah—but it seemed hard to believe any of them would have sent her over the edge to suicide after all she had withstood through years of controversies and battles. And it seemed even more unlikely any of them would have somehow drowned her at the lake without the police or the coroner seeing something amiss.

Maddy supposed it could have been a stranger who drowned Alex, but presumably the coroner had found no signs of struggle or of sexual assault, the common reason for the seemingly random murder of a woman, as she had learned from Wolf.

But did a sexual assault followed by three days in water leave recognizable signs? And what had the coroner found, exactly? Did Scott know—did he have the postmortem? Could she get it from him, to just have a look?

But what was the point of that? Maddy had her own work to focus on. Wolf was right that her margin for error was very thin, as she had gone into a field with almost zero new employment and few people retiring (even fewer dying!) to make room for the young. She could not afford to do anything but constant, top-notch research in her field, which required consistent focus *as a scholar*. Besides, Wolf had warned her that everyone who befriends a police detective suddenly starts thinking they see secret crimes everywhere.

The simplest explanation for this scene with Shugar was that she had simply drowned, whether by accident or a kind of purposeful recklessness, as Hank had suggested when he talked about "tiring her survival instinct" by doing dangerous things.

She let out another sigh. Thinking about all this just made her crave Wolf's company more. It felt so easy, talking with him about everything she had read and seen and heard. She could almost feel the downy comfort of knowing that, just by having him listen, she'd figure out what she needed to do the next day. He would make sense of her personal nonsense or put it all aside in a way that felt like a lightening of her load. That feeling of knowing he'd always feed her something good, put her to bed, and stay with her at least until she was deep asleep.

Lord, how she missed that feeling of his body wrapped around hers like a fine, lined cloak, warm and complete.

Perhaps she should have had intercourse with Maarten the night before. Perhaps that would have relieved her of this feeling of—well, of having a hole that needed filling. Instead Maarten had brought her to orgasm several times and kept his own clothes on—not that she had minded. Nor did he seem to mind it. It felt so very lovely to have someone remind her by touch of the objective delights of her body, to finger-paint her into beauty.

Why hadn't Maarten dropped her a text by now? Oh, that's right—she hadn't given him her phone number. She needed to get his number and text him when she got back or check her email. But all that email that would be from reporters. . . .

Maddy wondered again now if what she had felt briefly with Maarten was what Alex had felt with Whitaker. Had Alex bothered to come to New York because of how Whit touched her—or did she see the touch as the route to other good opportunities: excellent food and drink, trips to Europe and the Caribbean, and a piano?

Why the damned piano?

Perhaps Maddy would find out in a few hours at Steinway. If she could even just figure that out, she'd be better able to focus on her own work and stop thinking about this. That said, it felt inevitable that she'd start a timeline on her way home. No matter how much of her own disciplinary research she had to do, she knew she'd have to at least sketch a timeline on this. Just to see what happened in the last couple of days of Alex's life.

"It doesn't make sense"—that phrase Scott and Hank had used, the conclusion Whit seemed to also come to—*it doesn't make sense.* This was the mental and rhetorical space where the Church and the Church's minions—Maddy's parents, the Dominican Sisters, even the Georgetown Jesuits—had always insisted on inserting the supernatural. *God makes the sense.* But Maddy had always had to fill that space hastily with rationality, to keep stupid talk of God out. Just as she used to shove lumps of steel wool into the wall cracks of the convent dormitory to try to keep the mice out.

Funny how Wolf thought, like her, that *people* should figure things out? At least where crimes were concerned?

Maddy grabbed her phone from the nightstand and flipped it over in her palm a couple of times. She could ask Wolf this: What should she do with Alex's letter—the codicil to her will? To whom did one give such a thing?

She put the phone back on the nightstand, got out of bed, and pulled back the curtain some to let in more of the light of the street. Then she put herself in the center of the empty space of the room, centering herself in the light cast from outside, and stood on one foot, bending over perfectly straight, one arm in front of her, one out to the side, one leg stretched behind. There she balanced for a minute and then reversed sides. From this pose, she put both her hands down to take a handstand. As she pointed her toes to the ceiling, she could feel a real hangover coming on. She needed sweet fruit juice, coffee, bacon and eggs, and lots of water, just as Liz had taught her. Joseph had assured her that Whit's account would be covering her breakfast. Maybe it would cover two breakfasts, one now and one in the daylight.

She bent her legs behind her to form an arch, belly up, and then, after a moment, stood up. She went to the bathroom, emptied her bladder, drank two glasses of water, came back to the main room to pull the curtains fully closed, and went back to bed. She tried to settle into a good sleeping position. Then she tried to empty her mind. But she soon found herself meditating on the difficulty of reading Joseph.

How was it that he seemed to have no obvious ethnicity, no obvious class, no discernible accent? It was just like what Liz had once said about Maddy early in their friendship, how she seemed to be from nowhere, a kind of invisible woman. Had Joseph stepped up in class or fallen down to take this position he found himself in—an arranger for wealthy men like Whitaker? Was the fun of the game for him the challenge of maintaining his integrity in the face of so much social manipulation? Of participating in it? Of being no one and everyone all at once in that club?

. . .

"Hello?"

He sounded like she had woken him up.

"Hey," she replied.

"Hey. How are you?"

"I'm okay," she answered. "Can't sleep."

"How can I help?" he asked, sounding suddenly more alert and interested. She wasn't sure what to say.

"Hang on," he added, after a moment. "Who is this?"

"Maddy," she said, now embarrassed. "It's Madeleine Shanks."

"Oh," he answered. "Sorry—I thought it was someone else."

She wondered if she should hang up and let Hank think he'd just dreamed her calling—save herself the full-on immersion in embarrassment. But his phone would show the record of the call. Now she wasn't sure what to say.

"Where are you?" he asked, yawning.

"New York. Long story."

"Are you there because of Alex?"

"Yes," she answered reluctantly.

"Why?"

She shouldn't have called. She should have gone with the voice of Liz in her head telling her not to call Hank.

"Maddy," Hank said, sounding another notch more alert, "I'm not sure what you're doing, but I'm guessing you're following up on what Scott said to you?"

"How did you know about that?" she asked. "Did you plan this with him?"

"Plan what?" Hank asked, sounding genuinely confused. "Look, it's like one in the morning and I'm not even sure what we are talking about."

"I'm sorry. Do you want to go?"

"No, no, no. Talk to me. Please." Then he said in a more soothing voice: "Talk to me."

She felt an erotic twitch, and then felt annoyed with the twitch.

"What is your orientation?" she asked him, blurting out a question that had only just cohered in her brain.

"Orientation?" he answered. "You mean my sexual orientation?"

"Yes."

"I'm straight. I thought that was obvious. In fact, I think I told you that. Why?"

"What *kind* of straight? What's the real deal with you?"

He was quiet for a moment. She strained to find if she could hear any other noise in the background behind him.

"Listen," he finally said, in a lower voice. "I'm not lying here trying to figure out how to answer your question because there's anything abnormal—statistically or sexually—about my orientation. I'm trying to figure out what set you to ask this question. And to ask it with hostility. Because you sound somewhat angry at me about my orientation."

Maddy sat up and pushed her back up against the headboard. She realized he wasn't wrong; she was feeling a little angry, without any clear direction for the anger.

"I'm sorry, Hank. I'm disoriented. I drank too much tonight. And I am so, so tired. Should I let you go?"

"No," he answered firmly. "You woke me up. So, tell me why you're asking about my orientation. Is it because you know Alex was working on the book about sexuality?"

"Yes!" Maddy exclaimed as if someone had elicited from her a confession she was dying to make. "And it seems like everyone who seems perfectly ordinary has an orientation I've never even considered! Jesus Christ, Hank. Everett is Sophie. And my dean Scott Willingham is a cuckold fetishist?"

"Oh," Hank answered, and then he let out a small laugh. "You now know the truth about Scott, huh?"

She laughed back, not at all sure why.

"So, let me change my question," she said, closing her eyes to formulate

148

it clearly. "I withdraw the question 'What is your orientation?' My question now is: How did Alex Shugar classify you?"

He answered without pause.

"She told me I was a 'chase fetishist.' And don't go wracking your brain for some memory of a text about this, Maddy. It's not a term that exists anywhere. Alex just made up 'chase fetishist' when she was pissed at me one day because I was late again. We were going to be late to a curtain of a show she had wanted very much to see. She figured—correctly—I'd been busy pursuing somebody and had lost track of the time. She said that what got me off was not getting off, it was the chase. So she started to taunt me by telling me I was a chase fetishist."

"You mean pursuing women you haven't yet had."

"That's what *she* meant, yes," Hank replied.

"And you're suggesting that's not true?"

"Oh, no," he said. "It's true. But I don't think that makes me any kind of fetishist. I think it just makes me a perfectly normal man."

Maddy said nothing. He was hardly the first person to observe that men like a good chase. Or that some men like it quite a lot.

"Let me ask you something more," she said. "If what you enjoy is the chase, do you enjoy intercourse once it finally happens?"

"The first time, yes. The second time, usually. Maybe even a little more the second time—I think because it's proof I've really got her? The third time, eh. Then, less and less. Then I'd rather go looking again."

She was a little taken aback at the plainness of the formula.

"Honest, at least," she said.

"Too much, I fear. I don't think I've ever copped to that before, not out loud. Sounds a little cold, out loud. But I guess it's pretty effective for you to wake someone up in the middle of the night and hit him with a hard line of questioning. You do like the hard line of questioning, Dr. Shanks."

"I'm sorry."

"It's fine," he said. "It's not like my habits are a secret to the world."

"No," she agreed, thinking back on what Lew had said about Hank's reputation. "Can I ask you something else?"

"Sure. Would you like me to turn on a bright light and shine it into my own face? For effect?"

"How do you manage to get so many women to sleep with you? I mean, I know you're good-looking."

"Thank you," he said. "You *are* smart and observant."

"So, how do you do it?"

"I'm not going to tell you," Hank answered, laughing through the words.

"Why not?"

"I'm not giving away my secrets to you."

"It's not like I'm going to use them," she laughed back. "I'm not into women!"

"Well," he answered in a coy voice, "you might sell my technique on the open market. Then my tricks wouldn't have the advantage of exclusivity."

"Oh, come on. Help a good young researcher out."

"Oh, I'd like to help a good young researcher out. I'd like to help you out, Dr. Shanks."

She felt a flutter as if a bit of her skin on her chest had just morphed into a lively moth and lifted off. She inched herself back down the bed, her back now flat on the bed. Oh, what she wouldn't give to feel his body right there, right now. She realized her breathing must be audible.

"Tell you what," he said. "Why don't you close your eyes, think about when you're back in town and we can get together, and maybe for now, that would help?"

She said nothing but smiled at the feeling, the feeling of more of her skin morphing, fluttering to life, lifting.

"Call me when you're back."

He hung up.

. . .

"Hello?"

Maddy didn't respond. She hadn't expected to feel startled simply by the sound of Wolf's voice.

"Hello? Who is this?"

"It's me, Wolf," she answered.

"Rabbit? What's going on—are you okay?"

"I'm okay," she answered.

She could hear him fumbling to look at the alarm clock on his nightstand.

"It's three in the morning. What's going on?"

She didn't reply. She was wondering how it was she had dialed a number again, still in the middle of the night, without a clear plan of conversation. She felt stupid for calling and seeming to have nothing to say.

"Are you worried about the trial?" Wolf asked.

"No. I mean yes, but not right now. Right now, um, I had a question about a pork roast."

"A what?" Wolf yawned hard.

"A pork roast," she answered. "I've got a pork roast in the freezer. About six pounds, I think—kind of big—and I'm not sure what to do with it."

"Why did you get a pork roast if you weren't sure what you were going to do with it?"

"I didn't go get it. I came into it. Now I have it. What do I do with it?"

"Well," he answered, "defrosting is always a good first step with a frozen piece of meat."

He yawned hard again, and she could picture just how he looked doing so, the way he yawned asymmetrically, his lower jaw out slightly to one side, his eyes shut tight until the yawn subsided. Sometimes he shook his head a bit after such a hard yawn.

"Okay, Wolf, but then what—after it's defrosted?"

"Bone-in or boneless? Must be bone-in, at that size."

"Bone-in, I think," she said, trying to remember what the label on the roast in Alex's freezer said.

"It depends what you feel like eating it with, I guess. Do you want it as a single roast, with potatoes and greens and fruit? Or do you want to do seasoned Cuban and pulled—something like that?"

"Man, I miss your cooking."

"And I miss your eating," he answered, without hesitation.

"Have you ever cooked with sunchokes?"

"Sure," Wolf replied, "when I find them. Not a lot of people seem to want them, so maybe that's why you don't see them much. You aren't looking to do them with the pork, are you?"

"No."

They were both quiet for a long minute. She read it as a kind of quiet that felt not at all awkward—just the kind of quiet they had had a million nights in a row in Philadelphia, while she worked on her research notes and he read the newspaper or a book. Only it hadn't been a million nights. Just a couple of months.

"I was just going to say, Rabbit, that you don't call somebody at three in the morning to talk about pork roasts and sunchokes. But *you* would."

"Well, not with just anyone," she said, wondering if he could hear her smile. "I had an amazing meal tonight, so I was thinking of you—your cooking."

"Where was it?"

"New York, at a private club."

"New York?" he said, more intensely. "Private club? Why are you out east?"

"Long story," she said, realizing he must be assuming she was there for a man. She tried to think quickly how to change the subject and blurted out, "How is your wife?" before realizing that segue was just going to confirm his suspicion that she was sleeping around in New York.

"Same," he said. "There's a reason they call it a persistent vegetative state, Maddy."

She always felt out of sorts when in private conversation he used her given name.

"I'm sorry."

"With potatoes and fruit, or something like a pulled pork?" he asked. "Which do you want to do?"

"Which would you do?"

"It would depend on the weather. Warm weather, something more southern. Colder weather, potatoes."

"Trial starts Monday?" she asked.

"No. Doesn't look like it."

He didn't explain. Her pulse started to pick up. What did he mean it didn't look like it? She didn't want to ask.

"How's your job in Minnesota?"

"Good," she said. "I feel like I'm doing a good job. Two classes, you know. They're going well. A couple of places are looking to have me come give talks in the spring. So that'll be good on my CV. And I've got that conference presentation in Pittsburgh next week—remember, I told you about that a while ago? And this week someone asked me to join a panel for the interdisciplinary conference in New Mexico next summer. I said yes to that. They hold it there because hotels are cheap in hot places in summer. The university will probably pay for that trip. I'll ask."

"Good," he answered. "And publications?"

"I've got two I am sort of working on."

"Sort of? You told me those were very important for your career, especially at this stage."

"Yeah . . . "

"So?"

"The transition makes it hard to focus."

"You mean the trial makes it hard to focus."

"You know, Wolf," she said earnestly, "with classwork, there's always a clear deadline. I have to be prepared by a certain day and time. And I have to get their papers back to them graded by a certain time. I always meet deadlines. Same with talks. There's a deadline. No matter what's happening, there are the deadlines. I'll meet them. Publications are more amorphous. They feel like they can wait until . . ."

She wasn't sure the word.

"A resolution," he said. "I get it. Are you eating enough?"

"Yes," she said. "I came into more than the pork roast, so I'm eating a lot. I'm going to get fat once the weather gets cold and I can't go out and run so easily. And that happens early in Minnesota."

"You're never going to get fat, Rabbit," he said. "You move more than you eat."

It sounded to her like he had rolled over in the bed and switched hands for the phone.

"What did you mean, Wolf, that the trial isn't starting on Monday?"

He didn't respond.

"You're making me nervous, Wolf."

"The thing you said in the papers, the thing you gave away, about the faked text—"

"I didn't talk to a reporter!" she protested. "I told that to my seminar class, after class, when we were out, and I didn't mean to. And someone must have told a student reporter. I haven't talked to any reporters."

"Well, be that as it may," he answered, in that slightly cop-officious tone that she so disliked, "it all led to some kind of legal wrangling with his lawyers and the prosecutors and the judge, and now there's a delay of some kind."

"Shit," she said. "Shit."

"Look, Rabbit," he answered, trying to sound calm but sounding perhaps a little irritated, "I've been through enough of these to know there's no telling where it will go. I have in fact *told* you that. There is always a good probability of a miscarriage of justice."

"I've been preparing myself for that—since you told me."

She thought she sounded like a ditzy schoolgirl reciting her spelling homework.

"You're *not* prepared," he said plainly. "You're never prepared when you know what the truth is and they say you're wrong."

She didn't respond. She thought to herself there was simply no way the jury would conclude anything other than what was true: Wilhelm was guilty and should go to prison forever.

As if he could tell what she was thinking, he went on: "It's going to come as a great shock to you if they find him not guilty. Odds are good you're going to feel like you didn't do enough. Maybe you're going to feel that I didn't let you do enough. You'll make deals with the universe—that you'll do this or that if only the universe will let you go back and do it right, so that the verdict comes out right."

She still did not answer.

"My main concern at that point, frankly—I mean if it's acquittal—my main concern will be your safety. You and I both know he probably did kill Jimmy, and we still can't prove it. He's pretty good, that motherfucker."

He didn't often swear.

"Short-listed for the Nobel," she said quietly. "You know that Wilhelm was short-listed for the Nobel? They won't call me as a witness?"

"Looks like they won't. The prosecution team is working off direct evidence. And the defense doesn't want you on the stand. *Nobody* wants you on the stand. You're too unpredictable."

She knew he didn't mean it as a criticism. If anything, he probably meant it in admiration—that she said what she thought was true, necessary, right, without consideration of loyalties or long games or anything. But one can't very well say "you're too unpredictable" to someone and not have it sound like an insult.

"I'd be much more comfortable," he went on, "if you'd take Hunter and keep him with you. You can do what you did before—just tell people you have a seizure disorder and he's a medical service dog. No one needs to know he's a retired K-9. He's running fine now that his leg is healed. He'd be so happy to be with you. It'd make me feel a lot better."

"But I don't have a seizure disorder," she said, wondering if he could hear her tears starting to flow. "And I don't want to have to take care of a dog. He's better with you. You know you can leave him at the station when you're out working and then he has good company, he's not alone."

They were both quiet for a while except for her occasional sniffle. She wondered after a while if he had fallen asleep. She started to think about what the next few weeks or months were going to be like. She might be able to avoid seeing televisions and newspapers, but there was no way people weren't going to just keep trying to engage her on the trial. Not just reporters. Her students, coworkers, friends.

She started then to cry audibly.

"Rabbit," he said sadly. "It's going to be okay. You're strong, you're a survivor, and it's going to be okay."

"I hadn't really thought about it, Wolf. But no matter what happens—not guilty, guilty, mistrial, even if he stands up suddenly and has a heart attack in the courtroom and falls over dead right there—it's never going to leave me alone. I hadn't really thought about it."

"Yeah," he said, sighing hard. "Here's my recommendation: Think of it as a bad cancer."

She sniffled again.

"This is how you cheer someone up, Wolf?"

"It's like a bad cancer," he continued. "You go through the treatment. It wrecks you. You're never going to be the same. You're always going to worry it's going to come back, that the whole thing will recur. But you survive it, and you feel weirdly grateful that you're alive for a while longer. Maybe more aware of your life than most people ever get to be."

She stopped crying and went quiet.

After a minute, he added, "I guess what I'm saying, Rabbit, is you've been through this kind of thing before. It's the kind of thing that might destroy some people. But you take it, you absorb it, you survive it. You use it. You feed off it, even."

She said nothing. She knew he wasn't wrong.

"Look," he added, "when I took you to the prosecutors and had you tell them what you had found, what you had figured out, I could see you understood your part in this. You didn't make your part smaller than it was to save yourself, as some people would. You didn't make it bigger than it was to make yourself seem important, as some people would. You just understood you were a part of it, a part of it that had to operate correctly to get to justice. You can step out of this when it is done. You'll always have played that part. But it's a part you played, not all of you."

She remembered now that first time at the prosecutors' office and remembered, too, what Joseph had said about how he knew Whit loved Ally—that he made her presence larger. That was exactly what Wolf had done at the prosecutors' office. He had made her presence larger. It was how they had all figured out that he loved her, a fact that made them all unsure, uncomfortable, about whether he was right that she was right. Her time there would have been easier if he hadn't so obviously loved her; yet she was not sorry they all could see it as easily as she could.

"Wolf," she asked, "is there ever a marked end to playing the part? A time when one gets to take a bow and go back behind the curtain?"

He hesitated. She could hear him clear his throat and move around.

"I'll tell you what, Rabbit. When it is over—when the verdict comes in—I'll come to Minnesota and cook that pork roast for you. That will be the signal it is over. Leave it in the freezer until then."

She felt a sudden wave of relief, as if he had pulled her out of the way of a train.

"What will you do with it? With the meat?"

"You know I don't usually know what I want to cook until just before I'm ready to cook."

"Tell me what you think you'll do. If it were now. If it were right now."

"A kosher salt and thyme and garlic crust for the pork. Fresh chopped rosemary for the potatoes, maybe with a little lavender mixed in, to give it that slight grassy flavor, with the skins and the whites of the potatoes cooked crispy. The pork will be with plums and apples, maybe a few figs, with a little bit of orange rind grated in, maybe with a few buds of chamomile soaked in orange juice first. Some kind of bitter greens – broccolini or collards. Pinot noir or something similar. Something good for dessert. Whatever you want for dessert. Okay?"

"Okay," she said. "Crème brûlée?"

"Sure."

"Baked Alaska?"

"Uh, okay."

"Pineapple upside-down cake?"

"I've never made one," Wolf answered, "but I can learn."

"Blue Jell-O with mini-marshmallows?"

"No!" he replied. "A man has his limits. No blue Jell-O, no mini-marshmallows. Speaking of limits, I've got to go to sleep, Rabbit. I have to be up in a few hours."

"Good night, Wolf."

"Give me a quick ring when you're home safe in Minnesota, please? Oh, and check to see if the broiler where you're staying works."

He hung up. Now she felt even more awake from the sudden and unexpected feeling of joy. It felt like being with the prosecutors all over again.

Chapter 14

Maddy paused the car at the mailbox as she approached Alex's house. Opening it, she was surprised to see nothing had come in the two cycles of mail delivery that would have happened while she had been in New York. There was usually at least one piece of junk mail each day—a car insurance solicitation, a grocery circular.

But when she came into the house, the reason became clear: Someone had brought in the mail while she was gone, leaving it all on the kitchen counter.

The specially delivered letter on the top—not mailed but left in person— made clear who had done this: Everett Sophie. It was in a cream-colored envelope, addressed in elegant handwriting to "M.S., Ph.D." Maddy stood at the counter to read the contents.

. . .

Dear Madeleine (if I may),

I am writing and leaving you this letter because I know that you will be wondering about that envelope I gave you to take to New York. Mr. Whitaker called me this morning to say that you opened and read it at dinner last night. He said you now know that he and I already knew what that envelope would contain.

We didn't mean to use you in any way, or to be deceptive. There is a lot about Alex's death that feels unsettled, and I think we—Whit and I—feel unsettled. She left us each so suddenly.

When I called Whit about your request to talk with him a few days ago, he seemed very eager to meet you, and I think that at that time he felt as I did—that the envelope with the codicil in it made a kind of clever reason for you to go see him right away.

But you will be wondering why I sat for months on what was in that envelope, as it benefits me financially. By how much exactly, I don't know, but I know Alex's house was without a mortgage and certainly worth a fair bit. And perhaps there are other assets of which I'm not aware, like bank accounts and life insurance and the like. And now a brand-new Steinway.

I do know that it specifically leaves a little to Scott and Maya's son, and the rest halved between Hank and me. Alex showed it to me before she put it in the envelope and signed her name across the seal. She wanted me to know.

Before she died, it never occurred to me that that envelope would ever come to matter. Of course I put it in a safe place. But I assumed she would live many years more, that she would outlive me, given that I was ten years her senior. And I also assumed that within a few months of handing it to me, she'd find a proper lawyer to fix her will, making that "to whom it may concern" letter irrelevant from that point forward.

I fully expected that either her own lawyer would finish chemotherapy and go back to practice, at which time Alex would have gone to him and fixed her will, or—well, frankly, that he would die of his cancer, and Alex would go ahead and get another lawyer and fix her will. It never occurred to me she might die within about a month of handing me that envelope. It never occurred to me that she might die at all.

And now it all makes me wonder whether somehow she knew she would die, or thought she might soon.

I am afraid I am rambling and not telling you what it is I really need to explain. It seems selfish to focus on myself in the face of Alex's death. But I do need to tell you something and ask you to try hard to understand.

I've told you a little bit about who I am: that I live some of my time as Everett and some of it as Sophie; that I feel myself fortunate in being able to live this way; that there is a sexual component to it, which again I think is odd *only* in the statistical sense and not in the sense of there being a sexual component to my genders, because I do think that for most of us, gender is about sexuality. Why else do we bother to dress as men and as women, particularly when there is the possibility of romance or sex? Indeed, I've come to think, in talking with many people, that the time we feel our genders most acutely is when we are engaged in sexual excitement.

But that is a longer discussion for another day and only if you are interested in it, the way Alex was. It is certainly something Alex and I talked about a great deal, especially as she worked on her new project in the last year—an attempt to understand human sexuality, but more significantly what to do with sex *ethically*. I mention it to you here, the sexual component of my bi-gendered life, because it explains why I was afraid of the police knowing about the codicil to her will. The police, I think, would be nothing like Alex in their understanding.

You see, Alex bothered to make this significant change to her will, to add me to it, to put it into writing, to have it notarized, to show it to me, to put it in this envelope to save, and to give it to me. That was all her choice, but that's what she did.

That meant I *knew* about the change in her will—there could be no question I knew about it, and had it in my possession, too. I knew I could financially benefit from her death. Quite substantially.

And then, shortly thereafter, she died, under what might apparently be considered somewhat suspicious circumstances.

I mean, I know she drowned in that lake, and we all know she went swimming alone all the time. But she was not a weak swimmer. And it is not that deep a lake, I don't think.

So, was it going to be the case, I had to wonder, that the police might ask questions about who would gain from her sudden and unexpected death? And if I showed up with this codicil to her will in my personal possession right after she had written it, not long after she had died, would they become suspicious of me?

You might say this is just a rather dramatic, perhaps even paranoid, thought. But if you know the history of how other people have viewed persons of minority sexualities—and I am thinking you know some about it because of your work, perhaps?—then you will know that plain-vanilla straight people love to imagine that anyone with a variant kind of sexuality is a pervert and therefore also immoral. This is the plain-vanilla logic about us queers. It's not hard to look at how people from sexual minorities have been portrayed historically, when we've been visible at all, and to see the assumption there, that we are naturally inclined to be—well, callous, selfish, even murderous.

I can only imagine what it would be like for me to try to explain to the police how I live, and somehow it would surely come up if I were under their scrutiny. Particularly difficult would be trying to get past their under-standing of my bi-gendered life as a mere cross-dressing fetish of a cheap and comical type. I don't need that. The irony! There I would be, treated by the police as if I should be ashamed of myself, treated that way because of the death of Alex, the woman who understood that shame, not sex, was the real problem for humans.

It hardly seemed worth my safety to pursue what is just money, and money that for me would come attached to the tremendous loss of Alex. So, I just let that envelope be, although it kept troubling me that this meant I was keeping Hank from an inheritance he was rightly owed. I did not know how to reconcile that with my own needs. I thought I had to speak to Hank soon about it and maybe he would come to a solution—perhaps we could say Alex had given *him* this envelope. Or perhaps someone else would take it for us and not explain *where* it came from, and no one would question it?

Scott wasn't going to question it.

But Hank has a way of thinking that his point of view—which, like Alex's, has little patience for shame around sexual orientations, as none of the three of us ever believed they are chosen—should be everyone's. He simply didn't deal with the reality of *what is;* instead he thought in terms of *what ought to be*—acceptance of people like me. In other words, he would have pooh-poohed my fears about possessing this letter, my fears about the police, and he would have pushed me to be honest, just present the codicil to Scott or to the court or whomever and go from there. He would have made a mess of it the way he often did in his very pugilistic and male way. I didn't trust him.

I still don't trust him. It's not that he's a bad person. He's just not very good at delicacy or at seeing other points of view. (Alex would hardly have been called "delicate" by most people, but even so, Hank managed to stomp on her emotions sometimes with his skirt-chasing habits such that she'd come to me genuinely wounded, though feigning mere anger.)

It felt strange, though, to hold on to this envelope and do nothing with it—not just because of Hank getting half but because Alex wanted me to have the money, too, right? I have been thinking since meeting you that I could take part of the inheritance and maybe ask Lew to go away with me—perhaps Palm Springs or Miami—where we could spend a week remembering Alex together. And then I could take some of the rest of the money and give it to charities in her remembrance. Fund some women grad students, intersex rights work, medical clinics for the indigent. She would have liked that.

So, I thought to talk to Scott about the envelope and what was in it, but I don't really know Scott. Alex and I became friends after their divorce, and I knew from her that he doesn't feel good about his own sexual orientation. So I doubted that he could understand the difference between shame and my reasonable fear, and all of that again felt too ironic, bitterly ironic, what with Alex's thesis, that consent and pleasure are the key to moral sex, not normality and pride (as pride is always the flip side of shame, and she wanted *out of that* for us all).

(As do I!)

I'm not sure any of this is making sense to you. However, I have the sense from talking to you that you are naturally inclined to figure these kinds of things out—that your foray in Philadelphia had something to do with your personality—and I didn't want you to go too far down some idea about me without my explaining to you what must seem confusing. I am also asking you to understand that, while I do not have any shame about who I am, that does not mean that I'm not endangered. Particularly by people like the average police officer.

I hope you will consider that as you decide what to do with the codicil. I would appreciate if you would not do anything to endanger me.

And, if you are willing, I would appreciate if you would meet with me again and tell me about Mr. Whitaker. I am trying to understand the parts of Alex's life I never did grasp, as I suppose it feels like then I still have her here near me. The truth is that the months are passing, and she is slipping away. And it breaks my heart. I worry I am going to forget what her face looked like, that I will have to look at photographs to remember. I do not have a lot of friends, and I had none like her. Her absence feels like a hole in the sky into which the darkness falls and grows bigger and then spills back out on me.

Sincerely,

E/S

P.S. If you are wondering how I got into the house, Alex used to leave a key under a rock out front. I wasn't sure it would still be there. I was just going to leave this at the door if the key wasn't there. I will put the key back when I go. You should probably take it in.

. . .

Maddy pulled out the flashlight she knew Alex had kept in the kitchen drawer where she had also kept pens and scissors and the like. She went out the front door and turned over this and that rock, shining the light around, until she found the key. Once back inside, she locked the door and made a mental note to tell Scott tomorrow she was going to get the lock changed. She checked the back door, the one off the kitchen, and confirmed the bolt that went into the floor was set. That door, at least, was secure.

Looking through the remaining stack of mail, Maddy found one more envelope meant for her. This was on slightly yellowed stationery she recognized well, postmarked West Virginia.

. . .

My dear Madeleine,

Sister Mary Grace told me she already wrote to suggest you might want to come back here for the holidays. I know she writes this invitation to you every year, but this year I am also writing to urge you to come. I know you probably want little to do with us, but I also know that the situation in Philadelphia with the trial has to be a cause of enormous anxiety for you. It is for *us*, watching it and knowing only a little from the news reports what you must have gone through and be going through. We can tell you are trying to stay out of the public eye.

We continue to pray for you, and to pray that justice is done at the trial. Thanks be to God that you figured out what was going on! (How many people you must have ultimately saved with your given cleverness, only He knows.)

It might do you quite a lot of good to come here to be among people who will not judge you or pester you if what you need is quiet and peace. You know we will not require anything of you. You wouldn't have to sleep with the boarding girls. You can have one of the guest rooms. I know the morning call to prayer will wake you up too early, but you need not get up; just rest, or work on your studies. We won't ask anything.

We worry about you, and we often feel, especially Sister Mary Grace and I, that we sent you off into the world without *enough*. You needed more than we provided.

Detective Wolf wrote to suggest that we check in on you. (He gave me the address where you are now lodging.) He, too, is concerned about you, and feels we might be of assistance. Obviously, you need not wait until the holidays if you need a refuge. We are here for you as needed.

You will always be steadily in our prayers. We pray for your mind, your body, your soul.

Madeleine, please do consider the possibility that the mortal world is sometimes too much, and it makes sense to just stop for a while, and let justice be in God's hands. He often has a purpose that we cannot know.

All praise be to God,

Sr. Ruth, O.P.

. . .

Maddy put the letter down and picked up her bag to take it to the bedroom. She changed into her nightgown, pulled out her phone, and headed to the bathroom. She dialed the phone and then cradled it between her shoulder and ear, picking up her toothbrush to apply her toothpaste. She remembered for a moment how Wolf used a pink-colored toothpaste for sensitive teeth and how it had a flavor she couldn't stand. Although the scent of it on his breath did not bother her.

"Hello?" Wolf answered.

"It's me. Just letting you know I'm home. Safe."

"Thank you for letting me know, Rabbit," he said. And then, just as she started to brush her teeth, Wolf added the question: "Can I ask why you were in New York?"

"Work," she said, her mouth full of toothpaste foam. "Work," she said again, trying to be clearer to herself as much as him. She spit the toothpaste into the sink. "My dean wanted me to go interview someone there."

It wasn't exactly a lie.

"Ah. It's good to make your boss happy," Wolf replied, as if she needed this kind of advice. "Tomorrow, work on a publication—or your Pittsburgh talk."

"Tomorrow," she answered, filling her cup with water, "work on what you're going to do with the pork roast when this fucking trial is over. Good night, Wolf."

Chapter 15

Two days later, Maddy looked over what she had assembled on five sheets of a yellow legal pad and realized there was so much she still didn't know. And so much she now *wanted* to know.

She should have expected this. Whenever she sat down and timelined the findings of a project, she was surprised both by what she saw and what she didn't. That was, after all, the very point of the exercise—a kind of inventorying of one's knowledge.

She breathed in deeply and gathered up into a single deck the white index cards scattered around Alex Shugar's desk. These were the cards marked with dates, events, and sources that Maddy had used to assemble the timeline on the yellow notepad. She opened the top drawer of the desk, found a tan rubber band left by Alex, and looped it three times around the cards. Now she added one blank card to the top, slipping it under the band. She took her pen and wrote on that top card one word to the left of the rubber band

(*Last*) and one to the right (*Days*).

Yes. That's right. This would be like any other publication of hers. Sure, the topic was a little unconventional, but some journal would take the paper she envisioned:

The Last Days of Alexandra Shugar.

It was a good, strong title. Granted, it lacked the usual colon and subtitle of the standard humanities paper. And she knew that history journals probably wouldn't take the manuscript because, as compelling as it might turn out to be, the editors wouldn't see the subject as historical. (Too recent.) She needed peer-reviewed publications in *history* journals. But it couldn't hurt to have one publication in an allied field like literature and medicine, a logical field for a piece that would include a retrospective of Alex's work. Heck, job committees in medical humanities might prefer a candidate who had one solid publication outside her own field proper, so long as she had several within.

Besides, there was a good shot at getting any paper on Shugar published right now. The interest in her life was high because her death had come early. And a publication in hand was worth two in process. Various journals surely would be actively looking for overviews of Shugar's work. Of course, most of those journal editors would handpick contemporaries of Alex to do an *in memoriam* essay. But some editor would be willing to send this article out for peer review, particularly if the editor saw Maddy's name on it, given her own fifteen minutes of fame and that she was Shugar's temporary job replacement.

She could put it in her CV as "under consideration" while it was out for review. And if in the process of doing this paper she figured out why Alex died, well, that would be interesting—and not necessarily something she would *need* to include in the paper. And if she did *not* figure out why Alex had died, well, then she still got a peer-reviewed publication out of it. And then no one, including Hank, would think she was a failure at these things. And no one, including Wolf, could tell her she had wasted an enormous amount of time working on what she wasn't supposed to be working on.

"Work on a publication" was all Wolf had said. He hadn't said *which* publication.

"Listen," she had said to Scott Willingham, when she called him the morning after getting home from New York, after telling him she was getting the lock changed. "I've decided I am going to do a paper about Alex's last days, a kind of piece about the arc of her life's work using the lens of the last days. So I have some questions for you to help me fill in what I know about those last days. It's just a research paper."

"Oh," he said in a way that she could tell he got it. "Okay, I see, you're doing *research* for a *paper*. Of course, I would help any junior faculty member in the college needing some help with a *research project*. It's good you're working on a publication and that the job here supports that."

She wished he hadn't added that last bit, about the job supporting it. He made it sound as if, should she decide to drop it, she would be failing to fulfill the duties of her position.

She had also called Hank Merriman, to tell him the same basic thing, and then Everett Sophie Inskeep, asking each questions about the days just before and after Alex's death. Lew Meadows (Maddy recalled with relief) had been away on sabbatical in the period when Alex died. That meant she didn't have to ask him questions, and he didn't have to know—and tell everyone—what Maddy was working on. She could just tell him when the paper was coming out.

Now, she looked over what she had assembled on the pad.

Thurs/5-26:
9 a.m.10:50 a.m.—AS presum. taught her grad seminar [UMN course catalog; E/S recall]

Returned home to drop car, get bag, be picked up by Everett [E/S recall]

noonish AS dropped at MSP airport by Everett, for Delta Airlines #42, depart 1:30 p.m. [E/S recall; Delta schedule]

prob. arrived JFK about 5 p.m.; met by driver, to Whit's club [Delta schedule; Whit calendar; Joseph]

evening—dinner w/Whit; asked him for piano; stayed at RC; Whit visited her at RC [Whit calendar; Joseph]

Fri/5-27:
morning—Steinway, selected piano type, not clear why buying, but AS was determined to do it that day, annoyed it would take a few months to get delivered [Steinway rep], texted Whit to inform she had chosen one [Whit recall; last phone text from AS]

lunch alone MoMA, bought scarf for Sophie @ giftshop [Sophie recall]

late afternoon flight JFK-MSP (which flight?), picked up by Hank [Hank recall]

late dinner w/Hank on way home @ Cat's Corner Bistro, Hank and AS slept the night together at AS's [Hank recall]

<u>Sat./5-28:</u>

morning—AS planned long work ("writing") weekend, seemed to be doing fine per Hank [Hank recall]

mid-morning—AS had brunch w/Sophie @ Sophie's house, gave Sophie the scarf, AS planned writing weekend, Alex seemed fine per Sophie [Sophie recall]

?? evening

<u>Sun./5-29: ??</u> (long writing day?)

<u>Mon/5-30/Memorial Day:</u>

[[Mon Temps in low 40s in am, low 60s by afternoons [*Star Tribune* weather forecast, from library]—water would be v. cold for swimming]]

9:30 a.m.—AS texted Hank "love you"; Hank responded "love you back. see you later?" / no further response, not unusual per Hank to get no response back [Hank text record/recall]

9:32 a.m.— AS texted Everett Sophie "love you"; E/S responded "Love you and scarf!" [E/S text record] No further response from AS, not unusual to get no response back [E/S recall]

(otherwise Hank & ES left AS alone per "writing weekend" plan)

DROWNED —between 9:30 a.m. and evening based on text replies/ nonreplies

(wearing clothing and jewelry [Scott])

8 p.m.—Hank texts AS – gets no reply [Hank text record]

<u>Tues./5-31:</u>

morning—Hank & E/S (each) tried texting AS, then phoning AS – no response, phone kicked straight to voicemail [Hank & E/S text records/ recalls]

1 p.m.— AS doesn't show for meeting with grad students; students ask dept. sect. where AS is. Dept. sect. tells Scott she can't find Alex, Alex has not called in; Scott tries phone, kicks to voicemail [Scott recall]

4 p.m.— Alex doesn't show for dept. meeting, dept. sect. tells Scott. Scott texts Hank; Hank calls Scott, says has also not heard from her; worried. [Scott text record/recall; Hank recall]

5 p.m.—Scott goes to AS' house—no car, no Alex, no cell phone or computer. Calls Hank. Hank calls E/S. None had heard from Alex since Monday morning texts. Scott leaves note for Alex to call him. [Scott/Hank/ ES recalls.]

<u>Wed./6-1:</u>

8 a.m.— group decision to call police after Scott confirms no sign [Hank,

E/S, Scott]

9 a.m.— Scott and Hank file missing person together [Hank, Scott]

<u>Thurs./6-2:</u>

p.m.— Scott pushes police, police maybe make a few calls? [Scott recall; confirmed Hank recall] (Everyone told police she went swimming alone, per Hank—that this was their worry about what had happened.) Police tell Scott it's not uncommon for adults to disappear for a few days without explanation. (Police not really interested per Hank and Scott.)

<u>Fri./6-3:</u>

Midday—AS' car reported apparently abandoned at Cottontail Lake

p.m.—divers deployed, body found, Scott notified, he tells others [all]

[some police inquiries made; say "accidental drowning presumed" b/c no sign of foul play [*Star Tribune* 6/4]

<u>about 3 days later?</u>—approx. June 6?— police return jewelry [Scott/Hank recall]

<u>mid-July</u>—Scott bugs the police, then told "probable suicide" [Scott recall]

Maddy looked over this timeline once, twice, three times, making notes in the margins, adding a few stars here and there, drawing a box around the word "DROWNED." As if it needed emphasis.

There was so much she still didn't know, particularly about the two days—Saturday and Sunday—before Alex died. Had Alex wanted time alone for a writing weekend? Or had she been depressed and isolating herself?

Plenty of academics, particularly in the humanities, would lock themselves away for a few days to get writing on a publication done. But *had* that been what Alex had been doing that last weekend, or had she been going down a mental spiral alone? Secure the "baby" in New York at Steinway—cost Whit a pretty penny with a big, black metaphor on her way out—and go, leaving the instrument to arrive later like a ghostly orphan?

Were those last "love you" texts sent to Hank and Everett Sophie on the morning of just normal expressions after a couple of days of silence as Hank and Everett Sophie both seemed at to think? Or were they Alex saying goodbye?

Had she gone swimming in her clothes and with her jewelry on because she was lost in a moment after a long stretch of intense writing, pulled into the water of Cottontail Lake as if by deep instinct, the way Hank and Whit described Alex sometimes being drawn to water? Or had she gone in with her clothes and her jewelry because she was simply feeling done with the world?

Or had she gone into the water for some emergent reason—perhaps a person or an animal in trouble?

Or had someone been there with her and drowned her intentionally?

What had happened to Alex's research records and notebooks that seemed to be missing? Had she purposefully destroyed them before ending her life? The same with her cell phone and computer, which were missing, according to Scott.

Or had someone—Scott? Hank? Everett Sophie?— gotten rid of them when they realized Alex was in all likelihood truly gone? Perhaps to avoid the Gnat ultimately getting them?

Maddy's own phone dinged with a text. She opened it to read the message.

Maarten here. Liz gave me yr #.

She was trying to figure out how to respond when he sent another message:

Exciting to watch trial news knowing that was u! I M basking in yr glory.

She sighed and looked out the window for a good couple of minutes. Then she deleted the text, including Maarten's phone number, and went out for a run.

Chapter 16

Wolf stood up when he saw the two of them coming. He gave Maddy an awkward kiss on the cheek, tipping his head back to avoid hitting her with the brim of his baseball hat. She drew back quickly and stared down at the floor, noting to herself that she certainly had *not* thought that the next time she would see Wolf in person would be in some random Pittsburgh sports bar with Sophie at her side. She was already agitated enough from what had just happened at the conference. Wolf's unexpected presence made her no calmer.

"John Wolf," she said to him formally, making a stiff gesture while keeping her eyes fixed on the dark green linoleum floor, "this is Sophie Inskeep."

"Pleased to meet you," Wolf said, shaking Sophie's hand. "Are you also a historian?"

The three of them slid into the booth Wolf had been occupying while he waited for them, Sophie taking the inside seat, Maddy next to Sophie. Wolf sat in the middle of the bench on his side. Maddy realized he was purposefully making the conversation space into an equilateral triangle. Much as he might want to talk specifically with Maddy, he wasn't going to ignore Sophie. Maddy felt suddenly grateful for his small gesture of (as usual) simply accepting whoever happened into Maddy's life.

But what was he doing here? It could not be good.

"No, no, Mr. Wolf, I'm not a historian," Sophie said, glancing at Maddy just as Wolf did the same. Maddy realized from the way they looked at her that she must have a bad look stuck on her face, but she could not seem to correct for it. She turned her gaze down to the table.

"I'm an architect and interior designer," Sophie said, still looking at Maddy. "A new friend of Maddy's. I came along just for the day. We'll go back on the same flight tomorrow."

Wolf signaled to a waiter to come over to the table and asked Sophie what she would like to drink. The waiter put a black paper cocktail napkin in front of each of them.

"A glass of chardonnay would be lovely, thank you. Or whatever white wine you have."

Wolf ordered himself a beer and asked Maddy what she wanted. Now she looked up, staring at him intensely with what something like a scowl on her face. Why was he here? Why had he shown up in Pittsburgh to see her without even telling her he was going to do that when she hadn't seen him in months? Something bad about the trial? Something he had to tell her in person? Or had he somehow figured out what she was trying to learn about Alex Shugar?

"She'll have a whiskey sour," Wolf told the waiter, who promptly left. Maddy leaned her head over to the side and scratched her forehead several times. After an awkward silence, Sophie turned determinedly to Wolf.

"May I ask how you know Madeleine, Mr. Wolf?"

Wolf looked to Maddy to see what he should say. She gave him a small nod.

"Maddy lived with me as a boarder for a few months in Philadelphia," he said, "while she was doing her dissertation research there. I'm a police detective."

He waited for Sophie to realize what he was saying.

"Oh," said Sophie. "Oh! I see—that was when Madeleine figured it all out about Dr. Wilhelm. You helped her."

Wolf twisted his cocktail napkin around his left index finger, unintentionally drawing Maddy's attention to the glint of gold of his wedding ring. As shiny as ever. But of course it was washed frequently, with all his cooking.

"She didn't really need my help figuring it out," Wolf told Sophie. "She just needed me to believe her. Which I did."

He looked at Maddy again, meeting her eyes. For a minute, they simply stared at each other. Sophie said nothing and sat quite still.

"Where's Hunter?" Maddy finally asked.

"I left him with Bobby. I just came for the day to hear your lecture. Did you want me to bring him for you?"

"What are you doing here?" she asked, as if he had not just said that he came to hear her talk at the conference that day. "Was he found not guilty? Did they find Wilhelm not guilty?"

"Rabbit," he said, catching himself up just after saying it. "Damn it, Maddy, damn it," he added quickly, acting as if "damn it" was what he had said the first time.

He grabbed a little bit of Maddy's hair by her jaw and pulled on it like the chain of a lamp, as if to wake her up out of her strange ideas. He let it go a moment later.

"The trial only just started," he said. "It's going to take weeks. Remember, you told me on the phone the other night from New York that this was the week you were going to be in Pittsburgh for the conference? I realized I could just drive over and hear your presentation. I didn't think you'd mind. Sure, it's a haul from Philly, but I have an old buddy who lives not too far from here, a friend who I can see tonight, and I can be back home in time for late work tomorrow. Just thought it'd be good to come hear your presentation."

"Because you're just so interested in the history of anatomy?" she said, wondering to herself why she was sounding so sarcastic. "Something about the trial, Wolf? Is that why you're here?"

The waiter returned with the drinks, accidentally giving Maddy the white wine and Sophie the whiskey sour. Sophie switched the two glasses around.

"*Nothing about that,*" Wolf said, firmly and in a low voice as if trying to discipline Maddy with his voice as one does with a dog. "Nothing about the trial. I just came to see how you are doing since you called from New York."

"Want anything to eat?" the waiter asked.

They all shook their heads silently.

"Madeleine," said Sophie as soon as the waiter left, running her finger on the condensation of her glass meditatively, "I think you should tell John why it is you are upset. Otherwise he's going to think you are upset with *him.*"

Maddy looked up at Sophie. She found herself admiring the makeup around Sophie's eyes, so perfectly applied. Sophie's eyeliner looked exactly as it is supposed to, framing the eye to draw attention to the eye itself, the way a good frame pulls a painting forward. Maddy wished she could get her makeup just right, just like that.

"Can you tell him?" Maddy asked, lifting the drink to her lips and taking a long sip. "Can you explain why I'm so rattled?"

"Was it the photographer at your session?" Wolf asked. "That guy taking photos of you while you were trying to present, Maddy? You *know* that's going to happen. Press photographers are gonna show up when they know you'll be in public. They want recent photos for the news on the trial. They can't take any pictures in the courtroom to use. They can only do sketches there. And news outfits always want photos—sells papers better. It's why I made a point of hanging back, so that photographer couldn't see me there. Why I was wearing a hat. Why I didn't even tell you I was here until I found a place we could meet away from the conference. The last thing we need is a picture in the news of the two of us together in Pittsburgh."

His voice trailed off and he looked at Sophie as if he'd been caught.

Sophie put her drink down and reached across the table to put her hand briefly on his.

"John," she said, "if I may call you 'John.' It's not the photographer."

She pulled back her hand and took another drink.

"The session two slots before Madeleine's included a presentation by a critic of a late friend of ours. Wait, what am I saying? Maddy never met Alex—Maddy and Alex were never friends. Let me start over. That other session before Madeleine's included a presentation by a critic of a late very good friend of *mine*."

Sophie clenched her eyes shut momentarily and opened them again.

"Good lord. Let me try that all again. To be clear."

She breathed in and breathed out and started again.

"As it happens, a session before Maddy's panel included a presentation by a graduate student in philosophy at the University of Minnesota who is doing his dissertation work on the late Alexandra Shugar. Alex Shugar happens to have been a very good friend of mine—my best friend—and she happens to have been the faculty member whose classes Maddy has been hired to cover. We lost Alex only a few months ago. The fellow presenting was a young man Alex used to call 'the Gnat.'"

"Sorry, Ms. Inskeep, but I'm still not following you," Wolf said, looking over Maddy's shoulder at the bar TV. She realized he had probably picked this bar hoping the TVs around the room would remain set to channels dedicated to sports so that none of them would flash up news of the trial. He had probably also figured that other academics from the conference would not end up here.

"Well," Sophie said, "this particular graduate student presented an analysis of my friend Alex's work that was—disconcerting."

"Fucking wrong," Maddy said, drawing Wolf's attention back to the table. "Completely fucking wrong."

Sophie breathed in hard and stared up at the ceiling looking as if she could see something there that wasn't right.

"I mean," Sophie said to no one in particular, "I guess Alex knew that could happen. *Would* happen. She talked about how one lost control of one's narrative. The Gnat had been doing that to her even before she died. She would hardly be surprised it's worse now. That *he* is worse now. Saying what he wants as she can't defend herself. The dead have no rights, do they, Madeleine? The dead have no rights, do they, Officer Wolf?"

"I just can't understand," Maddy said, looking over her own shoulder for a moment to see what kept intermittently grabbing Wolf's attention, figuring it must be the baseball game on the televisions over the bar. "I just don't understand how that fucking gnat can get away with such blatant misrepresentations of Alex's work. He's just reading into it in ways that serve his purposes. He's reconstructing her identity, repeating over and over again these false representations, and the more he says it, the more true it will all become."

She crumpled up her napkin, threw it on the table, and drank down the rest of her cocktail.

"Slow down," Wolf said to her. "Slow down. What do you mean?"

"It's so ironic," Sophie interjected. "All of that time Alex spent talking about how there is a reality *beyond* the representation. And he's proving her wrong by just over and over again saying things about her work that aren't true, turning falsehoods into truths. As if he's doing some kind of exercise to prove that she was so fundamentally wrong about reality mattering? Using her own life—abusing her legacy—to try to prove she was wrong about reality mattering?"

"Makes me sick to my stomach," Maddy replied, signaling to the waiter that she wanted another of the same. "Could you *please* take off the stupid Mets cap, Wolf?"

He shook his head.

"If we do get photographed together, no one'll believe it was me in a Mets hat. Plausible deniability."

Maddy didn't laugh.

"Listen, I understand why what you're describing would be upsetting," Wolf said, turning his cap's brim slightly to the side. "Of course it'd be upsetting to see someone whose work you cared about be lied about. But presumably the evidence out there will outweigh whatever this twit—"

"Gnat," Maddy corrected him.

"—whatever he says," Wolf finished. "People in the field will see what she actually said, what she really thought. There are records. Published. *Actual* publications."

Maddy caught Wolf's apparent reference to Wilhelm's forged text. She shook her head briefly at him as if to ask him to stop.

"It's a mountain of work, undoing what the Gnat is saying about Alex's work," Maddy sighed. "Correcting a record being actively sullied is a mountain of work. You know that. You told me what it's like when someone messes with the evidence. Who has *time* to stop him?"

The waiter came and delivered Maddy the second drink and asked the others if they wanted more. They declined. Maddy took a sip of the second glass and found it like the first, pleasantly cold and tart. She wondered if she should order food. But nothing at a place like this would taste any good.

"And it's the tangle," Maddy added now. "He's purposely making a tangle. A scholarly tangle that'll wrap itself around Alex for years if he succeeds. Forever, maybe."

"And so it'll all become about *him*," added Sophie, with a tone of disgust. "So the Gnat will make *his* name, and make it big, using *hers*. How convenient for him that she's gone just in time for his dissertation! He takes over her space without her here to fight him. He stands on her tall pedestal as she has now fallen off. Just in time to finish his degree and look so impressive to job committees."

Maddy turned sharply to look at Sophie, her mouth hanging open a little. The idea hadn't really occurred to Maddy—and it obviously had not struck Sophie the way it did Maddy, the timing of Alex's death to the Gnat's dissertation and his career. The benefit of Alex's recent death to the Gnat.

Agitated, Maddy reached past Sophie and pulled the small plastic food menu from the little condiment stand at the end of the table. The menu was smeared with dried ketchup, making what was listed there seem even less appetizing. She put it back.

"Blah," she said to no one in particular.

Wolf pulled his wallet out of his back pocket, opened it, and removed a photograph.

"Maddy and Hunter," he said, showing Sophie the picture. "I keep trying to convince Maddy to take Hunter at least while she's in Minneapolis. Don't you think she should have a dog?"

Sophie smiled broadly at the image of Maddy with the white shepherd. Maddy took the photograph from Sophie and looked at it, and then looked up at Wolf.

"I don't remember you taking this," she said.

"Didn't," he answered. "Bobby did, when you were back in Philly—remember? Bobby printed it and gave it to me."

She looked at the photo again and then looked up to Wolf. She smiled a half grin at him and then just gave into it—the buzzing of the booze combining with the deep comfort of seeing him in the flesh, not just in her mind, not just in the occasional fleeting dream. She leaned the right side of her face between her index finger and thumb, the fingers forming a stand for her heavy head, her elbow on the table. The whiskey was making her so warm, as were her memories of trying to explain something to him. She wished he would take the stupid hat off so she could see his face better.

"How is Bobby?" she asked. "Is he even of legal drinking age yet?"

"Yes!" said Wolf, letting out a small laugh. "You don't have to buy him beer anymore. He hasn't called to tell you?"

"To tell me I don't have to buy him beer anymore?"

"No, no, to tell you about the song."

"What song?"

A sudden group cry came up from the bartender and a couple of people watching the TV over the bar, a reaction to some play. The bartender turned up the volume of the sound.

"He wrote a song about you," Wolf explained, speaking a little louder to overcome the noise.

"He writes a song a day," Maddy snorted, "So, there's one about me. Who cares?"

"Oh, you don't get it," Wolf answered, smiling at her suddenly improved mood. He poked at the back of her hand with his index finger. "This one's special. It's called 'Mystery Girl.' And it's actually kind of catchy. What's the line? '*Mystery girl, mystery girl, when are you going to discover I oh love you?*'"

Maddy groaned and put her head in her hands, but Sophie smiled as she could tell Maddy was not unhappy now.

"He told me he's getting it recorded professionally," Wolf added, "in some guy's garage, and he's trying to get someone from a label to pay some attention. He keeps telling everybody it's about you. I think he thinks it'll help his odds. Probably does!"

"I'm just a gimmick to Bobby!" she yelled with faux disgust.

"Well," Wolf said, now looking at the food menu himself, "you *are* a gimmick for his song, but he does still have a legitimate crush on you. And like I said, it's a catchy little tune, and you never know. He's been getting gigs in Jersey. One in Baltimore, even. He's not that bad."

"No," Maddy agreed, "he's pretty good. I mean, on the guitar, and as a singer."

She thought about Bobby's face when he was singing to her that night at the bar, when he had completely misread the source of her heart's open pleasure that day.

Maddy started to slide the photograph of her and Hunter into the breast pocket of her button-down shirt.

"Hey!" Wolf cried out, grabbing it from her. "That's mine."

"But I need a picture of Hunter."

"So do I," he argued, taking it back. "Any self-respecting guy has to have a photo of his dog in his wallet."

"Yeah, a photo of his *dog*," she said, teasing him.

He took another drink of his beer and let out a chuckle.

"I might keep a photo of *you*, young lady, if you were even half as well-behaved as that dog."

"If I was half as well-behaved as that dog, you would have succeeded in kicking me out," she said, forgetting Sophie was there. "You miss having me eat you out of house and home. Admit it. You don't know what to do with all the extra food."

"I've got a freezer. But it's true, no one has ever used me as a cook as well as you did," he answered her, also seeming to forget Sophie's presence.

"Not even Sergeant Blackmore? The noises he made at your barbequed ribs? Remember how Wes told him to get a room with the ribs?"

"You're right. You're absolutely right. I need to get a photo of Sergeant Blackmore to carry around with me." Wolf put the photograph back in his wallet and slipped it into his back pocket. "Speaking of food, I almost forgot I brought you something."

He reached down to his bag next to him on the bench and pulled out a jar containing clear fluid and orange chunks.

"Pickled pumpkin. Tried making it last week. Pretty good, I think. But you tell me."

Maddy opened the jar, releasing the seal, and pulled one piece out.

"Hey!" he said. "I thought you'd take it home with you and try it there, not open it here."

"I'm hungry," she answered, crunching and wincing a little from the sour. "Nice," she added. "A little clove? And coriander?"

She pushed the jar over to Sophie who reached in with two fingers and pulled out a piece. She chewed on it and also winced, smiling.

"Very nice. Not so good with this particular wine, but I bet it goes quite nicely with a whiskey sour or a beer. You should have warned me, Mr. Wolf, and I would have ordered the right drink for this special appetizer."

Wolf smiled at Sophie and took the jar, fishing out several pieces and tossing them into his mouth. He washed them down with some of his beer.

"I'm sorry Maddy and I are going on and on like it's old home week," he said to Sophie, though it was clear he wasn't sorry about anything.

"I don't at all mind listening. And it's delightful to see Madeleine happy for a change."

Wolf looked to Maddy a combination of pleased and embarrassed—that look he'd gotten when she showed up at his station that time with Hunter.

"Very kind of you to accompany Maddy all the way from Minneapolis, Ms. Inskeep," Wolf said to Sophie. "I appreciate you doing so."

"Well, the truth is that Maddy had noticed that the other paper, the Gnat's paper, was lined up before hers. She mentioned it to me when she called to tell me about her trip to New York. I wanted to come and hear what the young man had to say, now that Alex is gone. Before she died, you see, Mr. Wolf, my friend Alex had been pretty upset about what the Gnat was up to, and somehow I felt like, between that and Maddy presenting, it would make sense to come along. It felt like I should at least offer. And Maddy said she did not mind."

"The truth is," Maddy said to Wolf, "I was happy when Ev—when Sophie offered to come with me. And really she offered because I'd told her—well, I'd *whined* to her—about having to go to a conference where everyone was going to try to talk to me about the trial but where I couldn't say anything about it. I'd have to spend the whole conference trying to change the subject in every conversation. I don't want to know anything until it is over, you know. I figured if she came and stayed alongside me, I could keep telling people I'd talk to them *after* I finished talking to this nice woman Sophie Inskeep. I could simply not stop talking to this nice woman Sophie Inskeep, and so I could get my paper delivered, see what the Gnat had to say, and get out of here without having to talk to anyone else."

Sophie nodded. "The plan was to have everyone think I was quite pushy and good at monopolizing Dr. Shanks' time. Of course I'm happy to help her out. It wasn't too hard to get myself plane tickets and a hotel room just for tonight, and I was happy to do it."

"Well, thank you, again," Wolf said. "Maddy, I thought your own presentation went very well," he said. "You agree?"

"It went fine," she said, taking another sip, feeling such a good buzz. "But you know what I feel like? Like I'm a one-hit-wonder and everyone comes to the performance wanting me to sing that one hit song, and I keep singing something else."

She sighed, took another sip, and rubbed her eyes.

"Maybe when Bobby's song comes out, Wolf, they'll pay attention to him instead."

She sounded suddenly less happy.

Wolf changed the subject by asking Sophie about her work. As the two of them talked, Maddy kept wondering what Wolf would think if he knew that Sophie was a man—or male, anyway. Now she almost wanted to blurt it out, to kind of strike him with it— "Sophie is a woman and a man!"— like a slap upside Wolf's head. She couldn't figure out why she was feeling this sudden knot of frustration towards him. Was it that she just wanted his attention back now that it had turned to Sophie? Was it that she knew, now that she thought about it, that he would think Sophie some kind of sexual pervert if he knew about her life? Maybe she wanted Wolf to be unsettled in his simple, uptight, old-fashioned formulations around sex—wanted him to see Maddy wasn't the only person who knew how to feel good about sex—that Sophie did, too. Or was Maddy so frustrated now because she hated that she herself was so close to a guy who could be a judgmental social dinosaur about someone as lovely as Sophie?

No, she finally realized. She felt so frustrated because here he was—the man who had believed her about Wilhelm—and she needed him to believe her again, to help her again, this time about Alex. But he was probably going to be so angry when he found out what she had been doing.

Wolf and Sophie had moved on in the conversation, from the kinds of projects Sophie did to the winters of Minneapolis, when Maddy finally interrupted with a gesture. She opened her bag, pulled out the yellow legal pad with the timeline of Alex's last days, and slapped it on the table in front of Wolf.

180

Wolf quickly picked up the pad seeing that Maddy had put it in a wet spot on the table. He dried off the cardboard back of the pad with the edge of his shirt and then looked at the pages. He turned each page over the top of the pad as he scanned. It was near the top of the third page that he got to the capital letters around which she'd drawn the box: DROWNED. She could see that his color had changed, page by page. He had gotten redder and redder.

"Who?" Wolf asked, looking at Maddy. "Who drowned?"

"Alex Shugar," said Maddy. "You can tell that from the timeline."

She leaned her head back on the top edge of the booth's bench seat and closed her eyes.

"Why?" he asked.

"That's what I'm trying to figure out," Maddy answered without opening her eyes.

"No," he said, "I mean why are you doing this?"

"Publication," she answered after a moment, biting her upper lip.

"No. *Why*, Maddy?" he asked again. "Why are you doing this?"

"Publication?" she replied.

"Why would you?" he asked again. "*Why* would you take this on? Why now?"

"My dean is Alex's ex-husband," Maddy explained, opening her eyes and looking back at Wolf. "He suggested it would make a good project, figuring out her death. He suggested I would be good for this project. Turns out he hired me hoping I might take on this project, figuring out why she died. Found that out after I already had the job in Minnesota."

Sophie sat up straighter, putting her hands in her lap. With the exception of Scott being Maddy's dean and Alex's ex-husband, this all counted as news to her.

"Is it a *good* project?" Wolf asked, now breathing harder.

"It is a very *interesting* project," Maddy answered. "It is a very *complex* project. It is why I went to New York. Not for some personal reason."

"I see," he said, looking back through the pages.

"I don't know how to get the postmortem," she said, pulling the pad of paper away from him and putting it back in her bag. "I don't know how to get the autopsy results. You do. Can you? Seems like an important piece of data."

She yanked the jar towards her with two hands, unscrewed the top, and pulled out another piece of pickled pumpkin. She put it on her tongue and let it sit there. Her salivary glands seemed to be exclaiming at the vinegar and the salt.

"It's an active police investigation?" Wolf asked.

She ignored him, ate another piece, and had another sip of her drink.

"If it is an active police investigation," Wolf explained, as if she didn't know this, "they aren't going to release that information. I can't get it."

"I think you *can* get it," she said. "And I need it."

She tucked her chin to her chest and looked at him with eyes up-cast.

"I *need* it, Wolf."

"You *need* to focus on your work, Maddy."

"I can't. I can't. I've tried."

A tear started to form in each eye. She looked over at the television as music started to play.

"Oh, look, Wolf—seventh-inning stretch. Our song."

"We don't have a song," he said quietly. "And if we did, it sure as shit wouldn't be 'Sweet Caroline.'"

She stood up and pulled on his wrist.

"Come on," she said, "dance with me."

He stood up and walked with her to an open spot between some tables. She lifted her arms and clasped her hands behind his neck, and he did the same with his hands around the small of her back. The men at the bar started singing the song loudly while watching them dance. She became aware she had a strained, sad smile forming on her face, a knot tightening in her gut.

And then there it was—like a full-grown dog bounding into the room—there was his scent, flooding her sinuses right to her brain. His sweat, his beer, his shampoo. There it also was, the feeling of his neck skin against her palms, running all the way up and down her spine. And the sensation of his arms around her, like a life preserver thrown from the ship's deck rail down to the choppy water.

"Wolf," she said, when they were far enough away that Sophie could not hear, "I haven't told Sophie, but Alex's ex-husband told me the police said 'probable suicide.'"

Wolf tightened his hold a little but did not reply.

"I need to know," she went on, "why they would think that. Why would they say that, and not 'accidental drowning'?"

"You feel sure Shugar wasn't depressed?"

"I've talked to all the people she was closest to. They all say no. No way."

"Have you not told Sophie that the police think 'probable suicide' because you don't want to upset her, or because you think she might ... that she might have … "

"What I know is she's inheriting half of Alex's estate. Alex changed her will to leave half to Sophie only a few weeks before she died. And Sophie knew that."

"I see." He furrowed his brow.

"Sophie is awfully nice though, Wolf, and I don't think …"

Maddy didn't finish the sentence. After a minute, she pulled on the back of his neck with her clasped hands to try to grab his gaze.

"Wolf," she said, now looking him in the eye, "*please* get me the autopsy results. I can't focus. I need this. Not just because of my dean. It'll distract me from the trial back home."

She realized too late that she had just called Philadelphia home. She hoped he didn't take note of it.

"If it's an ongoing investigation," he answered, "there's not much I can do. I told you that already. You know that."

He reached around his back and took her left hand in his right, lifted it above her head, and spun her around.

"And you can't think of something else that would distract you from the trial besides another death? I bet you can."

She came back around to face him.

"Liz taught me that when a man is making you crazy," she answered, now spinning back the other way, "the only solution is to think about another man."

She paused, awkwardly meeting his eye.

"I mean—what I mean is—it's like when a *song* is stuck in your head. The only solution is another *song*. That's what I meant."

The TV and barroom singing of "Sweet Caroline" ended and the ballgame started again. Wolf let go of Maddie. He started to walk back to the table.

"Wolf," she said, pulling on his arm. "Listen—when something is making you crazy—I think maybe the only solution is to think about another? Wolf, I need . . ."

He turned and looked at her.

"I *know*," he said firmly, as if she had been so rude. "I *know* what that feels like."

Chapter 17

Nothing wrong with combining research and pleasure, she thought, as the tub continued to fill and the sound of water-hitting-water pressed hard on her eardrums. She had mixed research with pleasure at academic conferences and on visits to archives—on that trip to Philly too, right? Didn't *every* academic at some level pick her discipline out of pleasure? Berries and cream.

The doorbell rang once and then again in quick succession, pulling her out of her reverie. She turned off the tap, grabbed a towel, tightened it around her, and hastened to the front door. Peeking out the peephole and seeing it was Hank, she opened the door. The cool fall breeze pushed its way under the terry.

"You changed the lock!" Hank declared in surprise, walking in carrying a brown paper bag of groceries. "I went to let myself in out of habit, but my key didn't work."

"You're not supposed to be here for at least another hour!" she answered.

"Well," he said, closing the door behind her. "When you offer a guy the deal you offered, he's probably going to show up early."

He looked her over from bare toes to bright eyes and back to bare toes. She felt a bit as if she had just been visually licked by a giant cat. Then he smiled perfunctorily and walked around her into the kitchen. She followed him, holding the towel up with one hand and trying to fix her mess of hair with the other. The brief but hard run she'd taken not long before had left it hanging half out of the hairband. But if she were to use both hands to fix her hair, odds seemed high the towel would give way.

"What are we having?" she asked as he started to pull food from the bag. She soon saw it would be the same meal as last time—steak frites, salad. "Ah, you only know how to make one thing for a woman."

"Two. The other is French toast. For the breakfast. Say what you will, I'm a gentleman."

As he donned his apron and tied it behind him, he gave her another big visual lick.

"Why don't you lose the towel, Dr. Shanks? You seem kind of overdressed."

"Ha. I was hoping to get a bath before you got here. I'd just about finished running the water when you rang the door."

"So, go get in the tub. I'll bring you a glass of wine. You can enjoy that while I cook."

"Nice try," she said, laughing at him and tightening the towel.

"No, listen, I'll get the sleeping mask that is presumably still in my drawer next to the bed, so I'll be *totally blindfolded* when I bring you that glass of wine."

He stepped around her to walk to the bedroom and she followed. From the night table closest the door, he proceeded to fish out a black, airline-issued sleeping mask. He held it up triumphantly like he had just won a game of capture the flag and then headed back to the kitchen. She relented, walking to the solarium off the bedroom and getting into the bath. She could hear through the open doors that he had put on some music in the living room. The water felt the perfect temperature against her chilled skin.

Not two minutes later, Hank appeared, taking baby steps, the mask over his eyes, a glass of red wine in one hand, his other hand extended to feel his way along the furniture and walls.

"Marco," he called out. "Hey, Dr. Marco!"

"Dr. Polo," she answered with amusement.

"Dr. Marco!" he called again. "I'm glad you didn't move the furniture, by the way. I remember where it is."

He reached the tub, bumping into it slightly with his knee. Feeling around with his free hand, he found the top of her head. He carefully lowered the glass. She took it from him and drew a sip while he knelt next to the tub.

"Uh, aren't you supposed to go cook?" she asked.

"Just wanted to feel the water," he answered, running his fingers through it until he found her arm. Like a spider dashing up its web, he dragged his fingers up her arm following the line to her neck. She was glad he couldn't see her face. Her eyes would give her away, and then he could do anything he wanted.

Wait, she thought, *why not let him do anything he wants?*

Hank leaned in over the tub now, put one hand behind her head, and kissed her. All she could think, the way his lips met hers, was butter meeting toast. He leaned in a little harder, kissing her more fully. Sweet butter; perfectly browned cinnamon toast; that promise of a raisin . . . She closed her eyes and held the wine glass up in her left hand to keep it from spilling and reached her right arm around his neck to hold to him. She could feel the water from her arm soak into his shirt while his tongue greeted hers as if for years their mouths had been meaning to stop talking and eat. The sensation of her forehead and eyelids brushing against the slippery fabric of his silly blindfold felt exceptionally erotic.

After a moment he pulled back, leaning back on his haunches and rubbing his thighs.

"Sorry," he said, still blinded by the mask, "this stone floor is murder on the knees. Maybe I should just join you in there?"

"We're not having sex!" she declared, catching her spit with the tip of her tongue, swallowing, and laughing. "Go away!"

"What's that you say?"

He pretended to scratch his nose, creating a small opening at the bottom of the mask on one side. His tilted his head back, making it obvious he was looking her over.

"Wow," he said. He cleared his throat jokingly. "I mean, wow, nice kiss."

He pulled the mask down to obscure his vision again.

"Get out of here," she said, cupping her hand and throwing water on him.

"Wait, we're not having sex?" He pouted like a little kid. "But you said—"

"Yes, yes, if you answer *all* my questions, there's that—that's the deal. I'm true to my word."

"And your tongue really is, uh, as acrobatic as you?"

"As I told you on the phone, it's my homunculus. It's me in miniature. Front *and* backflips." She winked, forgetting he couldn't see her. "But we're not having intercourse."

"Why not?" he asked, pretending again to look sad. "I get the sense you want Dr. Polo, Dr. Marco."

"I *do* want you, Dr. Polo," she said, turning the tap with her free hand to add more hot water. "But *you* won't want *me* after we do it—you told me that yourself. And I want you to want me, 'cause that turns me on. So, we're not doing it."

"Ever?"

"When I don't feel like I want you anymore," she said louder, to overcome the sound of the running water, "*then* we can have intercourse."

"That'll be great," he replied, turning to leave. "I love having sex with a woman who doesn't really want me anymore. It's so hot."

He pulled off the mask and dropped it on the bed as he walked toward the kitchen. Then he paused about twenty feet away from her and turned around to look at her body again, standing on his toes to see better into the tub. He said it quietly this time:

"Wow."

He turned back toward the kitchen and left.

She looked down at her body refracted in the water and smiled to herself. Her legs did look particularly good these days, strong and feminine all at once. Her breasts might not be perfectly symmetrical, but whose were? And each had its own charm, the left so nicely rounded, the right looking like it might welcome a hand to finish the rounding. The combination of the cold run and the hot water had left her areolae and nipples a dusky rose.

She swiveled the faucet to the off position and leaned back, sipping the wine, staring now at her belly, her thighs, her bush. This was definitely the way to do research.

Right—*research*. What was it she should ask Hank? Before he kissed her, she had had a clear list of questions and topics to cover. She thought back to the plane ride home from Pittsburgh with Everett the day before to try to remember what Everett had said—all those things that Maddy had thought she should later check with Hank.

When she and Everett had arrived at the Pittsburgh airport to head home, their seat assignments were eight rows apart. Then, without much warning, a stranger had come up to the two of them sitting at the gate, holding out the morning paper with Maddy's photo in it from the conference the day before, asking loudly if she was Madeleine Shanks.

Everett had seen how this encounter startled Maddy into uncharacteristic muteness, though he could not have known it was partly because the stranger held an eerie resemblance to The Jerk. Right after the man went away, Everett asked Maddy if she wanted him to sit next to her on the plane to put himself between her and anyone else. She nodded repeatedly in silent answer, as if her neck were on a bouncy spring. So, Everett took their boarding passes to the gate agent and came back with a window and a middle seat together near the back of the plane.

Just after the aircraft took off, it shuddered and dipped to one side for a moment. Several people let out a small cry of exclamation and Maddy found herself rapidly making the sign of the cross—the fingertips of her right hand quickly touched her forehead, her chest, her left shoulder, her right shoulder. Everett looked at her, surprised.

"Stupid old reflex," Maddy said, smacking her open palm to her forehead. "I didn't mean to do that."

"Raised Catholic!" Everett declared, with a pleasant laugh. "I was, too."

"Really?"

"Altar boy. I always wonder if it was the cute outfit that got me interested in dresses and accessories."

"Did you keep anything—I mean, of the religion?" she asked.

"I like the practice of Advent. Lighting the wreath of purple and pink candles each day, taking us to the moment when the sun will start coming back. But that's more pagan than Catholic, I suppose. How about you?"

"I keep only the useful personal connections," Maddy answered. "One of my friends calls my old Catholic connections 'the rosary mafia,' but it's just some nuns I know who help me out. They are how I ended up bunking at Wolf's place. The place I'd arranged to stay in Philly fell through at the last minute, and the rosary mafia found me his place. Of course, he thought I was going to be a man—a young Catholic man named Matty. As in Matthew. He wasn't interested in putting up a young woman and certainly not a mouthy *ex-Catholic* woman. But I had no other place to go. So, he had to take me in. And feed me. But then he liked feeding me."

"So, he's Catholic? For-real Catholic?"

Maddy nodded.

"And he's married?"

She nodded again.

"And you're in love with each other."

Maddy didn't answer that. She looked at Everett's face and had felt as if her own face were suddenly twenty years older, like the skin stuck hard to the bone.

"I don't know what we are," she finally said. "We're on a murder together. Murders. Plural. Seven. Or five. Or ten? Five at trial. Two they can't yet prove. Three we weren't sure were murders. I was pretty sure. Well, so was Wolf."

"And his wife?"

"I probably shouldn't say," Maddy answered. And then she did say: "She's in a kind of coma from which she'll never wake up. He won't disconnect her because of his religion. She was in an accident with his best friend. He was also a cop—they worked together. There wasn't any good reason for her to be in that car with his best friend. So, everyone presumes it was an affair. The friend was killed." She paused. "Not good."

"No, not good."

"We're not lovers. I mean, Wolf and I have never kissed. Y'know, not more than New York kisses on the cheek at the start or end of a visit."

"Is that what lovers are? People who kiss on the mouth?"

"I guess I don't know."

She then changed the subject because the conversation had become too self-centered.

"Did Hank and Alex ever kiss? I mean, as lovers?"

"No," Everett answered. "They came together kind of by accident, like you and John Wolf did, and they weren't each other's type. He likes . . . quick rolls in the hay with pretty young things. She likes—I mean, she *liked*—sex and romance when it involved intense intellectual connection. People her own age. Kind of the opposite, Alex and Hank."

"Did you and she ever have sex?"

"No. We also weren't each other's types. She wasn't as feminine a woman as I am attracted to as a man. Sex should be had through the right connection. That's why, as a woman, I like being with men who are into who I am as a woman. Alex and I became the best of friends, though."

"I don't mean to be rude, but there're men who are specifically into your kind of woman—anatomically and everything?"

"Oh, yes," Everett had answered enthusiastically, "and they're very grateful to meet women like me, as we are them. We have places where we can find each other safely."

"They're gay?"

"Oh, my, no. Gay men are into *men*, Maddy—gay men desire *masculinity*. The men I'm with, they're specifically into women like me. They don't want a man in a dress. They want a woman with a penis. They're special that way."

"It's a marvelous feeling, isn't it, to be with someone who wants you for what you are?"

The way Maddy said it with such earnestness, the way Everett nodded slowly in return, it was clear Everett appreciated that she believed him—believed that they knew the same feeling. For a moment they both just stared out the window at the passing clouds.

"It's funny, when we were young," Everett observed, "they always had us picture people we loved who had died as being up in the clouds, in heaven. But it's just clouds, isn't it? Your first airplane trip ruins that whole fantasy that someday you'll see them again in the clouds."

He said nothing more for a moment and then asked:

"The trial—it's causing you a lot of anxiety, Madeleine?"

"A fair bit. I don't like strangers asking me if I'm Madeleine Shanks like I'm some freak celebrity. I never know what they're going to do—why they want to know."

Maddy had decided not to tell him the core truth of the issue: that her freak celebrity made her nervous that The Jerk would contact her again. The pushy stranger at the airport had made it feel quite possible.

"I didn't tell you," Everett continued, "I made a point of going this morning to the conference reception breakfast to try to talk to the Gnat."

"Did you!"

"I did. He didn't know who I was, and I didn't tell him. He was full of himself enough not to care. What mattered to him was that I was interested in his work. I'm not sure I learned anything useful, and I didn't even try to persuade him he's being a scoundrel, because presumably he either knows that or he doesn't care."

Everett paused and tightened his seatbelt a little as if the thought of the Gnat caused him turbulence.

"One thing I did learn—he plays piano. In a blues band."

Maddy's eyes widened.

"But why would Alex have wanted *him* over?"

"No idea," said Everett. "Maybe she didn't. Doesn't make a lot of sense. But then neither does the piano itself. I also learned that he was away the weekend she died, at a conference in San Francisco."

Maddy had said nothing in reply to this but thought about what Everett was really saying: Everett had been trying to figure out if the Gnat had an alibi for the time when Alex had died.

"Do you think Alex was depressed before her death, Everett? Or very anxious about something?"

"She was . . . different. But it didn't look to me like depression or anxiety. I told you before, it's almost like she had found peace, a vibrancy. I was seeing her less often just then, but that's how it was sometimes. You know, we had times where we were busy and didn't see each other as much and times when we were together more. Like every friendship, right?"

Maddy asked Everett if he knew who Alex had been sleeping with at the time.

"Besides Whit? No. She didn't always tell me. We each had some things we chose not to share. Partly for the discretion of our lovers and partly, I guess, to spare ourselves potential criticism from each other. We may have loved each other, but we didn't approve of everything the other did. It was simpler to keep some things to ourselves."

Everett put his palms down on his thighs and smoothed out the fabric of his pants.

"You ask me, was she depressed? I guess you must be wondering if she killed herself?"

Maddy did not answer.

"What I *do* know, Madeleine, is that Ally was talking to a fellow who's a psychiatrist, talking to him for at least a few weeks before she died. She told me a little about him. His name was Griffin—Dr. Jeffrey Griffin, I think. But my impression was that that conversation happened chiefly because he was interested in her work—similar to how she and I met, through her work, and she was interested in learning about his thoughts on human sexuality. He'd told her he'd seen some interesting things in the way of human sexuality."

"I should send *you* to talk to him, Dr. Watson!"

Everett turned a little pink. "I don't much care for psychiatrists as a class. Maybe Dr. Griffin is different but, in my experience, psychiatrists are always trying to find the reason you're supposedly wrong. I like feeling like I'm *right*. I'm alright. I know I'm alright. It's a much better way to live your life, figuring you're alright."

Maddy hadn't answered, but she knew what he meant. Her therapist at

Georgetown had the same philosophy as Everett—not to dwell in what could mean one was sick or broken but to recognize what made one healthy.

When the flight attendant came to offer drinks, Everett and Maddy had both taken coffee.

"It's just lovely to see the way Wolf cares about you," Everett said, turning a little toward Maddy after the stewardess had moved on. "It's good to have someone like that in your life. Ally was that to me. I'm glad you have Wolf."

"I wonder what he would think if he knew about *your* life, though."

"I think," Everett answered, taking a sip of the coffee, "I mean, I *suspect* that John Wolf is capable of getting around old-fashioned bigotry. He seems to have an open heart. Would you agree?"

"Yes. He has a very good heart. Somehow, he's truly forgiven his wife. And forgiven his dead best friend. And why bother to forgive someone who's dead? And he learned to put up with this pesky ex-Catholic girl who pokes at him too much and eats his leftovers without asking. He has a deep charity about him. Even about criminals—though I've noticed he usually saves his charity for the ones who haven't hurt anybody but themselves."

She took a sip of her coffee and thought about it a little more.

"Yes, Everett. You're right. Wolf could learn to like you as both Everett and Sophie as he did me. He would at least accept who you are, if not understand. He doesn't try to fix people. He just wants people to not hurt each other. If he understood you weren't hurting anyone, he'd be okay." She took another sip and continued her musing: "I mean, he'd absolutely think you're a *pervert*, but then he thinks I'm one, too."

She laughed and smiled genuinely at Everett, and Everett smiled broadly back. Maddy then held up her cup as if to say "cheers," and Everett touched his paper coffee cup against hers.

"Would it be too strange," she had asked Everett later, as the landing gear went down, "if you and I became real friends—I mean, given that Alex was your best friend?"

"No," Everett had replied. "I think Alex would've liked it, actually. And I'd like it. She always understood that the different ones had to find each other and hold tight."

· · ·

"Shanks!" Hank yelled from the kitchen, his voice coming through clearly over the music. "You have a rat!"

Maddy was just zipping up her jeans and coming out to the kitchen following her bath. She asked him calmly what he meant.

"I mean you have *a rat*." Hank was holding a meat cleaver in his right hand and looking agitated. "Turned on the oven and the damned thing came skittering out from underneath. Must've been under there for the warmth of the pilot light."

"A rat?"

"Pretty sure," he said, bending over and looking around the baseboards of the kitchen warily. "Too big for a mouse, not big enough for a possum. Definitely a rodent tail."

Failing to find the animal in the kitchen, Hank walked around the house closing doors. Then he went into the living room in a determined fashion with the cleaver, still wearing his apron.

"Pretty sure it went this way."

"Shit," she said. "*That's* what I heard moving around last night. Must've been because I left the door open while I was bringing groceries in. A field rat."

She remembered now the one that the cat at the convent had brought in one morning like a trophy, still half alive. The nuns had gotten into such an argument about what to do with the poor wild creature, with Sister Severe wanting simply to drown it without further ado, and Sister Anjelica crying about Saint Francis looking down, and Sister Ruth remarking on how this was why people couldn't seem to agree whether the cat was a proper domestic partner or a minion of the devil. It had been one of those moments when Maddy had found sudden delight in the spontaneous converse of these robed women.

Hank got onto his hands and knees to look under the armchair.

"You're not going to *kill* it, are you?" Maddy asked, trying not to sound too much like Sister Anjelica.

"Of course I'm going to kill it," he answered. "It's *vermin*, and it's *in the house*."

"You can't!" she yelled, pushing her way between him and chair. "If you kill that rat, I am NOT giving you that blow job!" (That was at least not something Sister Anjelica would say.)

Hank paused and sat up on his knees and looked at her with a confused expression.

"Seriously? You *want* a rat in the house?"

"Oh my God, no, I don't *want* a rat in the house! I mean, not a rat I don't

193

personally *know*."

"But you don't want me to kill it."

"No!" she yelled, gesturing with her arms and hands as if he were stupid. "I want you to *capture it and take it outside*. That rat has done absolutely nothing wrong. It's innocent! This is no criminal rat. My fault I left the door open. And if you kill it, I will *not* give you a blow job."

"You have the craziest terms for sex that I have ever encountered, Shanks," he replied, standing up, shaking his head, and handing her the cleaver.

"Fine. Go get me the oven mitts and a towel. I'll try to capture it and get it out of the fucking house. Just hope it doesn't bite me and we spend the rest of the evening at the ER."

She did as he asked, and they each proceeded to crawl around the room in silence looking for the animal. Hank finally figured out it had lodged itself behind the couch. He instructed Maddy to stand at one end and use a couch cushion to block the exit and to help him tip the couch over. After a bit of pandemonium, he had the frantic animal in the towel and hastened to the front door with Maddy.

"Shut the door behind you," he yelled at her, "so it doesn't go back in!"

He leaned over and dumped the towel on the ground and then pushed the towel around a bit with his foot to get the rat to leave. It soon went scampering off into the dark woods.

"Happy?" he asked her. He picked up the towel and held it out in front of him in two fingers.

"Happy as I can be knowing I was sleeping with an unfamiliar rat wandering around the house. Thank you," she answered, opening the door to let him back in. As he passed her, she took the mitts and towel from him to put in the wash.

"I'd be lying if I said I did it for you," he answered in an annoyed tone.

In the kitchen, he washed his hands twice over, once with hand soap and then again with dish soap, and then poured her a fresh glass of wine. He handed it to her, sighed, and took a sip from the glass he had poured himself earlier. They stood there quietly for a moment, just drinking. Finally, she put her glass down and hoisted herself on the counter to watch him again take up work on their dinner, as she had the last time he was here. She realized that she was already seriously at risk of again wrecking the evening with him. She wondered if she had been unreasonable. But she certainly didn't want an innocent rat executed on the rug, not with a cleaver she would be using for food.

She took another sip of wine.

"I guess we'd better have makeup sex," he said finally with a resigned sort of sigh, turning to her. "To cut the tension. No choice."

"No way," she answered, putting her glass down. "Then you won't even finish making me dinner. But I'll take another kiss like that earlier one in the bath."

"It's too bad I'm not into orgasm denial," he said with another sigh, "because then you'd be the perfect woman."

He walked over to where she sat on the counter and started to put his arms around her.

"Hang on," she said, putting her hand flat on his breastbone, "you're telling me there are men who are into *not* getting off?"

"They're into being aroused but denied orgasm, yes," he said, trying to lean in closer. "They might really like you."

"Why would anyone want that?" she asked, still holding him off with her hand. "It seems like a sexual paradox—getting off on *not* getting off? How does that even work?"

"It's a kind of masochism, I guess," he said, kissing her lightly on her cheekbone. He started to inch his kisses down her face, toward her mouth.

"So the orgasm itself is a disappointment?"

"I don't know," he answered. "I don't find orgasms disappointing. I'd be happy to prove that."

He reached her mouth and kissed her with a sort of breath in, so that she felt ever so slightly vacuumed toward him. She reached her arms over his shoulders and pulled his head closer to hers with her hands so that she could feel his mouth fully against hers. His hair felt so good in her hands—soft and clean and short. The back of his shirt was still a little wet from having had her arms around him in the bath.

She licked lightly the inside of his cheek and wrapped her legs around his back. He pushed up against her now, and she could feel his erection against the crotch of her jeans. He scooped one hand under her, wrapped his other arm fully around her back, and lifted her off the counter onto him while still kissing her. Pausing from the kiss, he carried her wrapped around him to the living room and fell down seated onto the couch, with her now on top of him. He pulled off her ponytail band and took up the kiss again.

She knew he must be quite practiced at this, and yet somehow it still felt like he had invented this particular kiss just for her.

After a minute, she paused to pull back and look at his face. He looked so serious about all this, it made her smile. She felt his cheekbones with the tips of her fingers and then leaned in to kiss him again as he leaned back fully back on the couch and she laid herself down on him. Her left leg pressed down between his thighs and again she could feel his erection against her. She pushed her thigh against it.

"Okay," he finally said, pulling back and sitting her up on the couch. "If we're not having intercourse, even after all that business with the rat, convince me it's worth putting up with more of your brutal questions. Because I know they're coming shortly."

"What do you mean?" she asked.

"Tell me about your planned, uh, *routine*."

She scrunched her eyebrows, giving him a confused look.

"You said you'd do acrobatic things with—with your, uh, mouth. And tongue. It's my impression gymnasts have a routine they do during a game?"

"A meet," Maddy corrected him. "Competitions are called meets."

"So, at least tell me of your planned routine for this meet, after I answer your latest barrage of questions. *If* I answer."

"Oh!" she said, suddenly realizing what he meant. She stood up off the couch and pulled the coffee table away to create a more open floor space.

"Well," she said, running in place and brushing the hair away from her face, "first you want to do a little bit of a run-up in a circumstance like this, to sort of set the pace. Get things moving. Then I'm thinking a somersault—you know, turning *all* the way around."

She crouched on the floor, somersaulted twice in a row, and sprung up.

"Then maybe a little motion going around and around?"

She held her feet in place, arms above her, twisting slowly around at the hips.

"With a surprise backflip to add a little excitement."

She flipped. She took a look at his face. His jaw was slack.

"A full turn and a round-off, maybe a front flip?"

She flipped again.

"And then, you know, more of same until the, uh, judge, let's you know your *routine* has—completed?"

She did a split—happy she had put on the stretchy jeans that gave with her movement—and put her hands up in the air.

He pulled his jaw up and gulped a little.

"And what's the finish like? I mean whatever you call the end of the routine."

She grinned at him like a woman who had just given a child an ice cream cone.

"How about I swallow and smile? Is that too crass and obvious for the judge?"

"Oh, not at all. That's my favorite kind of dismount," he answered. "My very favorite. That's a ten."

He heard the oven alarm go off in the kitchen and hastened back to check the potatoes. Maddy reassembled the living room and came back into the kitchen just as he was returning the potatoes to the oven. He reset the timer and put the steaks on the hot pan. He tossed the salad meditatively a couple of times and added a little salt and pepper.

"Well, then," Hank said. "Go ahead. Ask me your questions."

She asked him first to go with her into Alex's office to explain what she was seeing and not seeing. He followed her there and said that he did recall Alex recently disposing of most of her records on the intersex research. So, he said, he wasn't surprised that that material was gone. Alex had told him at some point she was doing it because her research and correspondence in that area was complete, and keeping it would leave her open to a scrutiny that could only be unhelpful. He told Maddy he had tried to convince Ally it was generally a good idea to keep such records, particularly correspondence that could not be replicated. But the Gnat had irritated her so and Alex seemed determined, and he saw little reason to argue with her.

Hank took a moment to go turn over the steaks and then returned. Maddy asked him to tell her what seemed *wrong* in the room. She pointed out the bottom bookshelf that was missing whatever had been there. He seemed surprised to find it empty. He bent over and ran his hand over it as if he were making sure there was nothing there but dusty outlines. He explained that had been the shelf where Alex kept years of notebooks—dozens of those old composition-style notebooks with black and white cardboard covers and black fabric binding in which she'd simply written whatever she needed to write down day by day: notes on research, to-do lists, short drafts of ideas and letters, recipes and grocery lists, contact information for someone she had just met, notes from talks. Why she would have gotten rid of these, he said he wasn't sure. They weren't anything like formal records, just Alex's personal jottings which she might look back on to find a phone number or a note to herself. He didn't think she would have had any reason to dispose of those, or any desire. So, where were they? Maddy said she had not found them.

As for the rest—the photographs around the room and the published books on the shelves —all that seemed normal, he said. Same with the drawer containing material for Alex's last book project, on sexual orientations; those files, too, seemed to be intact as best he knew.

Hank went back to the kitchen to pull the steaks and Maddy followed. He assembled a plate for each of them, and they sat down together in the dining room to eat. Maddy was deep into thought on the question of why Alex would have disposed of all those notebooks, if she had. Was it possible Scott had removed them?

"Any luck figuring out the piano?" Hank asked, as they each tucked hungrily into the food.

"No," she answered, grinding a little pepper onto her meat. "This morning I tried calling the piano tuner who came to tune Alex's piano when it arrived in case he might know why she got it. First, I had to figure out who that guy was. That wasn't too hard. I just called a random tuner and described this fellow, and he knew who I meant. But when I called the tuner who had come, he explained to me like I was stupid or out of line that the relationship between a tuner and a pianist is like between a patient and a doctor, and you don't just tell any old person what you knew about various pianos or pianists in the area. He said that in this area they all followed that basic code."

"Seriously?"

"Seriously. Quite a pompous ass, and it was clear I wasn't going to get anything out of him and that it was likely I wasn't going to get anywhere calling random piano tuners asking who might have been planning to play here."

Maddy took another bite, chewed, and swallowed. The fatty juice of the meat coated her tongue like a salty silk blanket. He did buy good steaks. And he knew how to cook them.

"You don't know anyone Alex might've gotten it for? To play?"

"Just Everett Sophie Inskeep," Hank answered. But Maddy remembered to herself what Everett had said: To buy a Steinway so that your piano-playing friend has it to play when she stops by is like buying a sugar plantation in case your friend takes two lumps in her tea.

"Can I ask you something, Hank? Something maybe kind of rude?"

"Apparently, yes," Hank answered, sliding a piece of potato on his fork through the salad dressing and then eating it.

"How come you don't mind fooling around with me here, in Alex's house?"

He put his fork and knife down and took a drink of water. Then he put his hands palms down on the table, almost as if he was going to rise.

"Here's the thing, Maddy," he said, looking her in the eye with an intense expression she could not quite discern. "I loved Ally. I loved her much more than I understood when she was alive. It was only really after she died—after I understood that she was never coming back—that I understood *how* I loved her. *How much* I loved her. I never really understood before that the way I saw her in everything. In the changing of the leaves that we took pleasure in every year together. In the performance of every show we saw together, even if it was bad. In an exquisite experimental result, which I knew I'd tell her about as soon as I saw her. Although," he said, smiling suddenly, "she would usually try to shoot down the results, to make sure it was bulletproof, to help me out. Or just to annoy me. Anyway, what I mean is this: Ally had come to inhabit all the parts of my life—well, most—so that it was like that old cliché: She was a part of me. When she died, it was as if parts of me . . ."

"Necrosed?" asked Maddy.

"Yes. Necrosed. That's right. They simply shriveled up and died off with her."

He paused and took another drink of water.

"I felt for a while as if I had parts of me that were dead that I was simply dragging around."

He looked slowly around the room, at the table and the chairs and the walls, as if he were visiting a sacred space, or an active archeological site.

"But Alexandra Shugar, PhD, was if anything a pragmatist. As am I," he continued, returning his gaze to Maddy. "It's one reason we got along. She had little patience for sentimentality and what some people would call propriety. She had no patience for fuss." Now he took a drink of wine. "So, I knew within a month of her death that she'd have little desire—*no desire*—to see me go on with my life as if I could not live without her. That *was* how I felt at first, honestly, like I couldn't go on. But I knew it wasn't honoring her to give up the will to live. So, I went on. Including sexually. Honestly, it's what she would've wanted. She would've yelled at me if I'd done otherwise."

"I see," said Maddy, taking another bite of meat. She felt partly like she should not eat during this rather frank explanation—that it would come across as insensitive. But she also thought that if she kept eating, he might keep talking and not stop himself from telling her so much. "But it must feel a little funny in this house? To fool around here?"

"Not really," he said. "Not as much as you might think. It's not like I ever fooled around with Alex, here or anywhere. We were never sexual together-er. And I was never sexual with anyone in this house. It was her place. So, being with you doesn't feel like it has any real connection to my life with Alex. It's just a house, Maddy. Alex isn't here anymore."

She took another bite and watched him out of the corner of her eye to see if she needed to prompt him further. She could see she did not.

"You know what Alex'd probably say to you—to your question—Maddy? That *it doesn't matter*. Seriously, she was very practical that way. I would sometimes think that she and I were about to have a difficult, horrible conversation—about something we disagreed about, about her frustration with me. And she'd suddenly tell me *it doesn't matter* and let it go. That's what she'd say about the idea of me fooling around with you here, I'm sure. She'd say: *It doesn't matter.* She always had her mind on bigger things." He watched Maddy keep eating. "She'd even encourage me in this case to see it doesn't matter. It's just a house. It's just a place. Pleasure matters. That, she believed. That, *we* believed. That *we knew*."

He chewed on his lip like he was trying to think of how to phrase something. As she waited for him to go on, Maddy picked up a potato with her fingers, ate it, and licked her fingers to taste the remains. Then she did the same thing again with another piece of potato. She caught him watching.

"I just love greasy, salty things," she said, shrugging and wiping her fingers on her napkin. "I'm an evolved *Homo sapien*."

He smiled at her and for a moment said nothing. Then he reached across the table and took her fingertips in his.

"Like Alex," he said, "you have a presence about you that feels—well, that feels bigger than the room. Like more than the room. Like it *is* the room? The house feels different as yours."

She pulled back her hand, suddenly feeling a little embarrassed, looked down, and put her hands in her lap.

"And much as it's true that many of the things in this house are still things that were hers," he said, as she looked back up at him, "you fill this house in your own way." He took a sip of wine and looked at her now with more intensity. "With your flips. Your laughter. And your sense of righteous justice for a fucking rat."

One voice in her head (Sister Thomas Aquinas?) was telling her that he was just saying these things to get her into bed. But another voice (Sister

Ruth?) told her she should just be grateful to hear his appreciation of her ways, that she should take it with grace.

"So, it doesn't matter," he said.

"It really doesn't matter?"

"It really doesn't matter. Besides," he said, lifting his fork and knife again, "why would I turn you down?"

. . .

As he inexpertly moved the two pieces of chocolate cake from a box to two small plates, Hank explained to Maddy he'd decided to pick this up at a favorite bakery rather than making her some dessert. He could not rival, he said, what this particular pastry chef did to combine the textures of soft and hard chocolate in the layers, and he thought she had to try it.

When she tasted the first forkful, she understood what he meant. She told him it felt like a chocolate French kiss. She moaned a little at the feel on her inner cheeks and tongue. He poured her a glass of port to go with it and had the same himself. The cake soon gone, they moved back to the living room. He pulled the coffee table back near the couch so they would have a place to put their drinks and their feet.

"I still have a lot of questions," she told him as they settled onto the couch.

"Well, for God's sake," he answered, leaning in to kiss her, "get them over with."

After a relatively short kiss, she pulled away.

"I can't get them over with if you keep kissing me," she laughed. "I mean, there's plenty I'd like to find out from you via the rest of my body, but I need my mouth free to find out what your head knows."

"Yes, that's it, use your mouth on my head. Do that."

She grinned at him and shook her head. He pulled away a little and got serious.

"Go for it," he said.

"Alex had a grad student who'd filed a complaint against her."

"The sexual harassment-related retaliation complaint. From Sarah." Maddy nodded.

"What about it?" Hank asked.

"Was Alex worried about it?"

"Not really," he said. "Not about herself."

"About who, then?" Maddy asked.

"About me," Hank answered, as if this was obvious. "The complaint against Alex—the complaint about Alex telling Sarah off—that probably wasn't going to amount to anything. But Alex figured, as did I, that I didn't need another complaint in my employment records. And it was just awkward, since people often assumed Alex and I were lovers, so they would figure, incorrectly, that Alex would be jealous of any action between me and Sarah."

"I'm totally confused—hang on," said Maddy, wrinkling up her face and staring at the fireplace. She felt a sinking feeling, like the atmosphere had just gotten measurably thicker. "*You* were the faculty member who Sarah was following around like a puppy and who finally asked her out? *You're* the person against whom Sarah filed the charge of sexual harassment that had Alex in trouble with Sarah?"

"Yes," said Hank, leaning back on the couch, looking uncomfortable. "I thought from your question that you knew that."

"Whoa," said Maddy, putting a little more physical distance between them. "What *did* Alex think of you and Sarah—"

"Well, Alex never would've *known* if Sarah hadn't *told* her," he answered in the tone of a child making an excuse. "I didn't tell Alex about my . . . pursuits . . . any more than she told me about hers. We just didn't discuss such things."

"But what did Alex think when Sarah *did* tell her about you?"

"Ally seemed generally annoyed about the whole thing. I guess she thought I shouldn't have put myself or her in that position. That it was an unnecessary complication for her at work."

Maddy suddenly got up off the couch and excused herself to go to the bathroom. She closed the bathroom door and flipped the lock, immediately regretting how loudly she flipped it. He would think she was feeling the need to lock herself up away from him.

Why *was* it such a turnoff to hear specifics about how a man had pursued other women? What did it matter that he'd asked Sarah out a while back? Was the problem in her gut that Sarah was professionally just barely junior to Maddy? That she was so much prettier than Maddy? Was this just a case of sexual competitiveness and a feeling of being that loser girl?

Or was it that Hank now seemed so obvious, like such an easy sexual catch that he didn't feel worth putting out for? That he was so easy, he made Maddy feel like she was too easy?

But, wait, that was exactly what she had liked about him—the ease. Right?

Maddy thought about what Alex would think of her whole flood of emotion as she emptied her bladder, washed her hands, and looked in the mirror. Alex would probably conclude Maddy was being dreadfully conventional, wanting a man to somehow come with a history in which he had wanted no other woman. Wasn't this just the way the world shamed a woman, teaching her to want a kind of purity in sexuality that became, in fact, a prison of shame?

She came back to the couch and sat down next to Hank, her leg just barely touching his, and finished off her drink. She could tell he was looking at her face to try to understand where she had landed in her momentary retreat. But she did not look back at him.

"Tell me about the book Alex was working on." She pulled her feet up off the floor and tucked them in next to her, keeping her eyes downcast. "More specifically, Hank, tell me about the thesis."

As if relieved she was asking him questions again, he answered without hesitation that the book, as he had understood it from Alex's descriptions, was largely going to be about a philosophy of sex, one that focused on consent and pleasure as the two elements required for ethical sex. He explained that it had started in some ways when Alex had met Everett Sophie and learned about Inskeep's life and sexual orientation. Alex had confessed to Everett that she didn't really get his sexuality. And Everett had replied that if he'd learned anything about sex, it was that you don't *get* sex, it gets *you*.

"You don't *get* human sexual interests," Hank said by way of further explanation. "They're all kind of crazy. Even heterosexuality. Why would you make opposites and then expect them to be attracted? Magnets are a rare sort of thing in nature—the attraction of opposites. But we don't *get* sexual orientations. They get *us*."

"You mean we don't choose what turns us on, what grabs us. And a lot of it is just inexplicable."

"Right. Everett is right. We don't get sex; sex gets us. So, how are we to *think* about human sexual interests, given that so many are unthinkable, or at least un-thought?"

"How did Alex think of them?"

Hank explained that, after reading into the history of what humans seemed to experience and after talking to many people with diverse sexual interests, Alex had concluded—as he himself had, as Everett had—that there was much we didn't know about where sexual interests come from, but that people didn't seem to choose them. If they *did* choose them, they would surely not choose interests that could in practice be so hard to fulfill, or even illegal and immoral to fulfill, as in the case of, say, pedophilia. Or in the case where a man is turned on by rape.

"There are men specifically *turned on* by raping?" Maddy asked, befuddled. "They don't just rape because that's the only way they can get sex?"

"Oh, little flower," Hank said in a seemingly sarcastic tone, wrapping his arm around her shoulder. "There's so much nastiness in the world I'd rather not tell you about. At least not tonight."

Seeing she didn't find this amusing, he pulled his arm back.

"But yes," he said, choosing the tone of a professor in class, "there are men who are specifically turned on by rape. And guess what? They sometimes become rapists."

She turned her head and looked him in the face, to try to read his answers to these questions. His answers all seemed clinical. Merely descriptive with perhaps just a touch of bedside manner.

She asked him whether there were really people specifically turned on by death—necrophilia? Yes, he said, but it didn't seem to be very common. Very uncommon, in fact. By young children? Yes, he said. More common than necrophilia, unfortunately. By pretty feet? Yes, he said. Surprisingly common.

She said nothing for a moment but got up off the couch, frowning. She stood up straight, put her arms up toward the ceiling, and then caught herself about to do a handstand. She stopped, embarrassed. She put her hands back down and cleared her throat.

"What was that?" he asked earnestly, sitting forward a bit. "What just happened to you?"

She could not tell if his interest was personal or scientific. She rubbed her eyes and answered, "Bad memory."

She looked down at her feet.

"Was the guy who took your virginity so young into your pretty feet?"

She understood by his softer tone that he wasn't mocking her.

"No. Not that."

She went ahead and turned away from him to take a headstand—one that would be facing him. For reasons she could not discern, she felt like answering him upside-down. Perhaps it was that it would be harder for him to read her emotions. A man who could not read your emotions could not make use of them.

"I came to realize much later—when I found out just last year that he'd moved onto another girl after he used me—that he was into pubescent girls. It wasn't really about me, as I once thought—back when I was young and stupid and I thought I was somehow special. Don't we like to think we're special? It was just about my body as it was then."

Her shirt had fallen down, showing a bit of her bra. She regained a standing position and tucked in her shirt.

"And he did what he could to hold my body there, in early puberty. Because that's what he was into. He was my coach."

"Gymnastics," Hank said nodding, as if she had solved a bit of a puzzle. She nodded back.

"He limited my calories. Said it was to win. He won!"

Now Maddy looked at him looking at her and saw in his face a raw sadness that reminded her too much and too quickly of the face of old Mr. Bleu, the next-door neighbor, standing at her mother's coffin. Her lip started to quiver. He stood up and pulled her towards him and held her tightly.

"Don't be stupid, Maddy," he said, brushing her hair with one of his hands. "Of course, it wasn't much about you. It was just about him."

She wrapped her arms around his back, clasping her hands on his sides, and let go with a hard cry for just a minute. She knew she'd have to push it out or have it linger.

As soon as the dumb surge of tears had left her, she pulled back and flopped back down on the couch, wiping her tears away with her sleeves. She took a sip of port from his glass.

"I'm sorry," she said, wiping her eyes again on her cuffs. She was glad she hadn't put on any makeup. Best not to ruin a good shirt.

He sat down next to her.

"You're sorry because a guy sexually abused you when you were just a kid?"

"Yeah," she answered, "that makes no sense."

"If it helps, I'm right when I tell you that it had nothing to do with you, really. He was just using you for his own sexual fulfillment—for what turned him on."

"And you're different how?"

Hank looked surprised and then stared across the room.

"Ouch," he said quietly.

"I'm sorry."

"No," he said, "no. It's a fair question."

He paused to figure out the formulation of what he wanted to say.

"Here's the thing. Let me try to channel Alex here, as I say this, to try to say it a little more sensitively than I am inclined to say things. When you were—what, twelve or thirteen years old?"

She nodded.

"When you were that age, there was no way you could understand and consent to that sexual relationship. It was effectively rape, Maddy. *Even if* your body responded to his touch, *even if* part of you felt good about how he made you feel, *even if* you thought you were quite mature mentally then because you knew you were smart, *even if* you didn't struggle against his touch, *even if* you kept going back to him, that doesn't mean it wasn't effectively rape. Because it *was*. You could not have consented to intercourse with that man."

Her ears were ringing a little, as if she were still sitting on the edge of the tub listening to the water from the faucet strike the water in the basin.

"No one has ever said it quite that way to me," she said, wiping her eyes for what she hoped would be the last time tonight. "But it helps. You're right."

"Of course I'm right," he said. "I'm always right. And sexually, with me— although I feel a little stupid talking about me here at all—but with me, you know what you're about sexually, now that you're an adult. And you even know *what I am about* sexually, because for some idiotic reason I told you what I'm into. And you can decide what you want. And I'll respect that. So, you gotta see it's completely different. *I* am completely different. And I'm not just saying that for my own good. Fortunately for me, and fortunately for you, I'm into women who can consent, and I respect what they decide. Believe me, I feel very lucky that's what I'm into, since I didn't choose it. I'm just goddamned lucky."

She sniffed and looked at him, scrutinizing his face. She was trying to figure out why she shouldn't just seduce him immediately and escape into that for as long as it lasted. He had just said one of the most useful things anyone had ever said to her. And she knew it. And he smelled now not only of his cologne and his skin, but of steak and port and chocolate, too.

"For example," he went on, perhaps seeing in that space between her eyes what she was thinking, "if you end this evening by deciding you don't want to do anything sexual with me—anything more than what we have already done—well, then I'll fully respect that. I'll have enjoyed what we did. But you don't and won't owe me anything more sexually. And I expect the same is true for you with me. If I don't want to do anything more with you—for example, if I think you are too fragile to ask you to go through with your lingual gymnastics routine—"

She smirked at his choice of words.

"—then I'll ask you to let me go without that, and I expect you'll let me go, respectfully."

"Duh."

"That's the *difference*," Hank said, putting his hand on her knee in a way that felt reassuring and not demanding. He squeezed her knee lightly and took his hand back. "The difference is mature, meaningful consent. In some circumstances without consent, one or even both parties may feel some degree of pleasure. You may have felt that with that asshole. The body responds to sex. That's nature. But it's still *unethical*. Alex had come to believe we needed both for ethical sex—consent and pleasure. I mean, it seems a little obvious, but it does take some working through. And she knew that some people were stuck, as it were, with sexual turn-ons that didn't work in the scheme of real life—the man turned on by raping, the pedophile, the hebephile."

He paused and held his index finger in the air, his brow furrowed.

"In fact, that issue—that very issue—of people stuck with turn-ons that could never work ethically—*that* was most of what we talked about at the last dinner we had, after I picked her up at the airport when she came home from New York. I remember it clearly now. She was for some reason *obsessed* at that point with the idea that there were people whose orientations could never really be satisfied—or could never be satisfied in a moral way. I don't know if there was some event or some conversation or something she read that had set her off on that?"

Hearing this, Maddy wondered what had transpired between Alex and Whit on that last trip—or between Alex and Joseph? Or Alex and someone unknown? Something that then made her buy a piano?

"She was fascinated at that moment," Hank went on, as if all this had dislodged the memory, "she was intensely interested in the problem of thinking about what to do with people for whom there was no way to have ethical sex of the kind they really wanted. How to manage the kind of people who couldn't be satisfied ethically."

"Like the rapist."

"Like the man turned on by rape," Hank answered. "He could role-play it with a willing woman, but never have the reality in an ethical way. Real rape would be illegal, immoral. As in your case, with the hebephile."

Maddy said she didn't know that term that he had now used twice— "hebephile" —though she had seen it in Alex's book project folders.

"A hebephile is a guy turned on by pubescent boys or pubescent girls," explained Hank. "Not into young children; men who are into young, prepubescent children are classified as pedophiles. The hebephile's into the pubescent. Hebephilia is not something a guy chooses—but it's obviously his choice whether to *act* on it. The asshole who used you, your coach, he wasn't just into your young body, he *acted* on it. And he should never've done that."

Maddy thought back now to what Wolf had tried to explain to her after he'd found out what had happened to her—that The Jerk had been into her girl-becoming-woman young body type. Wolf hadn't used the term "hebephile." Maybe Wolf didn't know that word. But he'd suggested what she sort of already knew: that The Jerk's particular turn-on explained in retrospect why The Jerk had held her back on calories and made her work so hard at gymnastics: so she could not go into normal puberty. So her body would remain just the way he liked it.

And Maddy remembered how, after he'd found out about The Jerk, Wolf had started giving her too much fatty food, as if he could go back in time and protect her. And, in Philly, her hips and her breasts had rounded out more as he overfed her. And Wolf had looked at her one day and noticed how womanly she looked, and he had looked pleased in a way that just confused her.

"What do pedophiles do?"

"You mean the men who are truly into young children? Either they rape young children or they find a way to stop themselves, to control themselves. They sometimes isolate themselves from children. Some of them—the good pedophiles—they don't act on the urges because they understand it's not moral or legal." He sighed, as if thinking about this made him depressed. "Sometimes you see a pedophile or a hebephile marry a small woman, a petite and flat-chested woman, a woman who looks a little childish. Coping mechanism."

"Really?"

"Really," Hank answered. "Makes it pretty damned awkward to know all this stuff when you meet a heterosexual couple where the woman looks like that. You gotta wonder about the husband. And whether or not she knows."

"So, Alex felt this was all pretty clear, and she was writing it up?"

"I think on the weekend she died," Hank answered, rubbing his eyes and letting out a tired breath, "she was working on the book. Writing intensely, working especially on the problem of desires and actions that were on the trickiest ethical lines. She told me that was her plan. I know she was using real-life case studies with pseudonyms to write up the ideas. Of course, she couldn't say her own ex-husband was a cuckold fetishist. Or that her own best friend was autogynephilic. Or that a colleague she slept with but didn't fuck was a chase fetishist. So, she was shielding identities, she told me. But she liked examining us all, I think, as problems—and she was always coming up with more problems."

"What do you mean?" Maddy asked. She wanted to slip her hand into his but resisted the urge.

"Well, some of it was thought experiments for her—I mean, I assume they were thought-problems. We were talking about them at that dinner, the last dinner. She asked me—say you used someone for sex, but the person never knew it—say, for example, you used her photo or looked at her through a window to get off. We talked about this problem, this moral problem. How are we supposed to think about using someone for sex who never knew you did that? What if you drugged a woman and used her for sex, but she never found out?"

"Well, using someone's photo seems much less problematic than drugging someone!"

"Right, sure," answered Hank perfunctorily, as if Maddy were an unimpressive student. "But this raised all sorts of question about what consent even meant. What *participation* meant. What *sex* even meant. Did we ever really consent to sex, not knowing what was in the other person's head? And what even is sex? If you went to the shoe store and a guy helping you got an erection because he was into feet, but you never even knew, is him putting a shoe on you the equivalent of your foot being raped? *You* being sexually assaulted?"

Maddy snorted at this idea.

"I'm serious," Hank replied, "and so was Alex. If a foot could be a sexual object to one party, if it were used without the consent of the other but she never knew, then what? I remember now, at that dinner, we got into this weird conversation—were we two accidentally making love even though we weren't having sex? What constitutes making love? Were words exchanged in this way actually a form of sex?"

"Oh, you are making my brain too full," Maddy said. She leaned her head on the back of the couch. "I'm not sure I can remember all this. Too much."

He said nothing for a moment. Her eyes were closed, her body still.

"Would you like me to go?" he asked.

"Yes."

He started to rise off the couch.

"But," she added, opening her eyes, "I'd like to go with you. By which I mean I'd like to go for a drive with you. That okay?"

"Of course," he said, turning to her and offering her his hand. "Of course."

They each grabbed their coats and headed outside, Maddy locking the door behind them. Once in his car, she reclined her seat a few inches so she wouldn't have to sit up straight. He put on some music she had not heard before—a kind of bluesy rock by a group he said was Canadian. He turned on the heat and opened the sunroof a little so that she could feel a marvelous combination of warm air and cool breezes. Then he pulled over suddenly for a moment, left to get something from the trunk, and returned with a lap blanket for her. She settled in under the wool blanket, watching the dark fields and woods go by as he drove a little above the speed limit down long back roads. After a couple of miles, he turned the dashboard lights off so they could see into the dark better.

She was thinking about what he'd said back at the house—his explaining how it was that, even though her body had reacted to the touch of The Jerk, even though she had kept going back to him, it *had* been rape. She had for so long wondered why she seemed to have a kind of residual trauma about it all, an ugly scar that surfaced without warning in dreams and in waking moments as if she had been a trapped victim, when she could recall what felt like agency of some sort. Rape didn't always look so simple as the paradigm.

And she thought, too, about how the whole thing had been so steeped in shame—The Jerk's shame at what he was doing to her, her own shame from it, the way the people who found out flailed about, trying to hide the shame more—her father's intention of killing The Jerk for taking his daughter's virginity, the priests bundling her off to the convent, no one really asking her what had happened. They'd ended up collectively piling all the shame on her, loading her down with it as if she were their donkey, sending her off into hiding, down into a one-way subterranean mine, as if sacrificing her in that way absolved them.

Alex hadn't been wrong about the difficult subject. Maddy had been made the difficult subject. The convent had been the house of the difficult subjects.

But Hank was right; she was a completely different person now. Or nearly completely? Getting to Georgetown and showing Abe Lincoln, in his big limestone chair, her emancipated-minor papers. Showing him the proof that no one could bundle her off that way again like the donkey of sin. No one could control her fate—at least not so glibly.

Soon, she couldn't stop thinking about how it was that when Hank turned the car around a bend, the air flow would turn, too, such that she could smell him a little better if he turned to the left. She wondered if the same happened for him with her scent when he turned the car to the right. She started to count on her left and right fingers how many times he turned left and right, remembering what it was Liz had said to her about the importance of scent to mating. She wondered to herself if she wanted to have sex with Hank, or see if she couldn't fall into the routine Alex had had with him—sleeping with him next to her, without sex, except for words. Was this why Alex had been talking just before she died about sex without words? Because she was wondering if one could have sex only through words?

But Maddy felt particularly clear in this moment that she wasn't Alex. And she did *so* want to feel Hank in her.

She put her left hand on his right hand on the gear shift. He turned and looked at her. From what she could see of his face in the dark, he seemed happy to see her sitting there. He moved her hand under his on the gearshift. His palm felt dry and warm. Out of the windshield, she could catch sight occasionally of the glint of a deer's eye, just off the road.

When they got back, he told her he would just do the dishes and go. She pulled a dish towel out of the drawer and dried what he handed her, meditatively putting each item back in its usual place. Then he made a move to leave.

"Hang on," she said. "You told me so much tonight. You forgot my part of the deal?"

He put his hand on her left cheek and kissed her softly on the right.

"You don't have to," he said. "I like just being with you. Never a dull moment. And I understand why your questions matter to you."

"But I want to," she answered, taking his hand and pulling him down the short hall to the bedroom, to her bed.

"Why would you want to?" he asked as she laid him back on the bed and leaned over him.

"Because," she said, "I learned a long time ago that I didn't have to be forever The Jerk's captive. My body is my own, to do with it what I like. I'm free. And one thing I like to do is to give pleasure to a guy I really do like. Take pleasure from a guy I want. It's hot. In a grown-up way."

She undid his belt and fly, pulled his cock out, and slipped it into her mouth.

"Oh!" he cried out and he leaned back harder. He made a noise as if to say something else, but quickly gave up and just groaned as she pulled off the metaphor she had suggested earlier. Somersaults, flips, turns of her tongue. And a little running in place, all at just the right times. And then a sort of split. He leaned forward a little to watch her at that moment, and when she looked up and he caught her confident eye, she could tell that the meeting of their gaze pushed him to the edge.

And when she had finished, she climbed up the bed to be next to him, took a drink of water from the glass she kept at the bedside, and then settled in, leaning her head against his shoulder.

"Thank you," he said. "Especially for that excellent dismount."

"Thank you," she answered. "It's good to be reminded of my emancipation."

"Anything I can do for you?"

"Not tonight, but thanks for asking."

She sighed, not sadly, and closed her eyes.

He sat up, leaned over, and pulled off his shoes before removing hers, too. Then he turned off the light, pulled back the blanket, and eased her into a space next to him, tucking her into the crook of his arm. He pulled the blanket up over them.

"Want me to stay?" he asked after a moment. "Whatever you need."

"Stay just until you're sure there isn't another rat in the house. Then you can go."

"You got it," he said.

He brushed the hair off her face and kissed her forehead. The intense warmth of his body, like a flood of summer sun, reminded her immediately of Wolf.

Chapter 18

Maddy found herself staring at the checkered fabric of the curtains in Wolf's kitchen. He caught her gaze and looked to where she was staring.

"You think the basil needs water?" he asked. He pressed the pad of his right thumb down into the black dirt of the pot on the sill. "Moist enough."

He went back to the stove to stir the stew. Maddy realized she had in the bend of her left arm, leaned up against her hip, four soup bowls. They were the broad blue ones that always portended something especially good from Wolf's hands. She could sense that Alex and Hank would be there soon. She set the bowls at the four places of his table.

"Alex and I will just talk about our work all evening. You will be bored."

"It's okay, Rabbit," he said. "That is what single malt is for."

His joke was recycled but she laughed at it anyway. She could almost hear her own laugh.

Was the trial over? Should she ask him? But she didn't want to know. She figured he would tell her when it was. He'd said that when it was over, he would come to Minneapolis and cook Alex's pork roast. And they were not at Alex's house; they were at his. . . .

She thought she could hear his heartbeat in her ear. But was it his? She moved toward him to see if the heartbeat got louder. Coming to where he stood, she laid the left side of her head against his back, her ear positioned between his shoulder blades, and listened carefully. There it was. She reached her arms around his waist and breathed in hard.

With his right hand on the long wooden handle, he kept stirring. But now his left hand and forearm wrapped over hers, fitting so perfectly, a dog in its own bed, exactly the manifestation of what he had said once, that there is an answer to every problem.

"But what's the answer to life?" she asked him now.

"Death, silly," he answered, as if he had known her thoughts. "It is the perfect answer. The question is, Rabbit, what is the answer to the problem that is *you?*"

"Do you mean me, specifically, Wolf? Or do you mean 'you' in the editorial sense?"

He laid the spoon aside in the red apple-shaped spoon rest he kept next to the stove and he turned to her. He looked at her for a moment and then planted a kiss on her forehead in the very place Hank's lips had left the watermark of a kiss. The two of them, Hank and Wolf, were drinking from the same bottle of scotch, to put up with her and Alex? And both kissing Maddy, each in turn, where the priests used to plant the ashes on her, with the pad of the thumb dirt black. (Moist enough.)

Chapter 19

"Talk to me, Alex," Maddy said, standing near the lake's edge in the heavy darkness of the night. Hearing no response, she tightened the hood of her coat and wrapped her arms around herself to try to warm up, her pupils slowly adjusting.

Alex, wake up and talk to me. I have woken Hank up from a dead sleep to have him come over to your house to get me, to drive me here. I asked him to turn off the car lights while I'm out here, but he's surely going to eventually realize that we are where you died. And I'm not ready to tell him what I've figured out in the week since I last saw him, when I went down on him in your bed. I don't want to tell him yet that I've found Parvus, your piano lover.

It has been a week, Professor Shugar. It has *been a week*. And not just because I had to grade forty-three papers, teach the two classes, show up for three stupid committee meetings, submit a conference proposal on deadline, and avoid about ten thousand reporters' calls.

It's been such a week, I think I must have run close to forty miles, all in all. I know I went to the gym three times. The assistant coach of the gymnastic team lets me use the floor if I go when they are on their break, fifteen minutes right around six o'clock. Sometimes she gives me tips. What is it about being upside down and then right side up that helps me?

I've talked three times to Wolf this week, and he still has not even *tried* to get me your autopsy results. He knows I don't want to hear about the trial—he tells me it is moving faster than they expected. I mean, Jesus, they tell me it has *slowed down* and then it has *sped up*, and I feel like I'm on a rickety rollercoaster run by some idiot teenager who is high.

Wolf thinks the only reason I'm asking about your autopsy results is that I'm trying to distract myself from the trial. He thinks I will stop being interested in why you died once the trial is over. So, he doesn't want to bother the police here with—well, *with me*, I guess.

I've tried to explain to him that I doubt I will stop being interested in your death after Wilhelm's trial is finally over. But I can't very well tell Wolf *why* I doubt it—that I've ended up just so deeply in your life, so far away from the disciplinary research I'm supposed to be working on. That I've fucked up that way again. That I can't stop wondering if one or more of the people I have met through you might have somehow gotten you here, to where you drowned. Followed you here. Pushed you to here. Lured you here. Or something.

That's why I didn't want to come here on my own. That's why I called and woke Hank up and asked him to take me for a drive and then directed him here. I could do that—direct him exactly here using his odometer—from having stared at that map so many times, wondering if the map might tell me something about why you ended *here*. I used the big county map book you had on your shelf. But you didn't mark anything in it, including this lake. Was it simply because this lake is only about eight miles from your house, easy to reach? Is that why you came to this one? Proximity? Or did this lake have a particular significance for you?

I wish you'd talk to me, Alex. You'd save me the trouble of needing the autopsy results if you'd just tell me how it is you came to drown here.

I guess that's stating the obvious.

It's funny, how the police get to control your body this way. They get to know what I can't know. Why is that? Why is the last history of your body rightfully *theirs* and not mine to study, to research, to understand? I feel like I ought to be able to just go ask. I feel like I should be able to fill out a requisition card and have them turn your body over to me, like at the archives. If you were dead one hundred years, I could look at your report and probably your body, too, if it were still with us. Fifty years, even. But you're not dead long enough to be history.

Which begs the question of what I'm doing.

Wolf warned me on one of those calls this week—now I can't even remember on which call—that if I have an idea that this might have been some sort of a crime, then I ought to be careful. I think he believes that because I don't sound worried about my safety, I don't think it was a crime.

He tried to get me to take Hunter again. But I don't see you wanting a dog in your house. You kept your house so neatly. I mean, the rat did find this and that, things left around here and there. It had made a little stash under your stove. I cleaned it out wearing your bright green rubber gloves the day after Hank caught the rat. I figured I should clean it out before I turned the oven on again. There was a hairband in his little stash—was it mine or yours? And the rat had apparently found a paperclip and some little electronic part of something, a piece of a walnut still in a bit of shell. I saved it all, his little stash of things, in a little plastic zip bag to show Liz when she comes and visits. She will be interested to see what a field rat does with himself in a house like yours.

I suppose a dog would be useful. It would have found the rat before Hank did. But then Hunter might have killed the rat. And I don't know what I'd do with a dog if I were *with* someone at your house. Having fun with Hank, for instance. It would just feel like the dog was judging me. Huh – maybe that's why Wolf really wants me to take Hunter.

I tried talking to Wolf about your idea that shame around sex, not sex, is the true "difficult subject." And he tried changing the subject. Too ironic. I was two gin-and-tonics in at that point, and with the gin-buzz and Wolf on the phone, I pushed it—I pushed the subject of sex, of shame around sex. And then Wolf just got angry at me and asked me whether it ever occurred to me that *pride* around sex might be my own difficult subject.

I asked him what he meant. He said that pride was, after all, the opposite side of the coin, the coin with shame on the other side. He said that he didn't mean that maybe my problem was pride as in the *sin* of pride, as in one being *boastful*. Because, he said, I wasn't boastful about sex like men are. He said he meant maybe my own difficult sexual subject was *pride* as in *dignity*. Was it possible, he asked me—and, oh boy, could I hear the annoyance in his voice—that my real struggle was with trying to find sex with some dignity, and failing over and over?

I hate it so much when he sounds annoyed with me like that. And I'm not even sure what he meant. I mean, I think I know. He has this idea that the sex I have lacks dignity. I think he's just wrong. I think he has a weird, pious view of sex—maybe that's what gets him off. What's the scientific name for that one, I wonder? I'll have to ask Hank.

But what he said made me unable to answer him for a while because I didn't want to fight with him. We just kept the line open in silence for a long time, until I finally said good night.

Anyway, as I was saying, the first time Wolf and I talked this week, he told me that if I think your death may have been a crime, I need to be careful, and not just in the way of making sure I lock the doors and letting people know where I am—letting someone know where I am and when I should reappear. (The thing you didn't do. But would it have mattered?) But also being careful in the sense of not telling everybody that I'm researching how you died. Because, he said slowly, as if I'm kind of stupid, on the off chance it *does* turn out someone had a hand in your death, then it's probably not such a great idea to suggest I'm on to something. Particularly given the trial in Philly and what the papers have said about my role in bringing Wilhelm to justice.

Assuming Wilhelm meets justice.

"Justice, this is Dr. Wilhelm. Dr. Wilhelm, this is Justice. You two need to meet. I think you will hit it off. Spend years together."

I guess it never occurred to me I'd be marked that way, seen as trouble by troublesome people. Seen as a kind of venue for troubled people.

I never thought about something else—that even if Wilhelm *is* convicted, I'm not going to be able to stop looking at the actions of troublesome people. Look at me looking at you.

Maybe I *can* confine myself to the troublesome things from a hundred years ago. But I'm not going to be able to *appear* to other people around me, living people, like I am not noticing what they're doing, noticing what they're saying that doesn't make sense. I have no poker face.

I suppose it is useful to the world, this idiot brain of mine. That was the point that Sister Ruth made in her letter, wasn't it, when she wrote I'd probably saved a few people. She was suggesting I'm an Instrument of God. God's tool. It feels a little that way, Alex. Like I have to keep fixing the results of his inattention, the way a woman has to clean up after a man. I have to do it because somebody has to do it.

And who assigns me the work, the unpaid work, but a man: Scott.

Wolf doesn't believe anything untoward happened to you. Wolf generally believes in police work. He thinks that if Scott was told "probable suicide" by the police, then the police *know* it was suicide and they're just not *concluding* it yet officially, because they're waiting for Scott to come to terms with it so he won't make an ass of himself or of them by objecting publicly to that ruling. But then I don't understand why they won't at least tell Scott their reasoning. It doesn't sound like they talked to very many people in concluding that's what happened. It doesn't sound like they're doing anything more but sitting on their asses, presumably paying attention to something they consider more urgent.

You know what, Alex? If they thought you'd been sexually assaulted, *then* they'd pay attention. Men pay attention to women's sex. Most men don't like the idea of a woman being violated because it's another man cheating in the game of getting women.

Wolf asked me this: If I thought someone had hurt you, who could it've been?

I just started naming off everyone's motive.

Sarah being angry at you—and probably angry at Hank, too—and wanting your job.

Everett Sophie and your money.

Scott and your money, presuming he didn't know you had altered your will. He knows a finding of something other than suicide means more money, money from your life insurance.

Hank seems unlikely. I couldn't come up with anything there. Call it bias, but I think I'm reasonable on that.

But then, speaking of my bias, there's the Gnat. The Gnat, who might have been worried you'd crush him before he succeeded at making himself important off your name. Your death is just so convenient for him.

And all that doesn't even count crimes of passion that might have caused someone to hurt you. And you were passionate, Alex. You whipped up other people's passion. Look at your piano lover, Parvus, who dragged me twice this week under the piano at Chez Jacques without saying anything.

Christ. *What* did you see in Professor Parvus? Why on earth would you have bought him a piano for your house, to have him there? The way he dragged me by the wrist—

But if I name all these motives off to Wolf—the inflamed passions, the attempts at professional climbing, the money, the sex?—he tells me the fact that I see almost *everyone* as having a motive means I am on to exactly *nothing*. Motive, he says, is the *easiest* thing to imagine, the easiest thing to invent. If you can see any tie between two people, you can always imagine a way the tie could lead to anger, fear, jealousy, defensiveness that becomes offensiveness, offensiveness that could eventually become murderous.

I know he's right. You know, in history, we only toy with motive here and there. I mean the good scholars. The good scholars leave psychological motive alone. It's just too easy to imagine. Just too easy to invent. It's too easy to look at Newton, conclude he died a virgin, and imagine his insane genius had something to do with that. It's just too easy to look at Leonardo and decide his sexuality explained all of his art. And you and I, we still believe in reality, don't we? We can't just go around imagining motives.

"Forget motive," Wolf told me. "You need to see if there were means. There might be more to it then, than simply evidence of drowning." But he won't get me your autopsy report, which might help me know that.

I just don't think you were depressed. And I just don't think you would have come here to swim with your clothes and your jewelry on a cold late May day. Everyone who knew you agrees you were sometimes unable to stop yourself from jumping into open water with your clothes on. You were like a Labrador retriever that way—impulsive around open water. But everyone who describes to me such an instance describes an instance in which you came upon evocative water *unexpectedly*. Here—you *drove* yourself here. This wasn't you accidentally coming upon water.

Or was it? Maybe you were having writer's block that weekend and went out for a drive and here this lake was. And you could not resist. And you simply drowned by accident. Got a cramp and drowned. Got hypothermic and drowned?

But you would have taken your jewelry off.

Anyway, I know Wolf is right that I shouldn't let on what it is I'm researching about you—but hiding that, well, that just makes it harder to ask questions of people. I have to throw in a thousand extra questions about things I don't care about to dull the sharpness of my real questions. And it is tiresome. Really tiresome.

Professor Shugar, you *know* how *good* research is done! You *tell* your librarian, you *tell* your archivist, you tell her or him bluntly and clearly *exactly* what it is you're trying to find out, because then they know which texts might get you there. You don't dance around what you want to know. You can't fucking go to your archivist and say, "Show me everything in nineteenth- century medicine" and hope that, through random chance or some miracle of divination, she gives you the volume you need to make the links at the core of your very particular timeline. It's like with a therapist or a doctor: you don't dick around. You tell them why you are there. But now, in all these conversations, I have to dick around.

That's what I tried to do with the Gnat—to get answers without saying what I'm trying to figure out—when I went and talked to him. This week, I showed up at his office hours to tell him I'd heard his presentation in Pittsburgh and to ask him why he's misrepresenting your work. Of course, at first, he denied any misrepresentation. Then he launched into quite a Shakespearean monologue about representation and misrepresentation. It felt like a performance designed to showcase his brilliance. And his stupid shaggy head of hair and his big hands—the way he waved them around like he was caught in a swarm.

I just sat there with my arms crossed. Didn't take him too long to figure out my bullshit detector is industrial-grade. He let on that you had started confronting him directly, repeatedly— which I'm not sure anyone else knew. Did you tell Lew or Hank or Everett Sophie? They never mentioned that things had ramped up *that much* between you and the Gnat in the couple of weeks before you died. He told me he'd told you his plans for a book about your work, a book that would change the public perception of you. You told him you wanted him to stop, that this pesky young man was not going to dominate a woman who was a scholar of your rank. And he told you the scales of justice are not so much held by a blind woman as held by whoever grabs them.

I don't think he meant to tell me all that. Because right after he said it, he seemed to discover me still sitting there, his audience of one. And he seemed alarmed to see me sitting there.

Of course, how do I know whether *anything* he tells me is true? He has Escher up all around his office, as if the posters are some kind of "Visitor, beware!" disclosure about his fucking attitude with regard to reality. He tried asking me about the murders in Philadelphia. After what Wolf had said about being careful, I told the Gnat that I wasn't the one who put it all together. I tried to brush him off. Well, that just led to him asking me more. I kept insisting that I wasn't very clever in Philadelphia; I had gotten far more credit in the press for catching Wilhelm than made sense.

There I was, downplaying my own intelligence and hard work to this twit of a man, misrepresenting the truth to *this fellow*, of all people, the one who thinks representation and misrepresentation are all the same, a decoration,

221

a garnish, a dance to be deployed to prove that our adherence to reality is just a childish phase some never outgrow. Jesus Christ. *Me*, lying to *this guy*, about myself, to try to help *you*. Irony overload.

And you know what came of that? He basically used what I was saying to threaten me. He suggested he was going to recount what I'd just said, maybe in a publication or a presentation, and tell everyone what I'd said about how I wasn't really the clever one in Philadelphia. He'd tell people I'd confessed to him that I'd just been held up by the press because I made a cute-girl character in a story. Said he was gonna seek out that student reporter who'd published the piece about me a couple of weeks ago and tell her all this—because, he said, it'd be fun to see if this took off as a story in the national press, to see what stories the current zeitgeist craved or was willing to sample. He said it'd be interesting to see if they would pick up—pick *at*—a story about the mis-representation of me. Like my life is an *hors d'oeuvres* plate?

And I thought, *Jesus Fucking Christ*. If he does that—goes around saying I said this to him—Jill and Andre are going to absolutely kill me. The prosecutors in Philly, Jill and Andre, would be furious with me if this gets in the press right now, and then Wolf would be furious. What if it ends up having an impact on the trial? It seems like my only hope is to get in touch with this student reporter in a preemptory move and say, "He's making it all up; he makes shit up all the time. Ignore him if he calls you." But if I say that, the reporter will look into it because she'll be curious. And the story is gonna become that the faculty successor to Professor Shugar, the great anti-postmodernist and champion of reality and justice, is now fighting the same old fight with this stupid awful gnat of a graduate student who had so irritated Shugar herself, fighting over—

I mean, what can I do, Alex? Simply hope he doesn't go through with it, doesn't tell anyone what I said, or that if he tells anyone that they don't believe him? And what do I do if he does tell people what I said? Lie about it? Say he's making it all up, what he claims I said, even though I told him those things? He is like the Venus flytrap of irony, Alex. He is like the fuck-ing Venus flytrap of irony. And I am a stupid, stupid housefly sometimes.

The most amazing thing? How did we get interrupted but by having his *girlfriend* show up at the door—my back was to the door—to say in a sing-song voice, "Time to go to dinner or we'll be late to the movie." I recog-nized the voice. Sure enough, it was Sarah. She looked more than a little stunned to see me. And the Gnat shared her expression when I turned back to look at him. I just took my bag and left.

And still, Alex, you say nothing. As if you knew all of this.

So, then, do you know I met up with your Dr. Griffin, the psychiatrist Everett said I should probably talk to? How is it, Alex, that Dr. Griffin seems to know so much more about your recent life than even Everett Sophie and Hank? He does *not* seem like someone you would have liked talking to. Yet, just like that, he solved the question of the piano! Well, not the piano, but the pianist.

I'd told Dr. Griffin that I wanted to talk with him because I'm working on a paper for a journal about the arc of your life's work, and that one of your friends mentioned you having had very interesting conversations with him. He seemed at first rather chilly toward me. But then he is a psychiatrist, so of course they are always all about that placid exterior. He's what, only late thirties or so? Not too far out of residency. But he puts on that air . . .

I think there are two kinds of psychiatrists: the ones who are *not* Freudian or Jungian or of any particular school who seem to be very interested in health rather than etiology of pathology. And then there are the others, like him, who seem to want to be mediums of psychic ghosts, who think there's a simple, personal, historical reason for everything that goes wrong in your life. Obsessed with *motive*, paying no attention to *method* in a life. He tried to poke at my background, and I let on nothing, which of course will just leave him suspicious and looking me up, I suppose. Like your Mr. Whitaker did?

Anyway, I lied. I told Dr. Griffin that your colleagues had described you as perhaps somewhat depressed when you died. I asked him if he thought you died when you were at a low moment in your life. Were you depressed then? He said yes, yes. And he added that you had revealed to him more about that than you had to other people, about your anxiousness about all that was going on and your sexual frustration. What was he talking about there?

He made it sound like he knew a lot about your sex life. At first, I thought I had hit a gold mine. But what Dr. Griffin told me didn't make a lot of sense. To be perfectly honest, Alex, he did not seem the sort of person you would tell more than you would Sophie or Hank or Lew, or even Joseph in New York, for that matter. Yet Dr. Griffin seemed to suggest that what he knew was not so much the details of who and where—not Whit and New York, for instance—but something about your inner experience?

It just didn't make sense to me. He didn't read as the person to whom you would bear your sexual soul. I didn't think you'd put up with a psychiatrist, at least not of this ilk. So how is it he seemed to know certain things about you?

So, I asked Dr. Griffin as politely as I could whether you two—he and you—were lovers, and he merely smiled a sort of Cheshire cat smirk and said there wasn't an easy answer to that. And then he said no, you were not lovers. What did that mean? No easy answer to whether you were lovers, but a simple answer—no, you were not lovers?

He said that the two of you had shared an intense interest in human sexuality. That you'd spent many hours together talking about the variety of human sexual orientation, behavior, identity, that you'd talked about what you'd observed, and he'd talked about what he'd seen. I asked him if you'd talked to him about the book I'd heard you had been working on. I couldn't very well tell him I had your book project files because I live in your house. He seemed very interested in what I knew about the book. He said yes, he understood you to be writing sort of case studies about people with this and that orientation or fetish. He said you'd asked him to read drafts, and he'd been advising you on the book. Huh. So, if that's the case, Alex—if you were showing Dr. Griffin drafts from the manuscript—why did Hank tell me that your habit was to show *no one* drafts until you had an entire work done? Was that just a lie you told Hank to stop him from bugging you for drafts? Or was Dr. Griffin lying to me for some reason?

I asked Dr. Griffin whether he was shocked when he'd heard you had died. First he said yes. But then he said he'd been one of the people to report you missing because he'd expected to hear from you and, when he didn't, he'd called you and gotten no response, and then he called your office. You hadn't shown up for work. So, he called the police to express concern.

"A great loss," he said about you then. "A great loss, really." He seemed to mean it.

It was not a simple thing to ask Dr. Griffin about the piano. So, I just told him that I'm your successor in your job, which was the source of my interest in your life's work, and that some piano sheet music had come in the mail to you. I said I'd been told you didn't play the piano, so did he know whom I should give it to? For whom you might have ordered piano sheet music, so I could get it to the right person? I told him I'd been trying to get things you left behind at the office to the right people, cleaning up.

He asked, very interested, what the music was. I hastily made up that it was some piece by Bach—the *Goldberg Variations* was the first piano music that came to my mind—and he "huh'ed" like that was very surprising. Like sheet music coming in the mail to you was *not* surprising, but *Bach* was.

I asked him again, who it might be for, so that I could give it to the right person. He looked a little stuck—like he knew but didn't want to say. Then he told me it would have been for Professor Parvus. Your lover of late. Dr. Griffin warned me that Parvus was a deeply unstable fellow, prone to anger and even violence. A man with whom you'd had a major relationship that disappointed you enormously, or, then he said, that made you nervous?

He started to dish. And then he just stopped. So I pushed him a little, to try to understand what Parvus was about, asking as if I were just a curious gossip-girl. It seemed pretty strange since not one of your friends had ever mentioned Parvus. And only Sophie seemed to know about Dr. Griffin. How many sections of your life are there that I have not even found? You're like a nightmare archive, Alex. Completely uncatalogued.

Anyway, Dr. Griffin told me that Parvus is a physics professor at the U and a professional pianist. Griffin said that the reason Parvus is at the U and not one of the bigger places for physics is not his ranking in theoretical physics, which is near the top of his subspecialty, but because the St. Paul Symphony puts up with him enough to let him sometimes play with them. Griffin said that Parvus has a reputation of being unpredictable, obscure, angry, libertarian, contrary, disconnected from norms. That your attraction to him in some ways mirrored the way Parvus and you viewed sex, as carnal.

This was all so much to take in, particularly without a notebook to write down what he was saying. I couldn't even figure out what Dr. Griffin meant by all this—about you and Parvus and sex—and I asked him what he meant and whether *he* also understood sex this way, as carnal. He turned very still and then said that he was just quite dully heterosexual himself. And he added that it was *you* who was hard to understand.

I had to jump-start the conversation at that point. I remember it felt as if I had pushed the car of the conversation forward and jumped in to pop the clutch, you know? It was clear Dr. Griffin could be distracted by sexual pathology, so I asked him about your relationship with Hank. He said you and Hank had a tense relationship because you wanted his attentions but could not hold them. He suggested to me this was part of your recent sadness and frustration—a sort of unrequited desire for Hank. Did you tell Dr. Griffin this thing about Hank and you? Your supposed unrequited feelings? Did you say it just to shut him up about something—give him something to latch onto and be fascinated with? Because no one else seems to think you had an unrequited sexual desire for Hank.

Griffin asked me then about Wilhelm and Philadelphia. So that made clear he knows who I am. I told him I wasn't in a position to talk about it, but he pressed a bit—he started to refer to details of the trial that must have been recently reported in the news. I was kind of stunned to hear what he was saying. I think the look I gave him, of confusion and fear, must have made clear I'm not listening to the news. Then he became fascinated by my apparent lack of knowledge, and he wanted to know what my role had been. I suggested to him, as I had with the Gnat, that I'd less to do with it all than the papers suggested—that it was the police, not me.

I said to him: Look, they're not even calling me as a witness, so how important could my role be? Why should I bother to follow it closely when I have plenty of work to keep me busy? And he seemed satisfied with that. He calmed down? When I looked at him and saw him that way, I must have looked at him funny—*when will I ever grow a poker face?*—and he said he was glad to hear that it was not something that was a cause of great stress to me, but that if it was, of course I could talk to him about it and he would be happy to help.

Griffin reminded me of what Everett Sophie said on the plane in reference to him being a psychiatrist—how some psychiatrists want to point to what's wrong about you and circle around that. Circle like a turkey vulture over a piece of roadkill on a busy highway. He seemed like that. But you were a *hawk*, Alex Shugar: You liked the pursuit of fresh meat, *the living*. You would not have wanted to spend time with a highway turkey vulture. So why would you have bothered with Dr. Griffin? Maybe because you and he *were* lovers, and there was something there?

God, now *I* sound like a Freudian, seeing sex in everything.

Dr. Griffin had ridden his bicycle to Espresso Royale, where we met, and his arms and legs were strong, his veins showing—you might have liked that? I do, usually. Not him, though. There is something wrong with him. I can't quite explain it, but it's hard to imagine you with him. Am I just projecting? He was so much younger than you, and everyone has told me you liked your own age.

I wish I did, Alex. I wish I had your taste, in men my own age. It'd be easier. I'm surprised Hank has stayed in the car this long, quiet. I wonder if he's fallen asleep. He's kept the car running, so maybe he is warm enough that he's fallen asleep. I hope so. I would rather he not figure out that we are at the lake where you died and interrupt my conversation with you tonight. (Not that you're keeping up your part.)

Hank has been flirting with me all week since that night he was at your house and I went down on him and fell asleep with him and had that dream about you and him coming to dinner at Wolf's. God, Hank is *such* a good flirt. So much wordplay this week. He used campus mail to send me a note written so that if anyone else opened it, they would have no idea who sent it.

"Come, here, Watson. I need you."

Hank keeps asking me if I want him yet, and I keep saying yes, and that that is why he might as well stay away, as he can't have me until I don't want him. He comes back with suggestions of how I could have what I want without giving him what he wants, so that we could still both have what we want: me, him; him, the unrelenting chase. He suggested I drug him and fuck him and he had me laughing so. He was driving me so to distraction—I think he was the only thing that kept me from giving up on existence this week. I pulled out his apron at one point, out of your kitchen drawer, and oh, it had *his smell*. His scent. Oh, God, Alex. That combination of his cologne and his sweat—the part of the apron that comes up just below his armpits, oh, man—and maybe a little whiskey?

You probably don't want to hear what I did with that apron.

I hope Hank didn't think when I called him and woke him up that he was going to get more than a drive to a place he wouldn't want to go. I expect that he could hear in my voice I wasn't calling for anything other than help. For a man who says he wants me so badly, he can be remarkably undemanding and helpful.

My dear Professor Shugar. Why the hell would you fuck around with Professor Parvus when you could have Hank? Even if Parvus can play the piano very well, what the hell? But I guess you knew you couldn't have Hank—if you have him, there he goes. You would have been disappointed in him, and he would have hated that.

But Professor Parvus, really? I asked around before going to see Parvus and heard only that you and he'd had some massive fight at the faculty senate—truly epic in that everyone seemed to know of it—even people who were not there. All were able to recount the episode as if it had been a battle recorded by Homer. Absolutely everyone knew of the fight. But no one knew of you being in a sexual relationship with Parvus. Only Dr. Griffin knew.

They all tell me your *bataille épique* at the faculty senate was about the role of the humanities and the arts in the university. They say *you* were arguing for the proper marginalization of the arts and humanities—arguing these disciplines were increasingly not worthy of being called scholarship, or even disciplines.

But Parvus—Parvus the physicist—who apparently ordinarily said absolutely nothing at all at any meeting, who was known for simply sitting through them with pencil and paper working out a science or math problem, or his grocery list or something, well, in response to your denunciation of the current state of the arts and humanities, he stood up and yelled at you across the senate floor about how you claimed to be a champion of reality but seemed to know not the least about the reality of the human world because you had no concept of the power of art?

People said the whole senate was silent for a good ten minutes while the two of you went at it across the floor, making the most extraordinary arguments about epistemology, the limits of the human mind, the point of the academy. . . . They say it was incredible. Exactly the opposite of what you'd expect. A physicist arguing for the arts and humanities. An English professor calling them all useless, praising the hard sciences.

So, I went to his office to ask about the piano I figured you must've bought for him. He was not there. I went again and he was not there again. The more I thought about it, the more I thought the piano must be something I have to understand to understand your death, Alex. If you wanted the piano for Parvus to play at your house, then I have to understand why— was it just to get him to your house?

So, finally, I just sat outside Parvus's office and waited. There was a chair outside his office, so I sat there grading papers figuring I had to grade them somewhere so it might as well be there, in his hallway. Eventually, he showed up. He looked down at me and asked me if I was a graduate student who was lost, because, he said, I was obviously not in physics. Had he seen what I was grading—essays without formulae—or is he just a sexist twit who assumes a woman doesn't do physics? I said no, I was not a lost graduate student. I am faculty and was found. He didn't think my joke funny. He unlocked his door, and I followed him into his office. He sat at his desk and started working as if I weren't there. I sat down across the desk from him and just watched him for a while.

I soon recognized that what I had heard about him was true—he was not at all normal. He simply ignored me, went about his business on his computer, took his empty water bottle to the fountain out in the hall and refilled it and came back drinking from it, simply ignoring me as if we were two strangers who happened to be sharing seats facing each other on a train.

After a half hour of this, of him simply not caring that I was sitting in his office, sitting across his desk from him watching him, I asked him: "Why did Alex Shugar buy a piano to have at her house for you, Dr. Parvus?"

His eyes flared and he slammed his hands on the desk. He got up and grabbed me by the wrist and pulled me out his door—I grabbed my bag as I thought he was simply going to throw me out and slam the door in my face, and I didn't want to leave my backpack in his office. But he slammed the door behind us both and marched me down the hall and out the building and down the path, still holding my wrist. I told him, loudly, "You are hurting me. If you will let go my arm, I will follow you."

So, he let go my wrist and kept storming forward, and I followed him, wondering whether I ought to be. We got to Chez Jacques, that jazz bar near campus. It was of course closed at that hour—it was only about two o'clock in the afternoon. He banged on the door, and someone answered and let him in—let us both in, saying nothing, and they locked the door behind us.

He went over to their piano and threw off the fabric cover onto the floor and sat down and started to play something furiously. I didn't recognize the piece, but I could recognize in it—well, I don't know how to describe it. Okay, this—this metaphor: I could recognize in it a conversion, the conversion of DNA to RNA to amino acids to proteins to cells to organs to life to—to a condor. *A condor.* You know what I mean? This transformation. From the core, the very core, to the thing that flies out from the past in all its enormity as if it owns the whole fucking universe, as if it rules the world, but is in fact on the very verge of extinction.

His face. He looked up and seemed angry that I was simply standing there listening to him play, watching him play, staring at him, watching the way he played. He stopped suddenly and told me I wasn't ever going to understand why you got the piano if I stood far away from it all. I couldn't figure out what he meant. He told me to stop being so difficult and gestured for me to get under the piano. I asked him in words if that was what he meant, that I should get under the piano? And he yelled at me "Yes!" as if I were the stupidest child on the face of the planet.

So, I took off my backpack and pushed it under so I could have a place to put my head, and I lay under there, on the hard floor of the club, and listened as he played on. His big feet were too distracting, so I closed my eyes. Now I recognized he had moved on to something by Rachmaninov, but it was the angriest version I had ever heard. No, not angry—*natural.* As if he was not drawing it out of his memory but was drawing it out of the atmosphere. The way the lightning rod on the convent chimney used to draw the energy out of the sky.

And then after some time of this, he seemed spent; he seemed to have

229

expended a furious energy, the way the sky does in the summer. He moved on to play a Chopin nocturne, and—Alex, it was clear he was remembering you. It was so clear to me at that moment that he had summoned you, invoked you. I thought perhaps he was remembering a time with you in your bath? The blue bottles, the stars, the steam on the windows? Eventually he stopped and looked under the piano at me, and I realized—I felt like an absolute fool, realizing that I had apparently been crying. My face was positively soaked.

I crawled out and wiped my eyes with my sleeves. I was on my hands and knees. I could see then that he, too, was crying, his eyes pleading with the heavens, his pupils almost straight up, the tears flowing straight down, and he looked back at me. I said to him, simply, "I don't understand." To which he slammed down the cover on the keys and just left.

The person who had let us in helped me up, helped me to sit on the piano bench, and he gave me a glass of water and a napkin, and I drank it and dried my face and left to follow him. But Parvus was long gone.

Two days later—Thursday, was it? —we had a repeat. I sat there outside his office. He let himself in without acknowledging me. I followed him into his office and sat across from him. I did nothing but watch him work. He lost his patience with something—me or his work or something. He grabbed me by the wrist and tossed me into the hall and locked his office behind him. He wandered down the same path and I followed. He banged again on the door of Chez Jacques. They let him in, as if this always happened, or happened enough—that he would come and bang on the door to be let in—they saw nothing strange in it. He ordered me again with an impatient gesture under the piano. He played now what I recognized as Beethoven, then Schubert, then Debussy.

This time I could feel you with us almost the whole time. I could feel that he had invoked you. That, as Persephone, you had emerged momentarily and brought him solace, even joy, peace from his torment. And this time, when he was done, he did not slam the piano keys' cover. He closed it the way one closes one's grandmother's jewelry box. Leaving me there again. Baffled.

I called Wolf and tried to explain this, what happened with Parvus, thinking maybe he could help me figure it out. But I could not find a way to explain any of it, and I just made a mess. Wolf got angry with me, listening to me describe what happened, and asked me why I wasn't focused on my work. We got into the most ridiculous argument. I don't even remember how we got there, but I said to Wolf, belligerently, that he probably didn't understand anything about you, that he probably hadn't realized Sophie was a male under her clothes. He told me of *course* he had recognized that. He asked me back, defensively, if I thought it was a good idea to befriend people who were not what they seemed. I thought at first he was slamming Sophie. But then I realized this was some kind of slam at me.

He got onto the subject of pride again. He said to me, "When did it happen, Rabbit, that only gay people are entitled to pride when it comes to sexual life? Why aren't you or I entitled to have some pride?"

I wasn't sure what he meant, but to have it on top of the—the recent performance of Professor Parvus, and all the reporters calling, and Dr. Griffin telling me of the bits of the trial, it just left me weeping on the telephone. Then Wolf was beside himself with guilt, trying to calm me, asking if he should call Liz and have her call me, telling me the trial was going to be okay, that whatever I'd heard, I shouldn't worry too much about it.

Well, Alex. I thought to myself that I'm just a stupid basket case and there's no way I'm going to make it through this year. You know what Hank told me last weekend that you would say? *It doesn't matter.* I wonder if that is what you would say now. But would you tell me I can just walk away from all these people and decide it doesn't matter?

If only you'd *tell me* what happened here. Was it this cold out when you came here last? Had it been a clear night just a few hours before you died, the way it is a clear night tonight? Had you slept that night, or did you stay up to see these stars? Well, they would have been a little different—the stars. It was spring, then. Now we are getting to the end of fall here. I can't quite remember how they rotate.

Did you lie in your bath, Alex, and look at these stars just before you died? I wish you'd talk to me. Tell me what matters. Just tell me what *does* or does *not* matter; give me a hint. Just tell me why you had your clothes on, your jewelry. Just tell me why you drove here. Just tell me how you ended.

But you are no easier in death than in life, Alex. You are *such* a difficult subject. The most difficult I have ever had.

Chapter 20

Hank woke to the sound of Maddy opening the car door. Sitting down with the door still ajar, she banged her heels a few times on the car's door frame to knock the dirt off her shoes. She pulled her feet in and slammed the door closed. Hank yawned and stretched and put his seat back up to a driving position.

"Back home?" he asked.

He turned on the headlights.

"Yes," she said, putting her hands in front of the heating vents to try to warm them up. He cranked the blower fan up to help her.

"Have you been here before?" he asked, as he turned the car around and headed slowly down the unpaved drive from the lake, back to the road.

She wondered if he understood where they had been.

"No," she said. "Have you?"

He didn't answer for a moment. He looked at her but couldn't see her face in the darkness. He pulled onto the paved road, gave the car more gas, and shifted from second to third gear.

"Do you keep contacting me," Hank asked, "because you think I'm going to confess? Confess to having killed Ally?"

His voice sounded a little angry, Maddy thought, and she wondered how she had given him this impression. She wasn't quite sure what to say or do.

She cleared her throat, realizing too late that must have made it sound like he was on to something. She had just cleared her throat because her sinuses were draining from the shift of cold to warm.

"You call me to her house," he said in an angry tone, "and then you call me to take you in the middle of the night to a lake, I'm guessing specifically the lake where she died, thinking that I'll tell you—what? That I did it?"

"No," she said, putting her hand on his right arm. He shifted hard from third to fourth, as if to pull away from her touch. She pulled her hand back.

She was suddenly so very tired now. Tired from the long week of stressful encounters. Tired from standing in the cold talking pointlessly to Alex. Tired from this tug and push with Hank.

He drove faster down the dark road. She could see an occasional light in the distance and wished for a moment that the headlights would not make it quite so hard to see the stars. She wanted the steady visual anchor of the stars to counteract the feeling that he was driving her too fast, too recklessly.

"Hank," she said finally, in a worn-out voice. "I'm not at all sure what I could have said to give you the impression I think you hurt Ally. I don't think that."

The warm air flooding the car was making her even more tired, and she yawned. He did not reply. She unzipped her coat to draw the car's heat to her chest.

"I think maybe somebody did hurt Alex," she continued. "Maybe not directly, maybe indirectly. But not you. Sure, you hurt her feelings sometimes. You made her upset sometimes with your—your ways. But you didn't hurt her intentionally or significantly. She loved you right up to the end. You loved her—you love her still. I get that."

He didn't say anything, but it felt to her as if he started driving more calmly.

"I know maybe you don't think it, but I think you're basically a decent guy. Remarkably kind."

After about thirty seconds, he reached over, took her left hand, and put it on the gear shift to hold it under his, like the night a week ago when she had asked him for a drive. He still said nothing.

"I don't call you to me," she told him after a minute of silence, "because I think you will *confess*. I just think you know way more than most people did about Ally, so, frankly, you're *useful* to me. But I also call you because I think you're ridiculously—anatomically—physiologically. . . . You are the best distraction from all the craziness of my life right now. The best fucking distraction."

She let out a little laugh at her unintentional joke. Without a sound, he squeezed her hand. She thought it funny, that squeeze. Such a statement of desire as made by her, she thought, ought to elicit some overtly sexy gesture in return. Perhaps his finger rubbing the side of her hand suggestively. But the gesture he had made—the squeeze—was of reassurance. Of simple comfort.

"You have this crazy way, Hank, of turning me on and then making me feel safe," she explained, "all at the same time. *That's* why I call you if I need to go in the middle of the night to a lake where someone died. I didn't call you to take me because I wanted you to come there to confess. I called you because I knew I'd be safe. And I'd get to smell you again."

That elicited a gesture more like she had expected. It was not a finger rubbed on the side of her hand, but his thumb and his pinky curled under the sides of her hand, just the way a beetle grabs ahold of a flower's stem in a sudden breeze, just the way a kitten on its back grabs ahold of a hand playing with its silky underbelly.

She used her free hand to brush her hair back off her face.

"Are you wearing an undershirt under all that?" she asked him.

"Yes," he said, sounding a bit confused.

"Were you sleeping in it before you came and picked me up?"

"Yes."

"Would you let me have it, before you go?"

"Why?" he asked, although he said it with a smile she could hear.

"Because I've positively worn out your apron, and now I think it probably smells more like me than you."

He said nothing for a moment. Then:

"I'll trade you the shirt for that apron."

The car picked up speed.

. . .

She changed back into her long flannel nightgown while he went into the bathroom. She climbed under the covers and was about to turn off the bedside lamp when he emerged, shirtless.

"Oh," she said, counting down his ribs as if they might not all be there. His collarbone crowned them so nicely, like the antlers of a healthy buck with a very handsome face.

She lay back, without turning off the light after all, and held up her hands in a gesture indicating he should hand over the shirt. She held it to her face and took a good long breath. It was just what she wanted—that homeopathic distillation, that elusive combination of his cologne, his sweat, his skin.

"Oh," she said. "Thank you. That's very good."

He went around to the empty side of the bed and crawled in under the covers next to her.

"What are you doing?" she said, laughing. "We are not having sex! I'm having sex with your shirt, not you. Get out of here—I'm not into threesomes."

He reached over her and turned off the light, in the process rolling her onto her left side and pushing his body up next to hers. She could smell his salt as he reached over her. Now he wrapped his right arm around her and kissed her neck. He always seemed to know how much moisture to convey, in saliva, in perspiration, in his breath, to make her wet.

"You can have sex with my shirt. I won't bother you two."

She pulled his rumpled shirt up again to her face with her left hand and slipped her right hand under her nightgown. She could feel his erection through his jeans behind her as he kissed the side of her neck again. She found herself involuntarily breathing faster, as if she had started the hard part of a good run. Soon, she reached her right hand around to find his, and pulled his hand into her crotch. His fingers immediately found her wet.

"Fuck," he said, drawing the word to three syllables. He kissed her earlobe and then bit on it lightly as if she might otherwise get away.

She reached down and took one of his fingers and pushed it into her so that he would feel just how much she wanted him. Taking the cue, he pushed two in now, then a little bit of a third, and stroked her in and out, as she started to moan and wince in pleasure.

"But Dr. Shanks," he said, quite quietly, "studies show that somewhere between seventy and ninety percent of women will not reach orgasm with internal stimulation only."

She could not think what to answer him in words, but her pelvic muscles all tightened in response. Now he did something with his hand just like he had done on the gearshift when he had wrapped onto her hand. Like a beetle. Like a kitten. She was trying to figure out what he was doing with his five fingers, with just one hand, to drive her so crazy—three fingers in and two out? Something with her labia involving his palm? Then the heel of his hand? His knuckles? But all she could do was clutch his shirt harder to her face with both of her hands and feel her muscles involuntarily pull at his strong hand.

"What are you doing with—"

"Shhh," he answered.

"But what are you—what anatomical method—"

"Shhh, Maddy. I'm not even here. It's just you and my shirt."

He worked her a little harder as his hand got wetter.

"But why does it feel so—"

"Why?" he said, now reaching around under her with his left arm, finding one of her nipples with his fingers through the flannel of the nightgown. She expected him to pinch, but all he did was hold it ever so lightly and give it a tiny tug. A most polite, tiny, little tug. She let out a sudden grunt and a hard shake.

"You don't have to figure everything out, Maddy. Stop thinking. Just feel. Just let it happen?"

After a moment, as if he had waited for her to clear her mind, as he worked her pussy with his hand and her breathing grew hard, he did it again—a most polite little tug on her nipple. She came with something like a moan that turned into a squeal as he held her tighter now, as if she might fall off the bed. She shook and shook for a moment, and he held her with his left arm still wrapped under her, his right arm now around her belly. Her large muscles gave off small spasms of aftershocks.

When she had gone still and had started to show the signs of falling into sleep, he rolled her on her back and carefully pulled her flannel nightgown back down to her knees, straightening it out. He got out from under the covers, and, standing above her, tucked her in. He put on his over-shirt, buttoned it up, and put his two hands softly on the sides of her head. He leaned down and kissed her on her limp lips.

"Sleep well, you," he said, leaving.

She heard the front door open and then shut, and she fell fast toward sleep.

Chapter 21

"Professor Shanks? There are, uh, some people here to see you?"

Maddy looked up grumpily from the text she had been reading all afternoon. Then she caught herself, worried she had just given this poor young messenger a dirty look. But it had been so delightful to be lost for so long alone in this particular piece, the English surgeon Percivall Pott's *Chirurgical Observations*, published in 1775. The volume included "Some Few Remarks on the Polypus of the Nose" and "Observations on the Mortification of the Toes and Feet," plus the better-known "Observations on the Cancer of the Scrotum," in which Potts had written of the association between the work of chimney sweeps and the development of scrotal cancer.

Reading this book at the lone table in the back of the locked stacks of the history of medicine library, Maddy had been thinking about trying to research and then pen a paper on the history of occupational diseases—something *different*, something having *nothing* to do with the politics of human specimen acquisition, something she'd never read about before. It had been for a moment just that lovely stage of reading a totally unfamiliar text where there's no particular point, no particular search, just a near-pure read. The textual version of playing with a happy puppy in your lap.

That was when this grad student who worked part-time as a library assistant had interrupted her.

"Sorry," Maddy said to the student, sitting up straighter in the unforgiving institutional metal chair and trying consciously to soften the look on her face. "I was just lost in this text. Do you know who's looking for me?"

Maddy had taken to reading back here with the chief librarian's permission. It was a closed and secured area, one not normally used for work at all—just for fetching books a patron might need—which meant that if reporters figured out that this library is where Maddy worked and they stopped by and she was hiding back here, it would look to them like she wasn't at the library at all. The staff could say she wasn't there, and it would appear true. It had happened twice in the past week.

But did this grad student know to screen the way the chief librarian did?

"I didn't get their names," the student said.

Maddy sighed. If she sent the student back out to ask names and purpose, it was going to be obvious she was hiding back here. So she was stuck.

"They're dwarves," the student blurted out now. "I mean, they're little people. Is that the right term?"

"Oh," Maddy answered. "I see."

She closed the book and told the student to tell the visitors that she'd be out in a moment. She reshelved the volume, tried to fix her hair, and picked up her notebook and pencil, taking them out with her. She opened the door from the stacks to the reading room and found a couple—a middle-aged man and woman—facing her.

Maddy held out her hand.

"I'm Madeleine Shanks," she said.

"Professor Shanks," the man said, reaching up and shaking her hand. Maddy involuntarily calculated which kind of dwarfism he had—looked like pituitary. Typically-proportioned limbs. The woman seemed to have achondroplasia; shortened limbs, with the tell-tale facial structures of the condition. Maddy shook the woman's hand, feeling the woman's short fingers in her own.

The woman was wearing a gold necklace with a jeweled pendant, and Maddy thought it especially pretty, with pink and light green stones.

"I'm Michael Wollinsky. This is my wife, Ela. We were hoping to speak with you."

"Of course," Maddy answered, trying to figure out where they might be most comfortable. "Would you like to speak here or go somewhere—a coffee, a drink?"

"If you don't mind," the man answered, "we would prefer to speak with you where it is most private."

Maddy looked up to see the grad student staring from the front desk. She looked embarrassed as Maddy caught her eye.

"I'm going to meet with these visitors in the break room," Maddy called to the student. The student nodded and turned her head quickly back to the desk.

Maddy showed the couple to the back room with the kitchenette. She closed the door and gestured to the chairs and table. She hastened to pull up a footstool from the corner for Mrs. Wollinsky. She then pulled an empty box down from a shelf and offered it to Mr. Wollinsky for his feet. She knew that people with short stature found it easier to sit in regular chairs if they had a place to rest their feet, just as average-height people prefer high stools to have footrests built-in.

Seeing the gesture of accommodation, the woman smiled at her husband and gave a small nod.

"Can I make you some coffee or tea?" Maddy asked.

"Tea would be lovely," Mrs. Wollinsky answered. "I take sugar, and my husband takes it plain."

Maddy filled the electric kettle with water and turned it on. She took mugs down from the cabinet and set up the teapot with two bags of tea.

"Mr. Wollinsky," Maddy said, "I know your name. You're a prominent lawyer, aren't you?"

"Yes," the man replied. "I'm with the Office of Civil Rights in Washington. I was appointed by the president."

"Yes," Maddy answered. "It's an honor to meet you. And Mrs. Wollinsky, may I ask about your profession?" (Maddy thought from the woman's leather portfolio that she must be used to business meetings.)

"I'm a certified public accountant. A reliable profession good for following Michael around as he's risen in his career, from local to state to national work. Not hard for me to find work as an accountant wherever we move."

There was a small silence as the tea kettle made the light groan of water warming up.

"Well," Maddy said, facing the counter rather than the table, "what brings you to Minnesota? Visiting friends or family? Giving a talk at the law school, Mr. Wollinsky?"

"We came specifically to see you," he answered.

Maddy did not turn around. All she could think was that these people probably assumed she had been following the trial. She felt now as if she had not done her homework and was about to be caught. By a law professor, no less.

"I know we probably should have let you know," Michael Wollinsky added, "but we thought then you might not see us. It is our impression you're generally not taking calls from strangers. So, we decided to take the chance that if we showed up, you would speak to us. We have friends we could always visit here if you wouldn't see us."

Maddy turned around now to look at them. She noticed anew how well-dressed they were. She now felt so very underdressed, in her untucked button-down shirt.

"Well," Maddy said, "there are a lot of curiosity-seekers, you know."

The couple let out a small chuckle together.

"Oh, we know what that's like," Ela Wollinsky said. "Do you mind talking with us?"

"Not at all." She poured the hot water from the kettle into the teapot and brought the teapot and the mugs over to the table. She fetched three spoons, paper napkins, and the covered sugar bowl. She sat down at the table.

"I will admit," Maddy said, "it confuses me that you'd come all the way from Washington to see me. If I had known who you are, Mr. Wollinsky, I would certainly have taken your call."

"There are some things best discussed in person," Michael replied. "Some things that can really only be discussed in person."

He poured tea into the three mugs. It was clear to Maddy he was thinking about how to start the conversation. She said nothing.

"We don't mean to bother you," Ela said, filling the silence. "To be perfectly frank, we want to understand from you what—what happened. Dr. Wilhelm's lawyers have asked us to be, in essence, character witnesses for him. And we *thought* that we were going to do that—it will likely be quite soon when they would need us, since we've been told the prosecution is getting ready to rest. But now, as the trial has been going on and we await our turn, we wonder—what we should say. Not say."

"I mean, we know our duty is to just answer every question truthfully," Michael added quickly and firmly, stirring his tea as if to emphasize the

240

point of law. "But we want to understand what we are walking into, as moral agents."

When Maddy didn't answer, he went on.

"When the news of his arrest first came out, we thought there was no way it could be true. We had both been patients of Dr. Wilhelm. He was very helpful to the whole community, you know. Very caring."

"I know," Maddy said. She took a sip of tea and spit it back into the cup. "Sorry, too hot," she said, wiping her mouth with a napkin. The tip of her tongue burned.

"You are the subject of a great deal of conversation in the community," Ela told Maddy. "People are trying to figure out if we could have all been so wrong about him. Well, not all thought he was a good man."

"You mean Jimmy Heathcote," Maddy said. "Jimmy had been telling people he thought it was no coincidence that many in your community who'd died of sudden heart trouble had been those who'd promised their interesting bodies to Wilhelm."

"But so many of us had promised our bodies to him!" Ela said, stirring sugar into her tea. "I tried to explain to Jimmy the statistics—if so many of us had promised our bodies, then it made sense that those who died suddenly had been people who had indicated in their wills that their bodies should go to him. It seemed merely a *coincidence*. The work Dr. Wilhelm was doing —the care he had given—"

"I understand," Maddy said, now stirring her tea and holding the spoon in the air to let the steam come off it. She wished she could undo the unpleasant sensation of her singed tongue tip. "I told Jimmy the same thing when we talked about it. That we had to think about the denominator."

"That must have been after you came and gave the talk at our annual conference? Did you go to New York to see Jimmy?"

"Yes," Maddy said. "He gave me the names of lots of people whose deaths he thought were worth looking at."

She remembered now the napkins she had saved—the ones on which Jimmy had drawn out rough timelines, the timelines that had immediately made her sympathetic to him. The police still had those napkins. Would she ever get them back? Would she ever get back all her original papers on Wilhelm and the file folders in which she had organized them? The police had given her photocopies of the papers, but she had specifically asked them also to photocopy and send her the notes she had scribbled on the file folders themselves. She felt somewhat silly bothering them for this as they pursued the prosecution. But she wanted her research, in case they asked her something, in case she felt doubt in herself. And she wanted them to know they'd better take *all* she had found seriously.

"Well, no one took Jimmy *all* that seriously," Michael said, startling Maddy with this parallel to her own thoughts. "Except, I guess, you."

"Some people did—they just didn't make it known. I learned that later. Too late. And I think I was just better primed than all of you," Maddy sighed, getting up to get herself a glass of cold water to try to soothe her tongue. "I was just better primed to hear Jimmy out."

"Primed?" Michael asked.

"When you study history, especially the history of medicine," Maddy said, returning with the glass, drinking a little and pouring some of the cold water into her mug to try and cool her tea faster, "you realize that sometimes men who did great things, made great discoveries and were great doctors, well, sometimes they also did troubling things. It's not unfathomable to someone who knows history."

For a moment there was only the sound of Ela's spoon clinking against the inside of her cup.

"*Unfathomable*," Ela said, putting her spoon down. "That's what it was, when we heard of the arrest. *Unfathomable*."

"So, you think he is an evil man?" Michael asked Maddy in a quieter voice.

"I don't think it's useful for me to think about good and evil that way," Maddy answered. "In stories, in the movies, in some popular history, we have easy stories of good souls and evil souls. In real life, in scholarship, we have complicated humans—humans who will sometimes act for personal gain, and for self-preservation, or for defense or promotion of their lovers or their kin, in ways that we can understand from afar are immoral. But within the minds of the immoral person, there is a rationality, a logic, often in keeping with the things in their lives that we see as having been good."

"What do you mean?" Ela asked.

"Dr. Wilhelm believed he was doing the community of people with dwarfism enormous amounts of good," Maddy explained. "In fact, he *was*. You weren't wrong in your basic reading of him. You weren't duped. He provided good care and excellent research. And he needed more bodies to do more excellent research, research that would lead to more good care. If he found a patient who he thought was suffering from their condition, and who he knew wanted to give him their body for his research, and it was a body type he needed in particular—"

"Why not acquire the body a little early and end the patient's suffering?" Michael asked.

"Basically, yes," Maddy answered. "Solving several problems at once. From his point of view."

"A grim thought," Ela said.

"So, you're saying he didn't do it for money, or anything like that," Michael added.

"Oh no," Maddy answered. "It wasn't for *money*. I mean, not directly. In a weird way, it was for *charity*."

Ela looked at Maddy, with her mouth hanging slightly open.

"He saw his work as charitable," Maddy said. "He was helping in the long run. There have been plenty of great men—maybe some women, too—in the history of medicine who have seen themselves as generals in a war against disease and pathology, a war in which the patients are the soldiers to be sacrificed by the generals for the greater good. To win the war. Some, like Wilhelm, hastened death with their research methods, although usually not *intentionally*, like him. This wasn't about money. It was about being heroic, in a way. A charitable hero in the larger scheme of things. He probably feels quite misunderstood now."

She realized suddenly how good it felt to talk openly in this way about what she had seen —how good it felt to explain the historical context that had allowed her to see it, to explain the psychology of Wilhelm. Maddy had not been out *looking* for trouble, *looking* for someone to accuse, when she found what he had done. It was just impossible not to see the possibility, knowing history, and then to look for the pieces, and then to present the evidence, just as she would any other research.

"Did he kill Jimmy?" Ela asked suddenly. "Do you think?"

Maddy looked Ela in the eyes and saw tears accumulating behind the dam of the lower lid.

"We could not prove it," Maddy answered. "That's why Jimmy is not yet a named victim. Well, that and it is a different jurisdiction—that one is New York, not Philly. But I feel pretty sure—and John Wolf, the police detective that I worked with—he and I felt pretty sure Wilhelm at least arranged Jimmy's death."

"Jimmy's death didn't look much like the others did," Michael said, saying aloud what they all knew. "But Wilhelm ended up with his body, too."

Maddy huffed.

"Yes, I assume Wilhelm did that just to prove his own invincibility," Maddy said. "I wonder if he was trying to prove to me—"

She didn't finish the sentence.

"That you could not win?" Michael asked.

"Yes," said Maddy. "It made me so angry. Jimmy was a good man."

"None finer," Ela said. "Prone to drink, prone to anger. But none finer. His parents never knew that."

Two tears fell down her cheeks, and her husband handed her a cloth handkerchief from his pocket. She wiped her eyes and cheeks and handed it back to him.

"Are you sure you are right?" Michael asked, examining Maddy's face with great scrutiny.

"No good scholar should ever be one-hundred-percent sure," Maddy answered. "But I feel about as sure as that the sun will set today and come up tomorrow."

The three of them sat quietly for a moment, each drinking tea.

"Your presentation at our meeting was very interesting," Michael said finally.

The way he said it did not feel to Maddy like small talk, but genuine.

"What did you find interesting?" Maddy asked.

"Well, how you traced out the history of exhibitions of little people, including times long ago when they chose to exhibit themselves—it had never occurred to me some of them would have done that so long ago, to improve their finances and have a better life. You know, exhibition's very controversial in the community. Serious acting is, of course, acceptable. But debasing comedy or sensationalistic reality TV—voyeurism, or anything like that—well, it's the source of many a spirited argument."

"It was either very brave or very stupid of you to present on the subject of exhibition!" Ela declared, and they all laughed.

"I figured you are all adults," Maddy said, "and you could handle knowing that history. There is no shame for you all in that history. It never occurred to me that some children at the meeting would attend my talk, and I had to wonder if I should say at the beginning that maybe this wasn't a talk for children."

"Our children need to know their histories," Michael answered. "As you say, there ought to be no shame in knowing our history. They need to know of our ancestors, not just the people to whom we are biologically directly related as family, but the people in history who share the experience of our body types. In some ways, they are just as much our biological ancestors as our families."

Ela nodded. "I loved the way you took us through the images from the medical books through time. I saw just what you mean in the pictures—how at the start, they showed us like real people, but how when medicine became so powerful, we started to look like specimens in their books. It was amazing to learn that even the father of modern anatomy—what was his name?"

"Vesalius," said Maddy.

"Yes, that Vesalius himself might well have had achondroplasia dwarfism! What a wonderful thought!"

"Would you like to see a first-edition Vesalius?" Maddy asked. "And some other images from the various centuries, of people with dwarfism? We don't usually take nonresearchers into the stacks, but I am sure the librarian would let me take you back and show you some volumes, and that she would get the Vesalius from the vault for us. There is a table back there where you can sit, and she and I can bring the texts out and show you."

Michael looked at Ela, and they exchanged a smile.

"That would be marvelous, Dr. Shanks," he said. "We would love to see these books. Shall I make a dinner reservation, so we can buy you dinner afterwards, as a thanks?"

"I would enjoy that very much," Maddy said.

She smiled broadly and stood up, taking the mugs to the sink.

"You will just need to wash your hands and dry them well before we handle the books. We all do that."

. . .

Maddy was still thinking about the dinner conversation with the Wollinskys as she neared home, chewing on the inside of her right cheek.

Her stomach was grumbling. She hadn't been able to eat much at dinner. Michael Wollinsky had informed her before they even ordered that Wilhelm had managed to wage something of a campaign to bad-mouth her in the community and the medical circles, and that more of it seemed likely to happen, implicitly or explicitly, when it was the defense's turn to make their case. Wilhelm had been using his allies, including powerful academic physician-researchers, to suggest through the medical and peer-support grapevines of little people that Maddy had been wrong, that she had been carrying out some weird vendetta or fantasy—perhaps that she had felt an unrequited love for him. Michael warned Maddy that she was likely to find it very difficult to overcome some of what was being said about her.

Well, what he said helped explain why she was not getting many new invitations to give talks. People were fascinated by her presence when she *did* show up to an event as announced, but remarkably few invitations to give public lectures had come in lately, and none from medical schools. Usually they liked inviting historians whose work had something to do with medical controversies in the news. Wilhelm's reach was long. This had taken away much of her appetite.

Even well into dinner, Maddy could see that Michael and Ela Wollinsky found themselves wondering anew if she might be wrong—not because she said or did anything that made them doubt her, but simply because they were struggling to imagine this doctor, whose clinic they had attended many times, to whose research unit they had donated money, could be a murderer. A murderer many times over.

"If he did what you think he did," Michael had said to Maddy at the restaurant, "then you *are* saying he is evil. And it is very difficult for one to imagine that one cannot spot evil. That one completely failed to see evil. We expect true evil to be self-evident. How could we not have seen it, if it was there?"

"I think an evil act, when seen plainly with temporal or geographic distance, *is* self-evident," Maddy had answered. "But often you can't see it around you in the moment. You think you are dealing with a good person, so you assume they must be doing good. You cannot see into someone's soul. And the person can distract us from their bad acts with good acts."

She tried to figure out how better to explain her thoughts.

"I can understand Wilhelm's personality, his character, his logic," Maddy added. "I can see back into those and see how they make sense in terms of what happened. I can't tell you anything about what an evil soul looks like. There is so much he did that was not bad, it could be hard to see it."

"The way you describe what happened and how, well, how *normal* terrible acts are in life and in medicine," Ela had responded, "there could be much more evildoing in the world than we realize. Done by people with motivations we normally understand. People with whom we are sympathetic. We miss seeing what is right there."

"I do think that is the case," Maddy replied. "I think it's absolutely the case that there is much more evildoing in the world than people recognize, and if they would get past the idea that they can judge souls, that only evil souls do evil, they might *see* the terrible acts that are right before them. They might see their own terrible acts."

She was thinking of The Jerk. And how long it had taken her to understand she had been truly wronged. Why had she never thought of it as rape until Hank had categorized it that way?

But she spoke now to her profession rather than her personal past:

"There are plenty of terrible acts committed by good people in medicine every day."

"If you are right, then God will judge Dr. Wilhelm appropriately," Ela said, nodding her head.

"I very much hope the jury beats God to it," Maddy had responded.

Now, her stomach still grumbling, Maddy pulled up to Alex's house only to find an old Toyota hatchback parked in the driveway. It had Minnesota plates and no bumper stickers. No one was in the car, and no one seemed to be in the vicinity of it. As she cautiously neared the house, she could see a light was on in the living room, and she could hear the piano being played. It had to be Parvus.

She found the front door unlocked. With some trepidation, she walked in and closed the door behind her, leaving her bag on the entry bench. She walked into the living room and found it was indeed Parvus. A fire was going in the fireplace. He paused his playing when he saw her.

"How'd you get in?" she asked. "I changed the lock recently."

"I've never been here before," he answered. "I didn't have a key. Alex didn't have the piano then. Why would I have come over?"

"How did you get in?" Maddy asked again.

"Picked the lock," he answered. "Not very difficult."

He started to play again. Maddy did not recognize the piece—it was some kind of jazz.

"It's a good instrument," he said, continuing to play. "You want to get under?"

"No. I don't want to get under. Do you want a drink? I'm getting myself one."

He nodded. "Whiskey, neat."

She got him what he wanted, pouring herself a glass of white wine from a box she had open in the fridge. She found a coaster and put it on the piano, putting his glass on top of it. He kept playing with his left hand and took a quick drink with his right.

"You shouldn't let yourself into other people's houses," Maddy said as she settled herself down onto the couch.

"It's my piano," he answered, shaking his head to move some stray hairs that had fallen over his eyes.

She had him talking for the first time. Perhaps she could get some answers finally? She might as well jump in.

"Who knew about your relationship with Alex?"

"Nobody," he answered.

He played eight bars more.

"Nobody?" Maddy asked, skeptically. "I know of at least one person who knew of it. That's how I found you."

He stopped playing and picked up his drink. He took a long draft and put it back down.

"Who?"

"Dr. Griffin. The psychiatrist Alex was seeing sometimes."

"What the fuck do you mean, Alex was *seeing* a psychiatrist? She wasn't seeing a psychiatrist. You mean *sexually* seeing? Like fucking?"

"No," Maddy answered, oddly annoyed at finding someone with coarser language and thoughts than herself. "Talking to him."

"You mean as a patient?" he asked with a skeptical tone.

"I don't think so. Anyway, she told Dr. Griffin about it. About your relationship."

"I don't believe you," he answered. He got up and poked at the fire, moving one log slightly.

"You don't believe me why? Was there some reason you had to keep your relationship secret?"

"No," he responded, now walking around the room and looking at the furniture, the art, the drapes, almost as if he were considering buying the place. "We didn't have to keep it secret."

"So why are you so sure Alex didn't tell anyone?"

"Because we didn't *talk* about it with *anyone*."

Now he wandered into the kitchen to look around more. She followed him. He opened and closed drawers and cabinets.

"It's interesting to see where she lived. I can see her here."

"Why didn't you talk about it with anyone?"

"If I tell you that," he answered, wandering into the dining room, "then I'd be *talking* about it, wouldn't I?"

She followed him as now he was headed for the bedroom.

"Hey, stay out of my bedroom."

"It was Alex's bedroom," he said. "I want to see the bathtub."

He walked into the bedroom and flipped on the light switch. He looked across the room to the solarium through the French doors and saw the tub.

"Ah," he said, without moving any farther. "I see it now. That bathtub. She liked it very much, she told me. She wanted to have that bath and the piano together."

He switched off the bedroom light and went back to the piano. Did he mean that Alex had ordered the piano just so Parvus could play it when she took a bath?

Not sure what to do, Maddy refilled her wine glass and returned to the couch. He started to play again, now scales, as if warming his hands back up. Even his scales sounded like real music.

"Why," Maddy asked, somewhat loudly to overcome the sound of the playing, "why was it a problem to talk about your relationship?"

"Can't you ever just shut up?" he asked, launching into what Maddy recognized as part of Beethoven's Emperor Concerto. She could almost hear in her head the orchestral accompaniment. His playing filled the room with such intensity. The fire picked up as if he were feeding it oxygen. She started to wonder how she was going to be able to go to sleep in this house knowing that he—or anyone—could get in by picking the lock. Tomorrow she'd call the locksmith back and get him to add a bolt she could use from the inside—maybe like the back door, bolted into the floor—to keep him out at least when she was here.

"You played for her at your *own* house?" Maddy asked, as he reached a point in the music that called for pianissimo. "On your own piano?"

He nodded.

"So why did she bother to get a piano for you to play here? Just because of the bathtub?"

Maddy expected him to give some explanation involving the need for discretion—some reason they had to move their coupling from his house to Alex's house. He didn't answer. She got up and stood at the side of the piano and asked him again:

"Why did she get a piano for you to play here? Just the bath? Why didn't you simply continue at your home? Did something happen?"

He stopped playing and took another drink.

"She became suspicious someone was watching us there."

"And you couldn't afford to be seen together?"

"Jesus, you're so stupid," he replied. "They're going to find that doctor in Philadelphia not guilty, aren't they. Because you can't think straight."

She wasn't sure how to respond. He had punched her ego hard enough that she was inclined to throw her drink in his face and tell him she was calling the police to report his breaking and entering.

"No," he said, now playing a Joplin rag she assumed was meant as a mockery of her intelligence. "I meant she was convinced someone was watching us, *through the window*. The idea had started bothering her. She wanted me to get heavy shades. I don't like that. I like to know when it's light and it's dark. It orients me. Plus, she was sure they would still somehow be there—she thought it must be someone in my neighborhood or something, someone who was fascinated by us. So she decided to get a piano for here. So I could play for her here. She said she had some friend in New York who would pay for it. It is a good one."

He picked up the tempo of the rag.

"I see," Maddy said. This was not at all among the possibilities she had considered.

He suddenly stopped and looked at his watch.

"Shit. I have a late-night lab meeting. I said I'd be there. I guess I ought to be there."

He closed the cover of the keys and stood up. He bowed rather formally and headed for the door.

The gracious bow took her by surprise.

"Don't come play without asking me!" Maddy yelled after him.

"It's my piano!" he yelled back, banging the door shut.

She stood in the living room for a moment, unsure what to do. Hearing the fire crackle and spit, she went to it and knocked it down some with the poker. She didn't want to have to stay up late waiting for it to go out. She wanted to get in the bath and talk to Alex. But first she went into the kitchen to make herself some food. The loss of her appetite from the dinner conversation had left her so hungry now. She heated some oil in the heavy cast-iron pan, chopped an onion, and threw it in. She started some water to boil for pasta. She pulled tomatoes out of the refrigerator, chopped those, and added them to the frying pan.

In her mind, she was again replaying the dinner conversation with the Wollinskys. How do you recognize evil? More specifically, why did it feel like Parvus was not evil even though he had broken into her house, called her stupid, acted like such an asshole?

Suddenly, remembering herself speaking with the Wollinskys so intensely over dinner, a thought stabbed through her. She hastened over to her bag, pulled out her phone and called Wolf.

"Hello?"

"What is the definition of witness tampering?" she asked, switching the phone from one ear to the other and heading back to the stove.

"Rabbit? What's going on?"

"What's the definition of witness tampering, Wolf?"

"Did you talk to a witness, Rabbit?"

"Yes," she said, swallowing hard. "Two. Maybe."

Surely this didn't count. If he'd just give her the definition, she could compare it to her conversation with the Wollinskys and figure it out.

"Who did you talk to?"

"A couple with dwarfism who came to see me—Wilhelm's lawyer wants them as character witnesses. And they came to ask me—well, everything, and I talked with them for a couple of hours. . . ."

For a minute, neither of them spoke.

"Stir the pan," Wolf finally said.

"What?"

"Stir the pan," he said. "I can hear you are cooking something and I'm afraid you are distracted and you're going to burn something. Stir the pan."

"Okay," she said, stirring the onions and tomatoes. "But talk to me."

"It's not a great idea, Rabbit, to be talking to people right now about Wilhelm and the trial. It's not a great idea to be talking about it to people you don't know. Even most people you *do* know. You know that. But no one is going to charge you with witness tampering for talking to two people who came specifically to see you and to ask you questions."

"Oh, thank God," she said, taking another drink of wine, and stirring the pan again. White wine made no sense with this dish. But it was what she had open, and she just needed to feel a little less of everything right now.

She started telling him rapidly about her conversation with the Wollinskys, gushing it out to him in a long stream, telling him what a relief it was to talk with people like them who understood Wilhelm. Wolf said nothing for a long time, just listening. Her manic monologue drifted around from the conversation in the break room, to showing the Wollinskys the books in the stacks, to the dinner conversation, to the measures she had taken to avoid receiving calls or emails from people she did not know, to the rules she had imposed on her students and colleagues about not talking to her about Wilhelm or the trial, to the way the Wollinskys seemed to have explained why she wasn't getting very many talk invitations, to the book she had been reading, Pott's *Chirurgical Observations*, to try to forget about it all. She talked as she dumped the pasta into the boiling water and added some chopped sausage and dried basil to the pan, drank more wine, filled a glass with water and drank that down, strained the pasta, and put it all in a bowl.

Finally, she paused talking to take a bite, standing at the counter.

"Rabbit," he said. "I don't think I understood how much this is stressing you out. Maybe I didn't want to understand."

She coughed a little, catching a bit of onion on her hard palette. She pulled it down with her tongue and kept eating.

"I'll see if I can get you that autopsy report."

"Okay," she said. She ate another forkful. "Could you get me one other thing, Wolf? Can you send me that shirt you sleep in? But don't wash it before you send it? I think it will help me sleep."

"Oh, come on, Rabbit. You know that's my favorite shirt."

"But I think it'll help me sleep, Wolf," she replied, with no sense of humor in her voice. "I am a little afraid I'm not going to be able to sleep soon, not until it is over."

"Okay. I'll send it to you first thing in the morning. You want Hunter now, too?"

"No," she answered. "Too much work, a dog. I can't just up and go to dinner with visitors with a dog."

"You can if he's a service dog," he reminded her.

"You're telling me I'm crazy, and a dog will keep me sane."

"You know you would sleep better with him next to you. And I would sleep better knowing he was with you."

"I would certainly sleep better with *you* next to me," she said, taking another mouthful of food. "So, you know what? Send your shirt, but with you in it."

He said nothing for a moment.

"I do love you, Rabbit."

"I know that," she said, feeling the buzz from the wine. "And me, well, I am in love with you. Isn't it strange that the addition of a preposition—I am in love *with* you—the shift from the direct object, 'I love you,' to an indirect object, 'I am in love with you," represents a more intense emotion? English is stupid. The direct object should be more intense. But I am in love *with* you."

"I know that. And I am so sorry you're having to go through all of this alone."

"I'm not really alone," she answered, getting up to check that the front door was locked. "I have friends here now. Just like Liz said I would."

Cradling the phone between her shoulder and ear, she pushed the bench from the foyer up against the front door. That way she would at least hear if someone were coming in, because the bench would scrape on the floor or fall over. Then she went to the dining room and got a vase to balance on the edge of the bench at the door, positioning it so that the vase would go crashing to the floor if anyone pushed the door open.

"I have friends here," she said again. "Good friends."

"Maybe they could distract you a little?"

"Everett—that's Sophie—Everett offered a while back to take me shopping, with Lew, my chair. That might work."

"That sounds perfect," Wolf said. "You can pick out something nice to wear for when we have the pork roast, have it to look forward to as something special. And you can invite them to join us for that dinner. But don't invite them yet, okay?"

"Okay," she said, walking to the solarium. She plugged the tub and turned on the hot water.

"Starting a bath?" he asked.

"Helps clear my head."

"I wish I had had a better bathtub to have offered you here."

"You gave me plenty," she said.

For a few minutes, neither one said anything. She could hear him putting a leash on Hunter and leaving the house to take him for a walk. He could hear her taking off her clothes for the bath.

When he heard the water turn off, he wished her good night. She wished him the same and hung up. She plugged in the bottle lights, turned off the overhead light, and stepped into the tub, lying back in the water. One more time, she ran through the conversation with the Wollinskys, telling Alex in her head she'd be talking to her soon about Parvus, but that first she needed to go over the mental transcript of the conversation with Michael and Ela one more time.

And it was just as she reached again the part about Jimmy Heathcote and his rough timelines on the napkins that she realized something: just as Maddy had made notes on her research folders, perhaps Alex had as well? Maddy had only been looking at the *contents* of Alex's folders. She had not looked carefully at the folder themselves.

She stepped hastily out of the bath and wrapped a towel around herself.

She went into Alex's study, turned on the light, sat at the desk, and opened the drawer containing the files related to Alex's last book project. Maddy pulled out the first folder in the set, one marked simply "Ideas." While the rest of the folders each focused on one particular sexual orientation, this was a fat folder of jumbled notes and seemingly random articles, a kind of miscellany. It was a folder she hadn't paid much attention to. Yet for some reason, Alex had filed it as the first folder, not the last, the way one ordinarily did with a "miscellaneous" file for research.

She laid the folder on the desk and looked over the front. Nothing but stray pen marks.

She looked at the inside of the front cover. Nothing but a smudge of copier toner from an article that had been pressed against it.

She looked at the inside of the back. Nothing at all.

And then she flipped it over and looked at the very back of the folder.

And there it was. A chapter outline of sorts. A list of people to be used as case studies in the book with a notation next to each regarding their orientation, an abbreviation that matched the folders Alex had made, about particular orientations.

"Everett Sophie – adsef." *Amoir de soi en femme.*

"Scott – c.f." Cuckold fetishist.

For Dr. Griffin, Alex had written "v?"—meaning, presumably, "vanilla." The question mark indicated she must have wondered if it was true, his claim that he was just typically heterosexual? There was no folder marked "v." But then why would one bother to keep a folder on "vanilla" heterosexuality.

In the list were names Maddy did not recognize and would have to look up, matched to abbreviations on folders for pedophilia, hebephilia, an attraction to sexual drama, foot fetishism, and more.

No listing for Whitaker.

No listing for Hank.

No listing for Parvus.

And for the Gnat, "D/S." Matched to a folder on "dominance/sadism."

Maddy started to shiver. She put the folder away and headed back to the bath. Then she stopped, paused, and went back to the front door to check the lock; the bench; the vase.

254

Chapter 22

It was a good thing, Maddy thought to herself, that the rest of the faculty in this weekly afternoon meeting of the Medical Humanities program were stuck discussing an administrative issue that had nothing to do with her position. Her limp brain made it impossible to concentrate. And it was a good thing Hank had been willing to come the distance that morning to give her a ride to school. She was too bloody tired to drive. Just before he dropped her off, he offered to give her dinner downtown and drive her home tonight, seeing she had fallen asleep on the way to school. Surely she would sleep hard tonight?

Last night, whatever energy her brain hadn't spent figuring out what to do if she heard the vase crashing to the floor had been spent trying to decide whether it was time to stop living far out in the woods. But she was saving so much money. And with a steady stream of reporters now calling, she was feeling again that intense need to save money. In case she had to run for a while, hide for a while. Because all this noise might drive The Jerk back out. He was just stupid enough to imagine she would want to see him.

What *had* happened with The Jerk after those two police officers came to Wolf's house and took his letter to Maddy about a year ago?

"Maddy, do you have anything you want to add on this agenda item?" Lew Meadows asked.

"No, thank you, Lew," she said, rising to refill her coffee cup from the pot at the side of the room. She tried to stifle a yawn.

A few hours before dawn she had gotten up to look at Alex's list again. Then she had gone back through the other folders, trying to understand which of the people on the list she was going to have to look at, and talk to—and which of the people on the list she was going to have to approach differently. The Gnat, especially. Had Alex really been sure he was a sexual sadist?

And if something about sex with Parvus was different enough that it made Alex not want to talk about it, why wasn't Parvus on Alex's list? Not even with a question mark, the way Dr. Griffin was there with a "v?", questioning his plain vanilla?

Maddy would try to learn more about Parvus from Dr. Griffin when she met him for coffee this afternoon. She understood why there was only his name—Dr. Griffin's—on the list without a matched orientation folder; no one would need to collect source material on plain-vanilla heterosexuality. Most of history was about it, even if Hank had suggested recorded history was a lie that way.

It was a funny thing about written records, Maddy thought to herself as the faculty kept discussing some curricular issue, a funny thing about records like The Jerk's letter, Alex's jotted list, the library's cataloguing log of Wilhelm's faked text. The historian builds a story out of these things, these written records. At some level, she must effectively assume that these documents on which her story is based were the way to know the truth about the past.

And they *were*, of course, often enough. The Jerk's letter was a kind of darkly magical document—a written admission of what he had done to her plus an admission of what he was doing to a new girl. It contained a truth about him that Maddy was never going to be able to otherwise prove so easily. The letter was irrefutable. In his own hand with his fingerprints on it. It was why Wolf told her it was *good* that The Jerk had sent it to her.

Wilhelm's faked text—another magical document.

She had the sense Alex's folders were the same.

256

But what of all the things that happened that never made it into writing? Had they not mattered? They could not be managed by the historian. So had they, in effect, never happened? All of the strange sex Hank implied had occurred throughout human life. The way Hunter had looked into Maddy's eyes, to look for her expectations about who was at the door. The way Wolf had held her hand when they left 30th Street Station, when he came to take her back home. All these things that were not recorded.

All the things Alex had not recorded except in her brain: whatever made her meet Parvus but not speak of their meetings; whatever Alex must have felt about his extraordinary piano playing; whatever joy she must have had doing ordinary things with Everett Sophie or Hank; whatever made her go into the water with her jewelry still on. All of these things had apparently been recorded only in Alex's brain, a text ruined as soon as death came flooding her body like a flooded library.

So too, all the things Maddy never recorded outside her own body—the experiences recorded nowhere but the imperfect cellular network of her synapses—these would simply die with her and effectively never have been. And her brain was the only place that held the last significant recordings of her own parents and of her sister. She had never written any of that down. Mr. Whittaker's staff at his law office in New York would never find any record of her father, her mother, her sister, except in the most cursory fashion—birth certificates, death certificates, autopsy reports, yearbooks, census records. Such thin records. Just wisps. And so, when Maddy died, when the neural tissue where her family still resided went dark and then decayed, her parents and her sister would truly be gone then, gone to any chance at history.

Perhaps human life was simply destruction of the memory of the dead through more death, the dead wiping out the dead, cleaning up after themselves before going and locking the door.

"Maddy, I feel like you are...distracted," Lew said, in a voice that sounded less annoyed than concerned. "Is it because the prosecution rested yesterday?"

She looked up. All the faculty were staring at her through the bubbles of saline filling up her chop-meat eyes.

"What? What did you just say?"

"Oh, I'm sorry," Lew said, more quietly than was normal for him. "I thought you knew."

Her heart suddenly went into overdrive.

"Did they call him as a witness?"

"You mean Dr. Wilhelm?" Lew asked. "He pled the Fifth."

To avoid the wall of stares from the other faculty, Maddy shifted her sights frantically to the clock on the wall, as if it could tell her how much time was left. How much time did she have before the judgment? If the prosecution had rested, that left just the defense. And how much counterevidence could the defense muster? Soon, it would go to the jury.

"How long?" Maddy asked plaintively, breathing fast, looking at Lew.

"How long what?"

"I have to go," Maddy replied, hastily packing up her things and looking at her watch, again as if the time of day meant something. She thought about calling Jill, asking her how long, asking her what they had presented and not. But if the prosecution had failed to present some key piece of the Wilhelm history, they couldn't very well just pull it out in closing arguments. It was too late to fix whatever they had done wrong. She should have been paying attention.

Chapter 23

An hour later, Maddy was standing in the order line at the Dinkytown Espresso Royale looking at her Alex Shugar timeline when she suddenly realized Dr. Griffin was also already here, two customers ahead of her in the line. She thought she should reach past the people between them and tap on his shoulder. But she wasn't quite done reading the notes from last time she'd talked to him, scribbled on the pages following the timeline itself. She needed to keep her story straight.

When she had called Dr. Griffin around noon, she had told him that she wanted to talk with him today because the trial was making it hard for her to sleep and she was worried about developing depression. Not incorrect, but not her motivation for calling to meet again. The truth was that she had decided even before the faculty meeting that she would go all-out on Alex's death just until the jury came back on Wilhelm. Try, while the trial finished, to figure out everyone around Alex, everything about Alex. And then

Maddy would stop, wherever she was in the Alex research, and just let it go. Because she couldn't do this forever. Alex needed to really end.

After so many phone conversations with Wolf, Maddy had come to realize that Alex had just been a distraction from Wilhelm, who in turn had just been a distraction from The Jerk. She needed to stop distracting herself with the hope that someday earthly justice would start working and focus on academic life proper. Which meant she needed to put a deadline on Alex.

Deadline. She'd better not use that term about Alex around Hank.

She started listening in on the conversation Dr. Griffin was having with the fellow waiting in line in front of him. While the cashier was stuck trying to fix the register tape, Griffin and the other guy were talking bicycles. This explained Griffin's anatomy; he was too thin and sinewy, like someone who biked too much. The other man had noticed Griffin's expensive bike outside and admired it. Griffin was describing other bicycles he had—one for triathlons, another that folded compactly for commuting—and they were talking prices, bike shops, the best shoes for this or that.

Maddy wasn't going to be able to concentrate on her notes as long as this was going on.

Unnoticed, she stepped out of line and slid off to the restroom. She leaned up against the sink to read more from her yellow pad.

Her notes indicated that last time they had talked, she had downplayed to Dr. Griffin her part in the trial. That much she remembered, because she had done the same with the Gnat after Wolf told her to be careful not to let people know how snoopy she was. (Well, this was awkward; first she'd told Griffin that she wasn't much involved in the Wilhelm case, then she'd called him today saying she was anxious about the trial.)

Her notes also reminded her that she'd told him she was working on a paper about the arc of Alex's life's work, and that someone had told Maddy that Alex had been talking to Dr. Griffin about her forthcoming book. He said that was right; she'd been showing him drafts.

Maddy had asked Griffin if Alex struck him as depressed before her death, and he said yes, she was anxious and depressed, and sexually frustrated. He thought the frustration was about Hank. Griffin had said (after a Cheshire cat grin) that Griffin and Alex were not lovers, but that they'd shared an intense interest in human sexuality. But then Griffin had told Maddy he was "quite dully heterosexual" himself. Not destined for the book himself, he said. (He must not have known that Alex had put him on the list with that "v?". Perhaps she didn't want him to know that she intended to use him as an example of what people expect—the plain vanilla man. His type was common enough that he might not even recognize himself in the book.)

Per Maddy's notes, Griffin did not seem to know about Whitaker and New York. But he definitely knew about Parvus and the basics about Hank. So he knew about Alex's local life? But he did not seem to know about Everett Sophie. So he knew about the local, but only some of it?

Griffin had also told Maddy that he'd been one of the people to report her missing. So, he must have expected to hear from her regularly. That made him an important source.

Maddy put the notebook back in her pack to wash her hands and then her face in the bathroom sink. She'd thought, before she'd met Dr. Griffin, that she had made some sense of Alex, understood who she was. But between Dr. Griffin and Professor Parvus, Alex now felt to Maddy like a narrative mess—a person without any consistency or predictability.

Turning the crank on the paper towel dispenser, Maddy dried her face and her hands. She pulled out a compact of powder and dusted her face to hide the blotches that were forming. She emerged to find Griffin had finally gotten his coffee and made it to a table. The line had shortened, so she gave him a wave and got herself a cup of mint tea. She didn't want anything with caffeine; she felt jittery enough.

"So, the prosecution finally rested!" Griffin said to her as she was sitting down across from him. "And today, the defense began its rebuttal!"

He said it like he was a sportscaster. Like it was a game. Maddy shrugged.

"But you said the trial was making you anxious?"

"I guess I go back and forth on caring," Maddy said. "I think I will look silly and stupid if they find him not guilty, and I'm at a challenging point in my career. So I'm anxious about that." She could hear Wolf in her head, coaching her to move to the topic of Alex soon, away from herself. "And since you said *Alex* was anxious and you helped *her* with that . . ."

"I'm not sure I did help her. I'm not sure our conversations did her any good."

"Oh, I expect she appreciated them," Maddy replied. "By the way, I did get the sheet music to Professor Parvus. Thanks for helping me figure that out."

"Oh! Did you just mail it through campus mail, or did you give it to him personally?"

"I was going over near his office anyway, so I dropped it by."

"And what was his reaction?"

"He grouched at me," she answered, sipping her tea. "He seems to be an unhappy soul."

"Yes. Very intense and no doubt very upset at the loss of Alex."

"Were they in love?" Maddy asked.

"I don't know," Dr. Griffin replied. "Alex didn't seem to have typical relations."

"Does *anyone* have normal relations?" She gave him a smile with one raised eyebrow as a prod. It seemed to throw him off.

"As a psychiatrist, I suppose . . . I suppose I would ask you what you mean by normal."

"You know, vanilla. Plain-vanilla."

"I'm not familiar with the term." He seemed to mean it. "Plain vanilla?"

"The kind of sex the world tells us is normal," Maddy said, looking around the room as if looking for a normal person. "Nothing kinky. Always with your romantic partner. Everybody has orgasms in all the right places."

"Oh," he said. "Yes, I suppose there are lots of those people." Then, after a moment's hesitation, he added, "Yes, for example, I would be called 'plain vanilla.'"

"You have a partner?" she asked, looking him in the eye.

"No, but I mean I would if I found the right person. But why are we talking about me? Are you attracted to me?"

"No! Oh, God, no!" Maddy blurted out, laughing at the thought of being attracted to him. "No, I'm just a nosy little fuck."

"Interesting phrasing."

This was not going well.

"It's very kind of you to talk with me," she said, drinking her tea faster to finish it off. "I guess I ought to make an appointment with you, properly. But I would first have to see if my insurance would cover it and if you'd take my insurance."

She wondered if it was obvious from her face that she had no intention of seeing him as a doctor.

"If you're with the standard university health policy, it would be fine," he answered blandly.

She pulled out her phone to text Hank, to tell him to pick her up ASAP, but in front of Chez Jacques three blocks away.

"Sorry," she said. "There's a grad student I just need to check in on—she's on deadline with a proposal, and I said I'd be available."

"That's fine. You do seem distracted. I think it might not be a bad idea for you to work with someone on understanding your anxiety. Are you currently in a sexual relationship?"

"No time for romance with the schedule I've got!"

"I didn't ask about romance, Professor Shanks."

"Well," she said, looking up from her silent phone to Dr. Griffin, "I guess that's something we could talk about—romance versus sex?"

"Certainly."

Her phone beeped with a reply. Hank could pick her up soon.

"Oh, crap," she said, "the student does need my help. I am so sorry to pull you to meet me here and then just leave."

"It's fine," he said, "no trouble. I'll look forward to seeing you."

He smiled perfunctorily. She dashed out the door, ducked around a building, and hurried down a back alley.

. . .

Maddy got into Hank's car exclaiming, "Thank you! Thank you!"

He observed aloud that she at least seemed to be much more alert than she had been that morning. He pulled the car out into traffic and started toward Interstate 35W to head for the restaurant downtown.

"I just had to get out of there," she said. "I was talking to this psychiatrist Alex had been seeing—"

"Alex was seeing a psychiatrist?" He looked at Maddy with a confused expression and then turned his attention back to the road.

"Well, *talking* to one. Anyway, *I* didn't want to keep talking to him. I mean, I'd like to understand what he knows about Alex, but—"

"What did he say?"

"He told me she was anxious and depressed before she died. And that she was sexually frustrated. About you."

"Are you kidding me?" Hank slowed the car for traffic as they crossed the Saint Anthony Falls Bridge and looked at her face again. He could see she was serious.

"Maddy, I saw Alex at most a couple of days before she died. We had dinner and spent the night together." He accelerated again, now weaving in and out of the rush-hour traffic that merged two highways in a tangle. "Ally wasn't anxious. She wasn't depressed. And she certainly wasn't sexually frustrated about me. She had no sexual interest in me. That was conveniently mutual."

"Well, maybe it wasn't at that very moment? Maybe days or weeks before, and maybe again sometime near her death."

"That makes no sense. What else did this psychiatrist say?"

Maddy hesitated as Hank kept changing lanes.

"What did he say?" he asked, glancing over at her with a tense look. "You don't want to tell me because you think I shouldn't know? Or you're worried I'll be pissed?"

"I have no idea what you'd think," Maddy said. As he picked up speed in an opening in traffic, she put her hand on the dashboard as if to brace herself. "Aren't you going too fast?"

"Jesus fucking Christ, Shanks!"

She physically startled at his outburst.

"Why don't you fucking drive yourself?"

She said nothing as he headed now for the highway exit. Why was she so damned good at making people angry at her?

"I'm sorry," Hank said, in a voice that suggested he wasn't sorry, "but you pop into my car and announce that my Ally was seeing a psychiatrist, that she was anxious, that she was depressed, that she was sexually frustrated with me, and you expect me to feel like you haven't just kneed me in the groin?"

"I get it," she said, massaging one of her hands with the other. "I'm bad at this."

He steered the car off the exit into the downtown streets. She was trying to figure out how she was going to get him to go over Alex's chapter list with her now that she had completely pissed him off.

"Look on the bright side," she said. "You could have my acrobatic tongue later?"

He didn't answer, but simply sighed. She thought he looked tired of her.

"Well," she said, switching to kneading her other hand, "I'm doing a great job of making you not want me, which was the opposite of how we were going to get to fucking, wasn't it? *I* was going to not want *you*." She pursed her lips. "Sometimes I think I do everything wrong."

She was about to tell him the light they were sitting at had turned green, but she thought she'd better not. A car behind them honked, and he started driving again.

"Let me ask you a favor," she said, "and of course you can say no. How about we don't talk any further until we each have at least a drink and a half in us? Would that be okay? I think I'm less likely to be annoying then, and you're less likely to be annoyed."

264

He nodded.

He parked the car in a lot at the corner of 10th Street and Marquette Avenue at the base of a building with a five-story mural depicting a giant piece of sheet music—black musical notations on a white background. It appeared to Maddy to be some intensely busy piece, seemingly written for piano. She wanted to ask Hank what song it depicted, why it was there, but she had just asked him for silence.

A little bit of ice had formed on the sidewalks, so he offered his arm. His thick wool coat felt good to grab, and his arm felt so steady, even if he was pissed off at her. They walked into the restaurant—a mid-level Chinese place with white tablecloths and a big aquarium—and the hostess seated them in a rounded booth. He ordered a beer, she ordered an umbrella cocktail, and they sat quietly without looking at each other. He checked his phone and then put it away. She pulled hers out, turned it off completely, and tucked it back in her bag. Wolf had called a couple of times earlier when she was busy, but he hadn't left a message. Presumably he was just calling to tell her the prosecution had rested. She could call him tomorrow—not piss him off, too, tonight. Everything could wait while she tried to sleep tonight.

The drinks came and Hank asked for just one plate of fried dumplings and another round of drinks. Maddy sighed. Based on the order of just one plate, Hank appeared to have little faith they'd be able to get back to a good place. She took a long sip of the cocktail, finding it too sweet and quite boozy. He drank down most of his beer in one shot.

He heard her sniffle, looked over, and said kindly, "Oh, Maddy, no, don't cry." She shushed him and pointed to their drinks, as if to say, "no talking until it's gone."

He took his napkin off the table and dabbed the tear in her left eye. Then he brought his face very close to hers. He held her chin and inspected her left eye carefully, as if he were a doctor-clown. He wiped a tear away from that eye. Then he turned her face and inspected the other eye. Seeing a tear there, too, he took his napkin and dried that one. He checked back to the left eye, saw another tear, and elaborately dried that one.

His silly miming and rapid turning of her face made her start crying more even while she let out a wet laugh. Now he mimed silent panic at all the additional tears. He put the whole napkin over her face and dried her face, rubbing it like she was a wet dog come out of a bath. She started laughing and crying harder. Then he held up the damp, messy napkin with both his hands, as if it were a curtain, and spoke to her behind it.

"I think that if we don't talk to each other and I just keep drying your waterworks, the people near us are going to conclude we are crazy. They're watching us. I think you should go to the bathroom and do whatever it is you ladies do to 'freshen up,' and then we should go back to drinking and not talking."

She nodded in agreement. She came back a few minutes later from the bathroom. The dumplings were there along with the second round of drinks. Hank served her half the dumplings and motioned that she should dunk them, giving the sauce a thumbs-up. She tried one and nodded that he was right. To make the appetizer last a little longer, she took the tiny umbrella out of her drink and looked up to the ceiling, holding out one hand, palm-up. She winced, like she could feel rain coming down on her hand. She raised the drink umbrella over her head and mimed to him a satisfied smile.

He laughed, had another dumpling, finished off his first drink and started his second. She did the same. Her second cocktail had come not with an umbrella but with a tiny plastic sword on which the bartender had lanced chunks of fruit. She started to eat the pineapple off the sword, thinking she should finish the fruit and pretend to kill herself Samurai-style, when he looked at her and gave her a real smile.

"Okay!" she said, gulping back half of her second drink.

"Okay! You say you do everything wrong, Maddy, but that was a very good plan you came up with."

"Now can I ask you about Alex's list?"

"Right after we order. Okay with you if I just get us what they do best?"

"Of course," she said, relieved. He called the waiter over and ordered a spicy beef stir fry, a vegetable plate with ginger, and some fancy dish involving a whole fish on a bed of rice noodles.

Maddy pulled out her yellow pad and flipped to where she had transcribed Alex's list that morning. Hank looked it over once and said that it made sense—that much of it was what Alex had told him she was planning to include in the book. He said he didn't know all the names, but it was the sort of list he would have expected of her.

For example, Hank said, he was not surprised to see who Alex was thinking of using as the case study on pedophilia. Hank had introduced the man to Alex for that very purpose. The man was, Hank said, a decent guy, a man who felt sexually attracted to children but who had made sure not to act on it, ever, not with porn, not with live action. On Hank's advice, the man had in fact had his physician administer him chemical castration—a hormone treatment that would radically lower his testosterone level, taking away most of his sexual urge. It wouldn't change the man's pedophilic orientation, Hank explained to Maddy, but it would leave him less horny. The side effects of the chemical castration gave the man breast growth and made him feel much less energetic. That, Hank said, was proof of how seriously this guy took his moral responsibility. Plus, he had arranged his life to avoid being with children. A good case for Alex to use for the book as she wrote about sexual orientation versus sexual acts, consent versus abuse.

The waiter came and delivered the food, arranging it all elegantly on the table. Hank dished Maddy out a sampling of everything, and then made himself a plate. But she didn't yet dig in. What about the hebephile, Maddy asked, knowing from Hank that was what The Jerk had been—a man interested in children in the early stages of puberty. She pointed out to him the name on the pad with an "h." written next to it.

"I also introduced Alex to *that* person," Hank said, starting to pick up a bit of the fish with his chopsticks. "*That* guy is in prison."

"Oh, that's nice to hear."

She picked up a big chunk of beef with her chopsticks and ate it as he nodded.

"That guy's exactly the opposite of the pedophile to whom I introduced Alex," Hank continued, pointing at the fish to suggest she try it next. "The hebephile she was going to write about, he's a guy who thinks he's perfectly normal—claims that girls all over the world are married off at eleven or twelve, so it's natural for him to want them as sex partners. Claims he only has sex with girls emotionally mature enough to consent. Claims they're truly in love with him, and he with them."

"How do you know all these guys with such problematic orientations?"

"I'm a sex researcher," he reminded her. "They come to me. Well, in the case of the hebephile, he wrote to me from prison, and I went and talked to him. Wanted to prove to me that he was perfectly normal. To help him get out of prison. Not a chance. In the case of the pedophile, he came to meet me at my office. He wanted to understand more about whether there was anything he could do to change his orientation. I explained that we have absolutely no evidence an orientation can be changed—at least in men. You women—well, feminine women like you—you are complicated creatures. But in men, we can squash the sexual urge with surgical or chemical castration, but we can't change what turns men on."

"He must have been so depressed to hear that," Maddy said, digging into the food more.

"He kind of knew it when he came to me," Hank responded. "I just confirmed what he already knew. It's funny, though—people think of pedophiles as Satan on earth. Yet this guy is one of the most moral people I've ever met. Imagine his situation, what he's endured to make sure he does the right thing."

"And the hebephile?"

"Easily one of the *least* moral people I've ever met. Absolutely convinced that what his dick wants is what is right."

"Sex does claim to have its own superior logic sometimes, doesn't it," Maddy observed. "This fish is amazing."

"Isn't it?"

They ate for a while in silence, making only small noises of pleasure. Hank picked up her notepad again and looked at the list.

"Alex didn't think I was worth a chapter? I don't see myself or anything seeming to indicate 'chase fetishism' on here."

"I guess not. I guess you convinced her your habits are perfectly normal."

"My habits, maybe not. The way I *feel* as a man, probably so. Baby, I'm just more in tune with my body than most people. More centered."

He held his hands in front of his chest, palm to palm, as if he were a pious monk. She laughed at him.

"Yeah, so, Alex picked someone else for 'vanilla.' Sorry, darling," she said to him, pointing to the line for Jeffrey Griffin, with the "v?" next to it.

"Who is that?" he asked.

"The psychiatrist," she said with a bit of trepidation given their earlier argument.

"Why the question mark for that one? Was the question mark put there by Alex?"

"Yes, that's how she noted it, and my guess is you taught—life taught—Alex not to believe any man who said he's vanilla?"

"True enough. But why would she bother writing about vanilla?" he asked.

"I wondered that, too. I guess you've got to present the control group?"

"I guess," he answered, "though it's not like she wrote like a scientist. She wrote so much better than a typical scientist."

"Well, maybe she *wasn't* going to write about him. There's no folder on 'vanilla' in her files."

"How would you even *do* a folder on vanilla?" Hank asked with his head turned a little sideways. "It's both everything and nothing in the history and philosophy of heterosexuality."

He looked further down the list.

"Whoa—did Alex really think the Gnat is a sadist—is that what the D/S is for?"

"Yes, she had him down as a sadist. I have no idea if she thought that or how she could have known. I tried looking at the file, but frankly I had to stop pretty quickly. The material in it wasn't going to help me sleep. Explain the concept to me? Gently."

"Sexual sadism?"

Maddy nodded.

Hank said it was at basis pretty simple: being turned on by hurting someone. Dominance was about having power sexually. Most people into sadism, at most they role-play it with someone who enjoys masochism, he explained. But the worst cases—

"Those are criminal," he said. "The worst cases don't want a partner who consents. That takes away the sadistic thrill."

"Rapists?"

"Of the very, very worst kind."

Maddy said nothing for a bit. She slowly chewed on a carrot infused with the flavor of ginger and finished off her drink.

"You want another?" Hank asked.

"Oh, heavens, no. I'll be asleep by the time you get me home. I think you want me awake."

"You really don't have to . . . I mean, later," he said, taking her hand. "I don't want to feel like I'm coercing you. I mean, in theory, sexual coercion could be crazy hot. But, in reality, I'm not into that."

"Do I seem coerced to you?"

"Women are hard to read," he answered with a furrowed brow. "Women who are smart and blotto are even harder to read. I generally take the cautious path."

He looked at her face now, laughed a little, and wiped a piece of food off her cheek with his napkin.

"I'd prefer we do what we did *last* time," he said, wrapping his hand around her and doing that beetle-on-stem, kitten-on-fist thing. "What we did after the lake?"

She let off an involuntary hum at the memory.

"But no, no," she answered him, pulling back her hand. "We have a deal about what happens after you so kindly answer my questions about Alex."

"Tell you what," he said, clearing a space on the table between them. "I'll arm-wrestle you for it. If you win, you do me. If I win, I do you."

"Deal," she said. She plunked her elbow on the table and met his hand. "But I have to warn you, I've been working out with a great assistant coach of the gymnastics team when our free time matches up. The uneven bars, and the rings—she's great, and I'm getting pretty strong."

She pushed against him.

"Wow, you *are* strong for a little thing," he whispered with admiration. Then he leaned in closer and whispered very quietly, "Oh, I'd like to fuck you, Maddy."

She pulled back her hand and called for a time-out.

"Hank, have you ever 'made love'?" she whispered, using her fingers to make scare-quotes in the air.

"Are you asking me if I'm a virgin?"

"No, you moron," she said, now speaking in a normal level of voice and picking her chopsticks back up to eat more. "I'm wondering if you've ever thought of fucking as making love."

"It's not a phrase I would use," he answered, grabbing a piece of beef from his plate and bringing it to her mouth. She accepted it. "Because, frankly, if I called it making love, a woman might take it to mean I love her when I don't. But do *some* people have sex with the person they love romantically? For years and years? And enjoy it? Sure. Some people do that."

Then he added, like he had just thought of it, "Jesus, that must make life a lot easier."

"I would imagine," she responded, licking her lips. "Super plain vanilla. Not like spicy beef."

"Super plain vanilla," he echoed. "You like the idea of super plain vanilla?"

"Plain vanilla is *the most popular* flavor of ice cream." She looked at his face, his handsome face, and added, "Vanilla can certainly be very tasty. Especially if done well, with good ingredients and not created with the fake stuff. But me, I like trying lots of flavors. Beef can be spicy-good. Life is short. My tongue is long."

"Wait, remind me why am I trying to win?"

He put his elbow back on the table and she put hers back on, too. He let her appear to be winning for a few seconds and then plunked her hand down to the table with his.

"Damn," she said. "Turns out you're stronger than me."

"Testosterone, my girl," he answered. "A fine endogenous substance, when it's not a criminal one."

He looked at her again. She could tell by the way he gazed at her that the years that had grown on her face since that morning must now be gone. He looked very pleased with himself. He wiped his mouth with his napkin and called for the check.

Chapter 24

The cocktails, the food, the good company—Hank tucked Maddy into the passenger seat with the car blanket, and she was soon fast asleep. She did not awaken until they reached Alex's driveway and Hank asked aloud what was going on. She sat up straight and saw that Parvus's car was back. Light emanated from the living room windows.

"Oh, no," she groaned. "Not now."

She pulled off the blanket, got out of the car, and went into the house. Hank followed her, gingerly closing the front door behind them. They could hear Parvus playing something—one of the Beethoven sonatas, Maddy thought. She walked into the living room and Hank followed.

"Do you two gentlemen know each other?" she asked, throwing her bag on the floor next to the fireplace. "Professor Parvus, Professor Merriman. Professor Merriman, Professor Parvus."

"Parvus?" Hank said, aghast. "What the hell are you doing here?"

"Merriman?" Parvus replied, ceasing his playing. "What the hell are *you* doing here?"

"Well, obviously you have *company*, Maddy," Hank said, starting for the door.

Maddy ran after Hank. She could hear Parvus starting to play again from where he had left off.

"Hank, I can explain. But you have to give me a minute."

"*He* has a key to your new lock?" Hank said, clearly asking a different question with that question. He was at the front door and opened it to go.

"He just lets himself in, Hank." Then she realized that didn't sound right.

Hank walked out briskly to his car and waved at her in a disgusted fashion. She watched him drive off. She slammed the front door and stomped back to the living room.

"You cannot just let yourself into my house like this!"

Parvus did not answer, so she walked right up to him at the bench. He just kept playing, answering in a calm voice, "I rang the doorbell. Twice. You didn't answer. Was I supposed to *wait*?"

"Yes! Yes! You were supposed to wait."

"Why don't you sit down and relax?" he asked. "You should thank me, anyway. Merriman is a cad, and you don't need to live like a slut."

She leaned in and slapped him hard across the face.

He stopped playing and got up. He looked somewhat crazy as he came toward her as she backed toward the couch. Of course, he always looked somewhat crazy, she reminded herself. So maybe it was fine?

She fell back to a seated position on the couch.

"Don't *hit* me just because I'm telling you what I think you need to know!" he yelled. "You want to understand Alex, and I'm trying to help you understand Alex, and you're fucking around with Merriman and *striking* me? What the fuck is wrong with you?"

She was trying to figure out what she was going to do. She was in no position to do an easy flip off the couch. He could grab her if she tried that. Run for it? He stood between her and the front door. The backdoor was locked with the bolt set into the floor—it would take too long to get out that way. Even if she could grab the house phone, Scott had finally turned off the landline at Maddy's request. Her cell phone was in her bag behind Parvus, still turned off. A sharp verbal response seemed the only defense.

"I'm sorry!" she yelled at him. "But you keep showing up without warning!"

"Alex got me this *piano*," he said, gesturing to it as if she was daft, "so I feel like I have to come and play it, don't you see? I mean, given that—given that I killed her!"

Maddy did not answer. Now she was thinking about the contents of the room, trying to figure out what she could grab to hit him again if she needed to. But she thought she'd better keep up the verbal punches in the meantime.

"You *what*? What do you mean you killed her?"

"Well, it seems obvious I killed her," he said, and he pulled at his hair for a moment with his hands. "I mean, it was an accident. But there you have it."

Maddy now realized where the expression "your heart in your throat" came from. Her body felt exactly that way, as if her heart had somehow ended up momentarily in her stomach and had then pushed up through her esophagus, to lodge in her throat.

"Did you tell the police?" Maddy asked sharply. "That you killed her?"

"Why would I tell the police? What would they care? She's dead."

"Did the police talk to you at all after she died?"

"No!" he answered, in something of a bark.

And then out of nowhere the doorbell rang.

She didn't move.

He didn't move.

The doorbell rang again.

"Aren't you going to get it?" Parvus asked. "You keep reminding me it's *your* damned door."

Maddy did not respond.

"Fine," he said, annoyed, "I'll get it."

He went to the door and opened it.

"Professor Parvus!" the visitor exclaimed.

"Do I know you?"

"No, sir, no. My name is Everett Inskeep. I am just a huge fan. I've heard you many times at the symphony. I always get tickets when you are going to play. I'm sorry, I must sound like a crazy groupie."

"It's okay," Parvus said, in his usual grouchy tone. "You must have come here for Shanks. She is in the living room."

Maddy heard the door close. She stood up off the couch and extended her hand.

"Everett!" she exclaimed. "Thank God you're here!"

"Maddy!" Everett answered dramatically, because he thought Maddy was

274

joking around.

He took Maddy's hand and realized she was shaking.

"Do sit, Madeleine. Everything okay?"

Maddy sat down next to Everett, close.

"Professor Parvus was just playing," Maddy said. As if that was enough to send him back, Parvus sat down at the piano. "He was playing the piano Alex got for him."

"Really!" Everett said. "Alex got it for Professor Parvus! Well, well. Alex knew how to book a pianist."

Parvus gave Everett a look of confusion and put his hands back on the keys. He started to play Debussy's *Clair de Lune*.

Everett could feel Maddy still shaking a little. He put his arm around her and pulled her closer. She laid her head on his shoulder and listened. The sound poured from the instrument like water down a brook. Maddy could feel Everett holding his breath in anticipation. She realized he was waiting to listen, as a fellow pianist, to what Parvus would do with the phrasing. Everett held so still, as if any movement might interrupt the beauty of the song Parvus's hands now sang. The way Everett was paying attention to the music made Maddy feel much calmer.

When Parvus finished the piece, he paused and looked to the couch. He gestured with his hand to Maddy, suggesting that she get under the piano. Everett simply looked confused at the gesture. But Maddy stood up, took a pillow from the couch, and climbed under.

"Hold on," she said, crawling out again just a moment later.

She got herself the blanket off the back of the couch and went back under, settling in with the pillow and blanket.

"Okay," she said.

Parvus began to play a classical piece she could not place. A nocturne. Something calm. Something *calm*? This from the man who had just confessed to killing Alex, albeit accidentally? He must be truly mad.

But Maddy knew that Everett wasn't going to leave her alone with Parvus. She could calm herself. The music made it easy, as she closed her eyes and felt anew that she had drunk too much. She could feel the high notes on her cheekbones and the low notes in her chest. Oh, if only Parvus hadn't been here when they'd arrived, she would be alone now in this wonderful atmosphere of music with Hank.

But wait, that made no sense. Without Parvus, there would be no music. And she wouldn't have been alone with Hank long, because Everett had just shown up. . . .

None of her thinking made sense. She was so dopey. Why was Everett here, anyway? She yawned and thought about getting back up and asking him, but she was just too tired. She felt as if the notes were pressing her into the floor, the way a grandparent lays a heavy hand on a baby in a cradle to coax it to sleep.

Now Hank was going to be mad at her, and for what? She tried to think about what she would say to him tomorrow. But all she could think about was how lovely it felt when he had had her elbow-to-elbow to arm wrestle at the restaurant, and how, when he was ready, he had laid down her hand, just like that. How charming.

The nocturne agreed: "how charming."

She started to drift into the dark of sleep. She could surely pull Hank back here soon. She could feel him already in the gentle notes, kissing her neck, his hand on her back.

Only it wasn't Hank. It was Wolf.

Wolf had taken her up to the roof of his Philadelphia house. And on this flat roof, he had a view, a spectacular view that went on for miles and miles. Pasture, rolling hills dotted with lollipop-shaped trees, the sky so blue. As if they were not on top of a house in Philadelphia but on top of a mountain in the warmth of the summer. As if it were West Virginia? But a little flatter. Wolf was standing behind her, his arms wrapped around her, kissing her cheek, and then her neck, and she realized he was happy. Not ashamed, not upset, not worried, not guilty.

And now he had his hands on her upper arms, turning her to kiss her on the lips, and she put her arms around his neck as she had in that Pittsburgh bar. She could feel his full embrace, his body fully against her own, the sun soaking them through, his desire soaking her through, as if somehow he were finally there, in her . . .

She awoke to Parvus letting out a little laugh.

"Good dream, huh?" he asked, looking at her under the piano.

Everett cleared his throat, embarrassed.

Where was she?

She could see the two of them leave the living room, toward the front door. The door opened and closed, with murmured words. Footsteps came back. It was Everett. She could hear Parvus's car start and drive off.

"Oh dear!" Everett said, in sudden alarm. "I forgot to call John Wolf back!"

Maddy tried to rouse herself, to get out from under the piano, but her body felt like lead. And she did not want to let go of this wispy feeling still in her, this feeling that she had finally really felt Wolf.

"John Wolf called me earlier, Maddy, because your phone was off and he was trying to call you and was getting worried," Everett explained, sitting on the couch and pulling out his phone. "John Wolf called, Maddy. Wake up. He found my number in the business directory and called. I told him I was sure you were alright but would come and see. He must be quite worried by now. How stupid of me, to come here and somehow forget to call him to tell him you were fine. But you were so rattled when I arrived, and then Professor Parvus's playing was so distracting."

Everett pushed redial on his phone and Wolf quickly answered.

"John, hello!" Everett said. "Yes, she's fine. She must have just turned her phone off or it ran out of battery or something. I'm here with her at, at her place, and she's fine. I'm sorry I didn't call you earlier, as soon as I got here. We got—well, occupied by a piece of music, of all things. And then she fell asleep, and I was listening to some more music and lost track of my assigned task. I'm sorry. I'm so sorry to have kept you waiting."

Maddy felt stirred awake by all of this.

"Ask him if the prosecution did a good job!" Maddy yelled at Everett. "Ask him that!"

"Madeleine wants me to ask you if the prosecution did a good job." A pause. "Yes, Madeleine, he says they did a very good job."

"Ask him how much longer before it goes to the jury!"

"Madeleine wants to know how much longer before the jury takes it." A pause. "He thinks just a few days. He says the defense is not calling as many witnesses as it had been expected to."

"Ask him if that is because of the Wollinskys!"

"Here, Madeleine," Everett said, holding out his phone, "why don't you talk to Detective Wolf yourself?"

Maddy shook her head as she crawled out from under the piano. She didn't want the Wolf in her dream to be dispelled by the Catholic police detective version on the phone. She stood up and stretched and yawned. Everett put the phone back to his ear. Maddy folded up the blanket and put it back on the couch.

"What's that, John? Oh, you're going to come when it is over and make us all dinner! Did you hear that, Madeleine? Well, that would be delightful. It will be lovely to see you again. And without a Mets' cap, I presume. Yes, great idea. I would love to take Maddy shopping for a new dress for the occasion! I know just the place. They have just the right kind of cut for her figure. Her *lucky* figure."

Wolf said something and Everett laughed a girlish laugh. Maddy gave Everett a confused look. She crawled back under the piano to retrieve the pillow and tossed it to Everett. Everett caught it in his free hand and arranged it on the couch.

"Maddy, John says the package for you, the one you asked for, will be here tomorrow morning."

"Oh, good," Maddy said.

She knew exactly what she was going to do with his sleeping T-shirt. She was going to put it on a firm bed pillow, dressing the pillow in it, and hold on to it while she fell asleep. She felt sure that if she could smell Wolf next to her, wrapped in her arms, she would be able to sleep with or without another new lock on the door.

But now she was thinking about the door, wondering if she'd be able to sleep tonight.

"Everett?"

But Everett was talking to Wolf about the weather.

"Everett!"

"What, Madeleine?" Everett asked, somewhat impatiently. "What is it?"

"Ask Wolf what happened to The Jerk."

"Ask what?"

"Ask Wolf what happened to The Jerk."

"Madeleine wants to know what happened to The Jerk, John." There was a short pause. "He pled guilty to avoid a trial. Three years."

Everett looked confused for a moment and then said, "Oh! It's over? The case in Philadelphia is over? Wait, I'm lost. This must be someone else? Oh, I see, it's someone else. John says to tell you The Jerk started serving a three-year minimum sentence a couple of months ago. Registered sex offender."

Maddy did a double cartwheel and felt a little bit of dinner come up in her throat. She could taste the fish again. She went to the kitchen to get a glass of water.

"She just did a cartwheel, John. Two. I'm truly lost. Who are we talking about?"

"Everett!" Maddy yelled from the kitchen. "Can you please stay here tonight?"

She heard Everett tell Wolf on the phone that Maddy had just asked him to stay.

"Yes, there's a perfectly comfortable pull-out couch in Alex's office," Everett said into the phone. "I know, because I picked it out. Of course I don't mind. I have to be up early, even though it is Saturday tomorrow. I have an appointment to see a client. But I can set an alarm. It's fine. Okay, I'll tell her you'll call her tomorrow."

. . .

Maddy collapsed into her bed and yelled again for Everett. Why was she yelling for him like this tonight? Was it because he reminded her of the nuns? But the nuns would never let her yell like this.

"Would you please read to me a little something while I fall asleep?" she asked, when he appeared at her bedroom door. "Wolf used to do that sometimes."

"Of course," said Everett.

Everett went to Alex's study and several minutes later came back with Whitman's *Leaves of Grass*. He turned on the light next to the grey velvet armchair near Alex's bed and then turned off the light on the bedside table next to Maddy. He settled himself into the chair.

"You know, Maddy, Professor Parvus isn't just a world-class pianist. They say he is also short-listed for the Nobel in physics."

Maddy started laughing. She tried to stop, but she could not.

"What's so very funny?" Everett asked.

"Wilhelm was short-listed for the Nobel," Maddy explained, stopping herself from continuing to laugh. "It's just so absurd. It's just all so absurd."

"John said I should take you shopping for a new dress for when he comes and makes us dinner. Why is he coming?"

"I want to know it's over when it's over. Whether it's guilty or innocent, I want to know it's over. He said he would come make the . . ."

She hesitated, not wanting to let Everett know Wolf would be cooking a pork roast Alex had bought. It seemed to much like serving someone their beloved pet.

"He said he would come make us dinner. He would like to see you again and meet my friends."

"That's lovely. Just lovely. I think Monday would work well for me. For shopping, I mean. I'll check with Lew. We can take you out for some dinner and shopping. Are your classes and appointments over by late afternoon?"

Maddy nodded and yawned.

"Can I just ask you one thing, Madeleine?"

"Of course," Maddy said, yawning again and settling more determinedly into her bed.

"Why did Alex get Professor Parvus a piano to play here?"

"They were lovers. She wanted him to come and play here for her."

"I see," Everett said. But it was clear he didn't see. Maddy had no energy to start to explain tonight. If she even *could* explain.

Everett opened the book, scanned through some pages, settled on one, and began to read from Whitman.

I have heard what the talkers were talking, the talk of the beginning and the end,
But I do not talk of the beginning or the end.
There was never any more inception than there is now,
Nor any more youth or age than there is now,
And will never be any more perfection than there is now,
Nor any more heaven or hell than there is now.

Maddy closed her eyes and brought back into her chest the feeling of that dream, of having Wolf hold her in that way. She could still feel a little bit of his heat in the sun, his strength, his joy.

Everett kept reading.

Urge and urge and urge.
Always the procreant urge of the world.
Out of the dimness opposite equals advance, always substance and increase, always sex,
Always a knit of identity, always distinction, always a breed of life.
To elaborate is no avail, learn'd and unlearn'd feel that it is so.
Sure as the most certain sure, plumb in the uprights, well entretied, braced in the beams,
Stout as a horse, affectionate, haughty, electrical,
I and this mystery here we stand.
Clear and sweet is my soul, and clear and sweet is all that is not my soul.
Lacks one lacks both, and the unseen is proved by the seen,
Till that becomes unseen and receives proof in its turn.

Maddy was already asleep. Everett could tell by the way she had completely stopped moving. She seemed barely even to breathe.

He turned off the light and went to make himself a bed on the couch in the study. He moved very quietly, not wanting to wake her. Wolf had said that she needed to sleep now. For what was coming.

Chapter 25

Maddy woke up in the dead-center of the night, popping out of sleep the way a submerged cork resurfaces in water, breaching the surface suddenly.

She got up quickly and looked out the front window in her bedroom to make sure that Everett's car was still there. It was. She went to the bathroom, emptied her bladder, had a glass of water. Then she wondered what to do. She knew she was awake in the way that would not let her simply fall back. Her urge was to turn *on*, not *off*, the lights.

She checked and saw Everett had closed the door to Alex's office, where he was sleeping. She figured she could run a bath in the solarium off her bedroom without disturbing Everett. A bath would settle her. She went to the tub, plugged in Alex's bottle lights, pushed the drain stopper into the closed position, and started the water. Soon the windows were fogging up with the steam.

Lying in the bath, she tried to clear her mind, to calm her head, to think only of the lovely dream she'd had under the piano, of embracing Wolf on the roof amid the green hills. But other thoughts kept intruding, and she finally gave up trying to fight them. Chief among them was trying to figure out whether it was worth continuing such a stupid push-and-pull with Hank. She regretted how he had departed, the way he had stormed off, misunderstanding the scene. For a tough-guy womanizer, he seemed to get his feelings hurt awfully easily.

Still, the way he had made her body feel was just so—well, it made her mouth water a little, thinking about it. It hardly seemed worth giving up on him now, even as she had the sense it would not be long before they would find each other tiresome sexually. He was bound to disappoint, not in bed, but in the after. He would surely feel the same about her. It was strange to realize, as she did now, that they would probably remain friends. She hoped so. She liked his company. He had a rawness about him that felt fresh. Cucumber? Carpaccio? No; ceviche. Don Juan of Ceviche.

What a stupid, weirdly masculine interaction between him and Parvus. The looks they had given each other. Maddy could only guess at how—and how hard—they had butted heads at the university. Perhaps over Alex? But it seemed as if Hank didn't know about Alex and Parvus, at least beyond the famous encounter at the faculty senate. Parvus did seem to know Hank's reputation. Was that information he had gotten from Alex or just from being on campus?

Parvus had seemed so strange, not just in his interaction with Hank. And yet Maddy still could not see any real vice in him. Yes, he had confessed to accidentally killing Alex. But what did he even mean? Whatever he meant, he had been genuinely annoyed that Maddy wouldn't herself answer the doorbell when it rang, when Everett had arrived. He obviously was not about to hurt her, certainly not to eliminate her for having elicited from him a "confession." He was no Wilhelm.

So, Wilhelm had refused to take the stand. No doubt his defense attorneys would explain it the usual way, that it was his constitutional right not to be subject to questions that might make him look guilty when he was not. No doubt he was appearing at the trial in his finest suits, wearing the glasses that made him look both imperious and vulnerable, a man deserving of deference. He would look presidential and grandfatherly, all at once. He would have all of the benefit of the doubt given to wealthy white men with impressive professional histories.

No doubt the defense was calling patients who would say that Wilhelm had saved their lives. Parents who would say he had rescued their children. Colleagues who would say he was a dedicated genius of research and patient care. Yes, his attorneys would bring forward doctors and researchers who would explain how laypeople misunderstand how deaths can just happen, deaths that look out of place but are, in fact, in a physically disordered population like this one, just part of the tragedy of the condition. Sad, not criminal.

Some of his colleagues would testify on his behalf out of loyalty to him and the profession, others out of empathy for him, and a few—perhaps more than a few—out of a classist attitude that nondoctors like this jury of so-called peers are not worthy to judge doctors. Some would do it, consciously or unconsciously, out of simple self-interest, knowing that if Wilhelm got off, he would likely reward them. And they could not *begin* to imagine him guilty. He was one of them. And they would not kill their patients.

She wondered now, if found innocent, he would come after her. Physically? Professionally? Legally, even—try to sue her for defamation? Or would he just move on in his life, satisfied with having dodged her bullets? How would he explain, if he was found innocent and went back to work, if more patients—or if no more patients!—died suddenly of heart failure? Perhaps he would stop seeing patients and solve his little conundrum that way. He didn't need them. He could go on just doing research and have plenty of resources, including funding and personal income, to be comfortable the rest of his days.

Still, she realized, what she had done would forever cast something of a cloud over him. But she knew from history that plenty of physician-researchers who had done horrible, unethical things to vulnerable populations went on to win top awards from their colleagues, be elected presidents of professional societies, all in what was seen as recompense for withstanding the unfair barbs of the non-MD "critics."

She was, after all, just a PhD. She would never win in that game. No matter how it turned out, the MDs would always see her as someone who, if she'd been any good, would have gone to medical school. The other PhDs would always wonder if she had been right or wrong about Wilhelm. The cops and the prosecutors, they knew she was right. But they would always see her as just a one-off egghead at best.

And Wolf?

She smiled.

Wolf would always see her as a mouth to feed.

She added a few gallons of warm water to the bath.

. . .

Wolf had somehow brought the queen-sized bed Maddy slept in up to the roof, and here they were, under the double quilts, the green one with the tumbling blocks pattern and the white one with the interlocking rings, just waking to the low sun coming up over the verdant hills. A mackerel sky was lit pink from the rising sun. She was pressed into the crook of his arm, her head on his chest, his naked body against hers.

"*Red sky at night, sailors' delight,*" he said softly. "*Red sky at dawn, sailors be warned.* Better wear your raincoat today, Rabbit."

She could feel in her body that he had been within her and would be again soon. But there was no rush. There seemed to be no one else within twenty miles, nobody but a few cows and birds, a couple of leaping squirrels. The bed was warm, the air still. She started to notice the music now, Debussy's *Claire du Lune* again, as if it were the birds singing it.

But no, it was piano.

She opened her eyes to find herself in Alex's bed, in daylight, and sat up. She realized it must be Everett playing Alex's piano.

Or was it really Parvus's piano, as he was its intended?

Or was it Whitaker's piano, as he paid for the "baby"?

Or was it Scott's piano given that, until someone official was shown the codicil, he owned everything of Alex's?

Or was it rightfully Everett's piano, given the codicil to Alex's will?

Half-Everett's, half-Hank's, with ten percent going to Scott's son. Everett would take the white keys, Hank the black, and the kid could get the bench.

Oh, stupid brain, ruining the pleasure of a heavenly dream with such earthly calculations. She sighed, got up, and took her morning handstand. It *was* rather wonderful to wake from a warm dream to the sound of such exquisite playing. She could not understand why Everett had been so besotted by Parvus's performance when he himself clearly played astonishingly beautifully, about as well as Parvus by Maddy's ear.

The music, the way it was being played by Everett, sounded as if it had been written just then, just for that morning moment, almost as if it was an ephemeral meal to be eaten and gone in a moment's time.

She stood back up, pulled on her nubby old bathrobe, and emerged to the living room expecting to greet Everett.

"I made coffee," Parvus said, seeing her out of the corner of his eye as he moved on to *Eine kleine Nachtmusik*.

Maddy wasn't sure how to respond. She said simply, "Thank you."

She went to the kitchen and poured herself a cup. She came back to the living room and was about to sit on the couch when the doorbell rang. Opening it, she found the locksmith.

She could see now, looking past the locksmith, that Everett's car was gone. There was just the locksmith's van and Parvus's car.

"Tried calling you," the locksmith said, "but your phone seems to be off. So I just took a chance and came over."

"Damn—right," said Maddy. "My phone is still off. And I'm sorry I had to call you back out again."

She gestured to him to come in. She shut the door behind him.

The locksmith held up his finger to his lips, to suggest she be quiet. Then he moved his finger in the air along to the music for a few bars, swaying his head with delight.

"That Professor Parvus is something, huh?" he asked rhetorically.

"How did you know it was him?" Maddy asked, her mouth hanging open.

"His car. Well, and the music," said the locksmith, and Maddy felt momentarily embarrassed these clues had not occurred to her.

"But wait," she asked, "how do you know him?"

"He likes me to keep changing the locks on his door randomly while he's out. He likes a challenging lock. I do it when I'm in his neighborhood. I'm not the only one. There are three of us playing his game. I have a new set from Europe I'm gonna give him soon. A very *interesting* new kind of design but still all mechanical. He'd better hope it isn't raining or snowing when he gets that one!"

"Well," Maddy answered, taking a sip of her coffee, "perhaps you can give *me* whatever lock will keep him out?"

The music had stopped, and soon Parvus showed up behind her.

"Hey, Marvin," Parvus said, as if he were expecting the man. "Want some coffee?"

"That'd be great," Marvin replied. "Just black."

Parvus headed to the get Marvin a cup as the locksmith called after him.

"Professor, this young lady would like me to put in a lock that will keep you out. As if!"

Parvus came back with a mug and handed it over.

"Nothing new?" Parvus asked Marvin.

"Interior chain?" asked Maddy, ignoring Parvus's question. "I mean, I'd love to keep him out when I'm *not* here, but it sounds like that's going to be near impossible. So how about keeping him out when I *am* here?"

"I could install a chain for you," Marvin said, "but he'd just as soon show you how he can open those from the outside. Pretty simple. But an internal metal slide version of a chain would work. Some hotels have those now. Those are very challenging to disable from the outside, and he's not going to want to damage the door."

"Damaging the door is cheating," Parvus explained.

"I can add the device. Would you like me to change the lock again, miss?"

"Why bother?" Maddy asked, resignedly.

"Seriously! Why bother!" said Marvin. "Let him break in. Can't get playing like this just anywhere, and here you got it at home."

"Lucky me," answered Maddy. "Lucky me."

The locksmith put his coffee down on the entry bench and went to his van to get the lock mechanism. Parvus returned to the piano and started on what Maddy recognized to be the *Goldberg Variations*. The very piece she had spontaneously told Dr. Griffin had come in the mail to Alex for delivery to Parvus. Did Parvus know that somehow?

The locksmith returned with his toolbox and the parts he needed and said to Maddy, "He knows this piece is one of my favorites."

"Let me ask you something," Maddy said. "Do you know of anyone else trying to keep him out?"

"No. I expect most people'd be happy to let him come in and play their pianos. But I don't think he does that for a lot of people. Is your piano special?"

"Special to him," Maddy said, and thought again about what Whitaker had said—that Alex had asked him for a baby, and he had been too proud to abort it after she died. Little did Whit understand it was another man's child. Although he had suspected it.

Within just a couple of minutes, the internal locking mechanism was installed. Marvin told Maddy he would very much like to stay to listen but had a long list of house jobs, it being a Saturday. She wrote him a check, groaning internally at the unexpected cost. She bid him a good day and went to the couch to sit and listen.

"You're not going to get under?" Parvus asked her.

"Why do you have me get under?"

"Alex used to do that. I thought you wanted to understand why Alex bought me the piano."

Maddy put her coffee down and sat next to Parvus on the bench, on the edge. She watched how his fingers moved along the piano, as if the instrument were a perfect prosthetic. Were it a leg, she thought, and were his pants of the right length, you'd never know the leg was made of wood.

"Parvus," Maddy said, wrapping her bathrobe a little tighter, "did you see Alex the weekend she died?"

He shook his head side to side.

"You didn't see her after she left for New York?"

He shook his head the same way again.

"So when you said, last night, that you had killed her accidentally, you didn't mean directly. You weren't there. You weren't there when she died."

Again, he shook his head, left to right and back again.

"Of course I was not there," he added after a moment. "I would have *saved* her."

"So when you say you killed her accidentally, you mean you had something to do with the state of mind she was in?"

Now he nodded: yes.

"And it isn't that she was depressed by you. It was that you had her rather . . . in a new state of mind? That you and she had enjoyed a kind of sexual connection that left her distractible? She was distracted. The way she was when she would lie under your piano."

He nodded again.

"I see. You think she went swimming and she was lost in those thoughts, and she drowned."

"She would get lost. She would lose herself in the sex of the music. Like you did last night, the way you did a little. She told me once she almost crashed the car because she was listening to the radio and Chopin came on, *Nocturne in C Sharp Minor*. That piece. . . . She would end up in an altered state."

He continued playing, long enough that it became clear to Maddy she would need to ask more to learn more.

"When Alex said there were no words for what the two of you were like together, sexually—and you said you can't talk about it—she and you didn't mean that you two *couldn't* talk about it. You didn't mean that there was a reason you had to keep it *secret*. You both meant something else. That there were *no words*. That there were literally no words."

287

"Right," he said. "We had no words. We found words unhelpful."

He played a bit longer and then said, "I find you annoying. Annoyingly nosy."

"I am exactly that."

She put her two hands atop his, to stop him playing. She held them in hers for a moment, and then she pulled his hands into her lap.

"Indulge me, *please*, Parvus. I know I never knew Alex, but I am devoted to her now, and I want to understand."

He looked her in the face. She could tell he could see plainly the earnestness of her request.

"Alex and I met in the argument at the senate," he began, in a voice that sounded to Maddy like the start of a lecture on a topic he found intellectually interesting. "She was arguing that the humanities and the arts had become, the way they are now practiced, quite useless—that science was the only thing getting us toward reality anymore. I explained she was being ridiculous to think that science was the only route. She was being ridiculous to think science was at all a route to understanding the human *experience*. Science is quite good for understanding the universe, the subatomic, perhaps gravity, even generalities about human life—disease, development. But it is quite useless, for the most part, with the individual human experience. There, the humanities and the arts can, through approximations and imitations, approach the capturing of reality . . ."

He paused, and smiled briefly. It was the first time Maddy had ever see him smile.

"We continued the argument that day at my office, after the senate adjourned. We continued the argument into the night, at my home. I remember I gave her a tuna sandwich, as I had that at home. And one thing that I realized—and noted to her—she was spending all of her time, all of her life, *in words*. She was always looking at words, at people's words, at what she could know through their words. Her data set on human experience was absurdly limited, particularly for someone who insisted unequivocally that there was a reality beyond representation. Why do just words?"

"Well, she *was* a literature professor," Maddy replied. "Her subject was *words*. The data of her discipline was *words*."

He pulled his hands away from Maddy and sat them in his own lap. He continued speaking as if she had said nothing.

"She said she understood what I was saying—that she had spent years working on thinking about the body beyond representation. About real flesh. I suggested to her perhaps she needed to stop thinking that words were the only way to access that, to access reality, because of course she would be disappointed if she limited herself to that route. That when she condemned the humanities and the arts, what she was condemning were just word games. She always talked about there being a reality *beyond* our representations, yet there she was, just like the people she hated in her own field, stuck in representing that *in text*—stuck in *words* about *words* about *no words*. So stupid!"

He puts his hands back on the keys, like a cat pouncing suddenly on a string.

"She needed some science, mathematical, quantitative. Or art without words. I could provide both of those. I could provide routes in and out without words. If she wanted reality beyond representation, that's where she needed to go, in and out of that reality, free of words."

He began to play something Maddy did not recognize.

"And so you tried to show her that place, the place one can enter and exit and be in without any words," Maddy said.

Parvus nodded.

"We were at that point in our debate both spent down. It was long after the tuna sandwiches. We had been arguing—talking—debating for at least five hours, maybe more like seven. It was so incredibly stupid at that point, *talking* about trying to get *away* from words. So finally I told her to *shut up* and just listen and see if she could understand. Well, she ended up crawling under the piano, to feel the music on top of her."

Missionary position, Maddy thought to herself. A reasonable place to start a sexual relationship with a piano. She herself had found it quite pleasurable the night before.

"She told me later she worked very hard to stop words forming just then. She wanted to keep arguing. But you know, she had a very strong mind, so she had the potential to go away from words. And she managed to do that—she just kept pushing away from the words, letting the notes come, allowing the phrases of sounds without words to reach her. She had something of a breakthrough, an epiphany. She felt a wordless existence."

"What are you playing now?" Maddy asked.

"Mendelssohn, dummy," Parvus answered. "*Song without Words*. You are not a very good listener, are you."

"Tell me more," she said, ignoring his comment. "About Alex."

"Little by little, she learned how to do it—to be without words. And we

289

learned to have long periods of time together without words—I don't just mean that we didn't speak; I mean that we weren't thinking in words. And she finally began to understand what she had been missing in her ideas. We would reach in parallel, and then together, a different place. And of course we did not speak of it. We could not speak of it."

He finished the short piece and sat quietly for a moment.

"I know," he said, now with his eyes closed, "I know that on the weekend she died, she was planning to write intensely. I think what happened, what must have happened—she told me before then, what was happening—she was moving from this place of so many words as a scholar and a writer to understanding how to go to a place that had a reality beyond words. Just being. And I think what must have happened is that she found herself in that place with too many words, and she had to leave it, so she left it, and then . . ."

"And then she drowned in it," said Maddy. "She drowned while in it, because she was in water when she got lost."

"Yes," he said.

They sat there, neither saying anything for a long time. Then Parvus slowly closed the cover of the keys.

He did it in a way that Maddy could clearly see him closing Alex's coffin. It exactly recalled to her the undertaker closing her mother's coffin. The last time she would see her mother's hands holding a rosary. She remembered wanting to look a little bit longer. The mortician's wife had done her mother's nails. Her mother never did her nails. Her father would have seen it as vain and feared her mother was being sexual, out in the world. . . . But there were her mother's nails, done just so, the rosary wrapped around her hand, the crucifix draped over the side of her hand.

Maddy's lip started to quiver.

"I did not kill her on purpose," Parvus said. "I did not want to lose her."

I did not kill her on purpose, Maddy thought, in her own voice. *I did not want to lose her.*

He stood up, went to the front entryway, and took his coat out of the closet where he had hung it when he'd let himself in.

Following close behind him, she saw that he paused to feel in his fingers the new internal locking mechanism. He tried it out twice, trying carefully to open the door with it set in the locking position. The door would only open two inches or so. He did this test as if he had to confirm it was what he thought: It was something he could not undo from outside, at least not without damaging the door.

He looked so sadly then at the device. He stroked it twice with one finger.

Maddy found herself suddenly overcome with regret at having had it installed. Here she was, locking a man out when his baby was inside. His child that had lost its mother.

"I promise," she said, swallowing hard, "I promise I will only lock it when I absolutely have to."

He left without reply.

Maddy stood with the door open watching his car go down the drive, watching, too, a delivery truck drive toward her. She presumed it to be bringing her Wolf's favorite sleeping shirt.

She wasn't sure she had ever felt so terrible for doing a thing to someone that she hadn't meant to do. She wondered if Parvus would ever come back. Her mother had gotten in a car, too.

...

It took a while to find the right tree but eventually she figured out which one it was, based on where it was, the look of the trunk, and the spacing of the branches above. She remembered to some extent the pull-and-step pattern she had taken when she had talked to Liz and then Jill on the phone a few days before the trial had started. She would use the same steps.

This time she had on hiking boots, the pair she had bought in the used clothing shop in Bloomington on Walnut Street. These made it significantly easier to climb than those dress boots had. Her dollar-store knit gloves got caught here and there on bits of the branches, but they also saved the skin of her hands from abrasion.

Before she had headed up, she had made sure her phone was tucked well into a buttoned pocket of her coat. She scampered up the tree, feeling the chill of the air more intensely as she rose higher. The sun was notably farther south compared to last time, the deciduous trees in this patch of forest losing the last bits of their leaves—except the oaks, the species that always held out the longest with hope of a longer fall.

Once she had reached a reasonably comfortable spot, about thirty feet up, she settled herself in and called Liz. She was glad when her friend picked up rather quickly and happily answered Maddy's questions about how things were in the lab, in her teaching, and with Einstein and Newton at home.

"I miss talking to you so much, Liz."

"I miss it, too, Mad girl," Liz replied. "But I'll see you soon."

Maddy asked what she meant.

"Wolf didn't tell you? He called and asked me to come with him when he drives out to see you, at the end of the trial. He's going to stop in Indianapolis and pick me up there so he doesn't have to dip down to Bloomington. I can find a place to leave my car in Indy. We'll drive the rest of the way out to the Twin Cities together. It isn't easy to get a leave around here, but Josh and LaToya in my lab group said they'd cover for me in lab and in class. And LaToya will check in on Newton and Einstein for me. They understand."

"Oh my god, that's fantastic, Liz!" Maddy cried loudly, spooking a squirrel below her. "I can't wait to see you. But how are you and Wolf going to stand each other in the car all that time?"

"Yeah, I don't know—maybe I'll read us a book out loud, about the Founding Fathers or Ansel Adams, or how to cook a country ham or something. And then we won't argue. Although we'll probably argue."

"Wait, why do you suppose he wants you to come?"

"Maybe he thinks you're going to be a basket case," Liz replied. "And we'll have to take turns holding a cool towel to your forehead."

"More likely he wants to avoid a situation where I could get him alone. He wants you as a chaperone! That's funny."

She blushed a little at the thought of being such a sexual pest to him.

"Perhaps," agreed Liz. "It being a terrible idea for you to sleep with him is *one* thing he and I *do* agree on."

Maddy thought about telling Liz about the dreams she'd been having and about seeing Wolf in Pittsburgh, but she didn't want Liz yelling at her. For the same reason, she had no energy to tell Liz about all she had been doing to try to understand how and why Alex Shugar had died.

"Hey, whatever happened to Maarten?" Liz asked. "He called me once, wondering why you weren't calling him."

"I've been into someone else."

"Let me guess. He's about twenty years your senior and basically unavailable."

"Yup. He's only temporarily available to me," said Maddy. "He tells me that after we fuck, he'll want to move on, because that's how he is. He enjoys the chase. The catch, not so much."

"He actually told you that?"

"Yes. Weirdly honest. Of course, I pinned him into a corner and he confessed that's his way. You know how I am, getting people to tell me things."

"Why are you bothering with this guy, Mad?" asked Liz, in a voice that sounded half concerned and half annoyed. "Why don't you try for someone your own age who *is* available?"

"Let me ask you something, Liz," Maddy answered. "Do you *choose* what turns you on? Do you choose *who* turns you on?"

"No. You know I don't."

"Right. I think I'm the same way."

Neither one said anything for a good couple of minutes. Then Maddy continued:

"Here's the thing, Liz. I don't know why this is what I'm into. I don't know if it's just how I would have been no matter what my life had been like—because evolution makes a woman want a guy with resources, a guy with a proven track record of securing resources, in case he gets you pregnant. Is that it? Or maybe it's what I'm into because of my awful father because, as you've suggested to me, I'm looking for a father to take care of me. Or maybe it's because of The Jerk. Maybe he cemented something in my brain that now I can't change, about sex being about a big age gap. A kind of classical conditioning around sex, a conditioning that I can't break. Or maybe it's because of my feminism, my erotic desire to basically take resources from powerful men but never be required to give them anything back—to have my freedom remain forever intact, be a whore or a prisoner to *no one*."

She paused, and hearing Liz say nothing, she went on.

"What I do know is that this is just how I feel. Guys like this are what I'm into—much older than me and basically not available. And I'm tired of having you act like there's something wrong with me, something I should be ashamed of, something I should try to change."

"I get that," said Liz quietly. "That's fair. That is totally fair."

They went quiet again for a long time. Finally Liz spoke.

"Are you up in a tree again?"

Maddy answered that she was.

"Yeah, I heard a bird again, so I figured you were in a tree. Why do you keep climbing trees?"

"I don't all the time. Just when I'm feeling up a tree."

"Makes sense," said Liz. "So, you following the trial?"

"Not really. Are you?"

"Only a little. The whole damned thing makes me scared for you. Honestly, I get so worried about you. I haven't been sleeping great, but I haven't called you because I haven't wanted to bother you when I know you have so much to deal with."

Maddy felt her eyes filling.

"Thank you," she said.

"Is Wolf worried?"

"Yes," said Maddy. "He called a few times yesterday, and I guess I should call him back at some point. But sometimes when he's worried, he just gets upset with me because he thinks I'm not being careful enough. I don't want to deal with that right now."

Maddy thought about the package that had arrived with Wolf's sleeping shirt in it. She hadn't opened it yet, partly because she figured it would retain its odor better if she kept it in the package until she went to bed, and partly because she felt so unsure that he had wanted to send it.

Liz sounded like she'd read Maddy's mind in what she said next:

"You know, Mad, I do get what you mean when you say you don't choose what you're into. I haven't been fair to you in assuming you can just change to a more convenient erotic target."

Maddy laughed at her terminology. Liz ignored her and continued.

"But it doesn't seem fair to Wolf to keep pursuing him sexually when he doesn't want you to do that."

Maddy didn't laugh now. She made no sound and didn't breathe for a moment.

"You know what I mean," said Liz. "He's been pretty clear with you."

"I know. You're right."

She thought now for sure that she should not have asked Wolf for his shirt. Her heart felt so heavy, as if Liz had accidentally dissolved away the lovely dreams of the roof of the house in the sunny hills, leaving her instead alone, in a cold parking lot with broken pavement under a cement-grey sky.

But Liz was right that Maddy had to stop projecting her desires onto him. No matter how overwhelming they felt.

"I know you love him," Liz added. "And Wolf knows you love him. He loves you. I mean he loves you romantically. Well, sexually, too. I said to him when he called me—to ask me to come with him—I said that I understand he feels about you as he would a daughter. And he said that, if the way he felt about you was the way a man felt about a daughter, he would be a terrible father, a very *immoral* father. And we both laughed at that."

Maddy smiled a little, in hope, hearing this. But then Liz went on:

"Still, he doesn't want to have sex with you, because of his religion and his wife. He didn't need to tell me that. You've told me that, and you know it. And as much as you and I think that that's stupid—having a stupid religion tell you what you can and can't do—there's a way in which he's not choosing that way of seeing love and sex any more than I am choosing to be into creative women my own age, or you are choosing to be into men who are old enough to be your father and who are not really available."

Maddy breathed in hard and let out a long sigh.

"This is making me feel so sad, Liz. I know you're right. But it is making me feel so sad."

"I'm sorry, Mad, I am. I want you to be happy. I wish you could be with the person you love. You've earned it."

Maddy started to cry audibly now, and Liz tried to say things of comfort, all the while worried Maddy would fall out of the tree.

"Maddy!" she finally yelled. "Listen to me! The good thing is Wolf truly, deeply loves you. And he's not asking you to stop *loving* him. He *loves* that you love him, I can tell. And *I* am not asking you to stop loving him. You just have to know you have to go elsewhere for sex. And sex and love don't have to be had together."

Maddy took a hard sniff in, and then spit out the snot that fell down into her mouth. It adhered to a branch below. She made a mental note to avoid it on her way back down.

"Okay," she said. "I know you are right, Lizard."

"And you know I will see you soon, with Wolf. And when I do, I won't give you any grief whatsoever about how the two of you love each other, because I know what both of you get from that is something you both deserve."

"Thank you, Liz," said Maddy.

"And I'll bring you a cake."

"Why are you bringing me a cake?"

"When something big happens, you get a cake. That's a law of nature. Trust me, I'm a scientist. When the trial ends, you get a cake."

"I do like cake," Maddy said. "And you know what kinds! Oh, and I have a present for *you* when you come."

Maddy went on to explain the rat that had come into the house and the stash she had found and saved for Liz's inspection.

"You're a true friend," Liz said. "You know what geeks me out. I wish I could bring you Newton and Einstein. I think you'd enjoy them."

"Maybe when I move to my own place," Maddy said. "I think sometimes

I'm too far from school, and it's time to move in closer."

"What are you going to do the rest of the day?"

Liz wanted to make sure Maddy wasn't just going to sit around stressing out and moping.

"Grade papers," said Maddy. "Really focus on grading a stack of papers. Really."

And that was true; after realizing she had chased Parvus off in a way that felt cold and heartless, she had decided she would try to stop thinking about Alex just for the weekend and try again to catch up on her classwork.

"And maybe get some exercise?"

"I've been working with an assistant coach of the gymnastics team now and then. She's good. And I'm running all the time, Liz." She added with a sigh, "Faster and faster."

Chapter 26

"Seriously, no, Maddy," Hank said, trying to peel her off him. "I have to go to my colleague's tenure party, or she'll be furious with me. And what if Sophie comes home?"

"Sophie said she wouldn't be home till at least midnight," Maddy answered, her speech a little slurred. "Come on, this's just follow-up *research*."

She took another sip of the cocktail Hank had made for her from Sophie's bar cart and gave him a mischievous smile.

"How can you be that drunk on one bijou?" he asked, shaking his head in wonder. "They're strong, but they're not that strong."

She didn't tell him that fifteen minutes earlier, she'd taken a Valium from a prescription bottle she'd found in Sophie's medicine cabinet. Just as Wolf had told her, when he talked to her on the phone but an hour before all this, this medication mixed with the alcohol made her not care about *anything*. Of course, Wolf hadn't meant to *recommend* it, she reminded herself as she tried to make some mental note of what was happening to her brain, for future reference in Alex's history. He had simply been describing what Alex had done in a greater quantity. But it now seemed to her a smashing idea, mixing Valium with a strong drink. An absolutely smashing idea. Sophie's living room looked particularly beautiful through this lens from this very pleasant couch. Oh, the crown molding! The old hardwood floors!

Sure, they were moving a little. The ceiling seemed to get a little closer to the floor, then pull away. Still, *nothing* was *bothering* her, and she delighted in this lack of sensation. Nothing at all was troubling her now. Not the trial; not what she'd done to Parvus; not the nagging feeling she'd seen someone near the house when she came back from the woods; not the letter she'd just found at the office, written by Alex about Sarah and the Gnat; not the other memo she'd found at the office, about the ethics committee; not the idea that Alex, her role model, had reached the point of taking on so much that she'd killed herself. Nothing.

Hank stood up to go.

"Oh, I see," Maddy said, pouting a little. "Your colleague who just got tenure will be *furious* with you if you don't show, because *she's* reserved you for the evening. I always forget to book early."

"Stop being stupid," he said, sitting back down next to her on the couch. "It's a party at her house with her husband and kids and everybody from the department. And she and I don't fuck around. Also, what's it to you? If you want to get laid, why don't you call Parvus? I came back to your place this morning and saw his car was *still* there. So I left again. I can't believe you even called me this evening. I kind of can't believe I'm here, but you sounded like you needed a ride . . ."

"Fuck, Hank," Maddy said in a drawn-out fashion. She thought she was sounding rather southern, like a southern lady in a small-town play. Well, except for the swearing. But even the swearing seemed genteel to her ear. "Parvus wasn't there *overnight*, Hank. I told you yesterday when you stormed out, he just lets himself in. See, he *picks the lock* to get to the piano Alex got for him. He's there to touch the piano, not me."

"The piano was for him?!"

"Yes," Maddy replied. "He and Alex were lovers by the end. So don't say I never get anywhere with my *research*. I got *that* far. He came to play it yesterday when you and I were out. He didn't know you were coming home with me. I didn't know he'd be there. Then he came again this morning. That was the third time he's come. Well, the third time I know of. He just wants the piano, not me. And I don't want him! Jesus, he's like thirty years older than me!"

"I'm like twenty years older than you, drunk girl."

He put his thumb just at the edge where her lips came together and rubbed gently for a moment. He was close enough that she could so clearly smell his shampoo.

"Well, so you're twenty years older than me . . . you're in my erotic target range then. All good."

He laughed at her.

"Where did you get that terminology, 'erotic target range'?"

"My friend Liz," Maddy explained, laying her wrists over his shoulders and trying futilely to pull him in for a kiss. "She studies rats. But it's 'cause she thinks humans aren't spherical enough. Humans are what she wants to study. Females are her range. Not spherical ones. Thinnish ones. Creative ones. With good hair. But for science, she says humans are too goddamned complicated, not spherical. You know what I mean—too, tooooo many variables with humans, not enough controls. So she uses rats. You can kill rats when you've come to the end of the study, and when you do kill them, with a tiny little guillotine, no historian yells, 'Objection, Your Honor! Objection!'"

Maddy started laughing and took another sip of her drink. She was almost to the end of it.

"Slow down, cowgirl," he said, taking the drink from her.

"You wanna be my horsey?" she asked, winking at him.

"Whatever kind of research you're looking to do," he answered, "you are making it hard for me to go."

He took her right hand and put it in his crotch.

"Oh, I do like that," she said, running her fingers firmly over his fly. "I do like that."

"Sophie never approved of me as it is," said Hank, "and if she finds me with you here on her couch—"

"She knew you were giving me a ride over from the U," Maddy said, trying to undo his pants. "I told her that, and she was *happy* you were helping me while she's out on her date. Help me out, Hank. Be a peach."

"Hang on." He hastened to the front door and back to the living room. "Okay, I set the chain on the front door."

He was standing in front of her, looking down at her. The way he looked at her in need, in want, it made her feel just so good. She realized this was a new sensation—the Valium and the alcohol making her feel so pliable but without the usual crazy rush of sexual desire. Just this woozy, free, erotic, floating buzz. She went back to undoing his pants, pulled his cock out of his boxer shorts, and pulled it into her mouth.

"Oh, you are *so* good at that," he said, his hands on her head, pulling his fingertips through her hair. She tried saying "thank you," but her full mouth made her mumble it in a way that made him laugh at her. She twisted her tongue around in her mouth, licking her lips as he was still there, and the motion made him groan.

"Oh, god, Maddy," he said, in a low voice.

She thought about answering "goddess" as a correction, but she decided to concentrate instead. She had her hands on his hips and did just a little bit of lingual gymnastics.

"Oh, god," he said again, and she glanced up to confirm she was doing it all just right. Her cheeks and eyes smiled at him in a way her mouth could not at the moment and, seeing that look on her face, with little warning he came suddenly and hard, holding onto her head to try to steady himself. In a moment he collapsed on the couch next to her. She picked up the drink and finished it off.

"Jesus, woman," he said, taking her glass and putting it on the coffee table. He leaned in and gave her a long kiss. She was struggling to remember how to kiss back.

"I like your research," he said now. "So efficient, too."

"That wasn't it!" she said. "That wasn't my research. That was just very pleasant *practice*, no theory. No research."

"Sorry," he replied.

"Oh, no sorry!" she said, pulling him back to try for another kiss. "No sorry. Not sorry at all. No sorry."

"So what was your research going to be?" he asked.

"Not too late!" she said. "Come up to the guest room with me. Do that thing you did to me last time. Don't talk, and don't let me talk. I wanna try no words. Not thinking, nothing mattering."

"Okay."

"Shhhh!" she said, putting her finger on his lips.

He scooped her up off the couch and carried her up the stairs. She watched the artwork hung along the stairs go by, step by step—black and white photographic prints, matted and framed.

Photos of Paris? The Left Bank? She tried pushing away the words—"left" and "bank" —picturing herself in a small boat, pushing off the stone wall lining the river in the photo. She focused as hard as she could on the image.

Just when she was starting to succeed, he laid her down on the bed. He had his lips on her neck and was unbuttoning her shirt. She was working on naming absolutely nothing. Yet she could not help but picture Michelangelo's God for a moment, pointing and naming this and that and this: button; mouth; nipple.

She focused all of her conscious energy, what little she could now muster, on the feeling of his soft lower lip touching the spot where her areola began and ended.

Oh.

Was this, then, where the world truly began and ended?

Didn't something so important in history *need* a name?

Chapter 27

"I almost forgot, Hank Merriman told me to tell you hello from him," Scott Willingham said to Maddy, sitting in the waiting room chair next to her.

Maddy paused grading the paper she had on her lap. She was trying to figure out what face she should make if she looked up at Scott.

She stared down at the array of magazines on the coffee table before them, as if the glossy covers could give her some acting direction. There was one magazine marketed to working mothers, with a woman holding a casserole and smiling like she'd just won the lottery; another one for runners, with a young man grimacing like he was lifting too heavy a weight; and one thick, high-gloss, out-of-season volume on Minnesota tourism, put out by the state, with a Nordic father-son team delighting over their catch of a big, healthy walleye.

Doctors' offices always had such weird collections.

"Oh, did he?" Maddy asked without looking up. "Hank Merriman said to tell me 'hello'?"

She grabbed the tourism volume and slipped it under the student's essay to make it easier to write comments on the paper.

"When and where did you see Professor Merriman?"

"Saturday night," Scott said, "at a tenure party. I told him that you called me to ask me to get you in to see Alex's doctor, to ask some questions. So he said to tell you he said 'hello' when I saw you."

Maddy almost laughed aloud at Hank's funny move, using a deanlette as a dumb carrier pigeon.

"Got it. Thanks. Tenure party for someone in his department?"

"Yes, Kali Ahuja. She's very good. We'll be lucky if we can keep her."

"I see," said Maddy.

She tried to hide her smile. If only Scott had known what Hank and she had been doing an hour before that party.

Of course, the only way *she* really knew what had happened between her and Hank up in the guest room of Sophie's house was to ask Hank by phone on Sunday—yesterday.

"You seriously don't remember what we did last night?" he had replied. "I carried you up to the guest room and, uh, did what you asked."

He cleared his throat.

"Three times. I mean, not all the same. Variations on a theme."

"Well, that's *very* nice of you," she said. "You are so accommodating."

He laughed lightly.

"You were *so* into it. I was *so* into it. I washed my hands before I left Sophie's, but . . . Well, one of our grad students handed me a beer when I got to the party, and when I raised it to my mouth, there was your lovely scent. Still on my hand."

"We didn't have intercourse, did we?"

"No! You seriously don't remember, Maddy?" Hank asked. "Were you on drugs or something?"

"Yes. Well, just one drug."

She told Hank she had taken a Valium from Sophie's medicine cabinet just after she and Hank had arrived at Sophie's house on Saturday night. When Hank left briefly to return a borrowed spare key to the neighbor's house, Maddy went upstairs to drop her bag in the guest room. She looked into the medicine cabinet in the master bath, found the bottle, and took one.

"You don't need a Valium to be with me, do you, Maddy?"

His tone was one of actual concern.

"Oh, hell, no, Hank," she answered quickly. She explained to him that Saturday morning, coming back to Alex's house from a foray out into the backwoods to call a friend, she thought she'd seen someone near the house, lurking about. She wasn't sure—but it all felt wrong—and it had scared her just enough that she decided to go to campus to work that day, not stay home, even though it was Saturday and it was a haul-in from Alex's place.

"You could've called me," he said. "I would've come over."

She ignored his comment. She didn't feel like getting into an argument about why depending on a man was not something she was going to do, especially when she had work to do. She explained that she had thrown some traveling necessities in her backpack—her toothbrush, her nightgown, a change of clothes—in case she decided she didn't feel like going home that night. She could always figure out somewhere to stay if she had to. Worst-case scenario, a hotel.

She'd gone to the main library to grade for a while, found a late lunch at the nearest Vietnamese place, and then gone to her own office, figuring her office was boring enough that it would be easy for her to concentrate. But she opened the door to her dark little office only to find it crammed with boxes that, it turned out, were full of records that had been moved out of Alex's old office.

She had called Lew to ask what was going on. He apologized profusely, explaining that the university was moving to clean up and paint Alex's old office to repurpose it. There were still papers there, and so the staff had just boxed them up and stuck them in Maddy's office, figuring since she was taking over for Alex, the boxes might include material she would want. Lew said he'd meant to tell Maddy, and she could just recycle the papers.

So then, of course, Maddy found herself poking through these boxes of Alex's, mostly to see if she could locate the missing notebooks and folders. Maybe Alex had left them in her office? Maddy ended up looking over the material for hours, pausing only to eat the leftover noodles and spring roll she'd packed up from lunch. The boxes contained mostly old student papers, exams, and essays that students had never picked up, plus old course materials, notes from university committee meetings, and the like. Maddy decided most of the papers were pointless to keep, so she dumped them into the big blue recycling barrel down the hall.

But two things seemed potentially significant.

One was a copy of a formal letter Alex had sent to Scott's office, just about a week before she died, marked "confidential." It stated that Alex had discovered bruising on Sarah's wrists and neck. When she'd expressed concern to Sarah about it, Sarah had said it was the result of a consensual physical relationship and had told Alex to mind her own business.

Alex had written in her letter to Scott that she was sending it because of her concern that Sarah was being subjected to physical abuse by another student.

Hank whistled at this news from Maddy.

"Was there an answer to that letter?" Hank asked.

"If there was, I haven't found it yet. I suppose I could ask Scott."

"So, what was the second thing you found?"

Maddy told him it was a series of back-and-forth letters that had started a few months before Alex had died, between Alex and the university's Institutional Review Board—the ethics committee that oversees human subjects research. The board had received an anonymous complaint saying that Alex was doing research on individuals' sexual orientations and histories with the intention of publishing a book on them, but without receiving board approval to do the study and obtaining written consent from the subjects.

"Oh, yes," Hank told Maddy. "I knew about that."

"Was she upset about it?" Maddy asked.

"Upset to the extent she thought it was *ridiculous*," Hank replied. "Which it was. A ridiculous amount of trouble that she shouldn't have faced. The board system was set up to protect patients in medical research. Well, you know this. You're a historian of medicine, so I don't have to tell you. It was set up to protect patients who were being used in *medical* research, to try to protect their rights when they were being experimented on medically by doctors. But the system has been extended now to cover a lot more."

He paused and then continued:

"You know, Maddy, in my lab, we go through application and approval with them all the time, for my sex research on humans. Fine. In the psych department, lots of us go through the process. For work like some of mine, consent to the research is necessary. We're strapping tools on people's genitals in the lab and seeing what turns them on. Sometimes filming them. They need to understand what we are going to do and consent before they join up."

Maddy tried for a moment to picture what happened in his lab. She could not.

"But Alex, as a literature professor," said Maddy, "she would not have expected to have to go through all that, just to write about *stories* as illustrations of orientations, especially when using pseudonyms for people who were knowingly giving her the stories."

"Right," said Hank. "She figured the complaint was probably made by some identity-politics activist who had wanted to make trouble for her. But there's no way to know who made the complaint, I expect. There was a professor in the law school helping her fight back against the claim she needed board approval for the book she was working on."

"Yeah," said Maddy. "I found that in the file. And it looks like the board was listening to her and the law prof, but they were also concerned about not getting the university in trouble."

"I get why you find the thing about Sarah troubling," Hank told her. "But I don't get why this thing with the board seems significant to you."

"It goes to her state of mind," Maddy said.

"You don't seriously think she killed herself?"

Maddy paused, and then told him:

"Hank, I asked my friend who is a police detective in Philadelphia, my friend John Wolf, to try to get Alex's autopsy results for me. And he finally did. He got them on Friday and had been trying to call me, but I had my phone off when I was with you. Anyway, he called me not long before I saw you on Saturday, while I was sitting in my office going through Alex's boxes. And he told me what they'd found."

She paused, and when he didn't say anything, she asked, "Do you want to know?"

"Of course I want to know," Hank said in an offended tone. "I'm not a delicate flower."

"The autopsy showed Alex had taken a combo of alcohol and benzodiazepine. Valium. She left a note in the car about how overwhelmed she'd felt. On the passenger seat, she left a bottle of gin and a prescription bottle of Valium and the note. And then she went swimming. In her clothes, as you know. With her jewelry on, as you know. She drowned. Cause of death was drowning."

Hank was very quiet for a moment.

Then he said, "Thank you. For telling me that. But it still doesn't make sense to me."

"You mean Alex didn't seem depressed."

"She *wasn't* depressed, Maddy. I've thought about it more and more. I've looked back at our texts, at our conversations around that time. The shit she was dealing with, I know it sounds like a lot. But this was all basically the kind of shit she'd been dealing with for years by that point. For years, she'd been coping with this kind of crap. She was strong. She was a fighter. She wasn't particularly anxious about this."

"Then why did she have a recent prescription for Valium?" Maddy asked. "Why did she leave a note? Why did she go swimming in her clothes in the cold?"

"Why did *you* take a Valium?" Hank asked back with hostility.

"Because I am so fucking stressed out from the trial! And I will admit it, Hank! Because my cop friend explained to me on Saturday afternoon that, if you take alcohol and a benzo together, like Alex did, you're not going to care about *anything*. I guess I wanted proof, Hank! That there's a great way not to care about anything, and I had access to it Saturday night because I rifled through Sophie's medicine cabinet, and you mixed me a drink from her stash."

He didn't answer her for a moment.

Then he said:

"I never saw Ally take a Valium. I never saw a prescription for it. And she wouldn't have hidden it from me. If she *was* taking it, she wouldn't have been ashamed of it. Sure, she drank. And sometimes explicitly drank to take the edge off. Sometimes we did that together. But she didn't take prescription drugs, not very often, unless it was like an antibiotic, for a serious infection. Her doctor gave her a prescription decongestant last year for a bad sinus infection she had, and it made her feel weird mentally, and she stopped taking it because of that. She didn't like feeling drugged on prescriptions."

"Well, the prescription for the Valium *was hers*," Maddy answered. "The vial was in her car, as was a bottle of gin. And there was a note, in her own handwriting, saying she was tired of it all and wanted to . . . to stop."

Hank said nothing again for a while.

His silence went on long enough that Maddy finally asked, "You still there?"

"I just don't believe it," Hank replied. "I'm not saying you're lying, or stupid, or your cop friend is lying or stupid, or anything like that. And I'm not saying I knew everything about her life. I didn't know about Parvus. Christ, I had no fucking clue about Parvus."

He paused for a second while she wondered if he ever knew about Whit in New York. Maybe he cared more than he admitted about her lovers?

"But look," Hank went on, "why would she have gotten Parvus a piano to play at her house if she was thinking about dying? Besides, she was too strong to have done that. If she was crashing from some problem, she would have told me. She would have told Sophie. She used us that way—I mean, I don't mean *used*. You know what I mean. She leaned on us."

"I do know what you mean," said Maddy. "But you can see why the police said 'probable suicide'?"

"I can see why they said that. I just don't think they're right."

After a little while, he let out a long sigh and asked her, "So, you didn't go home from the office last night because *you* were anxious?"

Now she felt foolish at having to admit to Hank that, yes, she was apparently not as strong as Alex. But maybe even Alex would say a serial-murder trial of a wealthy, prominent doctor was more stressful than anything she'd dealt with?

"I called Scott, right after I talked to my detective friend, and asked him to help me meet and talk with Alex's doctor soon, so I could ask about the prescription. Then I called Everett Sophie. I asked if Everett Sophie would come stay with me or if I could stay over there. Sophie said she had a date and she'd be out until at least midnight or maybe later, but I was welcome to go crash at her place, to go ahead and use the guest room with the queen-size bed. She said that the next-door neighbor had a key and would let me in. She said she'd call the neighbor to arrange it. I thought at first that I'd just drive over there myself, but then—well, to be perfectly honest, I didn't feel just then like getting in Alex's car."

"You didn't want to be in the car where you'd found out that she'd left that note, with the drug. Where she'd been right before she died."

"So," Maddy continued, as if he hadn't spoken, "I called you and asked you to give me a ride. And you did. When we got to Sophie's place, I put my bag up in the guest room while you returned the key and made me something good to drink, like I asked you to, and I looked in Sophie's medicine cabinet, figuring she probably had Valium or something else that would mellow me out. Most people hoard old meds, and most people her age have hoarded some good stuff. So I found what she had, and I took one."

Hank said nothing for a moment.

Maddy added, "I would say I did it because I wanted to know what Alex had felt. But I did it because I was just over the edge. Overwhelmed. I don't usually do that."

"You don't have to apologize for it," Hank said in a voice that sounded to Maddy like Sister Ruth at her best. "I get you're dealing with a lot. I'm just wondering if . . . if I should not have . . . if you weren't capable of consent and I should not have—"

"Oh, for fuck's sake, Hank," Maddy replied, sounding truly exasperated, "please don't second guess what we did. You have absolutely no idea how much I needed you just then. And I do remember clearly everything up until you laid me down on the bed. And the parts I remember after that. Let's just say, *Je ne regrette rien*. You?"

She could hear him breathe in and out.

"Well," he said, "I did *not* go wash my hands again after that, uh, after that first beer and the revelation you were still with me," he answered. "And all in all, I had three beers. Your . . . your *spiritual company* made that party bearable."

She laughed at his linguistic joke, and then wondered if she ought to be laughing so soon after telling Hank all she just had about Alex. Then she remembered what he'd said to her over that steak at Alex's dining room table, that Alex would not have wanted him to stop living just because she was dead.

"It wasn't just the Valium that made me dopey and forgetful," she said. "I was trying hard to clear my mind of words, to just focus on the feeling. Something Parvus told me Alex did with him. I think maybe it's hard to lay down memory when you're not thinking in words? I just focused on our bodies, mine and yours."

"Oh, you were focused," he said. "And I was focused."

"We didn't have intercourse?"

"No, really, *no*," he said. "And I would prefer when we do that, if we ever do that, that you be in a state to remember it."

"I'd like that," she said. "I like you."

"And I want you, too, babe," he answered. "Fuck, do I want you. Just say the word."

"I would. But I don't want you gone yet."

"We can always be friends after, Maddy," he said in an earnest tone. "I'm pretty sure we'll always be good friends. Or is that just a bullshit line?"

"It's a bullshit line," she said, laughing kind of wistfully, "and you're sweet to feed it. But that isn't the point. I got lots of friends, Hank. But none of them can do what you do."

. . .

"Dr. Shanks? Is this a good time?"

"Yes, hang on, Josiah," Maddy answered.

She put her hand over her phone's microphone, turned to Scott, and told him she needed to take a call from a grad student. He nodded. She stood up, took her things, and moved to a different part of Dr. Miller's waiting room.

She was glad to have at least a minute of distance from Scott's stiff demeanor. She could focus only so much on grading papers with him sitting right next to her. Especially since now she couldn't stop thinking about Hank and Saturday evening.

When Josiah had asked Maddy earlier in the day, after their seminar, if there was anything he could do to help mitigate the stress of the trial, she asked if he would give her an update that evening on the trial. She explained plainly to him that she couldn't stand to follow it but she also couldn't stand to wonder what she'd pick up randomly from people mentioning it. Josiah had said he understood completely and was happy to provide that kind of help. They'd developed an excellent rapport over the course of the semester, and she felt she could trust him to handle this request without making a big deal of it. There was good reason Josiah and Jenna were the students Lew most loved to hang with.

"Josiah," she said, taking back up the phone call, "you know you don't have to call me 'Dr. Shanks.' You can call me 'Maddy.' I've told all the grad students that."

"Dr. Shanks," Josiah replied, "when I get my PhD, odds are good with the way the market is that I'll never have job security. But I'll always have the title of 'Doctor.' So let me use it for you. Especially given that some people mistake you for an undergrad."

"Okay, okay," Maddy answered. "So tell the esteemed and barely employed Dr. Shanks what happened today at the trial."

"I had to miss a little bit so I have a little bit of it from Jenna. But she's reliable, you know."

"Ugh," Maddy answered, "it's not right for me to be asking you to do this. And now Jenna. You shouldn't be doing me favors as one of my students, and I shouldn't be asking."

"We're all glued to it anyway. It's not like you're asking us to paint your living room and babysit your kids for the semester. That's what some profs ask."

Josiah didn't let her answer as he launched immediately into a summary of what had happened with the defense now in the lead. Just as Maddy had expected, the defense attorneys had called other doctors to testify about the importance of Wilhelm's work, to say that, with relatively rare conditions like the ones Wilhelm was dealing with, patterns show up only in specialist offices simply because of the numbers needed to see the patterns. Statistics, they said, explained why Wilhelm saw the cluster of deaths among his patients. As to why he had so many bodies that had been promised to him, that was just evidence of his patients' devotion to his research.

"What did the prosecution do with all that?" Maddy asked.

"They kept cross-examination pretty short, maybe giving off a sense of being somewhat uninterested in these witnesses? I think they were trying to make the point that it doesn't matter what Wilhelm's reputation was—what mattered was what he *did*. The prosecuting attorneys asked the doctors if they could explain the notations in the logbooks, or why seemingly key pages would have been ripped out of the logbooks, and that went back and forth with the lawyers. The prosecution asked the witnesses who were doctors whether they pushed bequest forms on their patients, pressuring them to turn over bodies upon death. They had to admit they did not. They asked about the faked text, Schlesinger 1888. The prosecutors asked just enough to make the witnesses look uncomfortable and to suggest their testimony was weak in terms of relevance."

Josiah next told her that the defense had also brought forward three patients with dwarfism on Friday to talk about what a great doctor Wilhelm was, about why they were happy to know Wilhelm would have their bodies after their death.

"I guess it was supposed to sound all perfectly normal," said Josiah, "but the headlines on it were about as dark as you can imagine. 'I Would Gladly Have Given Him My Body.' And then the defense ran into a problem when the last patient they called mentioned that he never believed some other little person. Jimmy Heathe? Someone who had been saying Wilhelm was killing patients."

"Jimmy Heathcote," Maddy corrected him in a quiet voice.

"Well, the real issue was that the witness said 'Jimmy Heathcote, God rest his soul,' and then the defense freaked out, because it was clear there was *another* dead dwarf—I mean, *another* dead little person, one that we hadn't heard anything about? And he was someone who had been saying Wilhelm was killing patients? You know about that?"

"Yes," answered Maddy. "But I didn't know Jimmy had come up in the testimony on Friday. My friend from Philly didn't tell me. So, what happened when the witness said that?"

"There was some kind of huddle at the bench and after that the defense didn't call any more patients to testify. There was just the three who had already done so. And none of them were very convincing. They all sounded like they were besotted with Wilhelm, not objective by any means. Same as the doctors brought by the defense."

"Okay," Maddy answered. "Thanks. I hope you're not just saying what you think I want to hear."

"That would make me a lousy historian," Josiah answered, "and I do have some pride of profession, Dr. Shanks."

"Right, sorry. As long as I'm asking you to be my objective historian, what did you think of the presentation by the prosecution over the past few weeks? Was it persuasive?"

"Very," answered Josiah. "The documentation the prosecuting attorneys assembled, demonstrating the change in cause of death in this population over time, skewing towards earlier death than the subject population once someone signed a promise of his or her body over to Wilhelm—they brought in a great epidemiologist to explain all that data with graphs very clearly. The deaths congregating in his clinical population and no one else's, his grant applications boasting about the largest collection of specimens as the reason to fund him, his pushing bequest forms on patients. And especially the disjuncture between what he reported as cause of death on grant reports and publications and what medical examiners had found? *That* was damning. Too many cases of *that* to not be a real pattern! Plus Schlessinger 1888. Plus, the printer from Dusseldorf who confirmed he had made the text for Wilhelm."

"The printer testified?!" Maddy exclaimed, as quietly as she could in this doctor's waiting room.

"Yes, and you can't argue with a sturdy old German. And, well, I mean, the two nurses that testified about seeing Dr. Wilhelm in patients' rooms with mystery syringes just before three of the deaths. With no record of injections left by him with the charts. Then there were his logbooks, keeping track of all those patients with dwarfism, marking down who had promised their bodies, dates when they were due to be coming to see him, a column for when he'd gotten the body—circumstantial evidence, maybe, but, on the whole, those were creepy, and the defense couldn't shake that feeling that they were creepy. And the fact that the pages had been ripped out of the logbooks, and that they *had* the pages that had been ripped out, and could show what was on them, specifically the suspicious deaths. Why were the

312

pages ripped out, after you started asking a lot of questions—that's what we were all wondering, if it was so innocent? Plus the way he made sure he showed up quickly for the postmortems. Too convenient, his control of the whole scene, from clinic to death to postmortem. And with Wilhelm pleading the Fifth, there was no way for him to explain it all away."

"Okay, good," answered Maddy. She took a deep breath. "Good. So, more testimony from defense witnesses tomorrow?"

"No," said Josiah. "The defense went ahead and rested. Sorry, I thought you'd know that much."

"No," said Maddy, breathing out and in and out again. "Okay. Didn't know that. Okay. Did my name come up, I mean, in it all?"

"Only tangentially," Josiah said. "I get the feeling nobody really wants to talk about you. I mean, the lawyers don't want to talk about you. I know other people want to."

Maddy caught the reference. Earlier that day, she and Josiah and other students had come out of class to find two reporters waiting to try to talk to Maddy. It had grown impossible to even hide in the history of medicine collection's locked stacks because they would lie in wait. She was spending so much time hiding in the maps library between her classes and appointments, she was starting to think she should retrain in geography.

"Scott? Scott Willingham?" a nurse asked from the doorway between the clinic waiting room and the examining rooms.

Scott stood up and waved at Maddy, and Maddy thanked Josiah and asked him to call again tomorrow around five p.m. for another update. Maddy picked up her things and followed Scott through the door.

"Dr. Miller suggested you meet with him in his office rather than an exam room," the nurse said, walking them down a long hallway lined with doors to examining rooms, scales, and various educational posters. She showed them into an office and said Dr. Miller would be in shortly. She closed the door behind her.

Maddy and Scott each took a seat at the desk, facing the empty chair of the doctor. Maddy looked at the diplomas and certificates on the wall. She was relieved to see Dr. Miller's specialty—internal medicine. She knew it as a field whose members seemed to evince a natural affinity for historians. Not like surgeons. Not like the subspecialists.

"So, Dr. Miller is your doctor, too?" Maddy asked Scott.

"Yes," Scott answered. "You know, faculty tend to go to the university's physicians. It's just easier, being near our offices and all. Alex and I were both patients of Bob Miller for longer than I can remember. I think he'll probably agree to talk to you about her, as a favor to me."

Maddy hadn't told Scott what it was she wanted to ask Dr. Miller. She was hoping Scott would just make the introduction and leave. She didn't want to have to tell him what Wolf had found out about the autopsy.

The office door opened and a late-sixtyish balding white man came in and greeted Scott warmly. He had a pair of reading glasses resting against the top of his paunchy belly, hanging on a silver chain around his neck. A folded stethoscope was shoved into the right pocket of his long white lab coat.

Scott introduced Maddy by name, and then they all sat.

"How can I be of help?" Dr. Miller asked.

Scott looked at Maddy and Maddy returned the glance.

"Well, Bob," Scott started, "Professor Shanks is a historian of medicine, and, well, she is interested in Alex's death."

"Hobby of yours, Dr. Shanks?" Dr. Miller asked in a way that sounded like a friendly poke. "Philadelphia and Dr. Wilhelm's patients, and now Alex Shugar's death?"

Maddy wasn't sure what to say. She looked to Scott.

"Well," Maddy finally said, "the truth is that Dr. Willingham hired me on the faculty thinking I might be able to figure out how Alex died."

Dr. Miller raised his one eyebrow and looked at Scott.

"That's not it. I hired Dr. Shanks primarily because she's fully qualified," Scott protested, turning a little pink. "I mean fully qualified as a faculty member to teach Alex's classes and to be on the faculty."

"You're both acting like you have your hands in the cookie jar," Dr. Miller responded.

At that, he opened the big glass jar of frosted sugar candy on his desk and offered them each some. Each declined, but Dr. Miller took a piece and popped it in his mouth. He put the lid back on the jar.

"So, what have you found out, Dr. Shanks? I mean about Alex's death."

Maddy was taken aback by his blunt question, but then felt warmer to him for being so frank.

"Well," started Maddy, "as Scott knows, the police have marked Alex's death as 'probable suicide.'"

"Really!" said Dr. Miller. "That's surprising."

"Why would you say that?" Maddy asked.

"She didn't strike me as depressed," he answered, "and I'm surprised she didn't come to me if she was. She usually had no problem coming and

314

talking with me about—"

He looked at Scott before continuing.

"—about life circumstances, and her stress level and all. About anything."

"But you prescribed her Valium?" Maddy asked.

She made a mental note that Scott did not seem surprised by this question.

"No, I did not," said Dr. Miller. "Hold on, let me go grab her chart."

"You don't have it electronically?" Maddy asked.

"We do," he said, "but I keep a paper version for regular patients, so I can make notes that won't easily travel around. And so I can put supplementary material in."

He left the room for a minute and came back with a manila folder that looked almost two inches thick. Why so thick, Maddy wondered?

He put his reading glasses on and thumbed through the folder.

"Right. Just as I remembered. I saw her last about three weeks before she died. She had a suspicious mole and she'd made an appointment a few weeks earlier, and then came in for that appointment. I told her I wasn't particularly worried about it at that point, but we took a photo and agreed to keep an eye on it. She'd been out in the sun a lot, you know, swimming and walking, so I had asked her over the years to keep an eye out for changing moles and to let me know if one looked funny. Nothing in the visit notes about her being especially anxious or depressed. And I didn't prescribe anything."

He looked through the chart some more. Then he took his glasses off and let them fall to his belly shelf again.

"Alex didn't generally like drugs that made her feel funny," he added. "She generally refused prescriptions unless I insisted on something, and I only insisted on antibiotics, and only occasionally. Once for cellulitis. She was very healthy. She kept herself very healthy."

Scott was now sitting closer to the edge of his chair.

"So, if you didn't write that prescription, Bob, who did?" Scott asked.

Dr. Miller put his glasses back on and went through the folder again. Then he woke up his computer and pulled up Alex's electronic record.

"Nobody in this practice wrote that script. I can try to find out who did. Did she overdose on it?"

"Mixed it with alcohol, and went swimming in the cold," Scott said. "Left a note."

Now it was Maddy who edged to the front of her chair.

"How did you know all that?" Maddy asked Scott, her forehead furrowed. "Police told me."

"Why the hell didn't you tell me all that?" she asked. "Why didn't you tell me that at the outset?"

"Didn't want to bias you," he answered, sitting back in his chair. "If I'd told you that, you would probably have just told me they were right."

"So, I've spent months trying to figure this whole thing out, only to just get information two days ago that you've had *all along*?"

"How did *you* get that information?" Scott asked. When she didn't answer, he went on: "I'm sorry. You didn't ask me specifically."

Dr. Miller cleared his throat. Maddy looked at him and tried to read his face. He was looking at Scott rather as she imagined he would look at a suspicious mole.

"What else haven't you told me?" Maddy asked.

"I'm not sure what you mean."

"What else do you know that might have helped me get further than I've gotten with your little assignment?"

"I told you that you didn't have to pursue this question if you didn't want to," Scott said, holding up his hands in the air like she was sticking him up.

"Do you know where her computer or her phone is?"

"I told you that before. They were never found," Scott answered.

"Did you know that she'd ordered a grand piano?"

"A *what*? A grand piano?!"

"Do you know where the notebooks went," Maddy asked, "the ones that had been on the shelf in her office? Or the files that are missing from her drawers?"

"No," said Scott. "Those were all gone by the time we found out she was missing. I really don't know more than what the police told me. They showed me the note from her car. To confirm it was her handwriting. It was. Her handwriting on paper pulled out from one of her notebooks, those composition books. So it was clearly by her, left on purpose by her."

There was a pause as Maddy scanned her agitated brain for what else he might know.

"Look," Scott said, "I don't know why you're questioning *me* here. I thought you wanted to ask Dr. Miller questions."

Maddy ignored him.

"Did you know there was a codicil to her will? That it switched from leaving you everything to leaving most of it to Everett and Hank?"

Scott's head jerked.

"No," he said. "I did not know that. But why would it matter? I mean, why would that matter to me?"

"You knew she was working on a book about sexual orientations?" Maddy asked.

Scott nodded.

"Did you know someone had anonymously complained about her doing so?"

Scott nodded again.

"Was it you?"

"Was it me what?" Scott asked sounding genuinely confused.

"Did you make the complaint?"

"No! Why would I have?"

"Because," Maddy said, "maybe you didn't want her writing about you."

"What do you mean, writing about me?"

"Writing about your sexuality," Maddy explained. She glanced at Dr. Miller and he returned her glance. It felt to Maddy like he was telling her to keep going, as if he were coaching a medical student to push a patient harder in the history-taking.

"What do you know about my sexuality?" Scott asked defensively.

"I know Alex was planning to write about you, without using your name or any identifying details, as an example of a man who is into having his wife cheat on him."

"How did you know that?!"

"Do you mean how do I know *that* she was writing about you, or how do I know *what* she was writing?"

"What makes you think you know anything about my sexual life?" he asked angrily.

"Because," said Maddy, feeling strangely protected by Dr. Miller's presence, "because the manager of a private club in New York told me about it. Because Alex told him. Because *you* asked me to find out why Alex died."

Scott stood up suddenly and started to put on his coat.

"And are *you* planning to publish the findings of *your* research, Dr. Shanks?" he asked, buttoning up his coat. "Because if you *are* planning to publish the findings of *your* research, Dr. Shanks, you'd better make damned sure you have ethics board preapproval and the consent of your subjects. Or it will mean not only being promptly terminated but having a mark on your record as an unethical researcher. Try getting *any* job after *that*."

He left the office, slamming the door behind him.

Maddy sat very still. Her heart was racing. She was doing that thing she did sometimes, where she tried to figure out how to rewind time and, on the second, try not to be completely stupid. Not let her ego race ahead of her good sense.

Dr. Miller got up and came over to Maddy's side of the desk. He took hold of the chair Scott had been using and turned it to face Maddy directly. He sat down in it and then rotated her chair so that she would have to face him fully.

She looked up at him and swallowed. His face was very serious, very steady. Not unkind.

"Well, Dr. Shanks. If it's a hobby, you're awfully good at it. But it seems it may be a very *expensive* hobby."

She laughed a little at his joke, and then smiled as the tears started rolling down her face.

"I am a moron, Dr. Miller," she said. "I am a complete and utter moron."

"I think your problem is that you are exactly the opposite of a moron," he answered. "You're very smart, very smart indeed, Dr. Shanks!"

He reached across the gap between them and took her hands in his, holding on to them. After a moment, he clutched her hands a little tighter.

"I've been following the trial," he said. "You're right. Dr. Wilhelm most assuredly did it. The evidence is overwhelming."

"I'm very glad to hear you think so. But it's quite unpleasant to go through a murder trial," she answered. "Although I would be glad to have a whole jury say I was right, it'd be nicer if he just up and died."

"I'd imagine so," he answered. "And the prospect of going through *another* one, a whole 'nother murder trial, well, that might make one very inclined to accept a ruling of probable suicide."

She sat up straight and pulled her hands away.

"I wasn't accusing you of anything," he said apologetically. "I wasn't accusing you of missing something about Alex to save yourself."

"But perhaps you are right," she said, brightening strangely. "Maybe I've missed something because it is just easier to believe that—that the police are right."

"Maybe they *are* right."

"Do you think they are right?"

"Hell, no," he said, standing up and going to his shelf to get her a fresh box of tissues. He pulled off the cardboard seal and handed her the box. It was one of those institutional bulk-purchase boxes with tissues that felt like sandpaper. She wiped her face and blew her nose.

"Did the police talk to you after Alex died?" she asked him.

"No. I guess they saw no reason to talk to me, as I did not write the prescription? But Alex wasn't depressed," he said, sitting back down in his own office chair across the desk from Maddy.

She turned her chair to face him better.

"She wasn't anxious," he continued. "She didn't like taking prescription drugs. She didn't like going to doctors. She only just barely put up with me, and even then her friends often had to drag her in when she was vividly sick. Sometimes I thought she figured she was immortal."

"Did you know about her and Scott? Why they divorced?"

"Yes," said Dr. Miller. "I expect Scott might be horrified to know how many of us Alex told about that, but then Alex didn't have much of a filter, and she didn't think there was anything for Scott to be ashamed of anyway. She understood he didn't pick what lit his cigar. But Scott didn't see it the same way. He certainly never would have talked to me about it. But I probably shouldn't tell you that. He's still my patient."

"What do *you* think happened to Alex?" Maddy asked, leaning her forearms on his desk and grabbing his gaze as firmly as she could.

"I've no idea. But she did tick a lot of people off. And if she'd been writing about people's sexuality without their permission—"

"I think she had the permission of most of them," Maddy said, defending Alex almost reflexively. "Maybe not in writing, but they were cooperating with her on the book. Scott was a special case."

"Was he?" Dr. Miller asked.

"You don't seriously think someone killed her."

"What did the note say?" he asked.

Maddy dug into her backpack and pulled out the stiff cardboard express envelope Wolf had used to send her the shirt, along with what he had written down after talking to the police investigator in Minnesota.

"Hold on," Maddy said, "I have the note."

"What do you mean you have the note?!"

"Oh, sorry, I mean that I have a transcription of the note, read to my friend who is a Philadelphia police detective, read to him by the police here—so it's not the note, but it's what the note said."

She pulled it out and looked at it. She had looked at it three times, and every time she'd been struck by the strangeness of reading Alex's words in Wolf's handwriting. It was as if her brain didn't know whose voice to hear.

"Never rains but it pours," Maddy said, starting to read. "Don't know why it has to feel sometimes like everyone thinks every question I'm asking is forbidden, dangerous, offensive. Maybe it would be best to simply throw it all out and forget it. Wipe out the records and start over, or not start over. Do only what's required and nothing more. Teach, swim, sleep, read. Stop fighting. Stop picking fights I don't mean to pick. Stop."

"That's it?" asked Dr. Miller.

"Yes," said Maddy.

"That doesn't sound like a suicide note to me. Does it sound like one to you?"

"Well," said Maddy, "when you put it together with the bottle of gin and the Valium in the car—and the alcohol and the benzodiazepine in her blood—and swimming in the cold with her clothes on—that at least looks like someone not caring if she is going to die by going swimming. Don't you think?"

"I think, honestly," he answered, putting his clasped hands behind his head and leaning back, "I think I would be more inclined to think she'd accidentally killed herself if there *wasn't* this odd note and the benzo."

"Why?"

"Because the note doesn't sound like a suicide note, and the benzo doesn't sound like Alex."

"Well, the psychiatrist Alex was seeing—"

"Alex was seeing a psychiatrist?"

Now Dr. Miller leaned forward on his chair, interested.

"Not as a *patient*," she said, "talking to him. He had interesting stories for the book, I guess, and they were talking. Anyway, she was getting anxious in the weeks before because a lot was going on. Including with a lover of hers, a professor I've met who is pretty damned strange. She got him the piano."

"A piano," said Dr. Miller, nodding as if Maddy had mentioned a pathology. "Well, I'm not going to pretend I knew everything about Alex. She was a complicated person, Alex Shugar."

He opened her chart again and started looking through it. Maddy sat quietly while he did so. She wasn't sure what he was looking for, and she was trying to see what was in the chart. Now she realized why it was so thick.

"Why do you have offprints of so many of her authored articles in her folder?" Maddy asked.

Dr. Miller smiled.

"It's one reason I keep an old-fashioned chart even though the administration doesn't like us having charts like this. I add copies of what my patients who are academics have been working on—their publications. I ask them to bring me offprints when they come in."

"But why?"

"If there's one thing I've learned about academics," Dr. Miller said, "it's that they're always really working on themselves. I suppose any healthy person is. They just put their minds to it—working on themselves. So, if I am going to understand them, to be a good doctor for them, I need to understand a little bit about what they're working on in terms of research."

Maddy thought about this for a minute.

What was Hank working on? Proving one could not change one's sexual desires.

What was Liz working on? Female attraction and bonding mechanisms.

What was the Gnat working on? Remaking Alex Shugar in a new form, to force her to be someone she wasn't.

What was Maddy herself working on? People seen as abnormal. And what happened to people after they died.

Maddy looked down at her hands for a moment and was struck by the thought that they were starting to look just like her mother's.

"What are you working on?" she asked Dr. Miller, looking up.

"Diabetes!" he said laughing. He reached for another sugar candy and popped it in his mouth.

He went back to reading material in the chart. She had the sense he was simply looking for something he might have missed. Finally, he closed the folder without saying anything. He took his glasses down again.

"Who prescribed her the Valium?" Maddy asked.

"No one here. It's a controlled substance. I should be able to find out. But wait," he said, "why don't you just ask the police what doctor was named on the prescription bottle?"

"I can try," said Maddy. "But I can't do it directly. I got the information through my police detective friend in Philadelphia, so I'd have to ask him to ask them. I wish he had gotten that information on the first pass."

"I see," said Dr. Miller. "You know what? Maybe it's time you just went to the police yourself and explained what you've found and—well, they will know who you are, if you tell them. Ask them to tell you everything they know."

Maddy shook her head.

"You don't think they'd be exceptionally interested to listen to you, to work with you, given your celebrity?" Dr. Miller asked.

"They aren't allowed to tell me everything they know. It's an open investigation. And I think they'd see me as a police groupie," Maddy said, packing her bag back. "I think they'd tell me I just see things that aren't there."

"Is that what they told you in Philadelphia?"

"Some of the cops thought I was attention-seeking. Playing a damsel in distress And my detective friend told me that when people get to know a cop, they start thinking they're seeing crimes everywhere."

Dr. Miller nodded.

"Medical students start thinking they have every disease they are studying," he said. "Observer bias. I was sure I had five different fatal diseases in med school."

"So maybe I'm seeing something where there's nothing," she said, standing up.

"Or maybe you're *not* seeing where there *is* something," he answered, also standing up. "I'll see what I can find out about the prescription. Leave your phone number with me."

She took a pen off his desk and wrote her name and number on a sticky note.

"Text me to ask me to call you," she said, "and indicate it is you. I'm not taking calls from unknown numbers right now. Too many people I don't know calling me."

"Listen," he said, walking her down the hall back to the door between the clinic area and the waiting room, "I will talk to Scott and talk him out of being foolish, rash, about you and your job. He's just embarrassed. I can work on him. Don't worry about your job. If nothing else, he knows what I just witnessed, and he's not going to be stupid enough to fire you when he knows what I saw. It would look like personal revenge, a kind of cover-up of his sexual issues, and he wouldn't want the details of the conflict getting out."

Dr. Miller opened the door for her, adding, "Scott doesn't want anyone knowing about his—his interests. Not in a million years. You saw that for yourself. He's not a bad guy. He's just spooked by you knowing about his personal life. He's not proud of it."

Maddy walked into the waiting room and Dr. Miller closed the door behind her. She glanced up at the waiting-room TV only to see a short clip of Wilhelm walking out of the courthouse with his entourage of expensive suits. The screen soon cut to a reporter behind a desk, talking earnestly. Maddy was grateful the sound was off.

Chapter 28

Wolf probably knew what suicide notes normally looked like. As she drove hastily toward the university parking lot that usually had an open space this time of morning, Maddy thought about calling him to ask what he thought of Alex's message. He had only transcribed Alex's for Maddy, not commented on it. Did he have thoughts?

But then Alex wasn't a typical person. So, would comparing her final note to the typical suicide note make any difference?

Wolf had told Maddy once, so obliquely, about being present for a suicide. She had thought at first, as he was telling her about it, that it had happened many years earlier. But as he spoke, it slowly dawned on her that it had only just happened, so recently that the body might still be warm at the core. She remembered now how it became a night that she'd had to make them dinner. He wasn't in any shape to cook. She opened a beer for him and tried to figure out what she could make that would be any good, given what was in the fridge. While he'd gone to lift some weights in the basement and then taken a shower, she'd made a simple dinner of a small roasted chicken with vegetables, a side of rice. She'd done the chicken the way he taught her, cut down the middle in half, pushed down hard on a baking sheet, rubbed with decent olive oil and kosher salt and a little dried rosemary, cooked at a high temperature in the oven.

He explained to her over the chicken that he would have to go to the funeral that next day. He felt he had to go to apologize to the family for not talking the guy off the ledge. The dead man had been Jewish, so the funeral was going to happen fast. Not like the Catholics where you get a couple of days to prepare, to get everybody's clothes ready, to figure out what you're going to feed people after. Not like the wake for her parents and her sister that had gone on for three days, where everyone kept coming up to Maddy saying such stupid things.

"Your parents loved you so much."

"Your sister was such an angel."

"You'll be okay."

All of it was, of course, true. But these were stupid things to say. She much preferred the neighbor who came up to her, smelling of vodka and Noxzema, and asked Maddy in a raspy voice, "You want some money, kid?"

When Maddy nodded yes, the woman handed her three hundred dollars in twenties. Maddy had stuck it in her pocket and nodded a thanks.

It hadn't even been the sort of call Wolf normally went out for these days, now that he was a detective. But he had been in the vicinity. So, he'd gone to help his colleagues, to see if he could stop the guy. But he hadn't. The truth was that sometimes Wolf wasn't very persuasive.

"I know he was Jewish, Rabbit," Wolf had said, "so I hope they don't mind that I'm praying for his soul."

Maddy thought about what the Church used to say about suicide—no way do you get to heaven after suicide, thank you very much. That's why Wolf had been so off-kilter. The failure to save this guy must have felt like some kind of eternal failure on Wolf's part. She told Wolf she was sure the family would be grateful if he said that they were *all* in his prayers. He thanked her for that suggestion.

She hadn't told him how much she hated it every time someone told her they were praying for her soul. As if she didn't have to save herself. She was glad he understood instinctively never to say it to her.

...

"Thanks for doing the driving, Soph," Lew said, buckling his seatbelt in the back of Sophie's SUV. "I'll take you ladies out for dinner to that great French-Vietnamese place downtown after we're done shopping. My treat."

"Who says men don't know what women want?" replied Maddy from the front passenger seat.

"How's the heat back there, Lew?" Sophie asked, pulling out into traffic. "It's gotten so cold out."

"Just fine," Lew answered, as Maddy's phone rang.

She opened her bag to retrieve it.

"I forgot," she told Sophie and Lew, "Josiah is calling me. I asked him to call about this time."

Lew insisted she put it on speaker, so she did.

"Hey, Josiah," Maddy said. "You should know I'm with Professor Meadows in a car and you're on speaker."

"Hey, Dr. Shanks. Hey, Dr. Meadows. You two remember I want to meet with you both on Thursday morning?"

"Yes," said Maddy.

"Yes, Josey," said Lew. "We'll both be ready to go over your draft proposal. We'll make a point of discussing it a little beforehand, so we're ready. And then we can all go out for some Ethiopian after, okay? Tell Jenna she can join us. My treat."

"Sounds great!" said Josiah. "Very kind of you."

Maddy found herself wondering if Lew was buying her so much food because of the trial, or because of their salary differential. Or did he always treat everyone?

"Dr. Shanks," Josiah said, "can I ask you a question before I give you an update?"

Maddy said he could.

"Were you out clubbing all night?"

Sophie looked over at Maddy from the driver's seat with a bemused look. Maddy hastily tried to turn the phone off speaker, but Lew grabbed it from the backseat and spoke into it.

"Josiah! Josiah, tell Daddy what makes you think Auntie Madeleine was out clubbing all night."

"Well, there was the double-clutching of a large coffee and a large orange juice in the seminar, plus the arrival with sunglasses," Josiah replied. "Oh,

325

and same clothes as yesterday. Not that I'm supposed to notice that."

"So," said Maddy, embarrassed, "I guess my makeup refreshing didn't cut it, huh?"

"We have to work on your technique, sweetie," Sophie said in a quiet voice.

"Anyway!" said Maddy, louder than necessary. "I think you were calling with an update?"

"Right," said Josiah. "Not much to say. Pretty pro forma instructions to the jury according to the legal-beagle talking heads. And then off they went, the jury. Now they have it."

"Excellent!" said Lew.

Maddy turned and looked at him to try to understand why he would say that.

"That means it's almost over," he explained. "Pretty soon you can stop hanging out with the maps and go back to your natural habitat. You know, books stained with blood, books that smell of formaldehyde and mold. The *lady-like* stuff. Then you can get some publications done."

Maddy frowned and turned back forward. As her chair, Lew was obviously thinking what she had been thinking—she was fucking up, not getting done what she needed to get done.

"And then I can find you easily for lunch!" Lew added hastily. "Which is what matters in academic life." Lew leaned forward and poked Maddy on the shoulder. "Now, tell us where you were out clubbing on a Monday night, and more importantly, *with whom.*"

"Thanks, Josiah," said Maddy, grabbing her phone back. She took it off speaker and told Josiah she guessed she wouldn't need any more end-of-day updates unless something happened with the jury.

"Sorry if I said too much," he said, genuinely. "I guess I shouldn't have—"

"It's fine, really," she said. "It gives Professor Meadows something to *talk about.*"

She turned again to look at Lew and gave him a mock-scowl.

"As you know, he's always at a loss for things to *talk about!*"

She hung up and explained to Lew and Sophie that she'd gone out dancing at a gay bar the night before because she had so much stressful energy she needed to burn off. She figured a gay bar would be safe. She told them she'd asked Hank for a recommendation and he'd directed her to a place where the bartender and clientele knew him well, a place where he'd recruited subjects for his study of the genetic basis of homosexuality. She didn't mention that Hank had stopped by to see her and had asked the bartender

326

to take good care of her.

"And, well," she went on, "I felt like a moron for crashing a gay bar, but then I had a good time with one guy there, about my age. He had been a cheerleader in high school, and he knew how to dance with someone with my weird gymnastic moves. I ended up not in a condition to drive home when they were closing. The bartender gave me the couch in the manager's office. And I was just going to sleep there until I felt okay to drive. But by the time I woke up, it was morning, and I had to hustle to get to seminar. Living so far from campus is a real problem."

"A real problem if you go out clubbing on weeknights," said Sophie, chuckling. "Next time, take me and Lew with you. They never give me any trouble at the door if it's a gay bar."

"Why would anyone give you trouble at the door?" Maddy asked.

"The dance bars all card at the door, no matter how old you are," said Sophie. "Because of the cops. And some bouncers at the straight bars don't like it when your ID says 'Everett' and you look like an Evelyn. Assholes, if I may use the proper term."

"You should just get a fake ID like the underage kids do," said Lew to Sophie. "Easy-peasy. I'll go get one with you and have them take fifteen years *off* my alleged age. That could come in handy."

"But why were you needing to go dance?" asked Sophie, ignoring Lew. "Stress of the trial?"

Maddy said it was that, but also having met with Alex's doctor the day before. She told them what Dr. Miller had said, which meant having to tell them what Wolf had learned from the police. Lew and Sophie both went quiet on the news that Alex had taken a combo of gin and Valium and left a note that said she just wanted everything to stop.

Maddy let the quiet sit for a while. It wasn't that she thought they might tell her something she needed to know. (She was sure they would protest as much as Hank and Dr. Miller and Scott did that it didn't make sense.) It was, rather, that she thought they needed time to be alone with the memory of Alex for a moment, knowing what had been found with her.

"Dr. Miller called me this afternoon," Maddy said, breaking the silence as they entered downtown. "He found out who wrote the prescription. Alex got it from Dr. Griffin, that psychiatrist she was talking to about the book, the one you told me about, Sophie. And oddly, she didn't fill it at the university med school clinic pharmacy, the one near our offices, like she usually did with her scripts. She went somewhere else. Do you suppose she was ashamed of needing it?"

Lew immediately rejected the idea.

"Alex wasn't going to apologize to anyone for however she dealt with stress," said Lew. "Not her way of life."

"Did you find out where it where it was filled?" Sophie asked.

Maddy looked over at her and thought that Sophie looked funny all of a sudden. Stiff. Uncomfortable.

"Yes," she answered. "A place called Two Brothers' Pharmacy, miles from campus, and not on her way home, either. A little independent shop, according to Dr. Miller."

Lew and Sophie said nothing for a minute, but Maddy had the sense they were exchanging a look mentally.

"Two Brothers', huh?" said Lew.

"Yes. Why?" asked Maddy.

"It's a place . . ." Sophie started. But she did not continue.

"It's not the kind of place you'd expect Alex to go," Lew explained, "particularly how out of the way it would be for her. It's a place a lot of people in the community know. You can get your HIV drugs there without anyone giving you a nasty look."

"You can get your hormones there without anyone giving you a hard time," added Sophie.

None of them said anything further for a while. Maddy was trying to figure out—why Two Brothers'? Had Joseph in New York been onto something when he said maybe Alex had taken a woman as a lover?

. . .

Maddy tried the dress on again when she got home, standing in Alex's master bathroom to see it in the mirror. She shifted her weight to stand on tippy-toes in an effort to see the whole thing. It did fit her perfectly. No wonder when she had come out of the dressing room with this dress on, Sophie and Lew had kind of gasped and then gone quiet.

And then Lew said that silly thing: "Our little girl is all grown up!"

The robin's egg blue was perfect. Not babyish, not clubby, just . . . dreamy. The scoop neckline perfectly framed her face. The cut showed off her shape without quite screaming "hourglass!"

And best of all, after Maddy said she loved the dress but protested she couldn't spend so much on one piece of clothing given her salary and her

328

job insecurity, Sophie bought it for her as a gift. Lew bought her the heels and a necklace and even a clip for putting her hair up in a pretty twist and bun, just so. She tried the clip in the bathroom at home three times, until she got her hair just right.

Maddy wasn't sure she could wear this to a pork dinner with Wolf, but she was sure she'd wear it somewhere, sometime, and feel just as she did now: like she had managed to do something right. Like she had managed to make friends with good people. She almost wanted to send a picture of herself in it to the sisters in West Virginia. She thought they might delight in it. Here she was, healthy, happy, and properly accessorized. Looking like a grown woman, after all.

Maybe she should tell Hank to come over . . . But she wasn't ready for that, and she should sleep. He had been lightly texting her all day, all variations on *thinking of you*, followed by something more to make it clear how he was thinking of her. She guessed he had liked the way she danced at the bar.

She went to the front door, opening it to look out, feeling the cold immediately shoot up the dress and drape her bare arms.

No sign of Parvus. Probably just as well. Wouldn't he just say something stupid, finding her in this pretty cocktail dress and fancy heels, standing at the front door at ten o'clock at night, her hair done up?

She figured she might as well set the latch on the front door now.

But first, she sat down at Alex's desk and made a list of the things she had to do the next day. It was impossible to know how long the jury would be out, but once they came back, she told herself, she would stop pursuing the question of Alex. And there were still some things she wanted to know.

Call and ask Wolf to find out if the note was dated. Maddy realized in conversation with Dr. Miller that Wolf hadn't written down a date on the transcription. If Alex had dated it, it might give Maddy a clue about what day Alex had died. Alex had texted Sophie and Hank "Love you" on that Monday morning, Memorial Day, but then she'd been missing for a few days after. Was it possible she died not Monday, but Tuesday or even Wednesday, after isolating herself?

Call the cleaning woman. Sophie had said something over dinner to Lew about how nicely Maddy was keeping Alex's house, and that led to a discussion about how Alex had a housecleaner, something Maddy hadn't known before. The cleaning woman came on Saturdays because she worked a regular job during the week. So maybe, Maddy realized, she would know something about what state Alex was in that Saturday? Lew gave Maddy the name and number of the woman, Trish Hannigan, out of his little address book. He had the information because Alex had hatched a scheme to try to convince Mrs. Hannigan that a gay son was not the worst thing in the world. Mrs. Hannigan repeatedly talked to Alex about her son—about how the Church said he'd be going to hell, about how she was worried he'd never be happy or healthy—and Alex wanted her to meet Lew, to see that out gay men grow up to be just fine, especially if you love them. Alex's scheme hadn't worked out chiefly because Lew didn't want to be bothered with a cleaner on the weekends, but Lew at least had the information about how to reach her.

Call Dr. Griffin back. He'd called twice today, the first time leaving no message, the second time catching her at dinner with Lew and Sophie. Maddy had stepped out to take the call just long enough to tell him she was out with friends and would call him the next day. He said he was calling to make sure she was going to make an appointment to see him, that he could work around any insurance issue. She said she'd call him back tomorrow. She didn't much want to talk with him, but if she asked him about the prescription for Alex and the choice of pharmacy, maybe he'd tell her something useful. And she wanted to know if he knew that Alex had taken it with alcohol just before she died—that he had written a prescription that contributed to her death.

Call Dr. Miller, ask him to call in a Valium prescription for her at Two Brothers'. She wanted to go over there and get a feel of the place herself, to see what would happen if a woman who seemed pretty straight showed up to get a prescription of that sort filled there. Plus, then she'd have a handy stash of her own of Valium, good for not caring for a few hours, if the jury turned out to be bad at their job. She could fry herself a little in the span between the news of acquittal and when Wolf and Liz and maybe a cake arrived.

Call Scott back. During dinner, he had also left a message telling her she needed to call him back. What did he want, she wondered, and was he still going to be agitated about what she knew about his sex life?

Lord, what a lot of callbacks for someone who generally hated the phone and would much rather be alone with a book.

And there was one more thing she needed to figure out, but she wasn't sure how. Back in Pittsburgh, Everett had gotten the Gnat to tell him that he'd been away at a conference in San Francisco the weekend Alex died. But Maddy had realized that (duh) there were no academic conferences on

Memorial Day weekend, none that she had ever heard of, anyway. It was a funny time in the academic calendar, with some places on semester systems done with the year and others on quarter systems in the midst of finals. Plus, academic conferences in the humanities were never held on holiday weekends when flights would be expensive. And flights to San Francisco were always very expensive, as were hotels. So, had he been away?

She went to the front door and opened it to look out again. The air was so cold, she wondered why a deer seemed to be stirring in the woods. It should be bedded down.

And still no Parvus.

This time, after closing the door, she set the new inside latch.

She took down her hair and then took off the dress, unzipping it in the back carefully and hanging it in the closet on a wooden hanger fitted with a quilted fabric covering. She put on her long flannel nightgown and thick socks, removed her makeup, washed her face, and brushed her teeth.

Then she took Wolf's shirt out of the clean plastic bag she was keeping it in during the day and encased the firmest pillow in it. She turned off the lights and pulled it close. How was it he smelled sometimes of the game of baseball? Proletariat beer, mustardy hotdogs, relaxed crowds, and nine innings.

Chapter 29

So. Alex was in the closet. And she had been all along.

Maddy thought about calling Wolf to ask him to help her understand why it bothered her so much. And to help her consider whether it was meaningful that Scott was the kind of person who wouldn't think to mention this sooner.

Maddy had no sentimentality about human remains. What disturbed her about Wilhelm's collection had never been that they were *human*; it had been the way he had acquired it all. So why did it trouble her to learn that Alex was in the coat closet and had been there all along? Why did hearing this from Scott on the phone cause her to feel an urge to call Wolf and then to quickly pack up her bag, put on her coat, and head to Parvus's office in the hope he would be there?

As she walked across Washington Avenue and onto the university green toward Parvus's building, she reflected on the conversation she'd just had with Scott. She had returned his call from the history of medicine library after he had left another message saying she needed to contact him. On the call, he said nothing specifically referring to the conversation with Dr. Miller the day before, nothing about whether she might be in violation of university policy by looking into the lives of people who'd had relations with Alex. Instead, he was calling to insist that as executor of Alex's will, he needed to know where this codicil to the will was.

When Maddy told him she had it, he testily asked her why. She wasn't sure what to say. Should she explain that Everett Sophie had given it to her as a way to send her to New York to talk to Whit? That was surely just going to set off Scott again, a reference to New York. He would remember that Maddy had said yesterday that a manager at a private club in New York had told her about Scott's sexual predilections. Plus, there would be the reference to the affair of Alex's that had led Scott and Alex to realize what turned Scott on.

So, Maddy simply told Scott that Everett Sophie had given the codicil to her. It had been in an envelope sealed and signed by Alex and had been held for safekeeping by Everett Sophie.

"And you were just going to sit on it?" Scott asked. "For how long?"

Maddy didn't know what to say. It was a reasonable question.

"Well," said Scott, "if it is the case that I am not the chief beneficiary of her estate—which is fine with me, of course—I have a clear obligation to execute the will and transfer the inheritance to the rightful beneficiaries. It's a good thing I didn't already transfer the property to myself. That would have just made it so much more complicated. You should have told me about it the minute you knew about it."

When Maddy did not reply, he went on:

"You'll need to move. Soon."

She thought immediately of the bathtub and wondered if he would care if she took the bottles. And could she take Alex's good chef knife? And the fancy martini glasses? If Sophie and Hank were going to split it all, the two of them might not mind if Maddy took those things.

Maddy had started to think then about Alex's house being divided up and sold. Her car. Her daybed. The piano. What would be left then?

And that had been when it struck Maddy. She did not know where Alex was buried. Where would Alex's last place be? Where was the place on earth where she would return to dust? She asked Scott.

"Where is Alex buried?"

"Alex isn't buried," he replied coldly. "She was cremated, as per her wishes. After the autopsy."

"What did you do with her ashes?"

"They're in the coat closet. In a box."

Maddy felt then like a small bird had just appeared in her esophagus. Or was it in her trachea? A hummingbird.

"You mean in a box in *your* coat closet. At *your* home?"

"No," Scott answered. "In the coat closet at Alex's house—where *you* are living. I wasn't sure what to do with them. I didn't want them at my house, because my wife . . . My plan had always been to ask Alex's closest friends— the people who were closer to her than I was by that point—Everett, and Hank, and . . . but I guess I never got to it because I was waiting until . . ."

It was then that Maddy had found herself at the library reaching mentally for Wolf and then knowing she had to go see Parvus. He would know what to do.

Maddy couldn't shake the feeling that Alex should have *told* her that that's where she was. All the conversations they'd had, in the bathtub, in the kitch-en—couldn't Alex have just said to Maddy, "By the way, my remains are in the coat closet"?

But Maddy realized this was utterly irrational on her part.

Parvus's office door was open, and there was a short line of students waiting to see him. She took her place in the quiet, patient queue. She could hear Parvus lecturing a student and the student making noises like he understood what Parvus was saying. But the noises were not convincing. The student in front of her suddenly turned to ask her, "You here about the exam too?"

She shook her head. Now she was wondering where this student's body would end up. And the one in front of this one. And the one in front of that one.

"Your phone is ringing," said the student.

Maddy nodded, walked down the hall, and opened her phone.

"Bob Miller, Dr. Shanks, returning your call."

"Thanks," said Maddy. She found a spot outside a closed office door and sunk down to the floor to sit.

"I had a favor to ask," she said. But then she said nothing more.

"Yes?" he asked.

"Wait a minute," she replied.

She took her bottle of water out of her backpack's side pocket and drank down two gulps, hoping the hummingbird might stop flapping in her neck. Perhaps it was a dragonfly. A dragonfly with an iridescent blue body.

"Can I ask you something about Scott?" she asked.

"You know I can't talk about him as a patient. But hit me."

"He just told me, he just told me on the phone—after I've been living in Alex's house for months—that she's in the coat closet. That her cremated remains are in a box in the coat closet."

"So, okay. I see. You want to know what kind of guy doesn't think to mention this to a tenant sooner. Especially a tenant looking into the cremated person's death."

She thought she heard Dr. Miller laugh a little.

"He's a brainy academic, Dr. Shanks. Scott Willingham is an unsentimental, brainy academic."

He made a sound that sounded like a "tsk," or a pop of his lips.

"What can I say, Dr. Shanks? Yes. Yes. Most people might think to *mention* that the prior occupant was in the coat closet, sure. They show you how the keys work, they show you how the plumbing works, they mention the body in the closet, even if it's cremated. Does it bother you? Because I took *you also* for an unsentimental, brainy academic."

"It is funny, Dr. Miller," she replied. "I'm not usually disturbed by anything having to do with bodies. With human remains. In my work, I've been among so many, and it's my line of work in part because I don't mind being among so many. But Alex and I never met, and now I find out she's been in my goddamned coat closet all along."

Now he did let out an audible laugh. The sound of it made her a little less clenched.

"You know, as a historian," she continued, "you go *looking* for your subject. You look for her in texts, in records, in photographs. You talk to her in your head. It never occurs to you she might just be hanging out in your own coat closet without you knowing. All the times I grabbed my coat . . ."

"I can imagine."

"Anyway," she continued, "I was going to ask you a favor. Two favors. First, did you find out anything more about that prescription?"

"Not sure how much I should say," he replied, "but I called Dr. Griffin, and he acknowledged he had written it. So that was all legit. I told him about the cause of death and told him I'd looked up the Valium prescription. He told me Alex had been struggling a few weeks before she died. Anxiety. Some depression."

"But you didn't think so?"

"You know, I remember her on that last visit, about the mole, talking about psychiatrists in general," he answered. "Maybe she was trying to tell me something when she was talking about psychiatrists? That she was struggling? But then, she was so blunt, she would have just told me if she needed mental health care. I can't remember if she mentioned him specifically. It's so long ago now. I just remember an observation she made, because it was striking to me—that psychiatrists are all voyeurs, wanting to know your sex life. Like all internists are detectives, she said, and all surgeons are glorified mechanics. She had these kinds of spot-on observations—they made me look forward to seeing her on my clinic appointment list."

"But you still don't remember her seeming depressed or anxious."

"No," he said, "and I wouldn't give a depressed patient Valium, for God's sake. Maybe for anxiety, okay . . . Not my favorite approach."

"So, she didn't seem anxious to you? When you saw her last?"

"No," Dr. Miller answered. "But how often do we see what we're *not* looking for?"

Maddy wondered if he was referring to the box in the closet. What if she had discovered it one day and opened it and found what was in it? Would that have been less jarring than Scott's news today had been?

"So, the first favor was asking me about Alex's Valium prescription. What's the second?"

"I was hoping you'd give *me* a script for Valium, so I can take it over to Two Brothers' and have it filled."

He didn't reply.

"I want to see," she explained, "what Alex would have experienced there. I want to understand why she went all the way over there for it."

"Controlled substance," he said. "How about I call you in a script for something else over there? Want a prescription-grade vitamin?"

"I need to see what happens with a Valium script," she said, fibbing.

"Because you need to know if they ask you for ID and all that," he replied.

"Yes, yes, that's it. Just a *small* script?"

"You're not my patient," he said. "And what you're doing might be called 'drug seeking,'" he answered. "But I suppose I do know your reputation—what it is you *really* seek in your spare time—and I'm thinking I can probably trust you. Mind if I first look around the systems to see if you've gotten any similar script already? And ask Dr. Griffin to make sure he's not

336

also writing you one?"

"Not at all!" she said, feeling rather like she had scored unexpectedly.

"Okay," he said. "Give me your birthday, your address, the exact spelling of your name."

She did.

"Okay," he said. "I'll call it in to Two Brothers'. If I find you're clean."

She thanked him and hung up.

She looked down the hall and saw Parvus had just one student left waiting. She stood up, shoved her water bottle back into its pocket, and hurried back down the corridor toward his office.

Chapter 30

She had, of course, gotten back to Alex's house before Parvus. She had come pretty much straight home after running into Hank on campus, except for a stop to get a cup of chamomile tea to try to settle herself a little. But Parvus, he would have had to stop home to get what he would need in the morning if he was going to grant her wish that he spend the night at Alex's—not leave her alone.

She didn't pull the car into the garage, instead waiting in the driveway with the car and the heat running.

While Maddy now knew intellectually that Alex had been in the house all along, in her gut she did not like the idea of going back into that house alone. It wasn't so much that she needed someone to formally introduce her to the box ("Alex, this is Maddy—she's heard so much about you!") as that she wasn't sure how to think about the box itself.

Now that she knew, was she supposed to just leave Alex there on a shelf alongside summer and winter hats and holiday garland for the mantle? Or did she take Alex down and call Everett Sophie or Hank or someone and say, "Could you please come pick up your friend?"

Not Hank. Not after having seen him like that, less than an hour before.

She scratched her head and pulled her fingers through her sweaty hair.

Parvus would surely have some primal sense of what to do with this box of Alex's ashes. Maddy would just go with his sensibility. Indeed, it was the few cups of ashes that had once been Alex that made Maddy crave Parvus's rough, raw way. Charon, would he be, understanding how to ferry Alex across the River Styx. Alex had been long dead. But she needed the transport Scott had failed to arrange.

Maddy turned the car's heat down a notch and pulled out her phone to see if she had missed anything. No new texts, no new voicemails. The silence of the jury was making everyone quiet. Josiah, too, had not called. Presumably that meant nothing had happened that day. Just the jury still holed up, doing whatever it was doing. She thought about the possibilities, including the worst possible possibility: mistrial. She would almost take a full acquittal over a mistrial at this point. Living it all over again? No, God, no.

Thank goodness the person coming to see her and spend the night with her thoroughly disliked Hank. That made Parvus's company even more perfect. She did not want anyone who might say something happy and bright about Hank. Was there such a person, she wondered bitterly?

After leaving Parvus's office, she had headed to the parking lot where she had parked that morning. But on her way, she'd come across Hank. He didn't see her. She saw him, however—and he had been flirting with a woman right about Maddy's age, taking the woman's packages to carry for her, smiling at her, the two of them laughing just so . . .

Maddy told herself instantaneously that she was so very glad she hadn't slept with him. His dick must have been in so many women by now, heaven only knew what it carried. And he had been texting Maddy all week, telling her he wanted her while carrying on with this other woman? You'd think he could focus for at least a few weeks. No wonder Alex was thoroughly fed up with him sometimes.

Her phone lit up with a text.

Take you to dinner?

It was from Hank.

She sighed and turned to look out the back of the car for a sign of Parvus. Nothing. It brought her back for an instant to that car on the Brooklyn

Bridge, on her way to meet Whit, when she'd kept turning to see if Philadelphia was right behind her. Her phone dinged again.

Or bring you dinner?

She sighed again. What was she supposed to do with this?

Or have you for dinner?

She dialed him.

"Hey," she said rather coldly.

"What's going on?" Hank asked, seeming to get the tone in her voice.

"Nothing," she said. "Absolutely nothing," she said again.

"Something wrong?"

"I was walking to my car this evening and saw you on campus," she said. "You didn't see me. A little before six."

He didn't say anything.

"You were engaged. Deep in conversation. A very pleasurable conversation, by the look of it."

He still said nothing.

"Is she a grad student or junior faculty? Or undergrad? But old enough to drink at least?" Maddy asked.

He still didn't say anything.

She sighed, audibly. She did a quick survey of her head and realized that what she hated was not what he had *done*, not what she had *seen*, but how it made her *feel*. So damned inferior. She was too successful, too good a catch, to feel this inferior. What was this, junior high again? Why did she have to go this route? Why could she not just course-correct her stupid brain and genuinely say "fuck him"?

"I'm sorry you saw that," he finally said.

"You're sorry I *saw* it," said Maddy. "Not sorry that it *happened*."

"No, you shithead," he replied, startling her. "I'm not sorry it happened. You think you and I are exclusive? Even though you don't answer half my texts? Even though all we do is—"

"I'm not *interested* in being exclusive," she replied, curtly.

"I didn't think so," he said, "given that you told me you that you like lots of ice cream flavors."

"One at a fucking time," she answered. "One. At. A. Fucking. Time."

"Why?" he asked. "You said you're not interested in being exclusive."

She didn't reply.

"Never tried a Neapolitan life?" he asked.

They spent a good minute with neither of them saying anything. She

340

could picture herself poised, right arm up, stone in hand, looking into his glass house, where she could see this woman from the path, and Sarah, and Hank . . . Only the metaphor was all backwards.

She sighed. In response, he spoke again:

"I'm not sure what you want me to say. That you didn't see what you saw? That she was my niece or something? That I was just being polite to someone visiting campus? I'm not going to lie to you. Because I have nothing to be ashamed of. As even Alex would have to admit, much as she might get annoyed with me. I'm not going to lie to you."

"Good," she said. She meant it, and she sounded like she meant it.

"Also, you gotta understand, Maddy, I never know what is happening with you. And it seems clear that what's happening is that as long as you're into me, we're never going to fuck. And I'll be perfectly honest—yes, you give great head, but it's all getting a little old. I'd like to have some hope of eventually getting laid. Well and properly laid. The hope is what matters."

She said nothing. She could feel the defense mechanisms in her up at full guard. She could hardly blame him for getting tired of her unpredictability. Everyone eventually got tired of her unpredictability. Women friends enjoyed her spontaneity until they decided it meant unreliability. Men found her inconsistencies hot, right up until they found her chilly.

"Maddy?" he asked, his tone now more of a plead. "I would never have done that to you on purpose. I didn't mean to hurt your feelings. I am genuinely sorry I hurt your feelings."

She still didn't answer.

"You know I felt the same way about finding Parvus there that night, and then again the next morning. I get it."

The difference, she thought, was that she had never been interested in fucking Parvus. Should she say it?

"It's just human," he said, cutting off her thought, "to feel like you want to be *the one*. You want to win."

What was that her heart felt like? Cheese fermenting.

"Thanks," she said. She thought about what he was saying. Then she said again, "Thanks."

"Look, you know, you have to get what I'm talking about," he said. "A bird in the hand . . ."

"What can I say, Hank?" she replied with a sigh. "I just want your hand in my bush."

"Christ," he said, "you are really something."

She didn't reply.

"Do you want me to come over?"

"Not tonight," she said. Then she hastily added, "Not because of this. I found out—I found out something upsetting today, and I'm trying to figure out what to do."

"Are you okay?"

"I'll be okay. I asked someone to come spend the night here—*not sexual.* Just so I'm not alone tonight."

"You know anytime you need, I'll do that for you. *Not sexual.*"

"Yeah, right."

She saw Parvus's headlights pull in behind her. She hit the remote to the garage door to pull the car in and put the car in drive.

"Gotta go," she told Hank.

"Call me tonight if you need to talk," he replied.

Maddy parked the car in the garage, hit the remote again, and met Parvus on the driveway, her backpack slung over her right shoulder.

"Thank you," she said, as he got out of his car. "I mean, thank you for helping me."

"No problemo," he answered gruffly.

He opened the back seat of his car and handed her a bag of groceries. The end of a baguette was sticking out of the top.

"I wasn't sure if you had food for me," Parvus told her. "So I got enough for both of us. Not to be rude."

He went to the trunk of his car, opened it, and pulled out a gym bag. He handed that to her also as they approached the front door of the house. He pulled a small kit out of his pocket and started picking the lock.

"I have a key, you know," Maddy said, balancing her backpack, the groceries, and his gym bag.

"This is just as quick," he said, opening the door.

He gestured for her to precede him and closed the door behind them. He latched the door with the device the locksmith had installed, emitting an odd look of satisfaction at being the one to do the latch. She put the bags on the bench and took off her coat. She reached out to open the coat closet and then paused.

She looked at Parvus, and he looked at her. The look in his eyes, she thought, was one of a child temporarily lost—geographically, or in terms of social expectations, or something. She wondered if she looked the same.

After a moment, he took off his own coat, opened the closet, and hung it up. He took hers and did the same, and then he closed the closet door.

"I'm hungry, and I'm cold!" he said loudly, as if this would scare any ghosts. He took the sack of groceries to the living room, putting it down on the couch. Then he knelt in front of the fireplace, quickly set up wood and kindling for a fire, and lit it, blowing on the edge to help it catch. He took the blanket off the back of the couch, laid it on the floor, and started unpacking the food onto the blanket in front of the fire.

Maddy went to the kitchen to get some plates, napkins, utensils, and two glasses of water. When she returned, she saw he had a bottle of red wine, so she went back to the kitchen and grabbed a corkscrew and two more water glasses, figuring they'd be more stable than wineglasses on the blanket lying atop the rug.

He made them each a plate with a chunk of baguette, slices of salami, cheese, olives, and pickles. The cheese he cut up with his pocketknife, which he also used to peel an orange. He divided the fruit into its sections, giving her half of them and himself the other half.

She sat down on the blanket and leaned up against the couch, stretched her legs out, and started to eat. But before he started to eat, Parvus got up. He went to the coat closet and brought back the box that Maddy understood to contain Alex's ashes. He laid it down on the blanket, amid the open packages of salami and cheese.

"You sure it's the right one?" Maddy asked, eating a piece of the cheese. (Some kind of Swiss, she thought.)

"I took off the big rubber bands and looked inside," he said, rolling a small pickle in a piece of salami and eating it. "Can't imagine why Alex would have been keeping a box of ashes in the coat closet. So it must be her."

He sat back down, leaning against a part of the couch a few feet away from Maddy, and poured them each a glass of wine.

"To Alex," he said, raising his glass.

"To Alex," she answered, raising hers.

They both drank a little and stared at the fire.

"Why the hell would you hang out with Hank Merriman?" Parvus asked now with a tone Maddy took as genuine disgust. She wondered if he had seen Maddy almost run into him on campus after leaving Parvus's office.

"Alex used to do the same," Maddy said, with a nod toward the box. "Why did *she*?"

"I don't know," he answered. "I guess she saw something worthwhile in him."

"What do you have so against him?"

"He broke the heart of one of my post-docs," Parvus replied, eating a piece of salami with a slice of the cheese. "And I had no idea what to do with that. I couldn't very well offer her a shoulder to cry on—not appropriate—so I just, well, found it rather frustrating. Poor way to treat someone. And made me not know how to treat her. And Alex used to complain about him. Unreliable."

"I don't attempt to rely on him. That's my secret."

Parvus harrumphed at her. And Maddy realized her claim was untrue. She drank a little more wine to hold off eating more. She was trying not to gobble up all his food, to make sure he got as much as he wanted before she ate all she wanted. But the salami was good—dry, not too greasy—and the cheese well-chosen to go with it.

"Why do I hang out with Hank?" she asked aloud, as if asking herself. "Why do I? Well, when he makes me feel good, he makes me feel *very* good. I expect Alex felt the same in some way, although not sexually."

She watched the biggest log in the fireplace start to let off steam.

"The thing about a Lothario," she continued, "is that he knows how to focus. That's what makes him successful, I think. When he's focused on you, it feels quite like the sun. And I try not to get in situations where he can make me feel dark." She took another piece of salami and ate it. This pig had died for a good cause. She thought some more about Hank, about how he had made her feel dark that day. "You know what my motto in life is, Parvus? It is this: *If you're pessimistic, you're never disappointed.* I came up with that when I was fifteen."

Parvus snorted.

"That's a good one," he said. "I may have to use it." He took the metal poker and adjusted the fire a little. He sat back down after a moment.

"That morning when the locksmith came by," Maddy said, still staring at the fire, "after you told me about how it was with you and Alex, I asked Hank the next time he was with me to have no words."

Parvus squirmed uncomfortably, as if all his muscles had cramped.

"No, listen to me," she said, reaching out to him in a gesture of insistence. "The good thing about Hank is that he's like a tool, in a way. He doesn't mind being a sexual tool. So I tried it, to see if I could understand what you meant about Alex and the altered state."

"And?"

"Well, I was also two sheets to the wind, but it was—I think—I think I had some sense of what you meant. It was like he wasn't there, in a way."

Maddy was thinking of what Alex had asked Joseph on her last trip to New York—did it matter who we were having sex with? Alex must have been talking about Parvus.

"It was like Hank wasn't there. And neither was I," she said.

Parvus looked at her intensely.

"Yes, that's right," he said. "The person becomes a vector of something more."

"Like your playing," she answered. She realized it might sound like a saccharine compliment, but she meant it simply descriptively—his playing functioned as a vector of something more. "I think maybe sex can be a way to see more."

"My performance won't give you a disease," he mumbled.

"Did Hank give your student a disease?!"

"No. Not that I know of. I just mean a piano is never going to infect you. Never going to get you pregnant."

"Seems like it could break your heart."

"You *are* pessimistic, my girl," he replied. "Too much pessimism for your age. Too much trying to avoid being disappointed?"

They both stared at the fire now. It felt slightly intoxicating to her. The orange of the flames, she thought, looked quite a lot like a sunset, the thick trunk of wood in front of it like the earth, the flames of the tongue licking over the log's horizon. She started thinking about the imagination it must have taken for the revolutionary astronomers—Copernicus and Brahe and Kepler and Galileo—to have realized it was *not the sun* that moved. To have realized God *hadn't* built the universe in the way that would have made sense, with his own people in the motionless center.

How hard it could be to *see* what was real until you *knew* what was real. Dr. Miller's rhetorical question.

She broke the long silence, finally, with the thought.

"It must be difficult in physics, today more than it has ever been, to *see* before you know what you're looking for. And then do you just see it because you are expecting it? Not because it is really there?"

"You sound like the goddamned Gnat," he replied.

She was surprised he knew of the Gnat—but then, of course, Alex would have mentioned him. Maddy felt a sudden well of frustration that she had made no progress that day figuring out where the Gnat would have been the weekend of Alex's death. She couldn't figure out if there was a conference he might have gone to in San Francisco that weekend. If Alex *did* die on that weekend.

It wasn't clear to her how she'd ever figure this out. The police could. Maybe. They could ask questions she could not, call up records she could not. Had they bothered to look into anything? Had they even tried to figure out exactly what day she had died?

She had called Wolf earlier in the day, trying to get through her to-do list from the night before. Wolf told her that if Alex's note had been dated, the police detective reading it to him had not said anything about a date. And he thought his counterpart would have mentioned if it had been dated.

So that approach, too, was a dead end.

So many dead ends.

"Do you think," Parvus asked her, poking at the fire again, "that *your* field, history, is any better than mine at seeing something before you know what you're looking for? Do you think historians are somehow better at this business of investigation than physicists? How do you know what to look for?"

She didn't answer. Her silence was not because she didn't find the question interesting. Were humans easier to study than law-abiding physical processes one could literally not see? Yet what could one see in the mind of another? And she could not ever see Alex's death. It was all just as indirect as Parvus's work.

"There was one time," Parvus said, interrupting her thoughts, "when my little group was working on a deadline and my graduate student brought me a sandwich. I had asked him to get me tuna on rye. When he came back, I didn't look down at the sandwich he gave me. I just picked it up from the napkin and started eating it. I knew it was tuna on rye. And at first, it *was* tuna on rye."

Maddy was trying to figure out where this was going.

"After a few bites," he continued, "I realized this was *very* odd-tasting tuna on rye. I finally looked down. It was peanut butter on whole wheat."

He suddenly reached out and laid his two hands on the top of Alex's box. Looking at his hands laid out this way, Maddy saw for the first time the length of his fingers and the thick musculature evident on the back of his hands. The interossei seemed particularly prominent.

"One might conclude from that experience that one finds what one expects to find," Parvus observed. "I did, after all, quite clearly taste tuna on rye. Subjectively, it *was* tuna on rye. But eventually I found the presence of the peanut butter and the objective absence of rye."

She leaned forward on her haunches and ran her tips of her index fingers over the muscles on the back of his hand for a minute. They were remarkable. Parvus could tell from the way she was tracing out what lay beneath his skin that she had not seen a hand developed quite like this before. He held still so she could do what she needed.

She sat back and pulled his hands toward her, turning his hands over now, palm side up on her thighs. She took her middle fingers' tips and traced out his lumbricales, the muscles extending from his palm to the bases of his fingers.

"What's my fortune, O Gypsy?" he asked.

She gave him his hands back.

"To play for this unworthy soul," she answered.

He ate a slice of orange.

"Yes, well, first," he said, "I have to spend a couple of hours on a manuscript. You will need to give me a table with good light. Did Alex have a working pencil sharpener?"

"Yes," said Maddy. "I'll get it for you in a minute. After food. The dining room table will work well. We can turn the ceiling light all the way up for you. I use that space for work sometimes."

"What are you going to work on?" he asked.

He tore off another piece of baguette and handed it to her.

"I don't know." She let out a sad sigh.

"A manuscript, or grading," he said, shaking his finger at her. "(A) a manuscript, or (B) grading. I'm a full prof, and those are *still* the two choices."

"There's a research project I can't seem to . . ."

She did not finish the sentence.

"Finish it or abandon it!" he advised, first throwing his hands up in the air in a gesture of defeat, and then pouring them each an inch more wine. "You're an assistant prof? Non-tenure-track?"

She nodded.

"Finish it or abandon it," he said again. "You can't afford a knot."

She looked at him like a lost dog.

"Have you tried going to sleep?" he asked.

"I don't understand. Going to sleep?"

He stood up and added a log to the fire. Then he sat back down on the floor, leaning against the couch, a little closer to her, she thought.

"You look tired all the time. So try to go to sleep. Or work on something else. That's a classic way to solve a research problem. I've gotten many a fine paper out of a long nap."

"I'm not a scientist like you," Maddy answered.

"You're a social scientist. What's the problem? I mean, what's the problem you're working on?"

Maddy stood up and went to the foyer. She came back with her backpack, sat back down, opened it, and handed him the yellow legal pad with the Alex timeline and pages and pages of notes.

He took his soft eyeglass case out of his breast pocket, pulled out his reading glasses, and put them on, putting the case back in his pocket. He tried looking at the pad and groaned at the poor light. Standing up, he turned on the arched lamp that hung out over the couch. He sat down on the couch, just below the light, and began to read through her timeline and notes, page by page by page.

Finally, he handed it back down to her. By then, she had polished off the salami and olives and was poking through the grocery bag to see if he had brought dessert. He had: coconut macaroons. She took the notepad from him and opened the package of macaroons.

"I take back what I said," Parvus told her. "What you do isn't science."

She took a handful of the coconut cookies and passed him the container. He looked them over through his glasses, ate one, and then another. He licked his fingers clean and wiped his hand on his pants. Then he put his big right hand on top of her head.

She held still. She felt like she was a jar he might try to open. Would he put his left hand on her neck, as if it were the neck of a bottle?

"I'll help you after I've worked on my own manuscript," he said.

"Help me how?" Maddy asked, not moving her head.

"I'll play you Alex's music. You can try to not think. She used to not think."

"How did she not think?"

"Swimming, mostly," he answered. "She learned to swim indoors, too, under the piano or on the couch."

"But how?"

"You're a historian of science, woman. Think about it. Galileo, Newton, Einstein—they knew that we could not see what was real if we were bound by what we could see with our eyes. To know the real, you have to *allow the possibility of the unreal.* Or at least the unseen."

He kept holding onto her head with his strong hand.

"I would wager, Shanks, that you're like a lot of academics. You're an intellectual because you've seen rationality as an antidote to the spiritual—you see rationality as a repellant of hoo-ha."

He took his hand off her head suddenly and ate two more cookies. Her head felt strangely larger released from his firm grip. Like her skull was

348

bouncing back.

"You want me to *give in* to irrational hoo-ha?" she asked.

"For fuck's sake, no, of course not," he replied. "Give in to the possible realities, the ones that your mind ordinarily protects you from seeing. In this case, I would say stop thinking about timelines and actions and sources. They are getting you nowhere. You're focused on the wrong place."

"What's left?" she asked.

"What's left, Shanks? Tell me what's left when you take away timelines and actions and sources."

She did not answer. She was trying to think of what would be. If all the dates and people and actions were removed, or at least paused, what would remain for her to *see*?

"Color?" she asked.

"Yes, okay. Light waves. But I'll accept 'color.'"

"Scents?"

She remembered suddenly how she had known that the man who attacked her that night in Philly had recently been at the hospital—the smell of the soap from the hospital soap dispensaries, the same smell that was on Wolf's hands when he came back from seeing his wife.

"Scent. You a bloodhound?" Parvus asked.

She tried to focus again.

"Sound," she said aloud, "but then it's all *waves*. Light waves, air waves carrying scents, soundwaves."

"It's all waves, Alex!" Parvus said, laughing once sharply and tapping on the box with his foot. "Do you hear this? It's all waves. Shanks's found what you found. She's swimming!"

"But that doesn't answer *anything*, Parvus," Maddy said, in a kind of whine.

"You're thinking again. You need to stop thinking. Know, don't think."

He stood up and stretched his arms in the air and let out a growl of a yawn. He took off his reading glasses, put them back in the case, and put the case back in his pocket.

"Stop thinking, woman! Then maybe you can figure out how Alex ended up in this box. Now, get me the pencil sharpener. And make us some tea. Can't do good work on a manuscript on wine. Is that why you're not getting publications in?"

Chapter 31

As Maddy watched Parvus set up the living room the way he wanted it, she asked him if he wanted a whiskey now. After two hours of work at the dining table, he had suddenly stacked up his papers and put them away and moved with an air of purpose to the living room, as if he had an appointment there. He'd rotated the couch so that it was no longer in line with the piano bench but perpendicular to it. Then he'd moved the couch some more to get it just about three feet away from the piano, lined up right next to as if hugging it. He went to the solarium with equal purpose, gathered up the bottle lights, and set them up around the living room, plugging each in, bringing them to life.

Finally, he took Alex's box, placing it carefully on the floor under the piano about two feet forward of the pedals. After demanding an extension cord, he unplugged and repositioned one of the bottle lights to stand next to Alex's box, as if the bottle were a foot soldier guarding the tomb of a dignitary.

"Do you want something to drink?" Maddy asked again. "Should I have a drink?"

"You think alcohol relaxes the mind," Parvus said. "But maybe it just muddies it. Try swimming in clear waters for a change."

She went to the bedroom to get a pillow and heavier blanket than was on the couch as her body was getting cold from the late hour. The pillow with Wolf's shirt on it was still on her bed; she'd forgotten to put the shirt away that morning. She took that wrapped pillow and the warm top quilt from the bed.

Parvus was by that point sitting at the piano waiting for her. She was surprised to see him so patient. She settled herself down on the couch, facing him. She wanted to turn on her side, toward the pillow, to catch the smell of Wolf and baseball, but she figured Parvus was expecting her visible attention at least a while.

"Words are how people like you and Alex think," he said, seemingly undisturbed by the use of the present tense for Alex. "So reject words. Don't try fighting them—you can't fight words. That's why they're used for laws and treaties, tombstones and manuscripts. Just turn them into images and make them disappear that way. That's what she did."

"I will try," Maddy answered.

He got up and turned off the last lamp in the room and came back to the piano. There was now only the light of the bottles and the fire. He began to play something she thought she had never heard. She recognized her brain trying to name the piece or at least the composer and laughed at herself. The first thing she was doing was thinking about names—words!

She realized she must have laughed aloud when Parvus looked straight at her and smiled. He paused, walked over to her, clasped her head in his hands, put his lips near her forehead, and yelled, "Shut up, frontal lobe!"

He tucked the blanket around her, went back to the piano and, after a moment, began playing again. Maddy tried not to think about anything in particular and immediately started making lists of things she needed to get done: read Josiah's draft proposal; get Scott the codicil; check in with her billboard lawyer to make sure he had her new address.

She tried focusing on the image of her brain in her skull and then on Parvus's music. Now she found herself trying to anticipate the next note—not easy, as what he was playing was so different from his usual repertoire of classical solos. This was slow, modern, more chromatic than lyrical. She wondered whether he was simply making it up as he went along. But that did not seem to be the case.

Having the blue bottle lights here in the living room felt so different. The room was not big, but it was so much bigger than the solarium, and without the nearby windows to reflect the lights relatively intensely, the sense of being in the night sky shifted. She felt more as if she were out in a night desert, the sky far away and vast. She was breathing deeply, consciously, to try to enjoy the calm of Parvus's odd presence and the blue of the room. Now he was playing a note repeatedly, slowly, with his right hand, sweeping his arm slowly forward and back to cross the key, bringing the note forward each time it fell back. Now he brought his left arm forward, sweeping a single key, pulling his arm back, bringing it forward again, sweeping again.

Left hand.

Left.

Right.

Right.

Right.

Left.

And then she could see it—he was Charon in his vessel, slowly paddling across the River Styx—left side, left, then right, right, right, left, managing the current as he crossed. With Alex seated just about two feet in front of him, at his feet, in the bottom of the boat. The two of them silent in their journey together. No words, just the sound of the paddle meeting the water, the water meeting the side of the boat, the paddle coming back to the air and then meeting the water again.

Maddy closed her eyes and saw Alex swimming silently in the Atlantic night, her hair pulled into a tight braid, her black wetsuit hugging her body, white moonlight, the stars above, the caps of the waves peaking like the meringue tips of a lemon pie, the water lapping at itself, then lapping at her, her arm coming down on the water, the sound of the water, the waves pressing against the shore like a child pressing up against her mother's leg as she speaks to another mother and reaches her hand down to calm the little head, to say, "in a moment, in a moment, in a moment," the way the waves breaking on the sand say, too, "in a moment, in a moment, in a moment." The wave of water meeting the beach, turning into a wave of sound, barely lit by a wave of light from the moon.

And there was Whit—or was it now Parvus? —near Alex, equally silent, barely swimming, mostly floating, lost in the briny sex of the ocean, looking at Alex, seeing her swimming, feeling the envelope-lip spot where warm flesh meets cold water, the sense of enormity of the ocean, the ocean on the planet in the universe of stars. The closest star now so bright, Maddy's mother pulling off her little girls' shirts to send them into the edge of the water—the ocean saying, "in a moment, in a moment," her mother saying, "be careful, Maddy, not too deep" —but the deep is where the ocean shifts so delightfully, from pulling and pulling in, to lifting, holding.

And now Parvus had changed the rhythm of his paddling, as they were now approaching the other shore, with Maddy's mother there in a long skirt, her hair in a tight braid, to meet the boat, to take hold of the end and hold it steady against the shore as Alex crawled forward on the bottom of the vessel, holding the sides of the boat, coming to the front, standing to step ashore, while Parvus held the boat in place, his paddle used as a wedge, then as a rudder, then as a paddle again, to push forward again, to push again against the shore. And then, with Alex alighted, he pushed slowly back, turning his boat to return, turning away from Maddy's mother and Alex, turning back to the other side—

Now to take Wilhelm as his passenger? She could see Wilhelm waiting on the far shore for Parvus, his leather doctor's bag in his right hand, his black wool coat draped over his hunched body. Parvus paddled toward him, lifting his hand in a small gesture of acknowledgement, Wilhelm giving off a small nod in return. Maddy had a sense of the blackness of the water, black not from the depth but from the substance, something that would not reflect light, as if it had no surface but was only depth itself.

She opened her eyes and saw Parvus looking at her. He was sitting on the bench not playing, not moving. She struggled to fully open her eyes and focus.

"I would rather," Maddy said to him, pausing for a second, "I would rather you not take Alex away just yet—"

"She is still with us here," he replied. "Close your eyes again and see."

Maddy realized for a moment her fists were raised slightly above her abdomen, as if she were a child wincing from a touch to the belly. As if she were holding on to the sides of a ladder, steadying herself. She closed her eyes, her fists remaining as they were and, as Parvus began to play again, she could see she would climb up the ladder from the cool courtyard to the rampart of the old castle. There, up on the rampart, dirt had collected over millennia from the winds, and seeds had blown up too, and lush green grass and short weeds with yellow flowers had grown, and Parvus had laid the blanket from the couch for the meal. Alex was sitting in a sundress, a straw hat on her head, laughing at something in the sunlight, one hand atop her hat to keep it from blowing off in a slight breeze, the green hills the same green hills of the dream of Wolf's roof, the bed on the roof. Alex was reaching out to Maddy with something, a pastry dotted with powdered sugar and browned bits of toasted coconut. Maddy's mouth watered to see it and to see on the blanket, too, a plate of orange sections, each peeled of the white pith, each so plump, the fat and moist juice follicles pushing at each section's translucent skin—

So, too, Alex's body on the blanket, no, on the stainless steel table, peeled of the rind of her moist clothing, peeled of the pith of her damp underwear, the fat and muscle of her legs and arms and torso, swollen and pushing plump at her epidermis, ready for the pathologist's pocketknife, the pathologist reading off to the medical student scribe his findings, preparing to cut, Maddy understanding they would dispose first of the gut, to avoid putrefaction and flies—

But it was a *modern* room, of course, not a medieval anatomical theater, not a place where the dirt had blown in and the grass had grown, a *modern*, enclosed, climate-controlled room, so no rush, no rush. Yet the pathologist looked at his watch and saw he would be late soon to the lecture by the historian, and not very much of interest to see here, just what one would expect given alcohol and benzodiazepine and a note of resignation; in the lungs, water that would have damaged the surfactant, making breathing impossible even if the water had not taken the place of the air, perhaps some aspiration of stomach contents as the victim choked in the process of drowning, vomiting, breathing in the vomit; the heart would have accelerated and then perhaps gone into an arrhythmia and, if the consciousness was still operational, then there might have been some conscious panic, all the while with the brain saying *breathe, breathe!*, pulling perhaps more of the water in, flooding the cove that was Alex's lungs, her heart now in the hands of the time-crunched pathologist, the heart so still and firm—

—no, not a heart again? Not a heart.

"Wolf!" she yelled, sitting up, and Parvus stopped playing.

He came over and sat down next to her, sitting atop the edge of the blanket, pushing himself gently into the crook of her side formed between her pelvis and her ribs. She grabbed his right forearm in her wrist and said, "I'm sorry, I think I fell asleep."

He said nothing but took his left hand and brushed the hair off her forehead, stroking her head just as her grandfather had done during a fever, and she felt very small in the face of his large, strong hand.

"If I had gone swimming with her," she said to him, with a look of some panic, "I might have stopped her drowning."

"Yes," he said. "But you did not know she was going to go to the lake. I would have stopped her, too. I would have stopped her."

"I should have stopped my mother and my sister from getting in the car."

"But you could not know whatever you now think you should have," he answered, stroking her head again. "Time goes forward, and we have to go with it."

"As a wave," she said, gulping.

"As if a wave."

He used his left hand now to gently pull her tight grip off his right forearm. He laid her hands flat down on her belly.

"As if waves and particles all at once," he sighed, "time takes us forward."

"And the particles are . . . "

"Us, I suppose? What do you think the particles are?" he asked.

She looked at the blue light of the room and saw now that the last embers of the fire caused an orange glow to push lightly at the blue, as if the dawn were just beginning to break in the house. As if the house were the earth, a planet in motion, no matter the sense of still. She looked at his face looking at her face and could see yet his life in the pith that held his epidermis to his dermis to his muscle to his ligaments to his bone to his marrow.

"I think the particles must be the people, moving forward always," she answered.

"Yes?"

"Part of the wave of time but not the wave?"

"You must picture then the people," he said. "Or feel them? Smell them? No words. Do shut up, O Frontal Lobe. Do shut up," he said again, as if shooing out of the room a needy dog.

He got up and went to the kitchen, coming back with a glass of cold water for her. She sat up and drank, and he took the glass from her as she lay back down. He moved to the other end of the couch, pushing back the end of the blanket to her knees, lifting her feet onto his lap, starting to rub the balls of her feet and then her arches, slowly and gently.

"Are you not going to play more?" she asked.

"I will once I know what," he answered. "I believe you need your own music, not Alex's, now."

"But I want to understand what happened to Alex. I can stop it from happening again."

He sighed. He grabbed her ankles firmly in his hands as if she were a rabbit caught by this hunter, caught by the back legs. He shook her legs and feet a little.

"Whatever you do understand will die with you, Madeleine. If it ever comes, it will also go! Don't think knowing it will somehow keep you or anyone else from death."

She wondered in a flash where Wilhelm was, where Wolf was. She pulled her feet sharply away from Parvus, under the blanket, bringing her knees up to her chest, and she rolled over onto her side. There it was on the pillow, just a little bit of the smell of Wolf left, just a little bit of mustard. She pulled the blanket closer around her.

Parvus returned to the bench and began to play. Her brain cells quickly made the call: Beethoven, Sonata 8, the one called *Pathétique*.

Pathetic: yes, that was what she was. Pathetic. Unable to acknowledge the futility, playing the same game of hopscotch over and over, knowing she would lose again. Running to the same tree, knowing she could still climb only so high, for the tree would not grow at the speed she was growing. Dancing, spinning, her father telling her to stop, stop all this motion, sit down.

"What if it is *not* that?" Parvus asked her now, loudly, above the rapid jumping of his hands.

"What if it is not what?"

"Not that sadness," he answered. "*Pathétique.* That's not *pity*. You have got the wrong definition of '*pathétique.*' I can see it in your face."

She stretched out her legs and sat up, going over to the bench. She sat down next to him, hunched. He suddenly stopped playing, stood up, moved her to the center of the bench and sat back down, wrapping himself around her, one leg on each side of her, his front up against her back.

"Hold onto my legs," he said.

She did as he suggested, putting her hands on his thighs, just above his knees. He started playing again where he had left off.

"'Pathetic' can also mean simply 'of the emotions,'" he explained as he finished the first movement and slowly began the second.

She was acutely aware of being tired of his lessons. Not frustrated with them, simply worn out. He played and played, as if working his way through math-set problems, as if showing her a more elegant way to solve for *x*. As if he were showing her a simple math proof, as if she didn't know even one way to do the proof, for she didn't know what she was trying to prove. On and on went his playing. She leaned her head back on his shoulder and closed her eyes, loosening her hold on his legs.

For a moment, his nose became caught in her hair. She realized she must smell foreign to him, as he did to her. And what was it that he smelled of?

Salami from the dinner. Meaty, cured.

Pencil graphite from sharpening his pencils. A little metallic.

Smoke from having tended the fire. Wood turning to ash.

She leaned forward a little and laid her hands on top of his, catching them the way she imagined one might have caught a departing train in the nineteenth century. She quickly expanded her fingers so as to wrap them around his hands, to hold on. (A tiny girl standing on her grandfather's feet, holding his hands, as he dances her about the room.)

"You see, Shanks," he said as he kept playing, momentarily again sticking his nose in her hair, this time quite purposefully like a dog checking under a pile of leaves, "*there* is a nice particle-wave duality."

She understood he was talking about their hands, her hands distinct from his yet carried along with his production of sound, as if all one.

"You have latched onto dates and actions and sources, why?"

"Because" —she said, answering as if asked *what does two plus two equal?*—"dates and actions and sources are *knowable*. Objective points. Relatively objective points."

"But if it is neither wave nor particle but already always both?"

"I know, I know. The things that are subjective *do matter*. The seemingly objective is not the whole. The subjective is a necessary part of the light we see. It is the difference between the light itself and the color we see. The color we think we see."

"So, what is subjective in history? What is the thing that matters in history—your discipline—but is forever subjective?"

"The reading of character," she answered. "Character. The motivating force. Motivation. That which we know is always there, always pulling us down at the same constant rate, yet always invisible, impossible to show."

"Gravity!" he replied, as if she had truly taught him something.

He finished the piece, and said again, with satisfaction, "Gravity. *Character* is *gravity*. The motive force."

She thought of Alex's body, once drowned, sinking to the floor of the lake. Her eyes almost certainly open. Did she land dorsal or ventral, this fish of a woman? And how did her mother land?

Why did Alex keep turning into her mother tonight? The brown hair, pulled back in a braid sometimes? The approximate age of the subject at death?

Maddy let go of Parvus's hands, turned her body around on the bench, swung her legs over his, pulled herself properly onto his lap, wrapped her arms over his shoulders, and held on to him in a hungry embrace. He wrapped his long arms around her, pulling her close. She could feel the heat of his body like the heat of a fire that has taken the log.

Her breathing soon matched up with his, chest against chest. Slow, deep, full. No water in the lungs. He put a comforting hand on the back of her head, to lay her head down on his shoulder. He had been across the wide river this long day, over and over, but not in it, never in it. And here he was now, Charon, done with his day's work on the black water, come home to his daughter. His small and grateful daughter, who minded not at all that he smelled lightly of proximity to death: a little salami; a little graphite; a little wood smoke.

"Shush," he said. "Shush."

Chapter 32

Hank opened the door to Alex's house without thinking to ring the bell. He was clutching in his right hand a short batch of yellow roses dotted with baby's breath, wrapped in white tissue paper and held together with a shiny green ribbon embossed in white with the name of the florist: *Flowers by Jon Peter*. As this was an entrance Hank had made so many times with Alex— flowers by Jon Peter in the right hand, left hand free to open the door, a feeling of chagrin mixed with a sense of being misunderstood—he did not think to ring. Alex had almost always left the door unlocked, at least until going to bed, sometimes all night. And, because he had driven over in a long meditation on what Alex had helped him see about himself, he wasn't thinking of the present.

The sudden jolt of disorientation upon opening the front door came to him not just from finding Maddy (and not Alex) there, but finding Maddy in a pretty yellow cotton dress, matching the flowers in his hand, on her knees. She was just inside the front door in the foyer, praying the rosary with Alex's housekeeper.

Although they looked up and saw him, Mrs. Hannigan and Maddy did not get up off their knees or even pause in their duet of words—"Holy Mary, Mother of God, pray for us sinners, now and at the hour of our death, Amen"—but Maddy, with a quick upward glance at Hank, held up a finger in a gesture indicating he should stay quiet. She then pointed outside and flashed five fingers at him twice.

He read it right: "Give us ten minutes."

He backed out and closed the door. Maddy could hear him walk down the path, toward his car.

Maddy put both hands back on the rosary and kept speaking the words of the Hail Mary. She was observing the usual steady cadence. But now she nudged her left-hand fingers forward a bit on the loop of the rosary, to feel how close they were to the next Glory Be. Pretty close. She assumed her brain would kick in just in time as it had on the last, to say the right thing for the next Mystery when it was time. They were observing the Sorrowful Mysteries, given that it was Friday.

They were by now well passed the opening salvo, the Agony in the Garden—the suffering of Christ the night before he would be killed. Maddy had hoped that speaking of the anticipation of one's death would not set Mrs. Hannigan off on another tirade of tears about Alex's death. On the driveway, just after she'd arrived, Mrs. Hannigan had collapsed into sobbing right after Maddy had introduced herself and thanked Mrs. Hannigan for coming and helping her understand Alex's last days.

But, no. Maddy's naming of the Agony in the Garden, just like the rest of the rosary ritual, had done what it always seemed to do—sent the devout Catholic woman down into a mindless, prayerful obedience, one that required no thought, no reflection, no actual agony. Mrs. Hannigan just plugged along on the beads as if buying gas for the religion that was her car. Knowing the rosary would probably do this for Mrs. Hannigan was exactly why, when Maddy had called Mrs. Hannigan and asked her to please come over and try to remember what might have been unusual when she came to clean that weekend—and Mrs. Hannigan had said she did not want to be back in the house where Alex had lived before suddenly dying—Maddy had offered to pray the rosary with her. It would calm her as a llama does the sheep.

"We can pray for Alex's soul," Maddy had said. "Together."

Mrs. Hannigan would struggle to say no to that. The rule of the rosary was to pray it together. You couldn't cast the spell alone.

Maddy needed to meet Mrs. Hannigan here, not somewhere else, so that she could ask her to move around the house exactly as she would have done on a typical Saturday, to try to remember what was different (if anything) that weekend. Before Mrs. Hannigan arrived, Maddy had put on this conservative cotton dress like a good Catholic girl, adding a complementary cotton cardigan, a light blue number with flecks of yellow and blue in the white buttons. Looking in the mirror before Mrs. Hannigan's arrival, Maddy felt ridiculous, particularly with the prop of the rosary.

So, she had slipped off the underwear she was wearing and stuck it in her top dresser drawer, just to keep her sanity. She knew Liz, at least, would understand. She decided not to move the couch back to its normal place and not to move Alex away from her spot under the piano. It wasn't as if she could hide the piano and put the daybed back anyway. So that part of the room might as well be out of sorts compared to what Mrs. Hannigan would expect.

She did move the blue bottles back from the living room to the solarium so as to leave only one room, as far as she knew, significantly disturbed compared to what Mrs. Hannigan would likely recall . . . Maddy moved her forefinger and thumb to the next bead, starting again the dominant rosary prayer.

"Hail Mary, full of grace, the Lord is with thee, blessed art thou among women, and blessed is the fruit of thy womb, Jesus."

She noticed the pleasant smoothness of the bead between her fingertips. She had dashed out during a break from classes that day to Twin Cities Catholic Supply to get herself this rosary, picking out one that was pretty cheap but looked as if it could be dear. She did not want to offend Mrs. Hannigan's sense of propriety with one of those low-end types made of the cheapest plastic, seemingly held together by recycled dental floss. She had first found one at the store that was glow-in-the-dark, made of that creepy yellow-green plastic. Seeing it, she immediately remembered with a small laugh what had happened one night in the convent dorm in the dark when a girl named Meg had staged a one-woman play with a glow-in-the-dark Blessed Virgin Mary statuette. Too bad Meg had lasted only a week at the convent; they might have been friends.

A saleswoman had come up to Maddy and asked if she could help her, and Maddy said she was sorry for laughing, she was just remembering something from childhood, and she would take this other one, this rosary that was the color of espresso with silver metal loops. Probably hard plastic, the beads, but the texture made it look like they could have been made of decent wood. Eight dollars and ninety-five cents. The clerk had complimented Maddy on her selection. Maddy noticed, as the clerk took the beads from her to ring them up, that she smelled a little like a stale version of Sophie. Powder with a flowery overtone.

Mrs. Hannigan and Maddy had by now covered, too, the second Sorrowful Mystery, the Scourging on the Pillar, with Jesus beaten to a pulp, and the third, the Crowning of Thorns, the dramatic mockery of the once and future king. With the image in her mind of blood dripping down Jesus's forehead from the thorns, Maddy could not help but think of what Hank had told her that night over the Chinese dinner about sexual sadism. The deep cruelty being the chief source of excitement. How strange Catholics were to pray at the feet of a God tied and tortured. Who else worshipped a beaten God?

And how strange that, just a moment after this thought had come to Maddy, Hank had walked in, completely unexpectedly, holding a short bunch of flowers. Yellow roses. Not red, not pink, but yellow, matching this funny dress, as if he were here to take her to prom? She'd been able to smell the roses as she stood there with the breeze coming in behind him. Why had he come over?

Mrs. Hannigan and Maddy said in unison now, "Glory be to the Father, and to the Son, and to the Holy Spirit, Amen."

Mrs. Hannigan glanced at Maddy hopefully, and sure enough, Maddy's memory kicked in exactly where it was needed. Maddy said aloud, "The fourth Mystery, the Carrying of the Cross, Jesus having been beaten and crowned with thorns is given his cross to carry to the mount."

Mrs. Hannigan smiled at Maddy in approval. Only one more Mystery to go after this, and Maddy could remember that one ahead of time because it was easy: Dying on the Cross. Knowing she would not struggle for that one, Maddy could free herself fully to think of other things, the way she always had when praying the rosary as required, first by her parents and then by the sisters. New York potato chips, thin and soaked in salt. The mental crouch involved in doing a back flip. The way her lowest vertebra seemed to be reaching for her labia whenever she was kneeling like this, so upright. Especially when she wasn't wearing anything under the skirt of her dress . . .

Funny these compact rosary stories were called "mysteries" by Catholics when, in fact, there was no need for thinking, no attempt to discover anything new in this ritual. She had asked Sister Ruth once, "Why are they called 'mysteries' when they are named plainly as specific events?" And Sister had explained that while they seemed like events, they were events that could not be understood with the rational mind. The purpose of these events had to be revealed to us by God, because reason alone would not be able to deduce why God would allow his only son to be so mistreated.

Events that seem plain but are not deducible through conscious reason . . . how weirdly similar an idea to Parvus's? How strange a state Parvus had left her the night before, disoriented and unsure of everything yet somehow clearer about this—but about what? The subjectivity of history—the importance of character—the thing that could not be plainly understood but had instead to be felt, smelled, tasted. Maddy had spent the day trying to remember what she had somehow witnessed in herself the night before, what it was Parvus had said and asked and shown her, what she had learned. The only thing on which she felt clear was that Wolf had led her down the wrong path when he had said to her, about Alex's death, "Forget motivation."

Sure, Wolf had been right that one could come up with a hypothetical motivation for anything between any two people who had had any kind of relationship. But what he had missed was how she still needed to pay attention to character—character as motivating force, the gravity of history, the thing that pulls us each down. Surely Wolf believed in the importance of character?

(She could picture Wilhelm's face at the museum when a woman with dwarfism had come in, the raptor seeing the mouse from a hundred feet above. And Hank's face on the path yesterday, lit up, speaking to that young woman. And Wolf's face when he had knelt before Maddy, under the arrivals and departures board at the 30th Street Station, to ask her to please just let him help her.)

It was the character of Alex that had caused everyone who knew her well to say the same thing—"it doesn't make sense" that she would have killed herself. There was nothing *that* wrong in Alex's life at the time, nothing she could not handle as she had handled everything in her life so far. Then there was Hank's added insistence, again not wrong, that Alex would not have gone swimming with her jewelry on. Plus, Alex had just recently found this new place with Parvus, this new place of insight.

All of which meant only one thing. It wasn't suicide. And it wasn't an accident. So.

There was a thing that happened with scholarship, Liz and Maddy had found independently and then discussed intensely together, where you toil and toil and come to a very interesting conclusion, and then you look back in your notes and you see that you knew this at the beginning. You came back to where you started even if you had forgotten you started there.

It had always been what Scott had told her near the start, though he said only what it could *not* be: not suicide, not an accident. So, how would she figure out who had killed Alex? She knew she wanted Parvus to come back so she could see again. She wanted him to play on the piano whatever composition was on that musical mural near the Chinese restaurant on 10th Street. For reasons she could not ascertain, it felt as if the mural were important—it seemed as if Hank had taken her there specifically because he had known she needed to see a sign of Parvus on that wall. But what was she thinking?

She had gone through today in a half-conscious state that Parvus and that fire had induced last night, wondering at one point if she should even be driving, she felt so on the verge of disassociation. At the Catholic Supply store, watching the customers and clerks, seeing straight through to their characters as if watching them walk behind an X-ray and walk back out, the way she had always done with people, seeing right through them.

The woman with three children in tow, one toddling, one just barely walking, one an infant, and Maddy could see on her face she was coming in the hopes of some charm that would stop her getting pregnant again.

The old man there to buy a St. Jude medal to appeal to the patron saint of lost causes, and Maddy could discern it had something to do with the old man's own adult child. He must have burned through the other saints by now . . .

Then at Two Brothers' Pharmacy, where she had gone before rushing home from work to meet Mrs. Hannigan, Maddy had found herself in the same state. Only here, the customers consisted of a different cast:

A man with his eyes on the floor, mumbling to the clerk at the pharmacy pickup window. Maddy could see him fumbling to cover his wedding ring.

A drag queen shepherding a barely passing protégé through the makeup aisle, laughing loudly while explaining when one might use blue or purple mascara.

Maddy could see this was indeed the place Lew and Sophie had described—a place where the clerks were not going to give anyone a hard time.

When Maddy wandered from the birthday card section to the window to pick up her own prescription, seeing the mumbling man now gone, the clerk had said to her, "ID, please, sweetie," and when Maddy immediately produced out of library habits her faculty ID from the university and not her driver's license, the clerk had said, gently, "That all you have, hon? No driver's license?"

Maddy then fumbled through her bag, embarrassed, pulled out her license, and handed it over.

"Indiana, huh?" said the clerk, now with a little tone of doubt, looking from the photo on the card up to Maddy. The clerk took the license and went to pull the bag from the racks of readied medications. She then took the small bag and Maddy's license to show the pharmacist.

The clerk came back and said, not quietly, "You're not a cop, right?"

Maddy blurted out, "What?"

"Honey, it's a strange one," said the clerk. "Benzo, controlled substance, but only two pills? And you're giving me first a U. identification card and then an *out-of-state* license and, well, hon, listen, I'm not trying to give you a hard time. But we just don't need the trouble. So, tell me you're not a cop."

"I'm not a cop. My doctor called that in," Maddy added hastily, "Dr. Miller. And it's just two pills because my mother had a habit and I don't want to develop one, so he did it out of respect, you see. I just need it because I have to fly, and I'm afraid of flying."

"Uh-huh," said the clerk, in a tone that made clear she knew Maddy was lying. She asked if Maddy wanted anything else, and Maddy hastily pulled a pack of gum from just below the counter.

Such an upside-down place, Two Brothers', where the man with the downcast eyes and the drag queen with her rough protégé were read as perfectly normal, and Maddy read as suspicious.

. . .

Maddy heard herself launch a little too loudly now toward the end of the rosary, the atypical prayer near the end, "Hail, holy Queen, Mother of Mercy, our life, our sweetness, and our hope. To thee do we cry, poor banished children of Eve! To thee do we send up our sighs, mourning and weeping in this valley of tears . . ."

In a moment she and Mrs. Hannigan would stand up again and Maddy would offer her a cup of tea to be polite, and Mrs. Hannigan would say no, she just wanted to help Maddy with her question and go, thank you. Mrs. Hannigan would say that Alex was a beautiful and kind woman, that she died too soon, may God have mercy on her soul. And they would walk through the rooms in the order in which Mrs. Hannigan used to clean, and Mrs. Hannigan would tell Maddy in a rather perfunctory tone what she normally did and what she thought had been different that last time, as if she were handing off the job of cleaning to Maddy.

And Maddy would lie one last time to Mrs. Hannigan, just after Mrs. Hannigan embraced Hank warmly on her way back to her car.

"What a terrible loss, Mr. Hank! What a terrible loss it has been for us all!"

"Terrible, Mrs. Hannigan," he answered. "I miss her every day. Every single day."

Maddy would give her last lie then, while giving Hank a conspiratorial look. She told Mrs. Hannigan that Hank had known from Maddy that Mrs. Hannigan was coming, and the flowers he had brought were for *her*, so, here, she should take them.

"Yes," said Hank. "For all of the kindness you showed Alex over the years, Mrs. Hannigan."

The older woman wiped away her tears with her sleeves and then took the flowers. She smelled them three times before getting in her car.

...

"So, you don't care for yellow roses?" Hank asked, closing the door behind himself and Maddy, shutting out the cold air. He kicked off his shoes as Maddy did the same.

"You know perfectly well why I had you give them to her," Maddy said, crossing her arms and rubbing her biceps with her hands to try to warm up, having gone out with only her sweater to see Mrs. Hannigan off, having the cold air blow right up her dress. "How was it going to look to her, you coming here to Alex's home and greeting *me* with roses?"

"May I?" he asked, unbuttoning the front of his long, wool coat and gesturing to her to come and warm up against him.

"I suppose," she answered, pushing her body up against his, feeling his heat like a blast from a furnace. And there was his odor. She suddenly wanted to stick her nostrils right up against his neck and drink it in.

"So, what did you learn from Mrs. Hannigan?" Hank asked, wrapping the two sides of his coat as far around her back as he could, rubbing her back through the coat to try to transmit his heat faster.

"I'm not sure yet what I learned that is meaningful," Maddy answered. "Except one thing. She did not see Alex on Saturday. Alex wanted to be left alone for her writing weekend, so she asked Mrs. Hannigan if she could come to clean on Monday afternoon instead—Memorial Day—and that's when she came. Alex wasn't here."

Hank said nothing, but he understood what Maddy was saying: Alex was in all likelihood dead by the time Mrs. Hannigan had come to clean.

"And the police didn't talk to her?"

"No," Maddy answered. "They talked mostly to Scott, so far as I can tell, who probably sounded like he knew Alex's habits. Who knows if Scott even knew Alex had Mrs. Hannigan come every other weekend?"

Hank didn't answer.

"I'm sorry, I didn't know you were coming," Maddy said, releasing herself from his coat and turning to walk to the kitchen, thinking about what she could offer him to eat. She was wondering if perhaps now he would go, and she might convince Parvus to come back and help her again see Alex and the others.

But, oh, Hank did not smell of death. He smelled so like life. Like food.

"Wait, why do you smell like pizza?" she asked.

"Oh! I brought you a good pizza! It's in the car! In case you didn't like the roses as a way of saying again I am sorry. I just didn't want to pull it out in front of Mrs. Hannigan."

He rushed around ahead of Maddy to set the oven to preheat.

"We just need to warm it back up. It's got spinach and eggplant and peppers and fennel sausage. I think you'll like it. And I brought a good Sangiovese. Two bottles. Plus cannoli."

"Oh," she replied, looking at his ass as he bent over to reach inside the oven to pull out the pans stored there, to set the rack at the level he wanted. "Cannoli?"

She could feel the rush of her salivary glands, like children rushing to a delight.

"Do they know how to make cannoli in Minnesota?"

Her phone rang with a shrill burst. Seeing it was Wolf, she told Hank she would be right back. She hastened down the hall to her bedroom and closed the door behind her, opening her phone while trying to pull herself out of her sweater and out of this persistent fogginess.

"Wolf?"

"Rabbit? You home tomorrow afternoon?"

"Yes?" she answered, confused why he would ask.

"Okay, listen. Liz is set for me to pick her up in Indy."

Maddy was standing staring at the headboard on Alex's bed. It was covered in fabric, and she had never noticed until now how the black-on-white squiggle pattern looked a little like statuary marble shown in bright sunlight. She went up to the headboard, to look at it more closely.

"Rabbit? Did you hear what I said? I'm packing up. We are heading your way."

She ran her fingers over the fabric, feeling the raised pattern of the black stitching on the white. Her mind felt like a weight, dropping down suddenly, a bucket dropped down into a well.

"Rabbit?"

"What, Wolf?"

"We'll be there tomorrow, your place. Probably between one and three."

"But why, Wolf?" she asked, shifting the phone from one ear to the next. "Jury come back?"

"It looks like they may soon. Maybe tomorrow."

"But today is Friday. Can they come back on a Saturday?" she asked.

"Rabbit?" he answered, "You okay? Today is Thursday."

Thursday? She and Mrs. Hannigan should have been praying the *Joyful* Mysteries, not the Sorrowful. The Annunciation to Mary that she would conceive a son! The Visitation of Mary with Elizabeth, both of them pregnant! How did Mrs. Hannigan miss that Maddy had the wrong day? Had she been remembering the days of Alex's last weekend wrong, too? Or did Mrs. Hannigan just not know the rosary as well as Maddy did?

"Sorry," Maddy said, quickly realizing it would not be helpful to tell Wolf she'd just prayed the wrong mysteries. "I was thinking that, since I don't have to go into work tomorrow, it was Saturday. I was going to take a writing day tomorrow."

"It's okay," he said. "We don't know for sure about the jury—it seems too quick—but I thought we should come now. You've been so quiet?"

She wasn't sure if he meant lately or just now.

"Liz said it was okay with her, to come now," Wolf said. "She can always fly back to Indianapolis if it's going to be a lot longer. We can fly her back. We'll leave her car at the airport long-term lot."

"And you, Wolf? If it takes a while longer?"

"I can take a leave from work," he said.

"Isn't it too fast?" she asked him, running her fingers again on the fabric of the headboard. How was it she had never taken time to feel this fabric? How was it she had never seen how the squiggly black-on-white pattern looked like rough doodles of people, like crowds of commuters on the sidewalk of Sixth Avenue during the evening rush seen obliquely from a floor or two above, right near Penn Station?

"Wolf, can I ask you to find out something more? I want to know if Alex Shugar had a wound on her abdomen when she died."

"A wound on her abdomen? I think they would have mentioned it when they gave me the autopsy results, Rabbit."

"Could you ask?"

"I can try," he said.

They were both silent for a while. She wedged the phone between her ear and shoulder and used her two hands to pull Wolf's shirt off her pillow. She put the pillow back up against the headboard, folded his shirt roughly, and put it in her underwear drawer. Where was Wolf going to sleep when he was here, she wondered to herself? Where was Liz going to sleep?

Someone could take the pull-out couch in the office, and someone could take the living room couch . . . She couldn't sleep next to him. She didn't want to find her hand where it shouldn't be.

"Listen, Rabbit," he said now, "I will go call and try to find out, but do you need someone with you tonight? Until we get there? Should I call Sophie?"

"No, that's okay," Maddy said. "I'll ask another friend of Alex's. And I think I'll just try to put my phone down until you get here."

"Wait until I see if I can get you an answer on your question," he said. "I'll call you back soon, and I'll have a better ETA then, too."

"Okay," she said, and hung up.

She opened the door to the bedroom and the scent of the warmed pizza greeted her. Roasted tomatoes; sharp garlic; the fennel of the pork sausage. She was met at the kitchen door by Hank handing her a glass of wine. Should she swim in clear waters, without wine, she wondered for a second? And then she drank a little. It was tangy and smelled a little of violets.

"You okay?" Hank asked. "Everything okay?"

"Alex had her appendix out years ago?" Maddy asked. "Mrs. Hannigan said she did?"

"Yes," said Hank. "Emergency appendectomy. Why?"

"Did Alex have anything going on with her belly again—with her abdomen—just before she died? Or some other wound?"

"Not that I know of," Hank said.

He looked at Maddy quizzically. Maddy seemed to be looking at his belly. But she was, in fact, looking at the sink against which he was leaning. Mrs. Hannigan had said that Alex washed her hair in the sink that weekend. So, Mrs. Hannigan observed, Alex must have had a wound she was keeping dry, like she did when she had her appendix out, when Alex came home from the hospital and needed to keep the surgical site dry and clean for a few days, and she had washed her hair in the sink instead of in the shower as usual . . . But Maddy didn't tell Hank this. She looked back up and gave him a perfunctory smile.

"Would you stay tonight?" she asked. "Please?"

"What's up?" he asked.

"My Philly friend who called, he said the jury may come back tomorrow."

"I see. Of course."

He took the open bottle and walked over to her to fill her glass again. She had not noticed that she had drunk it all down.

"Not sexual," he said, politely. "My staying, I mean."

"Why not?" she asked, and now smiled at him in a way that must have looked, she thought, rather confusing.

"Ah, right," he said, putting down the bottle and turning to check the oven's temperature reading. "I turned you off yesterday when you saw me flirting with another woman. So now you're pissed and you don't want me. Which means now we can finally have intercourse?"

She knew he was kidding, but he didn't sound that way. He sounded simply annoyed. He leaned back against the sink. He picked up his own glass again and took a sip.

"That's fast for the jury to come back, isn't it?"

She nodded.

"So it must mean either complete acquittal or complete conviction?"

"Why would you say that?" she asked, jarred.

"They're not agonizing over some charge if they're coming back pretty fast. They're not debating much."

"Right," she said, nodding. "Right."

She was thinking about where she had left the prescription from Two Brothers'—in her backpack on the bench by the front door.

"Right," she said again. "I guess that means soon my life—well, I get acquittal or conviction, right?"

He didn't answer her.

"Let's just—just fuck," she said, though she did not put her glass down.

"Did you mean 'fuck it, let's just eat'?"

"No," Maddy answered, putting her glass down on the counter and hoisting herself onto it. She smoothed the dress out over her legs. "I mean let's just fuck, Hank. I have no idea what's happening to my life tomorrow. But I have the sense I might just die. So, let's just do it already."

He put his glass down on the counter next to the sink, walked over to her, and put his hands on her knees, feeling her joints through the starchy fabric.

"Maddy," he said, trying to catch her faraway gaze, "you're not going to die tomorrow. Whatever happens with the jury, you'll be okay."

"You know," she answered him, "one of the reasons I thought maybe it was okay that The Jerk was going to fuck me was that I thought, hell, I know I don't want to die before I have sex. And you never know when you're going to die! One of my classmates had just died from an asthma attack, just like that. You never know when it's going to happen. I didn't want to die a virgin. I knew that. I wanted to know what sex was. No one was going to tell me."

"But mostly," said Hank, "it wasn't up to you. The sex with him. Not really."

"No," she said, "not really."

She said nothing more for a moment, and he just waited. Finally, she sighed.

"If it had been completely up to me, Hank, even with the sense I might be trapped in my father's grip forever, I think I probably would have asked the universe for something better than what The Jerk gave me. Something a few years later. Certainly someone different."

She looked up and met his eye.

"And now you can," he said, taking just the end of her chin in three of his fingertips. "You can wait for something better. Something later. Someone different . . . I mean, different than me."

"You're not a jerk," she said, pulling his hand off her face and holding it in hers, looking him right in the eyes. "You're so not a jerk."

"Oh, but I am," he said. "And you know I am."

"But you're into mature women."

"I am," he said. "Your shape . . . Yeah, I love having my hand in your mature, healthy, perennially blooming bush, Maddy. You are a lovely, lovely, sexually mature female bird."

She laughed. He pushed the tip of his nose against her face and slid it up from near her jawline to her temple. Then he pulled back to look at her.

"Please, tell me you don't want me too much," he said, touching his forehead against hers.

He leaned in and kissed her lips tentatively. Then they kissed again, more deliberately. Two streams rushing down the same hill and meeting, tumbling over the rocks, the sunlight glinting on the wet, polished stone.

"Please, tell me you don't want me very much, Maddy. Just a little? Because I want—"

Her phone rang in her pocket again. She cleared her throat and smiled at him.

"Go check the pizza," she said, opening her phone and putting it to her ear. "Yes, Wolf?" she said into the phone.

"Rabbit? No wounds."

Wolf's voice sounded to her like a radio being played on a beach blanket five meters away.

"Slight bruising at the base of the ribs," he went on, "but no laceration. Also a slight bruising on the right calf. No recent cuts. Okay?"

"Okay," said Maddy. "What time will you be here?"

"Looks like around two, give or take."

"I'll be here," she said. "I'm going to put away my phone. I don't want to know until you're here with me, Wolf."

"I understand," Wolf answered. "Take care of yourself until I get there. Don't be alone."

She hung up.

"Everything okay?" Hank asked, pulling the pizza out of the oven and taking two plates down out of the cabinet.

"Yes," said Maddy. She handed him her phone. "Do me a favor and go hide this somewhere. And do stay the night? Best not to be alone tonight."

"Of course," he answered. "Whatever you need."

She thought to herself how he meant it: whatever you need. Which was why he wasn't so much a jerk.

He took her phone into another room, wandering the bedroom to the office to the bathroom. While he did so, she set the table in the dining room for the two of them, serving a slice of pizza onto each plate, topping off the wine, lighting the two tapered candles on the table.

"It must be," he said, coming back and sitting down with her, "like the ultimate dissertation defense—the jury, I mean. Only they're below you in the ranks of the intellectual, not above you. And the whole world is watching."

"Gee, Hank," she answered, "great job making me not think about it."

He apologized and served her another slice, as if to make up for it.

"You know you're right, right?"

"Yes," Maddy answered. "I think I know I'm right."

"Then whatever they say," he responded, "it doesn't matter. Sometimes people say I am wrong. But I go on in the knowledge I've been right. History will vindicate me."

"Hank, this historian will tell you it doesn't always work like that."

He reached across the table and took her right hand. He held it so tightly, as if she might wander off. He rubbed her knuckles with his thumb.

"Well, *I* think you're right," he said, after a while, "and I am always right."

"What the fuck do you know?" she answered, with a lopsided smirk, taking her hand back to eat more pizza. "What the absolute fuck do you know, Dr. Merriman?"

"I know you're absolutely brilliant, Dr. Shanks," he answered.

"You also know you can absolutely get up my skirt easier than *that,* at least with a hand."

"Fuck you," he answered, chuckling, eating more pizza himself. "I'm not saying it to get up your skirt. I think you're brilliant. And it's not because of what you can put together—though I do think you caught Dr. Wilhelm. It's because of how you can see things right without everything wrong getting in the way. You don't bother with convention. You and I are alike that way."

She picked up her napkin, wiped her mouth, and looked at his face to see if she saw her own. She could see, for the first time, hairs of his eyebrows that seemed a little too long, a little rangy. She could see some discoloration of his skin where crows' feet were forming.

"I feel so out of sorts from this uncertainty," she said, scrunching her eyes closed. "So out of sorts."

"Let me take you for a drive?" he asked. "And then run you a bath and put you to bed? I promise I won't go. You won't be alone tonight at all."

She nodded.

The prayer was stuck in her head as if it were an annoying song: *Holy Mary, mother of God, pray for us sinners, now and at the hour of our death, Amen. Holy Mary, mother of God, pray for us sinners, now and at the hour of our death, Amen. Holy Mary, mother of God, pray for us sinners, now and at the hour of our death, Amen.*

She wondered where Wilhelm was. If he thought the jury might come back guilty, what did he have to lose? The living being she thought she had seen in the woods the other day—

Well, what difference did it make? Eventually everything ended.

"Take me for that drive?" she asked, finishing her dinner and standing up. He nodded and blew out the candles.

...

Hank turned the heat up in the car as soon as the engine was producing enough, just a couple of miles from the house. As the car grew warm, he unbuttoned his coat with his right hand, his left hand on the wheel. On a straightaway, glancing over to Maddy, he could see her staring out the windshield, looking at nothing.

"You know," he said as he took the car toward to where the fields led to the wooded rural drive, in the rough direction of Alex's lake, "sometimes when I'm facing a tough audience the next day—when I'm going to say what I know is right but what I know they won't want to hear because it challenges their work or messes with their worldview—I just take a little while to relish my own understanding of the matter. There's a pleasant little high that comes from knowing you're right."

She didn't answer but nodded a little.

"Why don't you tell me, Mad, how come you know you're right?"

Her chest felt a little strange at his spontaneous use of the name Liz called her. Would Hank even meet Liz while she was here? And if so, what would she say? Would she give Maddy grief about Hank, after meeting him, or take seriously what Maddy had said to her about respecting the inevitability of her desires as much as Maddy worked to respect Liz's? Of course, Maddy never had to work to respect Liz's orientation; Liz was normal.

"Please tell me," Hank said, in his reedy voice, "my dear Dr. Madeleine Shanks, why you know you are right."

Maddy cleared her throat and began formally presenting to him the story of how she'd figured out Wilhelm had been attracting and killing patients to obtain specimens. It reminded her of when she had told her dissertation director this unlikely story.

"I went to the museum in Philadelphia," she began, "to obtain material for my dissertation. The archives there, on the collections, are quite solid. Substantial, reasonably well-indexed. No one else had spent much time looking at it the way I was doing."

She then described the history of acquisition from the eighteenth century forward, what she'd learned about who had obtained what from where—the use of executed bodies, a little grave-robbing, some prowling of wards to wait for death to release certain specimens to those who wanted to look inside, and the simpler, more modern, less nefarious path, of bodies in hospitals turned over to the anatomists, to medical schools, to well-respected researchers.

She told Hank about going to see Dr. Wilhelm's own collection at his invitation after meeting him at the museum, him thinking it would impress her, this young and bright-eyed historian of anatomical collectors in town for her dissertation, coming to see a famous doctor's collection. She told Hank how it had the opposite effect on her from what Wilhelm intended— how it made her wonder how he'd managed to get quite so many bodies of a particular type in so modern an era.

She'd had a bad dream about one of the specimens, she told Hank without elaboration. Then she started walking him through her research, step by step, what she had put together . . .

Listening intently, Hank drove on and on, through the night, more slowly than he ordinarily would, interrupting only now and then to express understanding with a "Hmm, I see," or to ask a very short clarifying question— "When you say 'he,' you mean who?" And little by little, it became clear to her that he understood fully just how dogged she had been, how clever she had been in certain parts.

When she got to the part about how Wilhelm's helper had finally told her what he knew, just before the helper killed himself, Hank looked to her like he might be sweating. But he did not stop, and he did not stop her. He was focusing so intently on the story that she wondered if he should even be driving.

But she pressed on, explaining what she thought they could prove about each death and what they could not prove about some, but what they suspected, or knew.

"Why didn't the defense claim this was all just done by Wilhelm's helper—the man who killed himself?" Hank asked.

"Because the deaths of Wilhelm's patients started long before their association—long before Wilhelm and the helper met. That wasn't going to work," Maddy answered.

"Why didn't they call you as a witness to tell the jury what the helper had told you about what he and Wilhelm had done?"

"Hearsay," answered Maddy. "They could not allow me to tell the jury what I claimed were the dying words of a suicidal man. Hearsay."

After that explanation, he was quiet for a time, and so was she. She realized now that she had never told the history quite like this. They had told her to keep it to herself until it was all done. Not even at the prosecutors' office had this history all been laid out by anyone quite like this. Perhaps at the trial, something like this story had been told—she could not be sure. But even so, it would have been told largely without her as a subject in the tale. She would, at best, be in the background. The prosecutors were going to focus on Wilhelm, *what he had done*, not on how Maddy had figured it out. Her subjectivity just complicated the story they were trying to convince the jury was clear, simple, objective—shocking, perhaps, but believable, and true.

But in this version of the story, the one she was telling Hank, she existed. As she laid it out for Hank like this, piece by piece by piece, she could see exactly why she knew she was right. And she existed. The objective truth was: she *was* right. The eyeless moon itself could look down to the earth and see what she had seen. Like the moon, she existed.

Now the stars looked to her quite sharp, bright, and beautiful, and the clusters of dark trees off on the horizon looked like strong, distant mountains. The orange lights of the car's dashboard seemed so clear and exact and perfect, like her knowledge, clear and exact and perfect, reading absolutely correctly the speed, the RPM, and the temperature of Wilhelm's long scheme. She was smiling broadly now. Smiling at the agreement of the stars.

Hank looked over at her and could see her pleasure. After a few minutes, he pulled off the rural road down a dirt path, put the car in park, and turned off the lights. He unbuckled his seatbelt and pushed his seat back as far as it would go, leaning the seat back to a low angle. He grabbed her left hand in his right, pulled it to his warm chest, and gazed at the ceiling of the car.

"See? You're brilliant," he said, now holding her hand in both of his, as if her hand were a dear prize. "Absolutely brilliant, my dear Dr. Shanks."

She laughed at him.

"You don't need to say that to get up my skirt."

"I know," he said, and he sat up a little and looked at her face. She thought by the way he looked at her that she must look young and happy. For he looked so young and happy.

"As you know," he added, "I know the way up your skirt."

He unbuckled her seatbelt and slid his hand up her thigh. He soon made the discovery she was wearing nothing underneath.

"Holy shit, woman," he said, becoming suddenly still.

"I didn't think it was possible to surprise you," she laughed. "Sexually, I mean. Anyway, yeah, I decided to take them off when I realized I was going to be stuck praying."

She took off her jacket and tossed it into the back seat. Then she climbed over the gear shift, turning herself to face him, her knees on either side of his haunches, her legs tucked into the space formed between his pants and his long coat. She leaned in and kissed him briefly, then leaned herself back, undid his belt, undid his pants, and pulled his hard cock out of his boxer shorts. She repositioned herself slightly and slid it into herself.

He gasped quite at the same time she did.

She couldn't remember now why she had been putting this off. To feel him slide along inside her, to feel the lovely run of his glans against her rugae, the moist vaginal ribs over which his erection now skipped and slid like a kid running his finger all the way across a keyboard. He was kissing her mouth, pulling her head towards his, as she kept pulling her hips forward and back, getting him to touch inside just the spots she wanted, a sensation that felt so like the perfect picking of a bush full of ripe berries.

She could hear herself vocalizing something, chanting almost, but it seemed as if someone else was saying all this—*oh, there, Hank, oh, please*—and he kept trying to catch her mouth with his to kiss it again. Now here was his finger, running ever so lightly down the moist interior of her labia majora, now glancing along her labia minora, so that her muscles startled and pulled at him harder.

She reached one hand behind her and put it between her legs, finding and feeling the base of his slick cock with the tips of two of her fingers, because she wanted to feel it there to know this was no dream, and he cried out "Maddy!" in a tone that was at once both adoring and scolding.

And now his fingers were fluttering on her as if his hand were a small and pretty bird, a very pretty *male* bird now in the bush, just as he had joked. But this was no joke; she felt as if her whole body was pulling at him now, wanting to pull him in so completely.

She leaned back a little farther and grabbed the base of his cock between the middle knuckles of two of her fingers to push him in deeper, and he cried again "Maddy!" in that same adoring-scolding tone.

And now she went looking for his mouth with hers, finding it, kissing him with her open mouth, wincing in delight as he glanced along her clitoris—she closed her eyes and saw suddenly a prim little dollhouse, made of glass, with two dolls locked in a dance, a man and a woman. Him and her. Her head felt simultaneously ethereally light and as dense as a black hole, as she could feel the action of a million of her cells, the wave of her hips striking his shore, coming back, coming forward again, *in a moment, in a moment*. Did she say that aloud?

"In a moment, in a moment," the words slurred, and then she let out a kind of screech at the feeling of everything in her truly being felt at once, and he yelled again, "Maddy!" but this time it did sound only as if he was the happiest man on earth to see her arrival. She could feel, then, his splash hot against her cervix, a fast burst of warmth, her uterus contracting like a cloudburst, contracting again, and again, her inner thighs suddenly so wet.

She fell against him and he locked his arms around her and pulled her in, kissing in a disorganized way at the top of her head, like a dumb pigeon pecking at crumbs on the sidewalk.

After a moment they were both still. She pulled herself off him and sat down on his lap across him, her feet draped over the gearshift, her dress wet here and here, and leaned into his chest and shoulder and neck. He adjusted his arms to wrap them around her and again kissed her head, here and there.

"Maddy," he said finally, "you're the only woman who—"

"Oh, dear God, Hank, *please*," she said, groaning and laughing, "don't start with me like that."

"No, listen," he said, "let me finish."

He kissed her once more on the top of her head, this time in a firm and steady way.

"I was going to say this: Madeleine Shanks, PhD, you're the only woman I've ever wanted to teach to play basketball."

She didn't answer for a minute. Then she asked him what the hell basketball had to do with anything.

"I don't know!" he answered. "I don't know. When it came to me out of the blue, earlier today—before I went to get you the roses—when it came to me in a kind of revelation that you're the only woman I've ever wanted to teach to play basketball, I realized I didn't know *what* it meant. I just knew it was true. That it felt like a very clear truth. It seemed important. So I was going to tell you that. With the roses."

She was trying to picture herself on a basketball court with Hank at the university gym late at night. But she felt like she might need to fall asleep fast, for just a few minutes?

"Putting aside the question of why on earth you would think the nuns didn't teach me to play basketball, why do you want me to know how to play?" she asked with a sharp yawn.

"I want to play *against* you," he explained. "I think you could have an amazing jump shot, and I want to try and play *against* it. More than once."

She chuckled and yawned again.

"Well, Henry Merriman, PhD, man, I'd like to teach *you* to spatchcock a chicken," she replied. "Because sometimes I just wish you'd come over and make me a goddamned *chicken*."

"I brought you a good pizza!" he reminded her. "And cannoli."

"Oh," she said, licking her lips. "That's right. Let's go back. I need cannoli."

But she didn't rise to get off his lap just yet. She felt so wonderfully spent.

After a minute, he said to her quietly, "Madeleine Shanks, PhD, you're also the only woman I know who, when she says she needs cannoli, I know for sure it's no metaphor."

Chapter 33

Maddy could tell Hank had succeeded in moving Alex's stereo to the bedroom when, from the bath, she could hear Ella Fitzgerald starting to sing. A few bars in, the singing paused. She peeked through the French doors of the solarium and could see Hank loading four more silver disks into the five-CD changer on the bedroom dresser.

Ella soon started to sing again. He came over and held out the small plastic bag she'd been saving for Liz.

"What's this?" he asked. "I found it on the dresser."

"That's what that field rat collected under the stove before you caught him and took him outside. I saved it up to show my friend Liz, the rat researcher."

"You *do* like studying collections," he answered, unbuttoning his shirt. He paused and held up the bag to try to see into it better in the blue-bottle light of the solarium. He had turned off all the other lights.

"A hairband," he observed, "and a piece of walnut, and . . ."

"Yeah," she said, "what is that other thing?"

He opened the bag and took out the electronic bit. He turned it over in his hand once or twice and then put it back in the bag.

"It looks like a piece of a device we use in the lab, from a type of camera we use for videotaping people who are there to participate in some of our experiments," he said. "I guess maybe I dropped it here? They are temperamental little devices. We're always having to fix them. But I don't remember having worked on one here."

He went back to the bedroom, put the bag back on the dresser, took off his clothes, and climbed into the tub with her. Seeing the water's sudden rise as he settled himself down next to her, she thought of Archimedes and his displacement experiments. He wrapped his arm around her so that she was leaning on his chest. She looped one leg over his. From all the movement, some of the water sloshed out onto the floor. It didn't much matter. She'd give the house one last good cleaning before she left it so Scott wouldn't get mad at her. (*Madder* at her.) And wasn't this, a bath with Hank, a fine way to say goodbye to this tub—if she must say goodbye to it? Here they were, soaking off the remains of their sloppy car sex. Scott would not approve at all. So Alex probably would.

Hank leaned over and kissed her briefly on the mouth.

"Ah, so that's what the cannoli tasted like," he said.

"I *had* to eat both. Because they were kind of soggy."

"No, no," he said, "it's fine. I told you that you could have both. And I meant it."

"Nice resource display."

"I'm no idiot, Shanks. Now that I finally know exactly what you feel like, I want back in."

She pulled on his wet chest hair curls by clutching them between her fingers and then took her hand from his chest to her face to smell it. He smelled even better when he was wet and so full of sex.

"I can see why Alex enjoyed this bath so much—and why you do," he said. "I've never been in it before."

"Really? Lately, I wonder, though, if I should be here alone and naked," she answered, "with all these windows. I don't mean in terms of modesty. I just mean in terms of safety."

He pulled her a little closer in a gesture that reminded her of how her mother used to pull her back from a rail.

"Alex had started to wonder the same thing," he said to Maddy. "After all those years of not caring. She wasn't ashamed, but there's a difference between shame and privacy. And safety."

"What did you say to her when she wondered this to you?"

"What was I going to say?" Hank asked. "She loved this tub in this solarium, with these lights and the stars, and I didn't want her to give it up. It was what settled her every day, on the days when she could be settled. And I wasn't going to point out to her that she was aging out of the range in which most rapists are interested. That's not the kind of thing you say to a woman friend."

Maddy laughed and slapped his face softly with her wet hand. He grabbed her wrist and kissed her open palm.

"You, on the other hand, my dear . . . You have not aged out of the range."

He reached around and pulled her body over to lay her atop him, her back against his front. She could easily feel his erection poking at her lower back. He leaned slightly out over the tub to grab the dark-brown bottle of lavender oil Alex had kept there. He poured a little on his left hand, put the bottle back down, and rubbed his hands together. Then he started to massage Maddy's neck, her collarbone, her breasts.

She reached her hands behind her, behind his head, interlocking her fingers behind the base of his skull to steady herself and to make it easier for him to touch her that way. He leaned his head forward a touch and kissed her left temple in the most erotic way she had ever had her temple kissed. It was as if his lips were on her pussy. No wonder it was called the temple.

Playing with her breast with one hand, he slid his other down between her legs. She opened them a little wider. He pulled his hand just an inch or so away from her and moved his hand back and forth, like the motion of the tail fin of a fish, creating an undulating steady wave of water to greet her clitoris, her labia, her vaginal introitus, over and over and over again. It felt to her almost magical, being so fully in the water yet also greeted, again and again, *by* this water, by his hand waving at her. She closed her eyes and could see him two station platforms away at Jamaica Station in Queens, no trains between them, smiling and waving to her with this back-and-forth motion. Sending the air over with his wave to kiss her on the cheek, over and over again.

She wanted to hear him call her name from that train platform in thrilled greeting—"Maddy!"—just the way he had when he had come inside her a few hours earlier. But she wanted first to feel just this wave, this kissing wave.

Is this why Alex had loved the water so? Had she opened her legs to the earth's waves this way to greet whomever had been her own personal Neptune—ah, Neptune, who seemed to be keeping Maddy now from sinking below the water through some trick of holding her with soft kisses on her temple, a light grasp on her breast, and the waves sent against her with his other hand. Such a fish, such a gloriously accommodating fish.

"Oh, Jesus, Maddy, your body," Hank groaned, now pushing his fingers lightly against her vulva, feeling the moisture that was so clearly hers, not water, pulling back his hand and making the waves again, grazing her clitoris with the side of a finger, her back now arched, her hands tightening against the back of his shoulders, his lips now on her neck, sucking softly on her carotid artery, seeming to coax the blood away from her brain leaving her dizzy and moaning. She screamed and he grabbed her as she came, pinching her nipple and thrusting his hand against her crotch, saying, "Yes!"

(As though he thought she was really onto something.)

In a moment he reached over and pulled the bath mat off the floor. He draped it over the far side of the tub, to drape her too, her arms hanging over, her head still dizzy. He entered her fast, fucking her from behind, his lower abdomen repeatedly meeting her ass, his hands running all over her back like a lion chasing an antelope running in circles, reaching down with both hands and pulling her apart a little, to push in deeper—

And she pushed back at him, moving ever so slightly from side to side, feeling as if she could feel him all the way up through her, right to the base of her throat, wanting to turn and take him now into her mouth. But he would have none of that, holding her there and fucking her harder and harder, until he came in her with a push that slammed her hips against the edge of the tub and sent a wave of water flying over the edge—

Almost immediately he apologized for banging her against the hard edge. But he stayed in her and on her, panting and (she realized, with self-satisfied delight) sweating a little onto her back.

"Oh, no, it's good, it's all good," she said, her voice funny, relishing the sense that she was buzzed in a way that might never go away if she could just stay here forever, her head so close to the floor but not so close that she risked hitting it, with him in her, with him on her, and in her, and on her, forever and ever, or at least a few minutes. (Amen.)

...

Maddy wasn't sure if she'd awakened because Hank was snoring next to her or if she would've woken up anyway. But here she was, awake. And there he was, snoring. Had he snored like this next to Alex? Had Alex just been a deep sleeper?

Well, it wasn't exactly a normal night for Maddy. Even after getting laid by Hank twice, she wasn't going to find sleep easy. Wolf was coming, maybe with a verdict. Liz was coming, and she could well be in a mood after driving overnight with Wolf. And here was Hank, snoring.

Maddy remembered the time Liz broke up with a woman for snoring. Liz had discovered that if she and her girlfriend did *not* have sex, the girlfriend slept lightly, without snoring. But if they *had* sex, then the girlfriend slept hard and snored like a bus. So, should Liz give up the sex or give up good sleep? She had put the problem to Maddy, and Maddy had shrugged in response, saying maybe Liz should sleep on the couch after she and her girl fucked?

The relationship was over a few days later.

"Can't choose between sleep and sex," Liz had explained, saying nothing more. They'd moved on to talking about upcoming conference options and the cheapest place to get toilet paper.

Hank wasn't snoring all *that* hard. Not like a bus. But it was loud enough to keep her mind alert. At least he was here, and she could wake him up if she needed him for anything, even just to tell her everything was going to be okay, no matter if the jury was stupid.

After the bath, he'd dried himself off rapidly, giving her a little more hot water out of the tap to keep her warm while he went off to toast a clean towel and her long flannel nightgown in the dryer, to make them good and warm. She hadn't asked him for that. But she liked that he went through this little bit of affectionate effort, wrapped in a towel himself.

While he'd gone off to the dryer, she'd lain back in the bath to stay warm, looking at the bottle lights, thinking she would take them with her when she left this house. She'd thought about what Mrs. Hannigan had said about not finding the big bath towel Alex had kept specially for after her baths, the kind of towel so large they called it a bath sheet. It would have been nice to have that. Maddy might have taken that with her too when she had to leave.

Hank let off a kind of snort and rolled over, still asleep. Maddy sat up against the headboard. Should she bug out to the couch? Or maybe take one of the benzos in her backpack? She looked at the clock—it was just before three. The pill would likely knock her out well into morning, leaving less of a span when she'd be awake without Wolf yet there. It seemed like a very good idea. Hank had told her he'd have to leave by nine for a search committee meeting, so there was no chance Wolf would arrive to find Hank, even if somehow Maddy slept until Wolf and Liz arrived.

She got up carefully so as not to wake Hank, pulled on the wool socks scrunched under her side of the bed, and went to the foyer. She found her backpack and rifled through it to find the waxy white paper bag from the pharmacy. She tore it open, pulled out the orange plastic vial, and went to the kitchen. She took one pill and downed it with a big glass of water, leaving the vial on the counter.

Then she stood leaning against the countertop, feeling a little cold, making a mental note that she should wash her sheets and make her bed before Liz and Wolf arrived. But mostly wondering about who had lured Alex to the lake, and how, and why. Was this the place Alex had stood when she had taken the Valium? Or did she take it at the lake?

It had to be someone Alex had trusted to meet there or to go with her. Her car had been found there, so Alex or—or the other person—had driven it there, driven Alex there. With whom had Alex felt safe mixing a drink and Valium and going to a lake? Or had she been unconscious by the time they reached the lake?

Maddy was glad she'd have to give up that car and the house soon to Scott. She had almost eaten through all of Alex's dry goods anyway. And much of the freezer . . .

The chill of the countertop edge against her lower back was soaking through her nightgown like a cold hand, and she was just starting to feel the drug's effect. It was a little like her brain had walked inside and shut the door, coming from a noisy street into a quiet office. She could still hear the noisy neuron equivalent of cars and people on the streets in her head, but they were being muted, gently faded out, like someone had turned to the left the volume dial on a radio.

Hank certainly hadn't done it. He would not have let Alex hurt herself and he would not have hurt Alex. If he had, he would not have forgiven himself. Not Lew. Certainly not Josiah. Probably not Whit. Probably not Joseph. Not Parvus—he wanted Maddy to figure it out. Same with Scott.

Everett Sophie? Sure, Everett Sophie stood to gain a lot of money, and the letter left for Maddy—asking her to be careful about talking with the police—would have been the perfect one to write to play on Maddy's biases. ("Please don't make the police interested in me, because they're all a bunch of bigots.") And yet Maddy could not imagine Everett Sophie hurting Alex either. She couldn't imagine Everett Sophie hurting anyone. Wolf's instincts and Maddy's instincts couldn't both be so far off the mark there.

Who was dislikable?

The Gnat, of course—and, like Sarah, Alex had some bruising—could Alex possibly have been involved with the Gnat sexually? It seemed so unlikely Alex would have been involved with him, much less trusted him enough to get into a situation where she had mixed Valium and alcohol and gone to the lake. But then no one had guessed that Alex had become sexually involved with Parvus, who, granted, was nothing like the Gnat in terms of awfulness, but with whom Alex had only been known publicly to fight, loudly and truly.

Could Alex have been sexually involved with the Gnat? Could he have killed her, either accidentally or purposefully, for his own sexual gratification? Or killed Alex with Sarah's help to meet their mutual needs—not so much their sexual needs as professional?

Of course, it could be someone Maddy didn't even know about. There was that. Alex had a complicated life. No one seemed to have known Alex was sleeping with both Whit and Parvus, so who else might there have been in her life as a lover, an enemy, a source of trouble?

Suddenly, Maddy realized the muffled noise of the car in her head was not imagined. Someone had driven up to the house and was at the front door, opening it. She grabbed the heavy cast-iron frying pan and moved to the front door, her heart racing hard. She was just about to scream for Hank.

But of course it was Parvus. Hank had not set the new latch, and she had not thought to set it, because Hank was here. She held the pan down at her side.

"Hank is here tonight," she whispered to Parvus as he quietly closed the door behind him.

He nodded.

"Yes, I saw his car," he whispered back.

Parvus took the frying pan from Maddy as if she had meant to hand it to him all along. He put it back on the stove, went into the living room, took off his coat, tossed it on the couch, and sat down at the piano.

He didn't yet open the cover to the keys. Instead, he started cracking each of his knuckles, one by one.

She flopped down on the bench right next to him and slumped like a rag doll.

"I can't figure it out, Parvus," she said. "I just can't figure it out."

Then, to her own surprise, she started to cry. She figured it must be some combination of the drug, the startle from the front door opening, the relief of the sex with Hank, Wolf coming soon, the jury deciding soon, the late hour—and perhaps also Parvus no longer smelling of ferrying death—all pulling her feet out from under her.

Parvus turned and put his big arms around her, then reached his right hand up again to hold the top of her head, to hold the jar of a skull that held her brain.

"I know, Shanks. I had a feeling about you—a strange feeling. That's why I came over."

"I can't figure it out," she said again, crying harder on his shoulder. He released her head from his hand and started stroking her head with his yardstick fingers.

"Why don't we try again?" he asked.

"What's the use?"

"Alex is the use."

He let go of her and folded back the cover of the keys.

"Parvus," she asked plaintively, "*why* won't you play the song on that building?"

"What are you talking about, Shanks?"

"The wall of sheet music. Those five-stories downtown, off 10th. Why won't you play it and let me *know* what it is?"

"Silly girl," he said. "It's Ravel, *Gaspard de la nuit*. Go back to bed, Shanks, and I will play it. Go back and see if you can't use your Gaspard *de la nuit* for something fucking useful. See if the asshole can't redeem himself. Help release your brain from its self-imposed prison."

She stood up as he started to play very softly. It did not even sound to her like music, it was so lacy and soft. She went to the kitchen to drink a little more water. Finding the prescription vial, she took the second pill, throwing the empty vial into the trash can below the sink. She went back to bed just as Parvus's song grew a little louder. She could not understand how it could grow louder in volume yet softer in feel.

Hank woke to the feeling of her climbing back under the covers. He sat up at hearing the music.

"What's going on?" he asked her, alarmed, rubbing his eyes.

"Parvus is here," she said. "To play."

"Why?" asked Hank. He looked at the clock.

"He says you should redeem yourself, Gaspard, asshole."

"What?"

Hank rubbed his eyes again, and then rubbed his forehead with his palms. Maddy could already start to feel the second pill pile onto the first. It seemed to her very clearly that the first pill was Parvus's right hand, the one that promised or threatened to open her skull, and the second was his left hand, the one that played the bass notes, as if all were normal.

But all was not normal.

"Just fuck me one more time, Hank," she said, lying back.

"Maddy, what's going on?"

"Just fuck me again, Hank," she said, "and please, stop talking."

This meditation by Ravel had to be, she thought, a determined wind in the tops of the trees, a voice from above speaking to the creatures of the ground, a tossing about of the creatures of the branches.

Hank stood up to close the door, but Maddy yelled at him to leave it open so she could hear Parvus play. She could see Hank was naked and tired.

He came back and climbed under the covers and pulled her close, saying quietly to her, "Okay, but I'm not an exhibitionist. That's not who I am."

That's not who I am.

Character and orientation, she thought. Character could be forced by motivation? Or?

He kissed her forehead as if by obligation. She could feel him moving to be on top of her. She could feel him playing with his dick in his hand, trying to get his erection going for her, and suddenly—well, there she was again: The Jerk playing with his limp dick, trying to get past the weight of his shame, to get his erection up, to get what he came here for, to push her two knees up for just two minutes, push himself in, and unload in her.

Why on earth had she just asked this of Hank?

Why was Parvus tickling the piano like it was not real?

Why was she crying again?

"Maddy, I'm sorry, this is not who I am," Hank said, and he lay back down on the bed while she stared at the ceiling and tried to figure out where the little bit of light was coming from.

He wasn't here for bad missionary sex with a crying woman. Of course he wasn't. Why would she even want that?

388

She pulled in a gallon of air to her lungs to stop herself crying, threw back the covers and got up, noticing she still had on her wool socks and her night-gown. She dragged herself into the living room and sat back down on the bench next to Parvus. He scooped his big right leg around her, missing barely a note in his playing as he reached his right arm over her head, pulling her into the middle of him the way he had before. She was the small Russian doll encased in him. She put her hands on his as she had before: the girl propped on her grandfather's shoes, reaching up to hold his hands to dance.

Now he was playing so calmly, so kindly. She could barely keep her head up. *Maddy,* Hank had said, *this is not who I am.*

It was what Wolf might as well have said to her. Why did she push men to where they did not want to go?

Was this going to be it for her and Hank? Just two rounds, one in the car and one in the bath, and he was really done with her, already? Or did he just mean that he didn't have it in him to fuck a crying woman, certainly not with another man a few steps away playing a piano bought for him by a woman they both had secretly loved so much.

This is not who I am.

Hank speaking the thing Parvus had pulled out of her the night before—character as the motivating force. Hank could not be moved from who he was to who he was not. And for Hank, for whom everything was about sex, orientation was character. Character was motivator. Which meant orientation was motivator.

Her head felt so heavy now from the drugs. No wonder—she thought in the heaviness—no wonder Alex had been so confused about Parvus. So confused *by* Parvus. If Alex had come to know and accept Hank's understanding of sex and identity, then all was about a sort of cement-set orientation. A baked-in sexual experience, a baked-in motivator that could never be shifted, no matter what.

Yet Parvus had shown Alex something else, something more interior, something perhaps changeable in sex. Parvus wasn't operating in the same physical universe.

But who was right? Parvus or Hank?

Maddy was struggling to keep up with his dancing hands, the benzo weighing her muscles down, leaving her like a dog that has to sleep. She gave up and pushed her way off, away from him, and staggered back to the bedroom. There was Hank, sitting up against the headboard, the blanket up to his belly, the bedside reading light switched on.

"Do you want me to go?" he asked.

She crawled in next to him and lay up against his arm.

"God, no," she said. "Don't leave me now. Don't leave me now."

"Okay, okay, don't worry," he said, pulling the blanket up around them. He inched them down some in the bed to be more comfortable. "I'm here."

He reached over and turned off the light.

"It can't have been you," Maddy said, in a groggy voice. "It can't have been you that killed Alex."

"Of course it wasn't me," he said.

"Not you. Not Parvus. Not Scott. Not Everett Sophie. Not Lew. Not Whitaker, and not Joseph."

"Who are Whitaker and Joseph?" Hank asked. "Are you dreaming of some childhood story, Maddy?"

He was twirling the end of her hair around his index finger, his other arm wrapped around the curve of her waist, holding her from tipping into the abyss of deep sleep.

"Maybe it's not your job to have to solve everything, Maddy," he said. "Maybe you should give yourself a break."

She didn't answer but sighed like she might leave the conscious world. All the words were leaving her, and she could not have been happier to say goodbye. They had stayed too long. They kept trying to pray, and she needed them to go. She wanted not the prayer, but the liberation from prayer. Her hand drifted to her crotch.

"I think, Maddy," Hank said in a very soft voice, "you're making me realize there is nothing sexier to me than a nubile woman in a flannel nightgown, falling into deep sleep. This comes to me as a surprise—this turn-on. You do surprise."

"I like how you fuck me, Hank," she said with her eyes closed, with a yawn. She was wondering how it could be that his smell was harmonizing with Parvus's left hand. Hank said something, but she could not hear it in words. It just sounded like music. All the words were gone.

Hank rolled her off him, reached down under the blanket, and pulled her nightgown over her head. At that, she opened her eyes. There he was, looking down at her, right into her, with a sort of stupid adoration. Not an ounce of shame in his face. Nothing but him emptying himself into her eyes. He yanked off each of her socks and then pulled up her left knee with his right hand and slid himself right into her. She thought for a moment that he blushed. He pulled up her right knee and pushed harder against her.

Parvus's playing grew louder yet a little more exquisite, she thought, as if he was telling her to go ahead, to find this answer. She thought she could hear his notes speaking, the cadence of Parvus's own true prayer, the push and pull and push of being, the way God had not *chosen* a name for each living thing on the planet but had merely *spoken* the names that were already there: lion, ox, wolf, and rabbit. But those words of God were not *really* words, they were the animals themselves, expressed in Parvus's heavenly song. She could see that there were all these things living together without the words, before words, in song. She could see the endless expanse of connectedness, a harmony ordinarily interrupted by the words that distinguished each. It was all connected if you could just hear those five stories of music.

Hank pulled back just to the edge and came forward, looking so earnest, and she could feel her own internal grab to keep him from going. Just plain and simple, his eyes meeting hers, neither blinking, but her breathing getting harder, gulping the air.

How could it be? How could it be? His face, perfectly fitting hers, the sun and the moon both up in the sky at once, over the green hills, over the earthly breakfast. And Parvus was playing the song of the morning creatures, the song of the brightening hour, and Hank moving in a counter rhythm to it. The words gone, Parvus found for her what is left: the animal character. And so Hank kept moving in her with his true purpose—and never had there been a truer purpose in her, either. Her muscles and glands kept answering his motion, the waves, the two of them carried on the waves, together, for a moment their desires perfectly matched, the orientations of their human souls perfectly aligned—

And then there it was.

There it all was.

There it all was, all so obviously connected.

Dr. Miller's name on her own prescription bottle. Dr. Griffin's on Alex's.

The drag queen's rough protégé at Two Brothers', barely passing.

What Alex had said to Dr. Miller about psychiatrists being voyeurs.

The overheard conversation on the tea shop line about bicycles.

The chapter list.

The missing folder. The *one* missing folder.

The missing notebooks.

What Mrs. Hannigan had seen in the kitchen sink—Alex's hair.

The bruise just under Alex's ribs.

Why Alex had bought the piano.

"Oh!" Maddy cried. "Oh, I know! I know! I know!"

Hank could see in her eyes something quite wonderful. She seemed barely able to stay conscious. Yet there, in the way her eyes looked, he could see it: perfect clarity. That joyful clarity of knowing, and knowing you are right.

Chapter 34

Full daylight, silence, and a hammer of a headache met Maddy when she awoke. What day was it? What did she have to do today? The clock said it was almost eleven. Could that be right? Then she suddenly remembered.

She sprung out of bed and moved quickly through the house to see if Hank or Parvus was still there. Neither. She found a half pot of cold coffee in the kitchen with a handwritten note: *Looking forward to having you on the court.*

In the living room, the couch had been put back in the normal place. Alex's box was gone from under the piano. She hastened to the coat closet, finding the box wasn't there either. Maddy ran to the bedroom and rifled through her drawers, trying to find where Hank had put her phone. She went to the bathroom and did the same, but she could not find it. She headed back to the bedroom to get dressed, throwing off her nightgown and quickly putting on her underwear, jeans, and a sweatshirt. Lacing up shoes felt like a time waster. She sat down on the foyer bench, pulled on her dress boots, and zipped them up. She grabbed her coat and keys and dashed out the door, putting on her coat as she rushed to the car.

Glancing around nervously as she ran for the garage, she locked herself in the car. She closed the big garage door after her, pulled out of the driveway, and headed to Cottontail Lake, driving fast in an illogical route that took her on long straight roads to make sure no one was following her.

It seemed likely, for reasons she could not articulate, that Parvus would have taken Alex's ashes there. She could tell him the solution first. As Maddy drove, the things she had realized all fell back into place in her consciousness, like water filling up an ice cube tray.

Alex had *indeed* written that note they found in the car, the car that Maddy was now driving. But Alex hadn't written it just before she died, and it hadn't been a suicide note. It was simply written during some moment in Alex's life when she was feeling overwhelmed and had taken a moment to jot her thoughts down on a notebook page, as she had so often made notes in her composition books. The page had just lent itself to the plan to try to make it *look* like suicide. The killer could have found that note weeks or even months before, going through Alex's things when she wasn't home. When he had hatched the plan, he would have known the seemingly despondent note, written in Alex's own hand, was available to him.

Alex also hadn't put the bottle of gin or the prescription vial in the car. Those, too, were planted. The prescription vial had never been touched by Alex—at least not while she was alive. (It would have been perfectly easy to put her prints on it after death, by just pressing her fingertips to it, here and there.) Alex had probably never been to Two Brothers' Pharmacy. The prescription had to have been picked up with a fake ID, maybe one that had taken advantage of Alex's androgynous first name, so that a person who looked like a man could present himself as Alex Shugar. Or maybe the killer had used an ID with the sex listed as "female," as that's what Alex's medical records would have indicated, but had cross-dressed to make the clerk think Alex was a transgender woman.

Regardless of how he did it, the person who picked up that prescription at Two Brothers' wasn't Alex. It was the man who had written the prescription: Dr. Jeffrey Griffin.

Shortly after she was found dead, Griffin could have told—and presumably did tell—the police that Alex had been suffering from anxiety and depression to explain the prescription and the note and paint the picture of a suicide. The police would have had no reason to think he was being anything other than helpful with this information about a suddenly deceased patient. That's why Griffin's view of Alex's state of mind in her last weeks differed so radically from everyone else's: because Griffin was lying. That's why Dr. Miller had seen no signs of Alex being in extraordinary distress when she came in for the mole check: because she *hadn't* been. Alex had never needed a psychiatrist—she had no trouble opening up to just about anybody. But Griffin had wanted to see into her sex life.

Yes, when Alex had observed to Dr. Miller "all psychiatrists are voyeurs," she hadn't mean it metaphorically. She meant, literally, that Griffin was a voyeur—a sexual voyeur. The "v?" on Alex's chapter list next to Griffin's name—it wasn't for "vanilla." A folder for the orientation matched to his name was missing *not* because such a folder had never existed. No, the lack of a folder matched to his name was *not* because he was vanilla and Alex didn't think vanilla was worth writing about. It was because the folder Alex had assembled had been about voyeurism, and Griffin had taken it.

Griffin didn't realize Alex had left a sketch of chapters on the back of the "miscellaneous" folder because he hadn't looked carefully at what she had written on the folders themselves. Neither had Maddy. He'd probably only looked at what was inside the folders to make sure there was no trace back to him. He'd probably left the rest of the folders there as a messy trail, just in case they decided maybe it wasn't suicide and wasn't an accident. Plus, taking *all* those folders would have set off suspicion, at least in Hank.

As for the missing composition notebooks—Griffin couldn't leave the set with just one notebook missing, the one with the page ripped out. So he had to take them all. The missing folders on Alex's intersex research, well, either she had disposed of those herself (as she told Sophie she was going to) or Griffin had taken those, too, to set any suspicion down the wrong trail.

Alex must have somehow figured out, not too long before she died, that Griffin was a voyeur, that he had been watching women—or maybe women and men? —for sexual gratification. Or maybe he just told Alex outright about his interests? People did have a way of telling Alex the truth. The bit of the camera device that the rat had found and squirreled away under the stove—Griffin must have dropped it in the house or something. For months, Griffin could have been letting himself into Alex's house so easily with the hidden key, to read the notebooks or to set up a device if he wanted to watch from afar instead of through the window as usual. Alex traveled enough to have made it pretty easy, and her travel schedule would have been partly public when she was away giving talks.

How had Alex and Griffin met? Maybe he had seen her in the bath on a nonspecific prowl of this neighborhood. More likely, though, like Everett Sophie and others, Griffin had come to hear some talk Alex was giving about sex or read some work by her and had ended up asking her to meet for further conversation. He probably wanted to know what this woman, so interested in sex, did sexually herself. That's how he tracked her to Parvus's house, to watch them there. Alex had sensed someone watching them because someone had been.

Eventually, Alex must have figured out his kink or he must have told her, though it seemed doubtful she realized—at least until very late—that he had been the watcher. He would have known that she had the belief that no one should be ashamed of their desires—only ashamed of problematic actions. Perhaps he had thought she was the one person he could tell about his desires. Perhaps he also saw no harm in his own actions, as he was just watching, and he thought Alex would think the same. It was just like porn, only the actors didn't know a stranger might consume their live performance. Alex must have thought it through, this philosophical question of voyeurism. Probably even talked with Griffin explicitly about it. If a man was watching two people have sex and getting off on it, but the two people he was watching never knew, was there a moral problem with that?

That's why she had that conversation with Hank about this very sort of problem at their last dinner together. Did the lack of consent to be watched matter, given that those being watched would never know? How was it different from a person getting off on the thought of someone else who never knew? Was it true that what you didn't know couldn't hurt you sexually?

No doubt Alex saw it as a fascinating philosophical and moral conundrum, one that *had* to be in her book because of how it pushed the question of what consent was, and what sex itself was—the very thing Hank had said they talked about at their last dinner. If a voyeur watched you and your lover having sex, was it an ontological threesome or simply two singular acts, one a coupling, one masturbation? Did you need to give consent to someone's desire to *look* at you? What if you had all your clothes on and were simply working your job, and someone wanted to watch you do your job because he desired you. Was that a sexual act to which your consent was required? If that was the case . . . well, if that was the case, then the world was full of people violating each other.

Yes, Alex would have seen the idea of voyeurism as something to compare to everything else she was looking at—Sophie dressing up and going out to the world because it made her feel sexually alive, the shoe salesman foot fetishist, the Gnat wanting to control and hurt others even through his rhetoric, the deeply moral pedophile who never acted on his desires, the hebephile who insisted he was normal, that girls of thirteen years could consent. Alex would have found voyeurism fascinating as an intellectual problem. She would have thought about how it was like the position she'd found herself in with Scott during their marriage when they both realized he had a cuckold fetish—that a man could want to "watch" his woman with another man, for his pleasure.

But, undoubtedly, she would have found it disturbing to find herself one of Griffin's subjects. Parvus said Alex had bought the piano because she thought someone was watching them at Parvus's house. Did she know it was Griffin? At some point, she probably knew. By that point, Alex must have been thinking not only about the philosophy and the morality of Griffin's habit of watching—of his getting patients to tell them of their sex lives so he could "watch," even as he got paid for his work as a psychiatrist—but also thinking about the illegality of what he was doing.

Alex must have been thinking about turning him in. Or he must have worried she was thinking about it. And being Alex Shugar—"rhymes with slugger"—she probably would have just outright told him how she saw it, that what he was doing was wrong. And her talking to him about it would have led him to think she might not just *write* about him (which would have been bad enough), but that she might turn him in. And even if Alex did not call the police, she could ultimately threaten his medical license, which would threaten his income, his status, his whole life.

Presumably he was the anonymous book subject who had written to the ethics committee to complain that she was writing about people without their consent. He was probably hoping to scare her out of writing the book, out of writing down his story and her analysis of it.

Perhaps his thinking was this: If *she* wanted to stop *him* from pleasuring himself without the consent of those he used as subjects, why shouldn't *he* stop *her* from pleasuring herself by writing about him, exhibiting his sexuality in her work without his consent?

He must have found a way, that weekend he killed her, to get her into conversation with him at her house. It probably never occurred to Alex that Griffin might go to this length. So she didn't think to protect herself. He must have found a way to give her a drink plus something laced with the benzodiazepine. Maybe he just made some cocktail that masked the drug.

He would have wanted some way to give it to her that wouldn't look funny on autopsy.

He must have gotten her far enough to the stage of unconsciousness to get her to the kitchen sink, which he would have prefilled with water, perhaps under the guise of doing the dishes? Or maybe she was unconscious by the point he filled the sink.

And there, there, in the kitchen sink, he would have held her head under the water.

The bathtub might have been easier for his plan from a physical standpoint. But in the solarium, there would have always been a risk of someone seeing through the windows.

Whether the bruises at the base of Alex's ribs and on her right calf were caused simply by him holding her down firmly, head in the sink, or by her struggling against him, or were there for some other reason, regardless, Griffin would have overcome Alex. He was bigger and stronger than she was, and he had the advantage of knowing the plan. And he was motivated.

This method—the sink—this was why Mrs. Hannigan thought Alex had washed her hair there. Because when Mrs. Hannigan came on Monday, some of Alex's hair remained in the sink. In his haste to get out of there, Griffin had not noticed.

Everyone had assumed the texts Monday morning to Hank and Sophie ("love you") had been sent by Alex. That she must have died at the earliest on Monday. But Griffin could have easily sent those texts from Alex's phone to put them off looking for Alex awhile longer than might otherwise have happened. It would have been easy for him to look at the text record to see the kind of messages she sent and to replicate a couple.

Now Maddy had reached the lake and saw it for the first time in daylight. The water was still and luminescent, the trees grand and noble. The scene of this wooded lake seemed to Maddy virginal. Innocent. As if it had never cloaked a murdered woman.

Maddy parked and got out of the car, buttoning her coat up all the way. Parvus was not here, and there were no signs of him or anyone. The heels of her boots felt a little unsteady on the gravel, and she noted it was just the kind of coarse gravel that wasn't easily going to capture traces of footprints. It might pick up the ghost of a bicycle tire, but only if one looked shortly after a tire had run over it—before weather had wiped it clean again. And, she remembered, it had rained not long after Alex died.

That conversation Maddy had overheard when she met Griffin at Espresso

Royale—the talk of his foldable commuter bike—it was clear he could have easily moved that bike from his car to hers when he transported her body here. Then he would have biked back to her house, put his bike in his car, cleaned her house of his deeds, and driven off. If anyone had seen him, he could have said he was there to see her because she had been in distress. But presumably no one had seen him.

Maddy realized, surveying the scene, Griffin could well have made a point not to bike straight away from Alex's car, to make sure he left no nearby trace of the bike. He could have carried Alex's body into the lake and then carried his fold-up bicycle to some other part of the lake, away from the car, to leave by way of the brush and woods, picking up the path to the road hundreds or even thousands of feet away.

The lake would have been very cold, and it would have been difficult for him to bike all the way back in soaking wet clothes. Perhaps he'd just left his clothes back in his car at Alex's house and worn a wet suit out here? But no, he would have dressed normally in the car, just in case he was stopped while driving on the way to the lake or on the bike ride back, in case someone saw him. So he must have carried his bike and his clothes from the car to the other side of the lake. But he would have had to carry out the big bath towel, too . . . the one Mrs. Hannigan said was missing, the one he presumably used to line the car to avoid a trace of his bike or Alex's body?

Maddy worked her way along the south edge of the lake, the side that led back to the road. The sun was coming from the south, casting long shadows of the trees, all the shadows pointing north together, as if they were compasses, redundant compasses. She picked her way through the brush, wishing she had Hunter with her. He would scamper out in front of her and be three times as good at looking for the towel. And she would feel safer.

Might Griffin try to find and stop her? Had Griffin guessed that Maddy was figuring it out? Surely he had. He did seem to be insisting she call him . . . perhaps with a plan to at least work out what she knew. But if he thought she was onto something, why hadn't he already tried to stop her?

Then she realized she'd barely been alone the last many days and nights. If he had figured out she was onto him, if he had been at the house, he would have seen other people with her, coming and going. There was the night Everett had stayed over. Then there was the night she had accidentally spent at the bar. Then there was the night Parvus stayed over. And last night, Hank and then Parvus, too, there with her.

There'd been just one night lately that she had been alone all night. It was the night after she had gone shopping with Lew and Sophie. That was the night she thought she had seen someone out in the woods when she had stepped out onto the porch. Why hadn't he taken advantage of her being alone that night?

Then she realized: At home after shopping and dinner with Sophie and Lew, Maddy had put on the cocktail dress Sophie had bought for her, donned the jewelry and shoes, done up her hair, and stepped out onto the porch, twice, dressed up, to see if Parvus had come. If Griffin had been watching and had seen her then, dressed up that way, he'd have figured she was expecting someone soon. He'd have thought she was not going to be alone.

Her heart picked up at the idea that she had perhaps managed to save herself simply through a thoughtless act of trying on what she'd gotten shopping that day. Wouldn't Sophie laugh to hear there was more than one way dressing up might save your life?

Oh, to have her phone, to be able to call Wolf and tell him all this. Of course, he'd tell her to get back into the car and drive to the police immediately. But would they believe her—would they believe this story, given how little evidence was left? A jotted chapter list by Alex on the back of a folder; whatever a pharmacy clerk might or might not remember about a prescription picked up months ago; Mrs. Hannigan saying she had seen hair in the sink; Hank swearing Alex didn't go swimming without taking off her jewelry.

Even if everyone contradicted Griffin's claims about Alex's state of mind around when she died, this was shit evidence. *Absolute shit.* And Maddy didn't want to go through another trial. Even if she had rock-solid evidence that Griffin murdered Alex, Maddy didn't want to go through another trial. And this was anything but a case of rock-solid evidence.

Maybe all it would take was a search warrant of Griffin's house and office? Perhaps there the police would find, if not evidence of premeditated murder, evidence of his voyeurism to support Maddy's theory.

But a *theory* isn't what you take to a jury, a bunch of random people likely to be swayed by personality, by someone's race and class and gender, by the rhetoric of a slick defense attorney in a three-thousand-dollar suit. Alex would never come across as a sympathetic victim to the average jury. It would be hard ever to paint her as a victim when she was deep into complicated sexual ideas and practices.

She was the ultimate difficult subject.

And then, just then, Maddy saw it out of the corner of her eye. It was lit just a little by the sun. A patch of light green that looked inorganic, particularly in the setting of these late-fall woods of brown.

She made her way to it and pushed back the leaves that had either blown over it naturally or been piled up by Griffin. Alex's bath sheet.

Maddy bent over and felt a bit of it between her thumb and forefinger. The fabric had become stiff from having been out in the elements, and it was a little faded, like a cloth left out on a clothesline all season. But it was unmistakably the match to the towels Maddy had been using.

Should she leave it here and go and get the police? But then what if Griffin got here before her and took it away, knowing she was onto him? At the very least, it stood as evidence someone had brought a towel from Alex's here. Forensics would presumably show that Alex had been wrapped up in it, or that a bicycle had been. She needed it to show the police, to get them to think past probable suicide.

Why hadn't Griffin come back to get it—why had he left it here? Perhaps because he did not dare be seen by anyone poking around these woods. No doubt, the more time passed, the longer people got used to understanding Alex's death as an accident or a suicide, the more confident he'd grown that no one would ever figure it out. Perhaps he'd even stopped thinking about the towel, at least until Maddy showed up. Or perhaps he had been out here to retrieve the towel but had been unable to find it?

Maddy picked it up now, holding out the corners in her two hands. It was a good six feet by almost five, and thick, like its mates that Maddy had been using in Alex's bath. There was no way Griffin was going to be able to manage this big, thick piece of fabric with his bicycle, unless he had brought some kind of special carrying system for taking it with him on the bike, and apparently he had not.

Realizing she should not have opened it, she folded it carefully now, three times over, trying not to get too much of herself on it, and rolled it up, leaves and all. She hastily found her way back to the car, put the towel on the seat next to her, and headed back to the house.

The clock in the car said it was almost one-thirty. By now, Wolf and Liz should be getting close. She would stop back at the house to see whether they were there, or whether Hank or Parvus had come back. (What had Parvus done with the box of Alex?) She would try once again to find her phone. And if no one was there and she couldn't find her phone, she'd take the towel and head somewhere—to work, or to Sophie's. She could leave them a note about where to find her and get away from the house.

Her head felt like cold slush, the effect of the drug still a little present, and her body felt so hungry from having had no food since the cannoli. She cranked up the heat of the car to at least try and warm up. Maybe she could grab something to eat as soon as she got back, just something to push up her blood sugar a few notches. Soon Wolf would be here, and he would know what they should eat . . .

When she told Wolf all this, about Griffin and Alex, what was he going to say? Was he going to drag her to the police? Or call the police to the house? And what then? Was she going to have to live through another whole cycle—police investigations, an arrest, the media, a trial? And was she going to become a complete freak now, the PhD who had caught two different murderers? Was this going to make it impossible to have a normal academic life, to get a job, to have students and colleagues take her seriously as an academic historian?

Maybe she should just take the sisters up on their offer and go hide at the convent for a while—at least next summer, when school would be out of session and she wouldn't have to stay on campus. Or she could go back to Indiana and stay with Liz.

God, she was hungry. And thirsty. She hadn't had anything to drink since the water with the drug at around three that morning. She was longing to get to the kitchen sink and drink down a few glasses of water.

But, oh, no. That sink.

She pulled into the driveway at Alex's, seeing no other cars. She would just run inside, drink some water, write a note to leave on the door for Hank and Liz saying they should come find her at her office, grab her backpack, and leave. She pulled up just short of the garage, put the car in park, and turned off the engine. She grabbed the towel out of the thoughtless habit of bringing inside what she had picked up while out, opened the car door, and—

As soon as she was standing, both feet on the ground, the towel rolled up in her arms, she saw him come around from the back of the garage: Griffin, dressed in hunter brown camouflage.

Chapter 35

Adrenaline was naturally selected in the evolution of *mammalia* as an excellent survival mechanism. It pushes the blood to the muscles, blows up the pupils, and yells at the lungs to open. But the initial surge of it is quite unpleasant. A bit like being hit by a bus.

Flooded with adrenaline, Maddy's brain triangulated faster than she could consciously process. Griffin had a rope in one hand, a hunting knife in the other, and he was coming at her from the left side of the garage. Leaving the car door open between them, dropping the towel, she ran around the back of the car toward the house. She soon realized there was no way she was going to get into the house before he got to her. She ran instead through the space between the right side of the garage and the house, tearing off into the woods.

It occurred to her after ten seconds that this had probably been the wrong way to go. If she had run to the road, she might have run to another house and found a neighbor. Or she might have spotted a car with a driver who would stop and help her. But then maybe there would be no neighbor, no driver. At least in this direction, she knew the way, and he could not chase her down with his car. Hopefully, even with his prowling, Griffin had not spent as much time as far back here as she had.

But damn, these stupid dress boots.

She could hear him behind her, following her as she leapt over the downed trees and dodged low branches. At one point, she stumbled briefly, but she rapidly regained her footing. Still, he seemed to be catching up. She ran a little to the north and then cut west. She looked back to see that, as she suspected would happen, he was taking the hypotenuse. He didn't know there was a wet spot there that she had been avoiding. He seemed to get temporarily stuck in the muck, giving her about twenty more feet on him.

She was heading for the tree she knew best from having climbed it twice. She'd never gotten to the top of it, but she figured that, if she did, the branches might hold her and not him. She was probably only two-thirds his weight if that. She'd turn her size into a strength.

But where was her tree? There was the white oak. There was the spinney of beeches. It was near here? There it was! The tree she did not know the name of, the tree to which she felt like apologizing for not even knowing its species. A fir?

She dashed up the remnants of branches at the tree's base, the stubs that provided a way to climb up the first ten feet, hoping he would not see which tree she had gone up. But the leaves had come down off so many trees and her clothes would stand out against all the brown.

Sure enough, soon he was at the base of her tree, panting. She was picking her way up, deeper into the thick middle, also breathing hard.

"Think you figured it out, do you?" he yelled up.

She did not reply.

"Come down," he said, breathing hard, "and I'll explain. It's not like you think. I can explain."

She did not answer again. She was wishing her body would stop its trembling, trembling that made it so hard to hold on with any confidence. The soles of her boots slipped against the branches. Sap and bits of bark stuck to her fingers and palms. She looked down and could see that he was beginning to assess how he would get up the tree. It appeared he did not have the experience she did in the art of tree climbing. His camo outfit must not be because he was an animal hunter. A hunter would know how to climb a tree.

Still, this was a pretty stupid plan on her part, going up the tree. There was no way out of a tree but one. A rat would never have made this mistake. Liz had taught Maddy that a rat always made sure to have two ways out in case a predator showed up.

"Think you're so clever, because of Philadelphia?" he said, now beginning to climb below her.

She was looking for something she could throw down at him. But there was nothing—no pinecones, no loose branches—nothing but her boots. And while those were slippery, they were at least better than socks for climbing this thing. The heels let her lock her feet a little as she made her way up.

She went a couple more branches skyward.

"The dwarf murders, those just made you think doctors are evil, right?" he asked. "Your mind is just confused from stress. Come down and I'll help you think clearly about all this," he said. "I'll help you feel less anxious, Madeleine. Come down."

"Fuck off!" she yelled at him, hearing her own voice carry through the trees. "I don't need to go through another fucking trial for another thing I never should have gotten mixed up in! You fucking, murderous asshole, I don't need to think about one more trial when the other one's not even done!"

She felt as if she were yelling pointlessly at the universe about too much homework. What the hell was this screaming at him going to achieve? There was no one within earshot, and he didn't care. In her head, she could hear the voice of Sister Severe telling her to watch her language, the way Sister had done when Maddy had referred to The Jerk as a fucking asshole.

"Wait," Griffin said, still climbing up.

She pulled herself up another level of the branches.

"Does that mean you didn't hear the trial outcome?"

She didn't answer.

"You didn't hear the news?"

"No!" she yelled at him, wondering what he meant. Had the jury come back?

"You don't know?" he asked.

"No!" she yelled again.

He paused and went quiet for a moment.

Then he said, in a lower voice, "It's over. Full acquittal. You were wrong, Dr. Shanks. Just like you're wrong about what you think about me."

Her right hand started to shake violently. She was trying to figure out why her right hand would shake so much more than her left.

"Full acquittal," he said again now. "You were wrong. Wrong, all wrong. It's going to be so embarrassing for you, I know. You don't need to embarrass yourself by being wrong again now, do you? Come down, and don't act like a child."

You're not a child anymore. What The Jerk used to say to her, to justify his ways. *They treat you like you're just a child, but you're so mature, Madeleine.*

She climbed one more branch up, right foot first up. The branch broke sharply under that foot and fell away. She threw her right arm around the trunk, steadying herself, to try another branch.

She understood she was already reaching the point where the branches were barely going to hold her. He was still a good ten or fifteen feet below her, unsure of himself. Some of the branches below him had broken. But he was making progress by staying near the trunk and holding on to branches above him to keep distributing his weight.

"Come down, Madeleine. I can explain everything and you can go on with your life."

Full acquittal? How could it be? *How could it be?* Everyone had said the prosecutors were good. *Really* good. Everyone who had talked to her about the trial said it was clear from the news reports that Wilhelm was guilty. Had they just been telling her this to give her some hope? Had the prosecutors totally screwed up the argument of the case? Failed to present everything they should have presented? Had the media twisted the reports from the courtroom, making the public think he was guilty while the jury had heard a more complicated and confusing story? Or was the jury just *that stupid*, that bad at following what they needed to follow, that swayed by Wilhelm's status?

There had been a moment, months ago, when she had thought to herself that if the jury came back with an acquittal, she would agree that she had been wrong and they were right. A good scholar knows that sometimes she is wrong—deeply wrong. A good scholar, particularly one conversant with the history of science and medicine, knows that sometimes smart people turn out to have been very wrong.

But just last night, she had laid it all out for Hank in the car. It had seemed so perfectly clear that she had been right. Wolf knew she had been right. And the prosecutors did. Hank said she was right. And Dr. Miller.

No, this acquittal wasn't about her having been wrong. This was about the problem of a jury. They weren't her peers, or Wilhelm's. These were random humans thrown together into a box, and random humans thrown together in a box make shit judges of the truth. There was a reason peer review was done by peers. Twelve random humans thrown together in a box like eggs in a carton as if they could be trusted with something this important!

"Okay," he said. "Then I will come for you."

He was slowly climbing higher.

"It was self-defense, you know," Griffin said now, almost as if speaking to himself. "With Alex Shugar. Self-defense. Just like this. I never should have been put in this position. This is all her fault."

Maddy thought about it. Even if somehow, miraculously, someone showed up right now, and he stopped his climb and retreated, and she went to the police and they arrested him, she was just going to face another carton of stupid eggs. Stupid, broken, random, dumb eggs.

She couldn't do it again.

She found the branch she wanted. It stuck out from the tree parallel to the ground and looked strong enough to hold her full weight. She secured her feet and her left hand. She pulled her right hand into the sleeve of her jacket to use the fabric of the sleeve to protect her hand. She rapidly rubbed her right sleeve along about two feet of the branch, top, side, and bottom, to scrape off as much of the loose bark and sap and pokey bits as she could.

She could see he was getting closer.

Now she stood up very carefully on her chosen branch, reached above her, and broke off as much as she could above it to make herself a clearing within the tree. She reached down below the branch and did the same, to the extent she could.

Then she started to prepare, mentally and physically, to position herself as she would with the uneven bars. These were certainly uneven bars. Well, they would have to suffice. For the so-called justice system was pointless. There was no *system*. No, there was no God to dole out the candies and the rotten apples, to hand out the keys to heaven and tickets to hell. The police were useful *sometimes*, but often not, which meant that in terms of reliability, they were useless. Sure, they had managed to put The Jerk away for three years. But only *three fucking years*? As if that was a logical equivalent to what he had done.

And Wilhelm. Wilhelm was going to walk—back to his mansion, back to his clinic, back to his life. And he was probably going to spend the rest of his life ruining her reputation. When she had been right. No, there was no justice system.

She thought back to the field rat Hank had almost killed with the cleaver.

How she had stayed his hand and made him capture the rat and free it. That was the kind of thing she had to do now. Only she was the rat. She would have to free herself.

She waited until he was just about in the right position, on a branch just below her, and she cried out, as theatrically as she could—

"Hank, thank God you are here! Up here! I am up here! Come save me!"

It did as she figured it would. Griffin looked down in panic. Maddy quickly put her two feet right next to each other on the branch, her hands just outside her feet, and raised herself upside down to take a handstand on the branch. She curled herself around the branch once in a tucked summersault, then, at the apex, extended her body out fully and spun around the branch, her body stiff as a long board, slamming the toes of her two boots straight into the back of his head. She came back up to the branch in a crouching position, her hands stinging from the abrasion of the move.

Griffin let out a cry at the blow, fell back a little, but then righted himself. She could see him glaring up at her, getting ready to come at her again. He looked like a guy who had nothing to lose.

Maddy turned around, now with the trunk on her left side instead of her right. If her last act was this act of judgment—of killing him purposefully while she accidentally killed herself—so be it. The world was foolish and pointless and, when she left it, she would no longer suffer its stupidity. Somebody would probably pray over her body, somebody would probably bury her, presumably next to her parents and her sister. But she wouldn't have to pay attention to any of it. It was all so stupid—when she had asked Parvus early that morning, "What's the point of trying to figure it out?" he had answered, "Alex is the point" —as if Alex, long dead, had anything to care about.

Dead, there would be no cares.

She raised herself up once more into a handstand on the branch and flipped herself once more around in a tight somersault, this time seeing him letting go of the tree with one hand, obviously planning to try to grab at her as she spun. Reaching the apex, she again lengthened her body out and came back around hard. This time she caught him with both her feet right under his chin, with a collision of the toes of her boots and the front of his neck in a moment of proprioception that felt quite like landing her feet on a gym mat, the way his neck gave a little.

He let go of the branches, shifting his weight fully to his feet, causing the branch below him to crack out from under him. With a muffled cry, he fell back, and back, and back, and back, branch by branch, finally falling freely for about the last twenty feet, headfirst, hitting the ground with a thud.

Maddy sat down fast on the branch near the trunk, as if she were playing a game of musical chairs and the music had just stopped. She threw her arms around the trunk and held it tight, wishing the tree would hold her back.

In a moment, she leaned over a little and looked down. He wasn't moving. She shifted herself some more to see better. His head a very bad angle to his shoulders. She thought this probably meant he had broken his neck.

But it was impossible to tell from here. And she wasn't going to climb down without knowing for sure that he was done.

A blue jay alighted on a branch near her, looking her right in the eye, cocking his head. He let out his corvid cry—"Ah! Ah! Ah!"—and took off again.

"Ah! Ah! Ah!" she yelled back at the bird, angrily.

How was it she was still here?

Chapter 36

The sky decided it should give a little snow.

Maddy wasn't sure how much time had passed, but the white flakes now falling, even though they fell lightly, added to her heap of self-pity.

She assumed Griffin was good and dead, but she was still afraid to go down past him. It had to have been at least thirty minutes and still he had not moved. He could not possibly be faking this. Anyone who had fallen like that, if there had been any life left in him, would have tried to get up again. And there had been no movement, none at all. People didn't fall like cats.

It was kind of remarkable how easy it turned out to be to kill somebody—not just in terms of the physicality but the psychology. She could see how it was that, if Griffin had convinced himself he had had to kill Alex (and Maddy) in self-defense, it wouldn't be that hard. As for Wilhelm, well, his motivation—the protection and advancement of himself, the protection and advancement of his research and career—that was something she could now also relate to. There had been an element of that motivation, too, in her move to kill Griffin.

So this is where her life had brought her: sympathy for the devils.

Wolf and Liz ought to be at the house by now. If they had arrived, Maddy realized, they would have seen her car there, with the car door left open and the weathered towel dropped next to it. What would they make of this, finding all that and Maddy not there? Wolf would probably panic. But would it occur to him to look for her back here?

She tried yelling, "I'm here! I'm up here!"

But no one answered. Not even the jay.

She had not had the chance to wash the sheets. Now, if Wolf broke into the house as he probably was going to do, he'd find her sheets smelling of sex. Then he'd assume the worst. Great. And she had nothing to feed him and Liz, nothing proper. Just maybe some bacon and eggs or simple chicken breasts from the fridge. And of course Wolf was going to call the police once she told him Alex had been murdered in the sink. And then the police were going to kick them all out as soon as it was clear they were describing the house as a crime scene. Where was she going to put them all up?

What a mess she did make of things. She should just mind her own fucking business in the future. Live in a series of good archives where reporters wouldn't find her and ask her how it felt to be so publicly humiliated, having supposedly wrongly accused a world-famous researcher of murdering his patients. Yes, she would retreat forever to archives. Assuming she could afford it. Assuming she wasn't going to prison for killing Griffin. (There was that.)

She felt anxious and low. But mostly she felt hungry. And thirsty. And cold. Her hands hurt like hell. They were torn up in places and stinging all over. And her upper back was weary from hanging on. She thought about singing, to try to cheer herself up.

A weird birdcall started from a ways away, from the direction of the house. Was that a crow? Maybe a raven? It sounded sharp and fast in repetition and low to the ground. Wait, no—it was a dog. A barking dog. Perhaps a dog with a person?

"I'm here, up here!" Maddy cried out. Then for a moment she wondered if Griffin might have had a helper and if she should not have yelled.

But no, no—

For then she heard it, clearly. It was Hunter's bark, the bark he would let out when thinking he was back at work as a police dog. The bark that said he didn't know he was retired.

"Hunter!" she screamed, as if she were drowning. "Hunter!"

Hunter came tearing up to the base of the tree, his white shepherd coat a burst of light on the shadowy forest floor. He stayed a few feet back from Griffin's body and anxiously looked up to Maddy in the tree.

"Hunter!" she cried, rarely having felt so relieved in all her life to see another living thing. She started to weep, still trying to say his name. Hunter bayed at her in confused greeting, mixing joy and upset. He nudged forward and sniffed at Griffin, then backed away again and ran toward the house. For a moment, Maddy felt her hope drain away. Then she understood what he was doing: going to make sure Wolf knew the way. (Humans could be so incompetent in the eyes of a dog.) All she had to do now was not fall out of the tree. That ought to be simple.

Soon Hunter was back with Wolf and Liz at the base of the tree, all of them panting. Hunter barked at Maddy repeatedly. Wolf told him to quiet down. Maddy could see Wolf kneel next to Griffin to check for a pulse and to feel his temperature. He stood back up and looked up the tree. Liz was carrying something—a white cake box. It looked to Maddy kind of squashed from the run.

"Rabbit?" said Wolf, looking up at her through the branches.

"Yes?" she said, a little like a guilty child.

"Are you okay?"

"I'm glad you're here," she answered.

"Come down?"

"Is he dead?"

"Yes," said Wolf. "He's dead."

She didn't reply.

"Did you want him dead?"

"Yes," she said. "He killed Alex. And he knew I had figured it out."

She could see Wolf and Liz talking about something, but she could not hear what they were saying.

"Mad girl?" said Liz now. "Could you come out of the tree, please? I brought you a cake."

"What kind?" asked Maddy.

"Carrot cake with lemon cream cheese frosting. It's kind of smooshed now, but I think it's really good."

Liz opened the lid, pulled out a chunk with her fingers, and ate it. Maddy realized that was exactly what she wanted to eat. Carrot cake with lemon cream cheese frosting. With hot, hot tea. A whole pot of hot black tea. And three glasses of water. But she didn't want to come out of the tree. It was going to be too, too humiliating to talk about the trial. And to explain why she had killed Griffin.

What if Wolf told her the evidence she had on Griffin was too thin to have performed an execution? Would she herself have to go on trial? She would just stay up the tree for a while more.

Hunter started to whine and bark at her again, and Wolf told him to quiet down.

"Rabbit, you're upsetting Hunter. Please come down."

"No," she answered. "Not yet anyway."

"Why not? He's dead, and we're here."

"Because of the trial," she answered.

"I don't understand," Wolf called up.

"Because of the outcome," Maddy called down.

"You're upset about the outcome? Their ruling?"

Again, Wolf and Liz talked quietly so that Maddy could not hear.

"Rabbit, about the trial, it's going to be okay," Wolf said, in as comforting a voice as he could muster. "I know it's shocking right now, but it's all going to be okay."

Maddy didn't answer. Of course he would say it was going to be okay. He always said everything was going to be okay.

Hunter started to whine.

"Shut up, Hunter," said Liz.

Then she yelled up at Maddy:

"Madeleine Arthur Shanks, you come down out of that tree RIGHT NOW!"

Maddy didn't answer.

"Her middle name is Arthur?" asked Wolf.

"I don't know *what* her middle name is," explained Liz, "so I used my little brother's. Don't you have to use a middle name when you yell at someone to get out of a tree?"

Wolf shook his head. He opened the lid of the cake box, scooped out a chunk of cake, and ate it.

"Oh, man, that's good." He called up the tree: "This cake is so good, Rabbit. They put just the right amount of sugar and lemon in the frosting. I think there's little bit of orange zest in there, too. Maybe even tangerine? Almond extract, I'm pretty sure. There's some amazing flavor in this cake."

Maddy sighed and started to work her way down. She carefully worked her way around the broken branch Griffin had been standing on when she had kicked him in the head and then the neck. She moved down a few more levels and heard a crack under one of her feet.

"Be careful!" Wolf screamed.

Hunter whined again. Maddy lowered herself slowly, bit by bit, finally finding herself on the branch she believed was the last one Griffin had hit. She paused there.

"Wolf?" she said, rather quietly. "How could they possibly acquit?"

"Because," Wolf said, "they'll understand it as self-defense."

Maddy didn't answer. She couldn't understand why he would suggest Wilhelm would be understood to have acted in self-defense against his patients. And why was Wolf using the future tense?

"What do you mean?" she asked.

"I seriously doubt the police are going to prosecute you, Maddy. But if it ever went to a jury, you would surely be acquitted. They would understand you were acting in self-defense. He was chasing you up a tree. With a rope and a knife."

"I don't mean that," Maddy explained. "I mean, how could the jury have acquitted Wilhelm? How could that happen?"

"What?" asked Liz, moving to try to get a better view of Maddy's face. "They didn't acquit, Mad girl. They came back today. Conviction on every count."

Liz patted Hunter on the head as if to convey to him her congratulations on the whole matter. He stood up very straight and wagged his tail.

Maddy grabbed the tree hard. She wanted to ask Liz to repeat what she had said.

But Wolf spoke first: "Of course, there will be appeals."

"Oh my God, Wolf, *shut up*," said Liz. "If you and Maddy don't stop annoying me, I'm going to take this cake and this good dog back to the house, and this good dog and I will finish off this cake without you two."

Liz gave Hunter a little bit of frosting.

"Don't give him sugar, Liz, it's terrible for his teeth," Wolf said. "Maddy, there *will* be appeals. I'm just trying to be honest with you."

Maddy thought about it, breaking through the fog of her hunger and her thirst, her cold body and her stinging hands. She realized that if Wolf had been lying about the conviction of Wilhelm just to get her out of the tree, he would not have mentioned appeals. So, there must have really been conviction.

Which meant the cake of this Friday would be joyful. Not sorrowful. She was still here.

Chapter 37

By Sunday morning, Maddy had grown tired of trying to get everybody to agree on exactly which body of water they should choose for scattering Alex's ashes. So, while Wolf was off at Mass, Maddy texted Parvus, Hank, and Lew and told them to just come to Everett Sophie's house at three o'clock, and they'd go together somewhere along the Mississippi. Maddy liked the idea of Alex swimming a long way before she reached the sea.

At roughly the appointed time, with Hank the last to arrive, the five of them piled into Sophie Everett's SUV, with Sophie taking the wheel. Parvus climbed into the front passenger seat and held Alex's box on his lap. With Maddy sitting in the back flanked by Hank and Lew, Sophie took off from Uptown to drive in the general direction of where the big river met the campus.

Forty-eight hours earlier, as Maddy, Liz, and Wolf ate more of the cake and waited in Alex's driveway for the police and the ambulance, with

Maddy drinking all the water available in Wolf's car, they had talked about where they were going to stay. Wolf confirmed what Maddy had suspected; the police weren't going to let them into the house once they knew Griffin might have killed Alex there.

"Let's pretend I don't know that and go in for now," Maddy said.

"Right, because a Philadelphia cop would not know this most basic protocol," Wolf answered. "Have more cake and get in the car if you're cold."

In response to Liz's confusion, Wolf explained that, while the crime scene had been spoiled for months—ironically, spoiled mostly by Maddy—the police still had to go through the motions. They would probably let Maddy retrieve her book bag, clothes and toiletries, and her phone if they could find it. But otherwise Maddy, Wolf, and Liz would have to bug out. Wolf suggested Everett Sophie would probably put them all up. And he noted that, given what Maddy had figured out, Sophie would probably appreciate Maddy's steady company at home while having to process the ugly truth of her best friend's end.

As Wolf wandered off down by the mailbox to call Everett Sophie to ask for emergency lodging, Liz and Maddy took turns throwing a stick for Hunter to retrieve.

"We did okay in the car, Mad," Liz said, as if reading the question on Maddy's mind. "Wolf and I took turns sleeping or keeping each other awake. When we got the call from the courtroom, Wolf was driving, so I put his phone on speaker. Someone from the prosecutor's office was in the back of the court. He was whispering to us about what was going on. I had to repeat some of it so Wolf could hear."

"But they don't let phones in the courtroom," Maddy said, throwing the stick for Hunter again.

"Yeah, Wolf told me later, when we stopped for the cake, the guy must've had a hidden microphone. Anyway—I don't think I ever saw anybody grab a steering wheel as hard as Wolf did while that guy relayed the verdicts. 'Guilty, guilty, guilty.'"

At that, Liz gulped, stifling tears. She bent down suddenly and gave Hunter a messy kiss on the top of his head.

"I just lost it crying. Like a fucking girl!"

She stood up and laughed at herself.

"Wolf had to pull off so I could get my shit together. We pretended it was because Hunter needed the walk."

She chucked the stick again and told Maddy that when, shortly after that, they hit the area of Minnetonka, Liz insisted they stop for cake for Maddy. She wasn't satisfied with the options at the first bakery so they went to another. Liz said she knew it was going to be a good carrot cake because the second bakery had that special kind of twisted white and red string to tie up the box.

"Aren't you glad we stopped to get it for you?"

And Maddy answered, "Oh, yes. So glad."

Maddy could not help but think about the fact that if Wolf and Liz had not stopped at two bakeries, they might have arrived before Maddy kicked Griffin out of the tree. Griffin might still be alive. And then she might have to go through another trial of another murderer caught by her.

Maddy also realized this: If Griffin had not lied and told Maddy that the jury had come back with a full acquittal, she might not have found it in her to try to kill him. But lying wasn't supposed to count as a mortal sin.

The sirens became audible just then. How funny, Maddy thought, that they used sirens even when it was all over.

. . .

Three hours later, after Maddy and Hank had finished the initial conversation with the police about what Maddy knew and suspected, Maddy took the possessions she could quickly gather. She was grabbing one of the blue bottles just as a police sergeant called out that he had found her phone. Hank had hidden it in the bathroom in an open box of maxi pads.

"Guess I'll never get those boots back," Maddy said as Wolf drove them away from Alex's home.

"Nope," he answered. "Evidence in a homicide."

"A *pair* of murder weapons?" Liz asked.

Her tone was joking, but neither Wolf nor Maddy answered for a good couple of minutes. Maddy figured she and Wolf were probably wondering the same things: Would she be charged with manslaughter? Or worse? Would what she had done to Griffin become public? Would Alex's murder become public?

"Ask Sophie to take you shopping for new boots," Wolf said finally, breaking the silence as he pulled the car into a grocery store parking lot. "She said on the phone you can stay with her long as you need. Said she'd be glad for your company just now. So, if you're moving in on her, we need to get a *lot* of groceries." He put the car in park. "Rabbit, don't go telling Everett

Sophie why you need new boots."

...

    Sophie steered her SUV down to West River Parkway, parking in a spot that looked legal. Craning her neck to look out from the middle of the backseat, Maddy could see a small fishing pier jutting out into the big river. The five of them bundled up and walked out to it, Parvus carrying the box.

    Maddy asked if this was a place Alex had ever gone swimming. In unison Sophie, Parvus, Lew, and Hank told her "no!"

    It sounded almost as if they were telling Alex no, that she could not swim there.

    "Much too dangerous," Hank added. Then he let out a sigh.

    They stood at the end of the pier for several minutes, saying nothing. Then Sophie began to recite from Whitman's *Song of Myself.*

I celebrate myself, and sing myself,

And what I assume you shall assume,

For every atom belonging to me as good belongs to you.

I loafe and invite my soul,

And lean and loafe at my ease observing a spear of summer grass.

My tongue, every atom of my blood, form'd from this soul, this air,

Born here of parents born here from parents the same, and their parents the same.

I, now, thirty-seven years old in perfect heath begin.

Hoping to cease not till death . . .

Sophie paused at that line. She tried to continue but could not. Lew cleared his throat and finished the poem's short chapter:

Creeds and schools in abeyance,

Retiring back a while sufficed at what they are, but never forgotten,

I harbor for good or bad, I permit to speak at every hazard,

Nature without check with original energy.

    They stood quietly a moment more, Sophie and Hank holding each other's arms and silently weeping, Lew wiping his eyes.

    Parvus secured the box between his left arm and his body, opened it, and scooped out ashes with his right hand. He threw the ash into the air over the river. Lew took a handful and did the same. Then Maddy, then Hank, then Sophie. Parvus looked into the box and, seeing there was a little bit of ash left, dumped the rest unceremoniously into the river. Then he threw the box and the lid in, too. They all watched as the cardboard washed downstream, bobbing gently in the current.

When they got back to the house, Wolf pulled Maddy into the butler's pantry and closed the door behind them to tell her the police had called. Maddy would not face charges in Griffin's death. The police had searched Griffin's house and office, finding Alex's phone, her computer, and her notebooks. They'd also found what appeared to be thousands of photographs and videos, a sampling of which confirmed Maddy's understanding of what Griffin had been doing.

With Maddy's hands still scarred and sore from the deadly gymnastics in the tree, Wolf helped her wash them now in the sink of the butler's pantry. Maddy said nothing as she watched the last of Alex's dust wash down the drain. As Wolf opened and closed the drawers of the pantry looking for a clean towel to dry her hands, she asked him about Griffin's collection of photos and tapes.

"Will the police detectives have to look at it *all*, Wolf?"

He nodded.

"Even though he's good and dead?"

"Good and dead," Wolf echoed her. "Leaving so much evidence."

Was he wondering what she was—whether they would find *her* in Griffin's stash? Perhaps that lovely sex she'd had with Hank three nights before in Alex's bathtub had been recorded somewhere other than Maddy's and Hank's brains. Would some police detective find that recording in the stack and, if he did, would he watch it more than once, ostensibly in the line of duty?

Maddy didn't know what to make of the fact that when she thought of this, she smiled.

Finding a clean towel, Wolf patted her hands dry. He took so long doing it, Maddy sensed he wanted to hold her hands, to see they were still alive. It reminded her of the way he had come to hold her hands in Philadelphia.

When Wolf opened the door from the pantry back to the kitchen, Maddy caught the sound of her friends talking and laughing. Liz was joking with Hank about how you can prove lesbians are real. Parvus was playing a Cole Porter tune on Everett Sophie's piano. Lew was singing the lyrics in his pretty tenor.

Seeing Maddy and Wolf emerge, Hunter came to stand next to Maddy. The dog put his nose high in the air, to better pick up the roasting pork. Seeing the dog out of the corner of her eye, Maddy realized she was doing the same.

. . .

Maddy and Wolf stayed up late that night, the two of them in their paja-mas sitting on the couch, Hunter asleep on the floor. She was finally ready to ask him about the trial—what had been presented, what had not, what had seemed to him a point for or against the prosecution. He answered all that and explained, too, on what bases Wilhelm might appeal.

"But he won't win," said Wolf, slapping his knee and surprising Maddy with this unhedged bet.

Maddy told Wolf she only wished she could know what Wilhelm's face had looked like when the verdicts were read.

"It isn't that I relish the idea of him suffering," she explained. "I don't give a fuck what he feels. I'm just genuinely curious how a person that arrogant receives the news that he has been found guilty by a carton of eggs."

At that, Wolf stretched his arms high in the air, gave off a yawn, and said she should go to bed. He walked her up the stairs with Hunter at his feet and knocked quietly on the door of the bedroom in case Liz was asleep. But Liz answered promptly, telling them to come in. She was sitting up in one of the two twin beds reading a nineteenth-century book she had found in Sophie's collection, on the fish and mammals of the boundary waters. Maddy climbed into the second bed and Hunter hopped up to join her.

"Good night, girls," said Wolf, closing the door behind him.

"Good night, girls," said Liz and Maddy to each other, cracking up.

"Hey!" he scolded in a hushed voice from the hallway. Maddy could just picture the faux-annoyed look on his face—the one he made when she stole food from his plate.

Liz and Maddy turned off the lights next to their beds and settled in, Maddy draping her arm over Hunter. As she listened to the sounds of Wolf using the bathroom and then going into the other guest room and closing his door, Maddy wondered what Liz was thinking about. Finally, she asked.

"I was just thinking about how much Wolf loves you. How goddamned lucky you are. So, what are you thinking about?"

"I was thinking about how I'm really behind on publications," Maddy answered. "You know—publish or perish."

"Yes," agreed Liz in a serious voice, "publish or perish. Stop with the mur-ders, Mad Girl."

"Tomorrow, Lizard," said Maddy, pulling Hunter a little closer to her chest. The dog let off a sleepy grunt. "After breakfast."

Maddy Shanks will return
in *Book Three: The Worst Thing*

Molly Macallen is the author of the Maddy Shanks
mystery series. Beginning with *The Index Case*, the series follows
the life of Maddy Shanks, a young historian of anatomy, as she
tries to figure out the truth behind a succession of suspicious
deaths – while also dealing with the challenges posed by her own
complex past and present.

Visit mollymacallen.com to learn more about the series.

Write to the author at molly@michigoose.com.

www.ingramcontent.com/pod-product-compliance
Lightning Source LLC
Chambersburg PA
CBHW031030030726
47497CB00004B/1076